"I KNOW THE RUSSIANS AND HOW TO *BEAT* THEM"

CIA Director Clark looked from Joseph to his watch. "All right, Professor. You've got one minute: talk."

"Thank you." Joseph dragged his hand across his mouth. "In a nutshell, I want to kidnap someone."

"Cherganyev?"

"No, someone bigger."

"Really. Who?"

Joseph told him. Clark's jaw fell.

"They're right about you, Professor. You're out of your friggin' mind!"

"I'm not. It can *work*."

Clark shook his head. "I don't see how."

"As I said, you don't know Moscow. You don't know Moscow's *underbelly*. There's a way to pull this off."

Clark's features softened. He stepped back and sat on the edge of the table.

"All right, Joseph. I'll bite. Start at the top, I want to hear everything . . ."

BLOCKBUSTER FICTION FROM PINNACLE BOOKS!

STARIK

JEFF ROVIN AND
SANDER DIAMOND

PINNACLE BOOKS
WINDSOR PUBLISHING CORP.

PINNACLE BOOKS

are published by

Windsor Publishing Corp.
475 Park Avenue South
New York, NY 10016

First Pinnacle Books printing: October, 1989

Printed in the United States of America

For Masha Bruskina,
Kirill Trus, and Volodya Sherbatseyvich.
—J.R.

To Murray Dorfman
in deep appreciation for the years
of encouragement.
—S.D.

PART
ONE

It was just after 4:00 A.M., Tuesday morning, when the pale blue Plymouth station wagon made its way along the C Street side of the State Department complex, past the long canopy and stately columns of the diplomatic entrance. The street was deserted, the only other vehicle a Dempsey Dumpster truck noisily making pickups two blocks behind them.

Despite the sparse traffic, Ambassador Anatoly Fedorsenko had instructed the driver to keep to thirty miles an hour. That way, when the driver was questioned, when the guards at the embassy gate made their report, when the KGB finished their investigation as to how and why it all happened, it would be clear that although the ambassador had defected, he had not run. He wanted Cherganyev to understand that Anatoly Fedorsenko was an opponent, not a coward.

Cherganyev, the old man sneered as he squeezed the round silver top of his cane. *Lenin Utra—the madman!*

Through the untinted window the ambassador saw a battered black van parked across the street, the red sticker marking it as deserted. He suspected it wasn't, any more than the dark windows were empty in the State Department offices or in the Federal Reserve Building across the intersection. He'd been watched every inch of the way. If any car came close, a fender-bender would keep it back; if the ambassador was attacked physically, a police officer or night watchman or civic-minded trash collector would suddenly appear. Ironically, the Soviets would have no choice but to publicly salute whoever cut the would-be assassin down.

The garbage truck peeled off down a side street when they passed the van. The van's healthy eight-cylinder engine hummed to life.

The Russian driver braked to twenty as the car rounded a corner. They rolled past a nondescript Oldsmobile Cutlass and vanished down the sloping ramp of the underground garage. When they were well within the tunnel, the ambassador leaned forward and touched the driver's shoulder.

"*Spasibo,* Nicholas," he said softly. "Thank you."

The young driver looked in the rearview mirror. He now knew what was happening, but he was bright enough to say nothing. He could report truthfully that he had been awakened by a call to his room, that they had been in no rush, that he had no idea what was happening until it was too late. At worst, he would be recalled to Moscow and reassigned. Or, Fedorsenko reflected, that's the way it would have worked under Gorbachev. Now—

The car halted before a maze of waist-high concrete blocks that permitted only a twisting passage. The driver entered slowly. As they drove into the labyrinth, spotlights were triggered automatically. A half-dozen men materialized, standing several yards apart along the route. Each man carried a submachine gun, its barrel trained past the car. The driver stopped. He wasn't surprised, but raised his hands just the same, making it clear that he considered himself a hostage. The ambassador sat still, squinting into a dark corridor to the right.

There was a rumbling behind them and the black van rolled down, followed by the Cutlass. The ambassador felt as though a door had slammed behind him. He silently cursed his old friend for what he'd made him do.

"Continue," the ambassador said, lightly tapping

Nicholas's shoulder with the head of his cane. The car edged ahead.

When they reached the end of the maze, one of the men in the tunnel pressed a walkie-talkie to his lips.

"Pier Three here. Tell Sailor One the cargo's in the hold."

The ambassador knew what was next. He himself must open the door and step out. He hesitated. He wanted to say something to Nicholas, not so that the driver would understand, but so that his words would get back to Cherganyev—and to his close friend Aksakov, whose opinion had always mattered so much.

I am not a traitor, I am a patriot.

But he refrained. Though he was exhausted from lack of sleep, eyes stinging, thoughts soft-edged, he knew it would not be dignified to use a boy as his messenger. The greatest lesson he'd learned in nearly fifty years as a diplomat was that appearance bolstered substance, not the other way around. So the lanky man said nothing as he stepped out.

No one moved to assist him as he rose slowly on his cane. He stood and squinted into the bright parabolic reflectors.

"I have come to request asylum," Fedorsenko said in a strong voice. Then he looked away, suddenly ashamed.

At once, two people walked from the dark corridor into the light, a man and a woman. The man was portly and balding, of medium build, dressed in a three-piece gray suit; the vest was tight, the jacket unbuttoned. The slender woman wore a smart black skirt and blouse with a stylish white jacket. She stood a head taller than the man and was about half his age, in her late twenties.

The man stopped, straightened. "Mr. Ambassador, I'm glad to welcome you as a friend."

"Mr. Secretary."

11

The men shook hands. Secretary of State Samuel Lawrence gestured to his side.

"You know my staff director, Julie Roberts."

He inclined his head. "Miss Roberts."

"Ambassador Fedorsenko."

"Come," Lawrence said. He hovered attentively at the side of the frail ambassador as they walked toward the elevator. The elevator operator, a security guard, stared past them, down the corridor. When they were inside, he punched the seventh-floor button. The armored door slid shut and Lawrence eased visibly.

The ambassador reached into the pocket of his square-cut British topcoat. "Do you mind if I smoke, Miss Roberts?"

She smiled politely and he withdrew a cigarette. Lawrence produced a lighter. Fedorsenko drew deeply, trying to subdue the last vestiges of anxiety. The Balkan tobacco tasted good, but it reminded him more than ever of home. He felt empty, and was suddenly looking forward to seeing Rosenstock. They'd had their disagreements, yet Rosenstock, among all of them, would understand.

The elevator eased to a stop and opened into a small, richly appointed anteroom. Lawrence gestured toward a six-paneled door to the right. "My office is right through here."

They stepped out, and the elevator door slid shut.

The ambassador said, "Everything is arranged . . . as we agreed?"

Lawrence smiled. "Yes. We'll be leaving shortly for the White House. The President will join us, of course."

"I assumed as much. When will Dr. Rosenstock arrive?"

Lawrence touched his lower lip. "Julie, have we located him yet?"

Fedorsenko grew wary.

"We think he's in Cambridge, but we're having trouble—"

"No!"

The ambassador stopped and thumped his cane on the floor once. His companions turnèd.

"I am seventy-two years old and my body is frail. My body, Miss Roberts, but not my mind." He touched a finger to his temple in emphasis, then glowered at Lawrence. It was not the practiced look of disapproval he used in public, but one of genuine disgust. "Secretary Lawrence, the talents and resources of every governmental agency are at your disposal. If Dr. Rosenstock were at a library in Khartoum, you could find him and *bring* him here."

"Sir, you overestimate our—"

"No!" The ambassador shook the tip of his cane at Lawrence's wingtip oxfords. "Dr. Rosenstock was part of our agreement."

Lawrence folded his arms and stared at the floor. The ambassador always fought for the smallest details in negotiations. Lawrence tried to decide whether Fedorsenko was merely being exigent or sincerely wanted Rosenstock at the meeting.

"As you yourself said, Ambassador Fedorsenko, time is important. Therefore, while we try to get in touch with Rosenstock, allow me to suggest the following. I believe what you're looking for is a balance of viewpoints in our meeting."

The ambassador pulled on his cigarette, huffed out the smoke. Lawrence took that as an affirmative.

"May I recommend, then, that Jim Clark be there to represent Rosenstock's point of view? Not only is Jim left of center, but he and Rosenstock are personal friends."

The cane thumped again on the hardwood floor.

"Don't insult me, Mr. Secretary. We both know that

13

as Director of the CIA Clark is already scheduled to be there. I like him, he isn't a *follower*. But he also is *not* Joseph Rosenstock.''

Lawrence smiled crookedly. The emphasis on *follower* had been meant for him. ''Are you saying, then, that you'd go back to your embassy after having come here?''

''Hardly. But I wasn't foolish enough to come with no other options. If I do not place a call within fifteen minutes, representatives of the People's Republic of China will arrive to offer me asylum. And rest assured, Mr. Secretary, I will leave with them.''

Lawrence's smile collapsed. ''Sir, even if we can reach Rosenstock, it will take at least two hours to fly him here. Why don't we start the meeting and—''

Fedorsenko held up his hand. ''Again, that's simply not acceptable. I'm well aware that Dr. Rosenstock disapproves of your policies. I believe he called them 'reckless' in the *Post*. I understand why you don't want him here, and I even sympathize.'' He took a step closer and pointed again with the cane. ''But now *you* must understand. I have not made myself an exile to take part in games. The meeting will be delayed until Dr. Rosenstock can attend, or there will *be* no meeting.''

''Mr. Ambassador, you'd jeopardize everything because of this?''

''Haven't *you*?''

Lawrence flushed, his jaw cocked to one side.

''Of course,'' the Russian shrugged, ''it's your prerogative to hold a foreign diplomat against his will and create an international incident. I will tell them I came here at your request and that you wouldn't permit me to leave. Something about alleged spy activity from our embassy.'' His eyes narrowed. ''Be advised, however, that Chairman Cherganyev is not Gorbachev. *Glasnot* is dead and purges are back in fashion. He and his storm troopers won't simply *detain* one of your representatives in retaliation."

Lawrence remained red but his expression softened. "I see." He gestured grandly toward his office. "If you'll come with me, Mr. Ambassador, we have fresh tea and vodka in my office. You can make your call and I can make mine. Julie"—he forced a smile—"talk to whoever is looking for Rosenstock and see what you can do about getting him here as quickly as possible. And when you find our esteemed Kremlinologist, stress that it is not I who am asking, but you. If we're lucky, he won't hang up."

The woman nodded once, and when her companions entered a drawing room she signaled for the elevator, rode it to the fourth floor, signed in, and headed for her office.

Julie couldn't help feeling sorry for Lawrence. Not only had the ambassador stared him down—no surprise there; Fedorsenko was a master at it, which was one reason he'd survived six regimes before Cherganyev—but now he had another petulant warhorse to deal with. The year before, when Lawrence hired her, he had said that the State Department was the only place in government where the higher the official, the dirtier the job. He was right. Even corporate lawyers spoke to one another with a thicker veneer of politesse than did diplomats.

Julie entered a code on the keypad beside her office door, went inside, and slid behind her desk. Punching up Rosenstock's name on her terminal, she moved the cursor, had the computer dial the number, then picked up the phone.

The truth was, no one was looking for Rosenstock. Lawrence simply hadn't wanted him here. As the phone rang, she found herself wishing she could leak this to the *Times* just to read William Safire's commentary. The two superpowers were about to go head-to-head, yet the President and his advisers couldn't even begin to devise a strategy until a misanthropic little academic arrived.

The woman drummed her red nails on the desk.

She wondered how the President would take the news that Fedorsenko wanted Rosenstock.

With temperance, she hoped. She shuddered to think what would happen if *both* of the most powerful men in the world started running around out of control.

2

The Metro inspector was returning from work as Panas Pavadze emerged from the apartment house. Panas bade the dowdy, middle-aged woman a pleasant good evening; she returned his greeting perfunctorily.

Sour-faced old hen! Panas thought as he stepped from the dingy old building. *What's the matter, didn't you get laid this year?*

But then, he reflected, if he had to work beneath the city instead of in elegance, and come home to one tiny room instead of four, he wouldn't be very pleasant either.

Panas went underground a block from his home and took the Metro to the Arbatskaya Station. There he stepped on the escalator leading to the platform level. He leaned against the railing on the right to let those in a hurry clamber by.

Anyone who noticed the tall, dark-haired man taking his time during the rush hour would have guessed, from his trimly tailored dark suit and polished shoes, that he was with the government. Who else could carry himself so proudly, so *slowly?*

They would have been wrong, but Panas did nothing to discourage the impression. Since Cherganyev had come to power and made militancy fashionable again, he had even taken to wearing his old regimental pin on his lapel, a mark of service in the Soviet navy.

Usually, with studied disinterest, he remained above the looks. Only now and then did his heavy-lidded eyes meet those of his admirers—the lovely young woman here, the anxious-looking man there. Though he had nothing whatever to do with the government, he enjoyed the fleeting sense of power.

Halfway up the long elevator, he glanced at the ponderous round clock hanging from the ceiling. It was 5:45. He was right on time. A brisk walk of four blocks, and he would be at work. He had an annoying visit to prepare for, from the Supervising Director of the Moscow Municipal Executive Committee, but that was still hours away. He would steal a minute here, a minute there, and have plenty of time to get his papers in order. It wasn't difficult to borrow time when you were the boss.

Panas reached the marble-floored main building, drank in the beauty of the sights and sounds that marked the beginning of his day: the red skies shining through high, arched windows: the drone of footfalls echoing through the cavernous station. Night was his time to live, to command, to serve. Night was glory.

What is this?

His nose wrinkled and he hesitated near the exit that led to a pedestrian overpass spanning the busy avenue. This night was different. The cool air was saturated with the sickening smell of fuel oil, far more than the odor of idling buses and lead-footed, low-gear taxi drivers.

What, then?

He looked at the faces of the people pushing their five-kopeck pieces into the turnstiles on the way in. Few looked up; something was on their minds. Then he placed

17

the smell, a particularly low grade of fuel oil burned by military vehicles, the kind that used to make him retch as a recruit more than twenty years ago.

Military vehicles, so close to the Kremlin?

Panas hesitated as people milled around him. He wondered if he should turn around and go home.

If only the Supervising Director weren't coming—

But he was. He would come to the restaurant to review the list of items Panas marked as spoiled after each weekend. Imported cheese. Preserved fruit. Smoked sturgeon. Of course, the items were neither spoiled nor thrown out. They quietly vanished from the storeroom and arrived shortly thereafter at the home of the Supervising Director. If Panas missed the meeting he would have to endure harsh words, perhaps even in front of his staff.

"Are you planning to stand there all night?"

A youth stepped on the back of Panas's shoe. Mechanically, Panas moved on. Breathing through his mouth to temper the taste of the air, he stepped outside and collided with a bulky militia sergeant who was rushing toward the station. The sergeant grabbed at Panas to keep from falling.

"What's your rush, Comrade?"

"I'm sorry—I wasn't paying attention."

The beefy man scowled. "Over here!"

"Pardon?"

Instead of repeating himself, the sergeant pushed Panas to one side, away from the rush of people.

"Stay right there!"

Panas felt his bowels constrict. "I'm sorry, sir, but I don't understand—"

The sergeant's features darkened and his hand settled onto his leather holster. Three soldiers stepped behind him. Eyes wide, Panas backed to the curb, exactly where the sergeant had pointed. The men formed a circle and talked among themselves.

Panas wished his wife were with him. Caterina handled crises so much better than he did. He watched from the sides of his eyes, saw the men point to the station.

Good, he thought, *they're not talking about me!* He raised his chin slightly, trying to look official. Perhaps he could turn this around. If anyone who knew Panas saw him, they might think he had something to do with all this. He gazed sternly toward busy Arbat Square. What he saw surprised him.

To his left, a convoy truck idled with a noisy rattle, its canvas top removed; soldiers with assault rifles sat shoulder-to-shoulder on the hard seats. Behind the truck, a line of armored troop carriers stretched to the first intersection, Kalinin Prospekt, then turned onto the broad boulevard and extended as far as Panas could see. In the other direction, on Gogol Boulevard, an army staff car was stationed by the bronze statue of Nikolai Gogol. Three officers stood by the hood, as grim as the mute figure above them. All traffic that tried to squeeze past the military vehicles on Kalinin was being directed not by the traffic police but by soldiers.

His gaze returned to the soldiers who had followed the sergeant over. They all had tawny complexions and shadowed cheekbones. Panas studied them as they received their instructions. Tatar, Kirghiz, or Uzbek—he couldn't place them exactly, but they were from one of the Central Asian republics.

Is there to be a celebration?

That didn't make sense. Nothing had been announced. Yet why else would these men be here, and all the vehicles? Despite the Central Asians, the troops were mostly regular Moscow units. Was there a terrorist alert of some kind? Had some group dared test Cherganyev's promise to level a hostile city for every Russian hurt by terrorist activity?

The sergeant sent his men into the station with a few

19

words and gestures. As they dispersed, he approached Panas.

Panas bowed slightly and smiled. The sergeant was unimpressed.

"Where were you running?"

"To work, Sergeant."

"At *this* hour?"

Panas's hands were shaking. He rubbed them. The façade of self-importance wavered. "I work at the Azov, sir."

"The restaurant?"

Panas nodded.

The sergeant eyed Panas's clothes. "The manager?"

"Yes."

"Name?"

"Pavadze," he said smartly. "Panas Pavadze."

"Party member, Pavadze?"

"Of course."

The officer noticed the regimental pin and seemed to relax slightly. Panas's breath, too, came more easily.

"Where did you serve?"

Panas told him. He'd been stationed on an aircraft carrier with the Baltic Fleet for two years, 1967 and 1968. What he didn't say was how much he'd hated it—the lack of privacy, of comfort, of dignity. The vile smells. The officers who broke your balls for no reason other than to break balls.

The sergeant straightened his belt. "I'm sorry to have stopped you, Pavadze, but we have orders to secure the area." He thrust a thick thumb toward the station. "In fact, if you want my advice, you'll go home. You won't be doing much business tonight."

"I'd *like* to go home, but I'm expecting the Supervising Director of the Municipal Executive Committee."

"Bah! There's no telling who will be director by to-night and who won't be."

"Why? What's happening?"

"Top secret matters," the sergeant said brusquely. "You'll find out when the Americans do. But look here—" He stroked his fat chin, came closer. "If your Supervising Director does show up tonight, mention that Sergeant Malkov of the militia treated you fairly. Sternly but fairly. Will you do that?"

Panas stood tall. "Of course."

"I know you will! A man doesn't rise without friends and good sense! And perhaps one day I can return the favor."

Panas bowed again. "Thank you, Sergeant Malkov. And—good luck with whatever you are doing."

The sergeant started toward the station, then stopped. "Pavadze!"

Panas turned toward the red brick building. "Yes, Comrade?"

The sergeant grinned, moved his hands as if he were cutting with a knife and fork. "I will tell you this much. Do you serve non-Party members?"

Panas shrugged. "I'm obliged to serve whoever can pay."

The portly man laughed. "That isn't what I meant, Pavadze. Later," he said again, "you'll understand later."

Panas turned back to the street. Now he was curious, looking forward to "later." It wasn't often that life held a mystery, and as long as he was safe behind his Party membership, immune to whatever was going to happen, he could savor the excitement. Of course he would recommend the sergeant! His nerves settled quickly and he told himself that he could afford to be generous. He'd joined the Party early enough. Unlike the last-minute converts, he was above suspicion. Things were finally good for him, and with Cherganyev in power, they were bound to get better.

21

Provided, of course, that no one found out about the food that wasn't really rotted or, worse, about the East German. The things a restaurateur overheard and kept quiet! If only the bastard didn't tip so well.

Panas put worry from his mind. Feeling invigorated, even light-hearted, he looked forward to a quiet night at the restaurant and an important event in the street.

3

Nona loved her little room.

Sometimes she just sat and looked around it. At other times, she was compelled to put her cheek to the cool plaster wall. To touch her home, her sanctuary.

Part of what she felt for it was nostalgia—memories of her mother, of a few cherished lovers. But a larger part of what she felt was comfort. Unlike others who had just one room in Moscow, she had her own sink, the bathroom down the hall was used by just one other family, and she rarely had to use the communal kitchen. On her inspector's salary she could afford items on the black market: tins of meat, fish, and fruit, things she could fix quietly in her room.

Quietly! she thought, shivering with contentment.

The rooms in the basement had more space—this one had been converted from a janitor's workroom—but people down there had to put up with noise from the rusty furnace and the rattling of the water pipes. After spending her days underground, amid the clatter of trains and heavy equipment, she preferred peace to freedom of movement.

And there were newer buildings too, which she could

probably afford. But what was the point of looking into them? There would be a ten-year waiting list—would she really need a new room when she was fifty-six?—and there was always the possibility that she'd be assigned roommates. Strangers. People might not like the music she listened to, or the poetry she read aloud.

There had been room enough here when her mother was alive; there was room enough now. Materially, Nona had virtually everything she required. She wasn't happy, but she was surely satisfied.

Nona stood on a chair to draw the faded curtain across the small window. When she'd come home from work, she'd undressed completely—carefully hanging her gray uniform in the tin locker that served as a closet—then pulled on a white robe and lay on the double bed that filled the center of the room. She'd contemplated rearranging the furniture, pushing the bed against a wall in the corner. Why keep both sides open if only one person lived there? It only cluttered things up.

But memories had distracted her, as they often did. She'd stared at the tattered couch her mother had insisted on carrying on their many moves, remembered making the tear on the armrest over forty years before. . . .

"Why can't you be more *careful?*" her mother had yelled.

Her mother had been so young then. Slender, her brown hair in a bun. Angry, but not hateful. Not yet.

Nona had apologized, sulked. She hadn't meant to scrape the twig across it. She'd been playing Baba Yaga, driving back the witch with a branch from an enchanted tree.

There had been so much room to play. Two rooms, each a decent size. A place for her dollhouse in the corner, a sewing table where her mother turned out a new ribbon or a bit of piping for her dress. Something to

23

make Nona happy when she came home from school with tears in her eyes.

She'd hug her mother, then weep about how they'd called her Comrade Elephant or stolen her chalk of slate so they could watch her lumber after them.

"Just words," her mother would console her, then take down her sewing basket and make the ribbon or piping on the spot. Then Nona would grab her rag doll, Olga, pull over her creaky rocking chair, and sit by the window waiting for her father. When he came home, she'd run to hug him and show off her adornments.

"And who is this angel come from heaven?" he'd exclaim, smiling, scooping her up in his big arms. She'd inherited her size from him. Also his imagination. They'd rub noses and he would hoist her onto his shoulder, walking her through the house, pretending to be the heroic giant Svyatogor. She would play the part of a pixie, and the two of them would search behind the sofa, under the bed, in the closet for the evil Wind Demon. . . .

Nona looked at the clock through tears. Six-ten, yet she was already tired. Or maybe she was just depressed; it was difficult, sometimes, to tell the two apart.

She looked out the window, at the lights of the hotel down the street. The drapes were thin and didn't block out the red light completely. But it diffused them, and if she used her imagination it was a vivid sunset and not glaring neon.

She fixed herself a light dinner of cheese and biscuits and unfolded *Pravda* on her small table. But the words were thick and she couldn't digest them. She read one paragraph over and over before pushing the newspaper aside.

She often though about her mother. After four months, the apartment still seemed empty without her. But tonight the memories were more upsetting than usual.

Why?

She suspected it had to do with the workmen she'd seen during her walk at lunchtime. They were standing on scaffolding around the History Museum at Marx Prospekt, scrubbing the bricks.

Her mother had pointed to just such a scaffold when they'd first moved to Moscow. "Your father puts those up, Nonatchka," she'd said. Nona had been very impressed. She knew that Pietr had fixed railroads before the war, but afterward could no longer walk as much as the job required. There was something called "shrapnel" in his leg. Whatever it was, it hurt, though, strangely, he seemed proud whenever he talked about it. And he talked about it a lot. He talked about the shrapnel and Stalin and a prosecutor named Vyshinsky more than he talked about giants and maidens and princes.

The war had hardened him, but what followed seemed worse. While there were still smiles and a rough hug for Nona now and then, the barrel-chested man didn't look at her the way he used to, or hold her mother, Anya, quite the same way. He seemed hard and distant.

Pietr's status as a war hero had earned them one of the new elevator apartments overlooking the river: two rooms and a private kitchen. He was named foreman of a construction crew, and there was always plenty of food on the table. But sudden noises upset her parents—doors slamming, cars idling outside the window, the elevator stopping on their floor. Then there were the veiled comments at dinner about people Pietr *used* to know.

"But, Papa," the eleven-year-old Nona asked one night, "why don't you know them now?"

Nona's question was answered with an admonition to "Eat your dinner," and she never asked again, though night after night there were always two or three more people whom her father no longer knew. They seemed to be either army comrades—officers, mostly—or Party officials or professors. Now and then he'd heard that a writer had been "taken," or a Jew.

Then, one night, Pietr himself didn't come home for dinner. Nona remembered her mother pacing, staring out the window at the street, drinking coffee, smoking cigarettes. Then the phone rang late at night and her mother pressed it to her ear. She'd wept as she listened.

"Detained? No, I won't worry." A long pause as she composed herself. "I love you."

It was August 24, 1951, and Nona never saw her father again. Seven weeks later an official statement arrived, telling them that Pietr Pietrovich Nemelov had been convicted of industrial sabotage and sentenced to ten years as a ZEK, a political prisoner, somewhere in the east.

She learned a new word: purge. She understood that night why her father always seemed to know fewer and fewer people, why entire families were suddenly forced to give up their apartments, as she and her mother were—

"Enough!"

Nona rose suddenly from her rickety wooden chair. Folding the uneaten portion of cheese in wax paper, she placed it in the wobbly icebox and stalked back to the table. She leaned on it, her eye resting on the small mirror hanging from a nail beside the door. She studied her face—so wide, with sad eyes, full eyebrows, and thick, frowning lips.

What was wrong with her? Her mother was at peace, her life *now* was good. Why let a memory upset her?

Because it's happening again?

No. Cherganyev was not Stalin. He revered Lenin, he did not destroy families. Whatever was happening tonight, the preparations she'd seen in the streets, the soldiers and military vehicles, it was innocent. The world was too dangerous for anyone as reckless as Stalin to rule Russia.

Nona sat heavily on the bed. She set the alarm clock, flicked on the radio, and listened to a Prokofiev suite, *Ivan the Terrible*. They were playing "Ivan Before Anastasia's Tomb," and it soothed her, caused her mind to wander.

She wished Georgi were with her. Not to make love, but to hold her. She smiled. Considerate as he was, Georgi was not a good lover—though she would never tell him that. It would destroy his poet's soul. The smile broadened. She wondered what kind of a lover Cherganyev would be.

"Bad," she laughed to herself. A girlfriend of hers at the Railroad Institute once said that men raise flags when they can't raise anything else. And if there were anything at which Cherganyev excelled, it was raising more and more banners.

Nona yawned. The music, the oboes, relaxed her.

She'd heard that her first lover, her cousin Dmitri, was now a leading physicist at one of the cosmodromes. She wondered, were she to meet him today, if he would apologize for what he'd done—forcing himself on her in a hay cart when she and her mother arrived destitute in Kiev.

Does it really matter?

She'd wept, then, for days, and felt dirty for months. After that, she didn't allow anyone to manipulate or control her. Even Nikita, her superior, knew just how far to push her. And Georgi—dear Georgi never pushed her at all.

The music seemed distant, and her breathing slowed. She felt safe, happy, and independent. As free as the sparrows that used to delight her as a child.

She was asleep when the music ended. Snoring heavily, she didn't hear the host announce the special broadcast that was soon to begin.

A broadcast from Arbat Square. A broadcast, he promised, "to stir the blood of every Russian."

A broadcast, he said, from the heart of Lenin Utra itself.

4

Joseph Rosenstock rubbed Edge on his round, lumpy face. The green gel foamed and turned white, and Joseph wiped his hand on a towel. He dragged a Bic razor up his neck.

"Shit!" The nick wasn't bad, but it stung. "See what happens when you rush, idiot?"

He tore off a sliver of toilet paper, stuck it to the wound, and resumed shaving. He hated doing stupid things, but it *was* 4:50 in the morning, and who the hell did he have to look good for, anyway? Certainly not Lawrence or the President, and he doubted Julie Roberts would be there.

For the mystery guest?

Julie wouldn't tell him what was up, which was smart. *She* was smart. Not only weren't the lines secure, but she wanted to make sure he came. And there was nothing like a political mystery to get an administration critic out of bed.

Joseph washed his face and didn't bother applying a fresh scrap of toilet paper. The cut looked as if it belonged. More than one critic had said his face was more like that of a prizefighter than an eminent historian, and Joseph had grudgingly come to accept that. The mouth

28

was set at a slight angle, and the bulbous nose was also lopsided; the ears were small and thick-lobed.

But no one ever criticized his big hazel eyes. Lively and intelligent, like those of a cat, they were the feature that people remembered.

He turned on the shower, stripped off his pajamas, and tried to imagine what that matter could be.

A situation, she'd said. That was political newspeak for a crisis. They hadn't called him when Cherganyev recently surged to power or, before that, for the Daniloff arrest, Chernobyl, the shooting down of KAL 007, or even when the head of the KGB, Andropov, came to the Kremlin. Now a car was on its way to take him to Hanscome, where a private plane waited. It had taken sixty-four years, but he was finally getting VIP treatment.

He grinned. *And if my track record is any indication, twelve hours from now I'll be heading to the Eastern shuttle in a dirty cab.*

So what? It'd make a great tag line for an op-ed piece.

Joseph tested the shower, adjusted the temperature, and stepped in. He plunged his face into the spray, washing away clinging remnants of sleep. His anticipation grew. For the first time in years he wasn't merely going to share his knowledge, as he did at the university, or flaunt it, as he did in his many essays and books. He was actually going to *apply* it. As much as he hated President Alexander, that felt good.

He shook his head, still trying to puzzle out what could be up. He assumed it wasn't an assassination or a military confrontation, since those were hardly the kinds of things one could keep secret. . . .

Joseph wagged a finger by his ear, as though cautioning himself. Leaning out of the shower, he yelled, "Lil, honey?"

A mumbled "Huh?" floated back through a pillow.

"Do me a favor and put on 'Headline News.' Watch

and see if they say anything about the Soviets. I'll be out in a minute.''

He got back under the water, scrubbed quickly. State didn't have the brightest people overall, and something might have leaked to the press. He'd love to walk into the room knowing what was up, just to shock the hell out of Lawrence and the President.

He pulled a towel around his shoulders and hurried from the bathroom. Lillian Rosenstock was propped on an elbow, staring vacantly at the television. A handsome woman with high cheekbones and short blond hair, she looked much younger than her fifty-eight years. She worked hard at her appearance, eating the right foods and staying in shape. Still, as she told her husband often, she was convinced he would outlive her; she had to put up with him, he did not.

Joseph used the light of the TV to select his clothing. ''Anything?''

Lillian yawned. ''They found a rock four-point-six billion years old.''

He frowned at her, walked back to the bathroom to dry himself.

Lil craned toward him. ''Joe, who is Julie?''

''Julie Roberts. You met her at that UN dinner for Fedorsenko.''

''The tall brunette? Pretty?''

''That's her. And smart. Lawrence hired her from one of those Wall Street law firms, the one Nixon used to be with.'' Joseph slung his towel over the shower rod, realized the hole he'd dug for himself. ''Yes, she's a remarkable girl. In fact, when I first met her, I told myself that if we'd had a daughter instead of two sons, she'd have been like Julie.''

Lillian said nothing. She twisted the edge of her pillowcase into a small, tight knot.

Joseph rubbed Right Guard under his arms. It was a

good try, casting her as a prospective daughter, but Lillian hadn't bought it. Time to change the subject.

"Lil, you awake?"

"Uh-huh."

"Remember the last time I was at the White House?"

Lillian nodded, but still didn't look over.

"Hon, remember? They had about forty of us come down when Cy Vance quit over the Iranian rescue fiasco?"

"I remember."

"Lawrence was one of the experts the President called in then, and I'll never forget how he looked at me when I suggested moving Mondale to State and having Glenn become VP. Carter at least smiled. He knew it wasn't a bad idea, even though he couldn't do it. But Lawrence gave me this idiot Marine *glower*, like I was army or navy *dreck*, and told me I was crazy. Crazy," he snorted. "You want to know what's crazy? Naming Lawrence as Secretary of State. The man who masterminded Grenada, big-stickmanship at its most inimical."

He came back into the room. The sports report was on and Joseph shut off the TV. Lillian pulled the covers to her cheek, watching as he dressed. In the light, his sense of style was merely awful; in the dark it was disastrous. She said nothing.

Joseph saw her watching him as he knotted his bow tie. "Something wrong?"

Her hair moved on the pillow. It looked like a no, but in the dark he couldn't be certain.

"You're pretty quiet. You sure you're not angry?"

"About what?"

"About me going to Washington. It's just a visit. I'll be coming home, probably before dinner. Maybe even before lunch."

Lillian turned away, and Joseph stopped dressing. She *was* angry. That was all he needed now: guilt. Just enough to distract him. He sat on the bed and stroked her hair.

"Why are you worried about Washington?"

"You really want to know?"

"Of course."

She faced him. "Because I have a feeling they're finally going to *want* you down there."

Joseph snorted. "Me? Not this administration."

"Yes, this administration! Who's smarter or cooler in a crisis?"

He kissed her forehead. "You."

"Really? Who's the one that took charge when the kids broke arms or legs? Who chased out the bats and snakes—"

"They've already got people in Washington who do those things."

"You know what I mean."

"Besides, talent doesn't matter as much as cronyism. Look at Lawrence, Perkiel, Kubert. Clark's the only one who got in on talent. This is an aberration, I guarantee it." He stood and finished fixing his tie. "I promise, we're not leaving Cambridge. We've got a good life here, and I know what your job at the club means to you."

"There are health clubs in Washington—and *I* know what government means to *you.*"

"Tsuris!" He threw up a hand to emphasize his disgust. "Nothing but trouble. And I guarantee you, by this afternoon at the latest, the U.S. government will *want* to function without me. It will *yearn* for it."

Lil stared at him as he folded his green blazer over an arm—his green blazer with the blue pants.

He smiled over at her. "Look, Lil, Sam Lawrence is in for the duration, two more years of this term and four of the next. He's pushy, smug, trigger-happy. You know how much you hate the haughty women down there, all the phonies? I hate Sam more. If I went to work with

32

him, I'd either resign or be arrested for murder. Justifiable homicide"—he waved his finger again—"but murder just the same. I'll be back," he assured her, kissing her on his way to the door.

"The navy blazer!"

Joseph stopped, looked at his arm. He smiled self-consciously and went back to the closet.

"Thanks, hon. I know what it took for you to do that."

She watched as he selected a new jacket and ambled away, saw the light go on in the study. He sat on the arm of the sofa and looked out the window.

"Call!" she yelled. "And you'd better call your office, too!"

Joseph raised his hand, signaled that he would, and went to the phone.

5

Joseph rang the history department and left word on the answering machine that he wouldn't be in—though he didn't say where he was going. All Dean Reynolds had to hear was that he was seeing President Michael Alexander. Tenure notwithstanding, Judie would dismiss him on the spot.

Joseph sat back down on the armrest and peered out at the driveway of their sprawling Tudor home.

He knew that Lil believed him when he said he hadn't slept with other women. But he knew she didn't trust him when it came to Washington. He hated the cocktail parties and the posturing, and above all he hated the bureaucrats. But that was intellectual discomfort, and he

33

could reason it away. Despite his denials, they both knew he'd take a government appointment in a minute.

He opened the window a crack, and savored the bite of the cold morning air. Even after ten years in Massachusetts, the sudden arrival of fall was a surprise. It hadn't been that way in Brooklyn, where he grew up, or in New Haven, where he'd studied and later taught at Yale. And it certainly wasn't like that in Washington. Fall tangoed with summer for a while in those places; here it hit hard and fast and booted summer out.

It was his favorite season, decisive and angry. It was comforting to pull an old sweater from the cedar closet and go walking through the changing foliage, to scoop up a football as it rolled loose across the footpath, or watch couples walk arm in arm, close together.

This was a better place than Washington, he tried to tell himself. Despite the faculty infighting and the students who knew everything at the age of nineteen, at least there was diversity. Time for himself and for Lil. A chance to get away and see the children and grandchildren. He would never have had that working at State or at the White House. And Lil would never last. She loved teaching aerobics at the club, working with the unpretentious people of Cambridge. She would be miserable trying to fit in with the snobbish, self-assured women in the capital.

Headlights brightened the road and lit the four walls lined floor-to-ceiling with books. He leaned forward, looking at the shrinking cones of light; the car sped past and he settled back on the armrest.

Of course, there was one thing he would have had in Washington: a chance to leave his fingerprints on history. He'd accomplished everything else during his career—won every important academic honor in the United States and Europe, written for and been written about in every national and professional publication in the States

34

and in the Soviet Union, served on international panels from which all other Americans had been banned. Maybe it was time to compromise.

Who am I kidding? he thought. No one was going to ask him to stay there. This was some kind of image-making bullshit to appease the liberal press or the Democratic Congress. When they were finished with whatever they needed him for, they'd discard him, just as he'd discarded them in the past.

His reverie was interrupted by another set of headlights, moving more slowly than the last. The car stopped beside the mailbox, then swung into the driveway. Rising, he pulled on his blazer and walked on tiptoes to the front door.

6

The twelve-mile ride to Hanscome Air Force Base took just over nine minutes. It usually took longer, but the driver, a bull-necked captain, was quiet and very efficient; he hit the Concord Turnpike entrance ramp at sixty and accelerated. He kept glancing at the clock beside the odometer, obviously keeping to a tight schedule.

Speeding through an open gate and onto Hanscome's innermost runway, the captain headed for a silver and blue Saberliner that shone brightly beneath the spotlights. The car stopped perpendicular to the staircase and Joseph let himself out.

The whine of the twin turbos drowned out the welcome of the copilot who came down the stairs to meet him. The young man led Joseph to the six-passenger compartment, then shut the door; the professor's face unscrewed as the thick carpeting and leather seats soaked up the residual sound of the engines. The copilot told Joseph to select a seat, then entered the cockpit.

Joseph flopped down, exhaustion quickly catching up with him. He opened his eyes wide to snap away the haze. As the plane began to taxi, he studied the walnut-grained console before him. There were earphones and radio dials marked for domestic and shortwave. Below it, in a matching wooden tray, were heavy bond writing paper, envelopes, two Cross pens, and a pocket dictionary. He wondered which Air Force muckamuck had spent taxpayers' money so he could write love notes to his mistress on twenty-pound cockle-finish paper. He knew that truly important memoranda were sandwiched between doodles on legal pads. His cheeks burned with the familiar loathing he felt for the indulgence in Washington, the fuck-you attitude that prevailed at all times except the two months before election day. He felt the old demons returning—the desire to serve, but also to change things.

Joseph had wanted to stay awake to contemplate what might be afoot in Washington. But, succumbing to the comfort of the seat, he napped until the Saberliner began its descent. Feeling more exhausted now than before, he glanced out the window, surprised that the aircraft had avoided the outlying Air Force bases. It touched down in a light drizzle at Washington National Airport, rolling to a stop on a section of the tarmac just beyond the TWA gate.

The copilot came back. "Welcome to Washington."

"I thought military traffic didn't land here," Joseph joked.

The young major grinned and looked with mock dismay at the pilot, a lieutenant colonel. "Are we military?"

The pilot gave his passenger a "Who, us?" look as the major heaved open the door and unfolded the steps.

Joseph sniffed the cool, damp air. Misty rain tickled his face. He was already uncomfortable; this *had* to be Washington.

A black Lincoln limousine rolled from behind the wing and a protocol officer jumped out. He snapped open an umbrella as he hurried toward the stairs.

The major stepped back so that Joseph could pass. "Have a good day, sir."

"I'll try."

The protocol officer reached the landing and stood sideways, motioning for Joseph to go down first. He tilted the umbrella over Joseph's head and followed.

As he descended, Joseph noticed blue and red lights flashing on the wet tarmac. There were two unmarked sedans waiting behind the limousine, with window-mounted flashers.

Dr. Rosenstock goes to Washington, he chuckled to himself as he ducked into the Lincoln. His good humor quickly dissipated. No one had come to brief him. Lawrence wanted to keep him guessing—or, worse, wanted to embarrass him.

The young man came around the other side and the mini-motorcade got underway, the cars hurrying down the field toward the Memorial Bridge. The young man beside Joseph said nothing.

The pricks.

Sending a lower-echelon employee had been a calculated snub, but Joseph could live with that. Playing games with national security was another matter.

So be it, Joseph decided as he stared through rivulets streaking the glass. He'd extemporized brilliantly in the past; he'd do it again.

And stick it to Lawrence the first chance he got.

7

As always, Panas found the sight of the Azov reassuring. It was a haven from the bustle of the city, from whatever problems he was suffering at home. He let his eyes travel possessively over the old stone walls and the high windows, then upward to the narrow tower that rose from one corner of the roof. The tower's small, silvered dome caught the last rays of the sun.

Panas climbed four cobbled steps and poked a finger into his vest pocket. Though the heavy beechwood door would be unlocked, he always touched his key upon entering. He wasn't a superstitious man, except when it came to black cats, spilled salt—and this. He was convinced that if he stopped the ritual he'd end up like his predecessor. And with Alexei nipping at his heels . . .

He twisted the knob and entered.

The stench of the fuel was supplanted by the smell of the flowers on the tables. Their welcome was like none other; a chestful of their breath lifted him to his toes, drew him in. He glided happily through the darkness, the only illumination creeping from beneath the double doors of the kitchen.

The splendor of the Azov's exterior was matched on the inside, but only when the lights were kept low. The massive beams overhead were pitted and grooved from two centuries of heat, cold, and insects; the rough pine tables were warped, and many of the fringed white tablecloths—magnificent in their prime—were stained beneath strategically positioned ashtrays and vases. An alert observer would also notice that the carpeting had been patched and repatched, that the original hand-fired china settings included many factory-made replacements, that most of the wineglasses, if tapped, responded with a tinkle instead of the bell-tone of crystal.

"Pavadze?"

"Eh?"

The manager turned toward a small waiting area to the left of the door. Behind the small bar, Alexei, the captain of waiters, stood frozen. Panas followed his gaze toward the two men sipping tea on the divan.

Who are they to address me like that? What is this, Pick on Panas Day?

They wore sport jackets, crewcuts, and unpleasant expressions. Then he noticed the holstered pistols poking from their open jackets. The *L*-scars on their foreheads.

Dear God.

Sredá-Grom.

"Panas Pavadze?"

"Yes sir—" Panas wanted to puke; he was barely able to push the words up his throat.

The men rose, setting their tea glasses on the brocaded fabric of the divan.

"Pavadze, your papers."

It was a brusque command from the shorter of the two men. He had a lisp, but it wasn't funny. Panas fumbled for his case.

"I have them right here," he tittered. He realized he was acting guilty, but couldn't help it. He knew exactly what had happened. Alexei, the dog, had reported his illegal activities.

The case slipped from his nervous fingers.

"Allow me," Panas said with a flourish, as if one of the others had dropped it. He bent, his stomach bubbling violently.

The man with the lisp stepped closer. Even in the dark,

39

Panas could see his downturned lips, his sallow face. Panas handed the man his documents.

"You'll find, sir, that everything is in order. I'm very careful about regulations. In the restaurant too. The health inspector is always thoroughly pleased."

Panas's heart galloped. It *had* to be the "spoiled food." He should never have let the Supervising Director talk him into it. He'd only have been the captain of waiters, but at least he wouldn't have the SG poling into his affairs. The fire crept up his breastbone.

The short man gave the papers a cursory examination, then dropped them on one of the tables.

"Many foreigners eat here, Pavadze. You speak with them."

The tone was accusatory, and he wished the man would stop calling him by his last name. It was intimidating.

"It's my job," he said, as pleasantly as possible. "I greet them, ask them harmless questions—do they enjoy Russia, how are the other restaurants." His mind said *Stop,* but his mouth raced on. "It is professional, sir, nothing more. Alexei, my fine captain of waiters here, can tell you—"

"Everything checks," the shorter man said to his companion. "He's the one."

Panas froze. *The one? No, God!*

"Come," barked the other, a brute with the face and arms of a bear. He had to suck in his belly to button his jacket.

"Come?" Panas blurted. "Where?"

Both men looked back at him. "With us," the shorter man said.

"I—I don't understand," Panas said bravely. "Why . . . I was just talking with my good friend Sergeant Malkov of the militia a few minutes ago, and we were both saying how proud, how *very* proud we were of—"

"Stop talking," said the bigger man, "they're waiting."

They? Who?

Panas pressed his lips shut. Trembling, he grabbed his papers from the table and followed the men out. Feeling an overwhelming desire to hold his wife, he hoped that Alexei—the traitorous bastard!—would at least have the courage, the *decency* to telephone her. Otherwise, Caterina might never learn what had happened to him.

After all Panas had gone through in forty-three years, he could not believe it had come down to this. He was being taken by the SG to an unknown location and an uncertain fate.

He wanted certainties?

There *was* one. He was certain that Alexei was watching him. Drawing his shoulders back and looking straight ahead, Panas made certain he marched proudly from his restaurant.

8

Joseph was traded again at the White House.

The protocol officer handed him to a Secret Service agent, who said exactly one word more than his predecessor: "Evening." After passing through a metal detector discreetly hidden in the molding of a doorway, Joseph and his new escort headed down a solemn corridor carpeted in red and decorated with paintings of the Spanish-American War. President Alexander had learned about the art from his wife and ordered the paintings brought up from storage. Having inherited Nicaragua and El Salvador from his predecessor, he liked to remind critics that war to the south was not unprecedented. Joseph hoped there were no paintings of either of the World Wars

The Secret Service agent was stereotypical—wiry, humorless, steel-eyed. But what interested Joseph was that his hand was constantly moving, casually brushing his belt, buttoning and unbuttoning his gray jacket, sliding up and down his tie. A hand in motion was able to get to a holster faster than a stationary hand; Secret Service people did this when a President was in the open or when several of the nation's leaders were in one place.

Joseph grinned. This *was* big. And while he felt utterly compromised being here, what elation! Now if only he could figure out what was going on . . .

They were headed for the Green Room, one of several conference chambers in the West Wing. Joseph stopped abruptly in the room's oval reception area. The Secret Service agent watched, puzzled, his hand hovering midway up his tie, near what Joseph presumed was a shoulder holster.

"There's a heavy smoker in there." Joseph pointed with his chin toward the mahogany-paneled door. "Balkan shag tobacco."

"I wouldn't know, Dr. Rosenstock." The agent's hand stretched toward the door. "Please come with me, sir."

Joseph resumed his shambling gait. His mind raced. If he was right, that could mean only one person. Fedorsenko.

He'd met Anatoly Fedorsenko five times: first in 1973, when they were both on the negotiating team that arranged the Apollo-Soyuz orbital flight; three times on TV panels (on the last, he'd lit a pipe to protest the Russian's cigarettes); and most recently at the UN party. They'd been civil to one another in 1973 and at the UN, but the TV appearances had been a different matter; the ambassador had been particularly incensed when Joseph insisted that it was the upheavals of the First World War that had enabled Lenin to come to power, and not a natural evolution in Russian society.

But then, Fedorsenko had to disagree, Joseph reflected. Otherwise, Cherganyev would have had his head.

So Fedorsenko was here, though Joseph couldn't figure out why. If there was a military crisis, he'd hardly have come to the White House, and an Alexander-Cherganyev summit would have been arranged during business hours. Hostages? Terrorists? Another nuclear leak?

In those cases, a low-level diplomat would have been dispatched, not Fedorsenko. That left only one possibility, incredible though it was. When Stalin consolidated power in the 1930s, he called his ambassadors home for consultations and then had them shot. Could that be happening again?

It didn't seem possible. This was *modern-day* Russia. Cherganyev had enough enemies at home that they would resist; the world press would eat Cherganyev alive.

Assuming, of course, that Lenin Utra gave anyone the chance. Joseph felt a chill in the small of his back.

The door opened soundlessly on oiled hinges, and Joseph stood for a moment on the threshold. Three men looked toward him as one. Seated on a Hepplewhite sofa was Secretary of State Lawrence. Behind him, by the unlit fireplace, stood CIA Director Jim Clark. Joseph smiled triumphantly. Across from them, Fedorsenko sat on a matching Hepplewhite sofa. Though unusually ruddy in the warm glow of the cut-glass chandelier, his leathery face looked drawn, his gray eyes unhappy.

Then Joseph was right. He regarded the ambassador, his own eyes gleaming.

"*Zdrahvojti,* Mr. Ambassador. The purge—it will be widespread? Bloody?"

43

Jim Clark slapped the marble mantel. "Full speed ahead!"

Lawrence frowned and rose. "All right, Joseph, two points for you. Now let's wait for the President, shall we?"

"Certainly, Sam." Joseph came forward, a bounce to his step, while behind him the Secret Service man shut the door. Joseph smiled wryly as he shook the Secretary's hand. "I just didn't want anyone to think I was out of practice."

"We read op-ed pages here. No one would ever accuse you of getting soft. Anyway"—he sat back down—"I appreciate your coming on such short notice."

"Your idea?"

Lawrence frowned. "But of course."

Clark came around the sofa and extended his hand. "Professor, it's good to see you again."

"Likewise. How've you been?"

"Busy."

"Productive?"

Clark snickered. "You know how it is. I spend ninety percent of my time justifying to Congress and the press what I do with the other ten percent."

"Sounds like academe."

"It sounds like everywhere," Fedorsenko said to himself, though loud enough for the others to hear.

Joseph turned. The Fedorsenko he knew was forceful, quick, arrogant. The man before him looked frail. He stepped around the low, marble-topped tea table where a copper teapot and a prismed decanter of vodka had been placed within the ambassador's reach. The teacup was dry, the tumbler full.

"I'm very sorry," Joseph said sincerely. He offered his hand; Fedorsenko laid his own inside it. "My own parents used to say of their own flight, 'It had to be.' Yet no one loved Russia more."

44

"Tell me, did they ever go home again?"

Joseph lowered his eyes. The ambassador's chest emptied slowly.

"I shall. Did they tell you what has been happening?"

Joseph shook his head.

Fedorsenko threw a harsh look at Lawrence. "I expected more from you, Mr. Secretary."

"Security," Lawrence replied with a shrug.

The ambassador drew hard on his cigarette. "Whose?" he muttered, then faced Joseph. "As you've surmised, Dr. Rosenstock, Cherganyev has moved quickly to consolidate his power. Several high officials have already been arrested, and just before I left the embassy I learned that General Grishena shot himself."

"At his command?"

"No, at home. They didn't even allow him that last honor."

Joseph ignored Lawrence's angry huffing behind him. "You were good friends."

"We *all* were. We fought together—with Cherganyev."

"Is Foreign Minister Aksakov all right?"

"So far. You know him, he's a bulldog when he needs to be." Fedorsenko stared at his cigarette. "But I love him. And I worry for him."

Joseph tapped his chin. "I assume, then, that you're defecting—but not in the customary sense. The fate of Anatoly Fedorsenko is not what concerns you."

The ambassador shut his eyes in accord. *"Spasibo,* Dr. Rosenstock. Thank you for perceiving that."

"A man like you—your loyalties couldn't have changed. Nor should they. You serve your nation well."

The ambassador smiled for the first time since leaving the embassy. "I was not wrong in asking for you."

Secretary Lawrence made a point of stepping between them and pouring himself some tea. He took a sip and set it down, remaining between the men. Joseph backed off with a sigh.

Moments later the door swung open and the President strode in. An aide pulled the door shut behind him. A tall man, several inches over six feet, Michael Alexander walked directly to the ambassador. Fedorsenko rose unsteadily on his cane.

"Mr. Ambassador," the President said, taking Fedorsenko's hand within both of his, "I'm sorry to keep you waiting. I had to have a word with Joe Orlando."

"The press has already heard?"

"From the Chinese, I'm told."

Fedorsenko stamped out his cigarette in a crystal ashtray. "They always *were* sore losers."

The President withdrew his pocket watch. "Joe won't be making any official comment until the regular briefing at ten, which gives us nearly four hours to sort things out."

Coughing, Lawrence stepped over and introduced Joseph. The President offered his hand.

"I've read your essays, Dr. Rosenstock. Don't pull any punches here, either. We need all the help we can get."

His candor caught Joseph off guard; he'd expected curt formality, nothing more. Joseph thanked the President and promised to do his best.

Much had been written about Alexander's charisma, and against even his hardened instincts, Joseph found himself under the President's spell. Part of it, he knew, was the stature of the office. The presidency had given even Nixon a propped-up splendor. But much of it was also this man. His height wasn't apparent on TV; in person he was tall and slender, Lincolnesque. His voice was low, starting from somewhere around the knees and gaining resonance; the blue eyes were hypnotic beneath bushy black eyebrows. His face, often described as gran-

46

itelike, was exquisitely chiseled: high cheekbones, a square chin, the nose long and straight, the forehead broad beneath dark brown hair. He'd been a TV reporter, local news anchorperson, mayor of Cleveland, senator from Ohio, now President. He knew how to convince and project and cajole.

If only he weren't so damn conservative, Joseph thought.

Following Lawrence's lead, Joseph sat on the sofa. President Alexander wished Clark a good morning, then stood facing the ambassador.

"Sam—want to fill me in?"

Joseph leaned forward with interest. The Secretary of State cleared his throat.

"As you know, three weeks ago Ambassador Fedorsenko and I met to discuss the sudden naming of Cherganyev as General Secretary of the Communist Party and Premier of the Soviet Union. The ambassador indicated to me then that there might be purges, and that if there were, he might consider coming here for assistance."

"Specifically?"

"A change. From within if possible, from without if necessary."

Joseph filled his lungs through his nostrils. He recognized the intelligence euphemisms: "within" was revolution, "without" was death. They were here to plot the overthrow of the leader of the Soviet Union.

The ambassador tapped a fresh cigarette several times on the top of his cane, and withdrew a fancy lighter from his jacket pocket.

"Before we discuss such an unprecedented act," he said, "I must stress, Mr. President, that it is necessary that Cherganyev be unseated not just for the sake of the Soviet Union, but for the sake of the *world.*"

Clark looked over from the mantel. He rarely appeared to be paying close attention to whatever was being said, but he never missed a word or nuance.

"Mr. Ambassador, I appreciate your concern about all the internal unrest," Clark said, "but our intelligence reveals nothing to suggest a radical change in international policy—"

"Speaking more frankly," Lawrence cut in, "I'd like to know exactly what it is you're offering us here."

"Offering?"

"If you and other officials are unhappy with Cherganyev, why should we become involved? The Politburo has removed leaders in the past."

Fedorsenko grew irate. "You don't understand. Even if there were enough support in the Politburo, which is doubtful, his spies, the Sredá-Grom, are everywhere."

"The Sredá-Grom," Alexander said. "The Lenin Utra thugs with the *L*s burned in their foreheads."

"Named after the day they were formed," Clark noted, "literally *Wednesday Thunder.*"

Fedorsenko nodded. "Only they're not just thugs. They're like Hitler's SS—autonomous, organized, and pervasive. The KGB protects Russia; the SG protects the party. Cherganyev has the power to pick off his enemies one by one. And the people are behind him. They've been very skillfully manipulated."

"Are they really that shortsighted?" Alexander asked.

"No, Mr. President," Federsenko replied. "That patriotic. Whenever President Reagan wrapped himself in the American flag, many officials and intellectuals cringed. But many *more* people rallied behind him. The commoners. The masses. They supported whatever he wanted, no matter how reckless it was. It's the same with Cherganyev. My country has always been run by a form of social contract: as long as basic creature needs are provided, the people will support whoever is in power."

"But you still haven't answered Sam's question," the President pressed. "Why should *we* interfere?"

The ambassador lit the cigarette. "Because a madman is now in control of the mightiest army on earth."

The President ignored the boast. "By 'madman,' you don't mean the things he's been saying about Lenin."

"Not at all. I hold Lenin in high regard myself."

"I understand. I meant no disrespect." It was a clarification, not an apology.

"By madness, Mr. President, I'm referring to the political equivalent of jihad—a holy war."

Joseph muttered, "Lenin instead of Allah."

The ambassador nodded.

"Holy war," the President repeated. "Is this a spiritual or a battlefield confrontation?"

"You still don't understand. Cherganyev has already *won* his spiritual war. Those who are not on his side will be converted. Those who are not converted will be dead."

"How, exactly?" Alexander asked.

"At home, the Sredá-Grom will handle the purges."

"And abroad," Alexander said, "you believe he'll go to war."

"He's that crazy?" asked Lawrence.

"That *devoted,"* Fedorsenko corrected. "you know that the group Cherganyev founded, Lenin Utra, is a political movement. But it began as something far more personal—what some would call a father fixation. Your national pride is spread over many political figures: Washington, Lincoln, Roosevelt. We have only Lenin, and long ago Cherganyev made him his."

"Lenin Utra," said the President. "What exactly does that mean?"

" 'Lenin Awake.' "

"His philosophy, you mean. Like Che in the sixties?"

"More than that. It's like a religion."

The ambassador noted the confused looks of Lawrence and the President. He poured vodka, took a sip.

"To understand his devotion, you must understand

what happened to Cherganyev. He was born in Kiev, father unknown, mother a prostitute—a working woman, his biography says. Anyway, the child was taken from her and raised in an orphanage in the Ukraine. Such institutions were run by the Party then. Socialist history was the only subject that mattered. Students learned that they were children of the Revolution, and that Lenin was the father of the Revolution. Most children accept that intellectually. Cherganyev also absorbed it emotionally."

Fedorsenko fortified himself with two quick sips, then stared into the tumbler as though it were a crystal ball.

"A teacher at the orphanage tells the story that Sergei Ilyich went into a trance the first time the children went to Lenin's tomb in Moscow. He jumped to the glass, put his mouth to it—like a sea snail sucking. The teacher needed help from a sentry to pull him away. A small child, yet as rigid as a corpse, pasted to the glass. Eventually, of course, he learned to control such displays, though his talk of Lenin was constant."

Joseph said, "He was a zealot during the war—"

"He was a *miracle*, Dr. Rosenstock. When the Germans invaded, he ran away from the orphanage. Others were content to surrender, but not Sergei Ilyich. He turned up as a messenger and spy for Russian units— still but a boy, mind you—sneaking through combat zones, building a network of other runaways and orphans, like myself." He paused and rubbed the head of his cane for several long moments. "For nearly fifty years I loved him." He shook his head. "I still do."

Joseph ached for him; Clark seemed suspicious. Fedorsenko continued.

"Many of those children were unable to adjust after the war. Accustomed to stealing, they stole. Raised on warfare, they fought. Many were sent to labor camps, a few were even executed. But not Cherganyev. He had learned in the orphanage how to internalize his fervor.

In 1945 he was recruited by the NKVD—now the KGB—and put to work in its Surveillance Service. He rose quickly, became a major at twenty-two. It was then, with great skill and dedication, that Cherganyev began building his hidden network, Lenin Utra."

"It was not part of the KGB then," Joseph said. "Actually, it was more like a fan club."

"A very dangerous one," Fedorsenko added, emptying the glass and refilling it. "Not only was it made up of fanatics but who would dare argue with reverence for Lenin? Even if one *had* sound ideological differences, as I did, no one wanted to make an enemy of the KGB. Of course, now that Cherganyev is in power, Lenin Utra no longer has to hide behind the KGB. Indeed, rivalry between the KGB and the Sredá-Grom is often quite intense."

"It sounds like the evolution of the Nazi Party," Alexander said gravely.

"Very much so, although in its early days Lenin Utra was quieter, more patient. They were content to leave foreign affairs in the hands of the leaders. Their efforts went to domestic control, primarily sabotaging moves toward westernization."

"Which Cherganyev did brilliantly," Joseph said, "maneuvering to have this one appointed a minister of trade, that one a store manager. He was like a chess master whose every move suited a master plan."

"Cherganyev happens to be a superb chess player," Fedorsenko noted. "Dr. Rosenstock, do you remember Vera's letter?"

"His first public move," Joseph said. "Vera was Cherganyev's mistress, since deceased. She wrote a letter to *Pravda* in 1985 and it became a rallying cry, sort of like Patrick Henry's 'Give me liberty or give me death.' In it, she said, 'I live in the Vinnickaja Oblast in the Urkainskaja Sovetskaja Socialisticeskaja Respublika and

I no longer feel proud to be a member of Komsomol. All about me, people pursue consumerism. Even my friends in the youth organization are free to wear blue jeans and listen to loud music. This can only lead down the path to destruction. Yet it is tolerated by our leaders. I ask why?' "

The ambassador raised his glass. "You have an excellent memory."

"I don't understand," said the President. "What does the letter have to do with—"

"Cherganyev? This was *samokritika,* public self-criticism, unseen since the death of Stalin. No letter is published in the Soviet Union that does not reflect the goals of Soviet leadership, meaning that years before he officially took power, Cherganyev was already in control. Vera's letter was a seed, and soon there were many such seeds, a map of Cherganyev's progress. In *Trud,* the trade union journal. In the youth organization's *Komsomolskaya Pravda.* And in the army's *Red Star.* Lenin Utra infiltrated those areas slowly, methodically, *successfully,* until there were enough people in place to give Cherganyev supreme power."

"And now?" the President asked. "What does he want next?"

Fedorsenko's expression was grim. "Cherganyev loves Lenin, but in a way he is also in competition with him. He wants to be *more* than Lenin."

"What can be more than a legend?" Alexander asked.

The ambassador drew on his cigarette and answered simply, "A god."

9

The SG men escorted Panas around the corner and ushered him into the backseat of a small black Moskvich. The sallow man drove, steering onto broad Kalinin Prospekt and darting between the troop carriers. His burly companion stared out the front window, alternately cracking his knuckles and tapping on the metal stock of his machine pistol. There was no conversation and neither man looked at Panas, who gazed forlornly out the window.

Panas tried to imagine what was in store. He wasn't surprised that they hadn't bothered to question him. Experts were waiting to do that at SG headquarters. But as he thought things over, he realized it didn't make sense that Alexei or the Supervising Director would have turned him in. They had to know he would incriminate them when questioned.

What difference does it make who betrayed me, or why? he asked himself. He was doomed. Tears formed in his eyes.

Through their blur, he realized suddenly that the car was not headed toward Dzerzhinsky Square, site of the SG center. They had swung around from Kalinin to Arbat Street, past the red stone Metro building where Panas had exited. His heart swelled as they turned into Gogol Boulevard and slowed. Perhaps they were simply going to make sure that he did indeed know the sergeant, and then let him go!

Suddenly hopeful, Panas noticed now that in the few minutes since he'd been here, a division of combat-clad troops had assembled, rank upon rank, facing a tall concrete building, the General Staff Headquarters of the Red Army. Panas was surprised to see that they held placards bearing the portrait of Lenin and the inscription LENIN UTRA. The portrait and legend had become more commonplace over the past few weeks, yet for it to have supplanted the traditional regimental banners amazed him. Even Stalin, at the height of his powers, had not tampered with military tradition.

The Moskvich jounced across a corrugated artillery ramp laid over the curb. It eased into a narrow passage the soldiers had left on the sidewalk, before the wall of the General Staff Headquarters and out of the way of the military vehicles. Lieutenants and their captains pressed against the wall to make room, stealing surreptitious glances at the car inside before swinging their gaze back to the troops that stood at parade rest.

The bearlike man ordered Panas to get out. Panas thanked him for the ride, opened the door, and found his legs wobbly.

The small agent got out. "This way."

Panas followed him toward the front door of the building. More curious now than frightened, he noticed that the troops had left a clearing farther along the sidewalk. A clutch of civilians was silently huddled there, some staring at the building, others gazing expectantly at Panas.

He was suddenly terrified again. *Are they waiting for me? Am I to be shot?"*

His escorts stopped. The big man jabbed Panas's trouser cuff with the toe of his shoe.

"Stand with them."

Panas stepped forward. *We're all going to be shot,* he thought, looking at the thick ranks of soldiers. *No chance they'll miss. Oh God . . . God!*

From a doorway, another man in a sports jacket watched him closely. In the glow of a nearby street lamp,

54

Panas saw the telltale scar on the man's forehead, the red *L* burned in the flesh of Cherganyev's elite. Panas's arms shook violently in his sleeves. He looked away and stepped to the back of the group.

The stench of the fuel in the air made him want to retch. He was reminded of photographs he'd seen of French and Polish partisans during the Second World War. Rounded up, gunned down. Was this a random act designed to put fear in the hearts of Muscovites?

They didn't have to make any examples on his behalf. He vowed that if he survived, he would take his membership in Lenin Utra more seriously, become an activist.

Panas studied his companions. Most seemed worried, especially the older ones. There were about twenty people in all, men and women, old and young. Some wore uniforms. One woman just in front of him had on the blue linen coat of a doctor. That reassured him somewhat; they wouldn't kill *her,* he reasoned.

Behind him, the SG car pulled away and an identical one arrived. The occupant—tall, goateed, professorial-looking—was sent to join the crowd. In silence he took his place beside Panas, his mouth an unhappy crescent.

Several minutes passed. Panas tried to count the portraits of Lenin. That failed to distract him, and he looked up at the matchstick array of antennae on the roof of the building.

The SG man in the doorway leaned toward him.

"Not yet, Comrade."

Panas shot him a surprised look.

Not yet? What had he done? He'd simply looked up at—

The roof. The man was still staring at him, so he dared not look back. But something was going to happen there. An acrobat would perform. They were there for newspaper photographs, to show that a crowd had gathered to watch. Or maybe a huge banner was going to be unfurled, a grand new portrait of Lenin. A cross-section of people would be photographed before it. This was all harmless, celebratory. No one was going to die.

There was a knock on the door where the SG man was standing. He came forward.

"Look up at the building," he said in a clipped voice. "Do not look away—"

Seven stories above, a window exploded outward. Shards of glass rained down, followed by a man. An officer. Falling. His uniform fluttered in the breeze, and his scream was shrill. Panas stared with disbelief as the man's eyeglasses flew off, his arms crisscrossing in front of his face. His legs kicked like those of a baby. He hit the street with crushing impact just a few meters in front of the group. His body seemed to collapse into his shoulder, his head snapping back. Glass from the window tinkled around them, some of it landing on Panas's hair and shoes. He didn't budge.

Before the group could quite comprehend what they'd witnessed, an officer broke from the phalanx and covered the body with a brown army blanket. The dead man's blood soaked through the fibers. Somewhere in the group, an old man began to weep.

Panas thought, *Quiet, old fool, you'll get us in trouble!* But the SG man didn't seem to hear. His eyes were on something beyond the group, in the distance.

Panas stared at the moist blotch that turned the blanket purple. Why had they been brought here to see a man fall from a window? Never mind whether he'd jumped or been thrown—why have an audience?

Someone whistled two sharp notes from the front rank of soldiers, and Panas saw automobiles working their way around the military vehicles. The ranks parted and the SG man sprinted through to meet a black ZIL limousine. The car nosed into the clearing, stopping just beside the dead man, and the SG agent opened the door. He stood at attention.

Only the front of the car fell within the cone of the street lamp. Beyond it, someone emerged from the backseat. The broad figure was followed by two others, men in military uniforms. All three stepped into the light.

Panas gasped.

One of the newcomers was Cherganyev.

10

The silence in the Green Room was oppressive. No one moved.

A god! Joseph thought. The last world leader who had aspired to godhead was Hitler, and he hadn't led a nation armed to the teeth with nuclear weapons.

It was Clark who finally asked, "So while Cherganyev honors Lenin and the past, what does he do for an encore?"

Fedorsenko said softly, "Foreign adventures. That will not only satisfy his ego, it will rally the people. Especially if he can create the impression that Russia is a victim."

The President's expression was stern. "Jim, how'd your people miss this?"

"It isn't his fault," Fedorsenko said. "Cherganyev evolved the plan alone, sitting in Lenin's study. Orders were passed not by computer, whose electronics can be tapped, but by fountain pen."

"Lenin's?" Joseph asked.

"Of course."

"Will he move against China or the West?" Clark asked.

"China cannot be intimidated; we've been trying for decades."

"Europe or the Middle East?"

"Cherganyev will present a peaceful face to Europe, hoping to drive your NATO allies from you."

The President slid his big hands into his pockets. He stared at the woven eagle beneath his feet. "Israel, then."

Joseph watched as Fedorsenko put his mouth to the tumbler. He was clearly delaying his answer. It was the point of no return, Joseph surmised. Defection was about to become treason. From the look in Fedorsenko's eyes, he obviously hadn't expected it to hurt like this.

"Yes, Israel. Specifically, along the West Bank of the Jordan. He plans to have a small band of volunteers invited in by the Arabs, then pit them against the Israeli army."

Lawrence leaped from his seat. "That's insane! The Israelis wouldn't tolerate the Red Army on their border. They'd find an excuse to wipe your boys out before they could blink."

"*Precisely.* And that massacre will be followed by Cherganyev rousing the Russian people and the Arab world both to vengeance. The ships and troops will already have been prepared—and in the eyes of the world Cherganyev will have *every right* to mobilize! He will have been attacked."

The President shook his head. "I can't believe it. Even Cherganyev isn't mad enough to tempt another World War."

"You're missing the point. Cherganyev doesn't believe he *will* start a war. He has proposed this action before, but each time the Politburo had the power to keep him down. Generals Popov and Grishena were always particularly effective in arguing against such a confrontation."

"Winning, but never convincing Cherganyev?" Clark asked.

"One cannot argue with faith. Cherganyev believes that Lenin will protect the Soviet Union from harm. And when the purges are finished and the Politburo falls completely under Cherganyev's control, he will not only have a shield but also a *mandate* to succeed."

"And there's *no* one who will stand up to him?" Lawrence asked. "Not Aksakov or Popov?"

"Would you? I didn't come here because there were alternatives, Mr. Secretary."

Lawrence sat back slowly. The President asked Fedorsenko how much time they had.

"There will be speeches and ceremonies first, to impress the people. And an escalation of the purges, of course." The ambassador shifted his head from side to side. "A few weeks at the most. Maybe days, once he's learned that I've been to see you."

President Alexander resumed his pacing. "Sam, should the Israelis be told?" His voice was thick but calm.

"I don't see that there's a choice."

The President gnawed his lower lip. "Jim, what's the status of Project 17?"

"It'll be green-light in about a month."

The Russian asked, "Project 17?"

Clark looked at the President, who nodded. The CIA Director said casually, "Bioengineered viruses. If Israel goes, they plan to take the world with them."

"They'd unleash biological warfare?" Fedorsenko asked with amazement.

"Not warfare," Clark corrected. "Annihilation. The Israelis have a nuclear arsenal of about 150 bombs, but they don't have the resources for mutual assured destruction, and they don't trust us to use ours. So they came up with these germs and stockpiled them in the Negev and at sixteen other sites—enough bacteria to wipe out every living thing bigger than a micron." He snickered mirthlessly. "What they've got makes the fungal toxins you've been raining on Laos and Cambodia look like manna."

At the UN, Fedorsenko had denied the "yellow rain" that poisoned crops and made those governments dependent upon the Soviet Union. He didn't deny it here.

The President's shoulders rose and fell. "Is there any way to get in and neutralize them?"

"The bugs, no. The silos? Possibly. They're all computer-controlled on site. But I wouldn't bet the planet on it. Each of those installations has nearly enough contaminant to knock out a good-sized city. All we'd have to do is screw up on just one and a few million people would buy the farm."

"Insanity!" Fedorsenko wheezed.

Clark agreed. "If our enemies don't get us, our allies will."

"Ambassador," the President said, "if we were to tell Cherganyev about the viruses, would that temper his ambition?"

Fedorsenko shook his head. "Even if he believed you, Mr. President, it wouldn't change a thing."

"What about the fact that you've told us his plans?" Lawrence asked.

"He won't care. He believes in the manifest destiny of the Soviet Union. His goals depend upon destabilizing the Middle East, upon having your allies stray farther from you as they measure their oil reserves."

The President's face remained expressionless. "And assuming Cherganyev *is* able to shake up the Middle East without destroying the world, how far does he intend to go?"

Fedorsenko laid the stub of his cigarette in the ashtray, and his veined hand curled into a fist. He measured each word of his reply.

"As far as you let him! The key, gentlemen, is to answer each move with power. When Soviet ships and planes go on red alert, place your fleet in the path. Match every move, ship for ship, plane for plane. When he sends his troops to the Israeli border, make certain yours are on the opposite side."

"Wouldn't he attack just the same?"

"Not if your European allies are still with you. And it's important to remember that if we act fast, before Cherganyev has had a chance to complete his purges and rally support, there will still be opposition at home and among Cherganyev's own allies. Quiet, but present." The ambassador's fist unclenched and he reached slowly for his cigarette. "But most important, gentlemen—as you do these things, do not talk to Cherganyev. No open diplomatic contacts. No secret diplomatic contacts. No UN resolutions. Be silent. Persuade your NATO allies *not* to try to act as go-betweens. Stall for time and make a temporary retreat the only acceptable answer for him."

"A mind like a chess master," Joseph muttered. "Cherganyev won't accept a loss or even a stalemate."

"Very true. Which is why, while one hand stops his armies, the other must work toward the . . . *change* we spoke of."

The President thought about it. He looked at Clark; Joseph sensed something unspoken passing between them.

"Gentlemen, I suggest a break. Sam, you and the ambassador talk names of people we can count on over there. Dr. Rosenstock, I'm sure, would like to rest after his trip. Jim, give me ten minutes and we'll meet in the Oval Office."

Clark nodded and the President strode toward the door. He hesitated and half-turned back.

"Dr. Rosenstock, wasn't it you who wrote last month in the *Post* that I was reckless?"

61

Joseph wilted a little. He didn't want to be sent home, not now.

"Yes sir, I did."

"Assuming I did in fact order the Stealth bomber tested over Soviet airspace, do you still feel I was wrong?"

Joseph hesitated, then nodded. The President smiled.

"I'm sure Cherganyev would agree with you, but I'm also sure of this: when faced with a chess master, it's often best not to play the game, but to threaten to clear the board. And if you *do* make that threat, your opponent had damn well better know that you can do it." He regarded Fedorsenko. "Rest assured, Mr. Ambassador, I have every intention of answering power with power."

The President left, and Lawrence rocked on his heels. "I believe, gentlemen, that's two points for our side."

Joseph didn't agree, but he didn't argue. He'd known, of course, that Alexander was fond of his armed forces, but the implication that he'd scramble a radar-proof nuclear bomber as a first resort? Between Alexander and Cherganyev, there wouldn't be a scoreboard left standing.

What's more, he couldn't understand Fedorsenko. The ambassador knew the rules. There were other ways to intimidate Cherganyev, the standard ones: sending ships and troops steaming toward the trouble spots; an increase in top-secret radio traffic, gibberish to confuse the Soviet code-breakers; new pictures from spy satellites, which the enemy would also intercept. Among the lot of them, they could even have figured out something new and creative. Yet Fedorsenko had said nothing in response to Alexander's threat. Was he too old to care, too tired?

Or perhaps he was too jealous. He had no family, just his country, and he'd lost it to another man. Would he rather see it destroyed? Could they trust his judgment in this matter?

Joseph's head spun. He had to talk to Clark, a sensible man. Without intelligence reports, the President could do nothing. And right now, Joseph sensed that doing nothing was the lesser of two evils.

11

Cherganyev stood beside the car while the two men—generals—walked in different directions, splitting to review the troops. When they were gone, Cherganyev went to the blanket.

Panas could see him clearly. Given what he'd just witnessed, Panas knew it was incongruous to smile. But he couldn't help himself. He was awestruck at seeing any celebrity in the flesh, but to behold the most powerful man in the world—the most powerful man in history—made him forget his fears. His love was absolute. He hoped that the Chairman was not upset by this man's death.

Panas basked in Cherganyev's presence. The leader was larger than he would have guessed—beefy, even a little soft-looking. His face was rounder than the newspaper photographs had hinted, and his complexion was pale.

But he burned with power. He wore a light gray suit and a black worker's cap, the flat kind favored by Lenin; beneath the short brim his eyes were deepset and riveting. He stopped beside the body. Like two small machines, his dark eyes moved from the blanket to the crowd to—

Panas!

He realized with a jolt that he had locked eyes with the Chairman. Panas was unable to look away, nor did he want to. Even when Cherganyev looked at others, singling them out, Panas continued to stare.

Then the Chairman spoke.

"This did not have to happen!" he bellowed, hands apart, palms upturned. "This man held a high position in our military, but he did not honor Lenin. When he realized the error of his thinking, there was only one honorable thing for him to do." Cherganyev lowered his hands slowly, like the pope. "We salute General Popov for having done that. But this did not have to happen." His eyes returned to the crowd. "And each of you was chosen to be here to help ensure that it does not happen again."

Panas was transfixed. He had been *chosen* by Cherganyev! The memory of Sgt. Malkov faded to insignificance.

Malkov! Panas realized, suddenly, what the sergeant had meant when he said, in parting, *"Do you serve non-party members?"*

On a platter. A cruel joke from a little man. He pushed the officer from his mind, stared at his new leader.

Cherganyev had lowered his hands and was drawing a finger across the crowd.

"You are all Party members employed in a place where you meet many people. You are professors. Physicians. Reporters. Restaurateurs."

Panas swelled with pride.

"Others will betray us still, but what you must do is make it clear to those you meet that Lenin's Great Bolshevik Revolution is reborn. You must report that you have seen tragedy befall those who ignored the will of the people. You must tell them that even they would be wise to join our renaissance, prudent enough not to stand in our way."

Cherganyev spread his hands again. "This did not have to happen." He stared again at Panas. "Comrade, there is a message on buildings all over this land. What is that message?"

Panas prayed that his bowels wouldn't open or his voice fail him. He prayed, too, that the smug men who had brought him here were watching.

He said clearly, "Lenin lived. Lenin lives. Lenin will live."

Cherganyev smiled like a proud parent. "Again. Louder."

"Lenin Lived! Lenin Lives! Lenin Will Live!"

"Once more."

"Lenin *Lived!* Lenin *Lives!* Lenin *Will Live!*"

The troops picked up the shout. It spread like a wave across the boulevard, thousands of voices in unison.

"Lenin Lived!"

The wave became a single chorus.

"Lenin Lives!"

The wave rose proudly, confidently.

"Lenin *Will* Live!"

Panas's groin tingled with excitement. *He* had unleashed this, and he shouted louder than he could remember ever having shouted. He wanted to add words. *"Bless Cherganyev! God praise Lenin! Lenin is God!"*

With supreme effort, he refrained. He turned his enthusiasm into volume rather than improvisation.

"Lenin Lived! Lenin Lives! Lenin Will Live!"

His eyes were fastened on Cherganyev. The Chairman was staring at one of the portraits of Lenin, his lips moving in private communion.

To hear what he's saying! Panas thought. *I would give a week of tips to find out!*

He suddenly became aware of the doctor looking at him, her expression more severe than before.

Still glowing with pride, he bent toward her ear. "Is something wrong, Madam Doctor?"

The woman pointed behind her. He looked. A trio of SG men came from the building.

"So?"

"Honor!" she yelled. "The man was forced to jump."

Panas recoiled. Was she mad?

"You'd be wise to keep quiet! I have friends who disapprove of such mutterings!"

"You fool! No one has friends. No one has a *future!*"

Cherganyev nodded toward his two generals, who were standing at either side of the General Staff Headquarters building. They raised ceremonial sabers, and at once the soldiers dispersed, double-time, in all directions.

Panas ignored the woman, and asked the man beside him where the soldiers were going. The man shrugged; Panas shrugged. Did it really matter? Glowing with pride, he rejoined the chant.

The doctor watched lines of soldiers snake through the streets.

"Fool," she repeated to herself. "They go to unleash insanity on us—on the world."

12

Joseph and Clark walked slowly down the corridor. A Secret Service agent followed several steps behind.

The men hadn't seen each other since an arms-control summit two years before, which Joseph was covering for a book. But there was no chitchat; there never was when Clark was working.

"So, Professor, what do you think about Fedorsenko?"

Joseph raised his shoulders. "Fedorsenko's been a key official since Stalin. That's a lot to throw away by coming here. But he also wasn't himself in there."

"Maybe he was just tired."

"No, it was more than that. He's *scared.*"

"He's always been a hell of an actor."

Joseph shook his head. "I've seen him when he's playing to a crowd. This wasn't an act. Besides, what does he gain by lying to us?"

"For starters, he can discredit us in Western Europe."

"How?"

"Think it through. Suppose the Arabs invite Soviet forces to the Middle East on maneuvers. And suppose we do what Fedorsenko says and send our troops there. Also on maneuvers, with the Israelis. And suppose, while we're there, the Syrians and Jordanians muster troops along the borders, not a Russian among them. They provoke an incident, make sure we're involved, and who comes off as the aggressors?"

"It's possible," Joseph admitted, "but I don't think Cherganyev would go through all this just to embarrass us. Gorbachev or even Brezhnev—yes. But given Cherganyev's missionary zeal, Fedorsenko's scenario makes sense. It's imperialism, pure and simple."

"And you still don't see the value of Stealth?"

Joseph frowned. "Don't tell me you do!"

"I believe in covert solutions to most problems, Joseph. That's why I left the Air Force before Vietnam. You don't saturation-bomb villages, you slice out one leader at a time until they start seeing things your way. But do you want to know what you're really up against with Stealth, Joseph? You're fighting precedent. And when a President has a precedent that worked, arguing against it is like pissing up a rope."

"I don't follow—"

"All the President has done was to dust off a plan drawn up by the Truman administration when we were the only ones with the Bomb. The philosophy was and is simple: an enemy shapes up or gets shipped out. Why do you think North Korea finally went to the peace table?"

"He was going to bomb them?"

"Publicly, he spoke about avoiding another Hiroshima and Nagasaki, but in private, he planned to level P'yongyang and Hamhung."

"Even so, we're no longer the only ones with the Bomb."

"In effect, though, we are," Clark said. "We're the only ones who can deliver it unseen and take out the nerve center of the enemy."

" 'Take out'? Jim, you're talking about destroying eight or nine million people and a city that's older than God."

"Assuming, of course, that it gets that far—"

"It *will*," Joseph cried, "believe me. Cherganyev won't back down. He saw how the press roasted Alexander for the last flyover. So what happens this time? You get Stealth airborne and Cherganyev keeps on pushing. He doesn't think you'll actually drop the Bomb."

"In that case, *he's* responsible for what happens, not us."

Joseph's frown deepened.

"Besides," Clark said, "what about the casualties we'll *all* suffer if Project 17 gets a green light? How many Israelis will die on the West Bank if there's a war over there? In my book, it's better to lose a half-million enemies than a half-million or more allies."

"Better? Whatever happened to finding a solution short of mass murder?"

"You think we aren't trying? Professor, if you've got

a way of discrediting Lenin Utra fast, I'd love to hear it. I've got three of my top people working on ideas—but so far, everything we've come up with runs the risk of making a martyr of Cherganyev. And you know what happens then. Cherganyev loves Lenin, but the Sredá-Grom loves power. *They* wouldn't hesitate to use nuclear weapons to take the Middle East.''

Clark had a point, but the alternatives caused Joseph's stomach to boil. ''Christ, whatever happened to the hot line?''

Clark grinned. ''The hot line's been a placebo since Johnson got pissed at Gromyko once and yanked it out of the wall. It gives the public a sense of confidence—but a military strike does that and more. It gives us leverage. Remember how Qaddafi calmed down after Reagan zinged Tripoli?''

''Big deal. Iran and Syria picked up the slack. Fear only works as a policy.''

Clark frowned. ''I hear what you're saying, and as I told you, we're all trying to find other solutions. Not just my people, but we're also moving out our conventional forces, taking our case to the UN, and the other major step we've taken.''

''Which is?''

''Breaking security. Telling Fedorsenko about Project 17. He's asked to have lunch with the Polish ambassador; we're going to allow it. If nothing happens, fine. But if Fedorsenko is jerking us around about his defection, or if he's really convinced that the Russians and Israelis are going to go toe-to-toe, he may send word to the Kremlin about the bugs. If Cherganyev didn't know about them before, he may change his plans.''

''Or he might launch an all-out peremptory attack on Israel.''

''That's doubtful. The Israelis would still have time to open the silos.''

"It's doubtful, but it's not impossible."

Clark pursed his lips. "No, there are no guarantees. That's why the Good Lord invented places like Cambridge, places where people who understand too much can escape the madness of reality." Clark smiled. "The truth is, Professor, I envy you. If I didn't hate teenagers more than I hate bureaucrats, I might join you there."

They stopped beside a six-panel white door. Joseph felt as though his head had been squeezed. He stared at the floor, his breathing shallow, his head light.

Clark studied his companion. "You look like hell. I know you're a Ramada Inn man, but I had one of the secretaries book you a room at the Watergate—I thought you'd appreciate staying there."

Joseph mumbled his thanks.

"Soak in the tub, have a good brunch on us, get some rest. I'll call as soon as anything develops."

Clark left then, and Joseph continued down the corridor, the Secret Service agent still following a few steps behind.

Sleep won't cure anything, he thought. *What we need is for Stealth to drop a bomb on Washington.*

Joseph thought back to how bothered he'd been when Alexander appointed so many military men to key positions. A brigadier general as ambassador to Israel. A former Air Force contractor as Attorney General. Even Clark, for all his liberal leanings, had been an ace fighter pilot in Korea. He'd never liked the message Alexander was sending to the world, but now the appointments frightened him.

Joseph reached the end of the corridor, and was surprised when there was no one to meet him. Since there was a room, there must also be a car; shrugging, Joseph stepped outside while, behind him, the Secret Service man quickly pressed a walkie-talkie to his lips.

The bright morning caught him off guard; he thought

70

time had stopped in there. He was stunned even more by the gaggle of reporters waiting in the drizzle. They approached as one, and though no one seemed to know who he was, they knew something was up and threw questions at Joseph as a car drove up. Their words were a blur of overlapping sounds.

"Sir, did you meet with—"

"—is Ambassador Fedorsenko inside—"

"—the rumors we've been hearing about purges true or false?"

Joseph wouldn't have answered, but a tall man with a round face came scurrying from the White House corridor to make sure. Joseph recognized him from the UN party: Lenny Wengler, former public relations head of the NAACP, now Alexander's deputy press secretary.

Wengler went around the car, away from the reporters, and climbed into the backseat. Crawling across the seat, he pushed open the door so Joseph could get in.

"Sorry to have left you like that. I didn't know you weren't staying with Clark."

"Good system you've got."

"No one ever tells us anything. We lower-echelon types are supposed to read minds."

As the men switched places, Wengler shielding Joseph from the crush of journalists, a microphone was poked between them. Scowling, Wengler turned behind him to face a persistent man from ABC.

"Sam, get that thing out of my—"

"Lenny, what's the story?"

"There'll be an announcement later, you know that."

"Later'll miss 'Good Morning America.' Just tell us if the ambassador's inside."

"Ten o'clock!" Wengler pointed to his watch in emphasis as he slammed the car door behind him. Joseph saw Sam's face gnarl like a tree knot, saw his lips continue to move as the car pulled away. Being a freedom-of-the-press man from way back, Joseph felt bad. But it was just as well he hadn't talked to them, for what could he possibly have said—other than, *Get your bureau chiefs out of Moscow, my friends, we're planning to destroy the city!*

13

There was a world above and a world below. The one above could be familiar and warm, but it could also be oppressively lonely. Nona was glad she could exchange one for the other.

Each day, the escalator would make its long descent to the tunnels. And during the ride, Nona would be transformed. In the soft light of the station, surrounded by marble columns and magnificently detailed wall mosaics, she would leave the girlish part of herself behind and become an adult. A professional. She would report to the office of Nikita, her supervisor, and get her assignment for the day.

"Clock the trains coming in to Dobryninskaya Station. Report those that are not precisely ninety seconds apart."

Or, *"Watch the turnstiles for anyone who tries to enter without paying. Take their papers, write down their names."*

Sometimes the transformation was essential. Like today. She had delved too deeply into the past the night before and she felt hollow, unhappy. Work was what she needed, even work as dreary as what was in store for her today: finishing up her monthly inspection of the tracks. She'd spend her first five hours on the line from Rechnoi Vokzal in the northern part of the city to Khakovskaya Station in the south. Then she'd collect Nikita to make the trip through the unused trunk, the eighth Metro line.

She hoped that would chase away the memories so she could enjoy her one day off: twenty-four hours every Wednesday. Time to relax, time to spend with Georgi. She hoped it didn't snow, so they could be outside. She also hoped he was in a good mood. That was selfish, of course, but when he was depressed he brought her down—despite the smiles she put on for his benefit, the jokes she told.

The morning inspection revealed that the north-south tracks were fine. Nona rode a succession of head cars, studying, in the bright glare of the headlights, the left side first, then the right. She noted on her report that the maintenance chief was to be commended.

Then came the tour Nona never enjoyed.

It was just after one o'clock in the afternoon when she stepped onto the flatbed repair car and stood beside her supervisor. She wore a thick wool sweater beneath her uniform jacket. The Metro tunnel was dark as well as unheated, the blackness making it seem even colder.

Cold, too, were the memories it evoked.

The eighth Metro line was quite different from the others. Those were broad and concrete-walled; this one was a black tube carved from the rock, wide enough to carry a single electric coach. It ran from the sub-basement of the Council of Ministers Building, through the footing of the Kremlin Wall, and under Red Square before heading south. It ended quietly beneath the Moscow River, not far from the Vobriev Highway.

Dubbed the "Stalin Express" by the gulag slaves who built it, it was constructed for just one passenger, Stalin, so that, if necessary, he could leave the city undetected.

Few people had known about it, then; her father had worked on it. "Doesn't it tell us something, Nonatchka, that a man who plots and murders and betrays must live in fear?"

It did, and how she wished Stalin had needed to use

this route and had vanished before terrorizing Russia, her family. The sense of emptiness began to return, and she forced herself to concentrate on the job at hand.

Since the track did not join with any other, the only way to inspect it was on a flatbed car. She'd appropriated this one from the crews who used them to repair tracks at night, when traffic was light. The coach which had been assembled here for Stalin now sat idle beside the tracks, used to store Metro equipment ranging from shovels to cement to dynamite.

Pulling on expensive gloves, the supervisor pushed a red button and Nona gripped the rail at the front of the car. She had no gloves, and her hands stung from the cold of the pitted iron bar. The small cart creaked and moved slowly forward.

The fumes of the sputtering gas engine were different from the ozone on the electrified tracks. The gas wasn't tart but light, heady, intoxicating. And the chugging of the engine was reassuring, as if she had a companion.

A friend, really, for she already *had* a companion: Nikita, her supervisor. But he didn't work as hard as she did, or as hard as her comrade the engine. He came only because he had to, because he knew the tunnel better than anyone else.

As he reminded her each time they took their monthly tour of the tunnel.

They moved more slowly than they could have walked, the cart geared for traction, not speed. Nikita peered down, a lantern on either side of the front rail lighting the tracks. The stark glow gave the bald, hawk-nosed man an evil cast.

"I worked on this line, Nona, did I ever tell you that?"

Every month, she wanted to tell him, but she let him talk. He wasn't evil or even harsh, just meticulous. Unimaginative. Afraid to depart from routine. She studied

74

the tracks on her side, looking for rust or any sign of crumbling in the railbed.

"Only fifteen, that's all I was. The men were in the army, so prisoners and boys like me did all the work. Drilling, dynamiting, carting out the rock, setting the ties. If you'd ever tried to use a little mallet and a dull chisel to chip out the bed for a railroad tie, then spike in the rails, you'd know what blisters are!"

Nona continued to stare ahead. She knew what blisters were. She got them when she pulled track switches manually to make sure they were working, carted heavy petrol cans to the flatbed on the mornings when she had to inspect repair work before trains were allowed through, or crept into drainage pipes to make certain they weren't clogged. She got them on her feet, constantly, as she stood on the platforms, marking what time the trains arrived and departed. They were what made her skin rough, masculine instead of feminine.

Nikita threw a spindly arm toward his left. "See where we are? Of course you can't. You'd have to know this place like I do. We're passing the foundation of Lenin's tomb. We had to reroute the wiring of the tomb when we built the tunnel. I pulled the cables through myself. Imagine, only a boy of fifteen doing such important work!"

He pulled the old iron lantern from the railing, and held it well over the side.

"Look, you can see the very spot. There—just below that outcropping."

Nona looked over absently. A thick bundle of cables ran along the top of the wall, held in place by big metal brackets. They disappeared into a large hole beneath a pyramid-shaped rock that jutted from the wall.

"My hands bled, but what a good feeling! Suffering for Lenin. Cherganyev should give me a medal!"

His voice rose, echoed through the tunnel, died. He shook his head.

"Up ahead we started to hit sand. Do they ever think about it, I wonder, those who ride around in comfort? Do they ever marvel at what we did to make their lives easier? Sand! If you're digging a tunnel, sand is your enemy. Each time it starts to slide back, you have to run like a lunatic. Everything can fall in on you in an instant."

Nona understood the feeling. She felt like that at times, especially when she thought about the past, about her father. As if grief or emotion would smother her. The only difference was that there was nowhere to run, except to sleep.

Or to Georgi. How she wished it were he on the flatbed instead of the wiry little supervisor. She could listen to *him* talk about anything, especially his work.

The reached a wall of moss-covered cinder blocks, the end of the tunnel. With a sigh, Nikita pressed a button that sent the cart shuttling in reverse. They turned to study the tracks as they passed over them again.

"Ah, you don't know the half of it," he complained as they passed the tomb once again. "Remind me, when we have the time, to tell you of the water pocket we hit while digging. We were cut off from the outside for hours!"

He *had* told her about it, more than once. "I will," she promised as the cart reached the narrow tunnel, carved from stone, that led to a catwalk in an adjoining Metro.

When they reached Nikita's booth on the platform beneath the Council of Ministers Building, he generously agreed to fill out the forms so that Nona could leave. She knew he did it so he could sign his name in both spots— inspector and supervisor—but Nona didn't mind. Promotions didn't matter, anonymity did—being left alone

76

to enjoy music, Georgi, new clothes now and then, interesting novels.

Her private thoughts and memories.

Bidding Nikita good afternoon, she hurried up the narrow stairway and through a gate marked Do Not Enter. There was still time to do some shopping before she was supposed to meet Georgi. She needed a new winter coat, stockings, a scarf. She would have time to get at least the scarf, but only if she found something delicate and attractive.

She entered the chrome-and-tile lower lobby of the building, then rode an escalator to the main lobby. Nona squinted as she stepped through a revolving door into a side street off Red Square. She stood for a moment, allowing her eyes to adjust to the brightness.

And she knew at once that she'd be doing no shopping today.

14

Joseph was awakened shortly before noon by the rattle of a key in the door.

Housekeeping. He'd forgotten to put out the Do Not Disturb sign. Where was the Secret Service when it was needed?

"I'm still in here !" he shouted, and was answered with an apology in Spanish. *"Gracias!"* he yelled as an afterthought, hoping the woman had heard.

He used the remote control to flick on the TV, curious to see how the press briefing had gone.

Cartoons were on. His mouth tasted foul. Coffee, he

thought, and went to call room service. As he reached for the phone, it rang.

"Joseph?"

It was Clark.

"Morning, Jim. I mean—good afternoon. How are things?"

"Not quite what we'd hoped."

Joseph was suddenly wide awake.

"Can you be downstairs in five minutes?"

"I'll be there in three."

He hung up and bounded from bed. He wouldn't bother shaving; he hurried to change. As he did so, "Washington at Noon" came on.

"There is big news today from the Soviet Union," said the anchorman.

Joseph froze with his pants half on. He reached for the remote, punched up the sound.

"As we reported earlier, a complete news blackout has been in effect for several hours. This, in the wake of the defection to the U.S. of their ambassador, Anatoly Fedorsenko. Now, the new government has sent soldiers to place all Americans under house arrest."

Joseph was dumbfounded. The anchor introduced correspondent Jack Gish at the State Department.

"Good afternoon," Gish said. "Jay, in a terse statement, the Soviet Embassy here in Washington announced that the Council of Ministers of the Union of Soviet Socialist Republics has ordered all foreign journalists, diplomats, technical personnel, and most foreign nationals either residing in or visiting the USSR to remain in their quarters until further notice. This order includes a ban on all communications with the U.S. Soldiers of the Red Army have been instructed to enforce the order to the letter, and a spokesperson stressed that failure to conform will result in immediate imprisonment and prosecution according to law."

78

Joseph whistled. "They'll do it, too."

He continued dressing. It was a hell of a law, Article 19 of the 1981 code governing the rights of foreigners in the USSR. What it meant was that they could shoot anyone they wanted. Nick Daniloff had been lucky—the spy that the United States traded for him was of low rank and more trouble than he was worth. But if the Russians intended to hold thousands of American citizens hostage until we gave back Fedorsenko—

Or worse, he thought, *what if Cherganyev doesn't intend to turn them loose at all? If we block him in the Middle East, he starts putting Americans on trial. If we send Stealth over there, we make a lot of widows back home.*

Joseph tied his shoes and listened as the President was quoted as being "extremely concerned for the safety and well-being of citizens of the United States now in the Soviet Union," while Secretary of State Lawrence affirmed the administration's "determination to take every step necessary to ensure the rights of Americans under international—"

Joseph snapped off the TV. Maybe Lawrence *had* to posture like that, but bullshit made him angry, clouded his judgment. He had to remain above that, think of some way they could *really* help the Americans—apply his talents, his knowledge.

He felt a rush of energy.

Downstairs, the driver from the previous night was waiting. When Joseph climbed into the car, the hotel doorman shut the door without hovering for a tip.

Everyone pitches in during a crisis.

Joseph chastised himself for being cynical. It was Washington that did this to him, all the façades and hollow party lines obscuring the good that men and women did.

Joseph drove a palm against his forehead. "Women— oh shit!"

"Is something wrong, sir?"

"Yes. I'm dead."

"Sir?"

"I forgot to make a call."

"If it's important, we can stop."

"It's important, but it's also too late. Never mind."

Lil would kill him. She had no idea where he was staying; even with the world spinning toward hell, his wife would expect a call. And she'd be right. Being insulated, losing touch with humanity was what drove men to send Stealth bombers from Edwards Air Force Base to the Kremlin.

Joseph spent a frustrating half hour in knotted midday traffic as they made their way to the White House. This time, a velvet rope had been stretched around the entrance to keep reporters back. It was easier to avoid them now, though Joseph still hated to ignore their shouted questions.

Joseph was met by another Secret Service operative—the corridor was now full of them—and was hurried to the antechamber where he and Clark had parted the night before. The CIA Director was still wearing the same clothes and he looked haggard; he was bent over a table. With him were three aides wearing neat hair, polyester, and expressions like startled deer. They relaxed when Clark waved Joseph over.

"Hear the good news?"

"Only what was on the tube."

"The house arrests? That's just a sideshow, to thank us for Fedorsenko." Clark tapped photographs on the heavy burl table. "No, this is the really big news."

Joseph glanced down at a mosaic of eight-by-tens. "What am I looking at?"

"Photos from the Talos III satellite. Here"—Clark pointed with his index finger—"are KGB personnel carriers leading army tanks into position around the Kremlin. These are the forces they used on our people. There"—he pointed to photos on the right—"are KGB vehicles from Leningrad arriving at the Finnish border. Looks like they're massing to seal things up nice and tight."

"So much for Fedorsenko's time frame."

"Blown to hell. What's more, they've obviously got the hardware to do the job."

Joseph's mind was racing. The arrests were not just to limit information leaving Russia, since spy satellites and operatives on the ground would see what was going on. Most likely the blackout was to keep people at home completely in the dark about military encounters until Cherganyev had done more rabble-rousing.

"Anything in the Middle East?"

"Nothing out of the ordinary. Regular Russian communiqués with Arab extremists, shipments of weapons, advisers coming and going in Syria."

"Mischief-making, you mean."

"More or less. But that can change in an instant." Clark scowled. "What they're doing here is setting up the ground rules. They realize Fedorsenko probably spilled his guts about the Middle East. They're letting us know, first, that they don't give a shit how much he told us and, second, if and when they move, they're going in with this kind of commitment. Enough men and machines to take on the Israelis . . . and anyone else who comes along."

"I notice all the forces are conventional."

Clark glowered, dark bags beneath his eyes. "Yes, Joseph, they're telling us that, too. No nukes. There hasn't been any unusual radio traffic to their silos and the cosmonauts on the MIR space station haven't been instructed to activate *their* supposedly nonexistent nuclear arsenal. Are you saying that that makes Cherganyev a pillar of restraint and the rest of us irresponsible?"

"All I'm saying is that it fits right in."

"With what?"

"As Fedorsenko said, it's a case of godhood. Cherganyev doesn't see himself as Alexander or Charlemagne, he sees himself as Christ."

"Then maybe someone should just tap him on the shoulder and remind him that missionaries bring food and Bibles, not tanks."

Joseph wagged a finger as though correcting a student. "Not always. Let's not forget the Crusades and the Inquisition. This is a holy war. Cherganyev is looking to convert, not slaughter. And if he must destroy, he wants to do it selectively—surgically, with conventional arms."

"That doesn't make him any less crazy in my book. What bothers me now is how *you* feel about him."

"What do you mean?"

"You sound like you're enjoying this."

"Well, yes, I am fascinated, but—"

"But *nothing!* I can't afford to have advisers on my team who are partial to the sick bastard."

"Partial? Jim, I'm a historian, not a politician!"

"And I don't give a rat's ass where any of this belongs in a historical context. Convince me you aren't so fascinated with Cherganyev that you'll look for ways to protect him."

Joseph didn't know how to respond. He tried to tell himself his patriotism wasn't being questioned, but he realized that anything he said would either damn him or sound like pandering. Clark correctly interpreted the silence and grunted.

"How the hell did we get off on this, anyway?"

Joseph managed a crooked smile. "You're tired and I'm worried."

"Make that two orders of worried, to go. I know you'll do the right thing, Joseph. I—"

The door of the Oval Office opened and both men

turned. They knew at once something was very wrong. Vice-President Kubert stood in the doorway, his round face pinched.

"Jim, the President would like to see you both."

Clark studied the man. "You look sick. What's wrong?"

"There's been another defection."

Joseph blurted, "Aksakov?"

The Vice-President shook his head. "Not a Soviet. It seems our ambassador in Moscow has been escorted from the embassy."

15

The sky in Moscow was heavy, holding snow, but the air was cold, refreshing. Nona sucked it in. And swore at herself.

She should have known to avoid Red Square. Every day since Cherganyev had come to power there'd been a display of some kind: military exhibits, entertainers (though never near the Mausoleum), speeches, and crowds. Always crowds.

But today had promised to be worse. When she'd come to work at four this morning, soldiers were everywhere. The newspapers at the kiosks said they were there to participate in ceremonies—but at the hotels? And the foreign embassies?

Now the square was packed, with soldiers and schoolchildren, teachers and factory workers, entire office staffs and many municipal employees. And she remembered why: Cherganyev made a pilgrimage to Lenin's tomb every Wednesday afternoon at two, marking the time and day Lenin Utra came to power. She looked at her small watch. It was 1:50. Nona didn't dare leave. KGB were prowling everywhere, and here and there she saw hard-looking men and women with a telltale *L* burned into their foreheads—the Sredá-Grom. Georgi called them priests, for their sole function was to make sure that Lenin was accorded the proper respect. Ordinary citizens might well be stopped if they tried to leave the square, asked what could possibly be more important than celebrating the memory of Lenin. But a municipal employee would certainly be arrested for shaming the city they served.

Nona would be trapped here until three, when the ceremony was over, then held up another half hour while the crowd dispersed. It wasn't how she wanted to spend her time off. Georgi might think she'd been held up and not wait for her.

Her shoulders drooped. Why hadn't she thought to come out some other way?

Her mother had often said it: *Nona's biggest problem is that her head is always in the clouds.*

She looked around. People clustered around her in their orderly groups. She was taller than most, and felt like a magnet as men and women milled about her. The people had obviously been bused in from outlying areas. Most of them stood in groups carrying neatly lettered signs. LENIN'S REVOLUTION REBORN—TEXTILE WORKERS OF VNOKOVO. WE STAND SHOULDER TO SHOULDER WITH LENIN—STUDENTS OF ROSTOV-ON-DON SOCIALIST VICTORY SCHOOL. The latter were first-graders who wouldn't have reached Lenin's belt buckle, let alone his shoulder.

She suddenly felt ashamed. What right did she have to judge these people, to be so cynical? Was it because she was stuck here, unable to hold her lover? Or was it something else? The supervisor and his little game with the form? The armed soldiers in Moscow! She hadn't seen that since her childhood, the purges. Was it the eighth Metro and Stalin, were memories doing this to her, bittersweet thoughts of her father?

KGB agents walked figure-eights through the crowd while the Lenin Utra police stood in shadows. Both groups stayed far from the eyes of the television cameras perched in the reviewing stands, parapets that rose like marble wings on each side of the Mausoleum. The cameras, steel-gray boxes with VREMYA emblazoned in red on the side, panned slowly back and forth across the packed square. The news program would be airing the footage later that day, as it had every Wednesday since Cherganyev came to power. Nona didn't own a television, but she had paused to watch them in store windows, had heard Nikita and others talk about the show. At one time it had shown glimpses of the world; lately, it had been filled with documentaries about Lenin and reports on the evils of capitalism.

What about the evils of my bad luck?

There was no way she could stay here for an hour, Nona realized. She'd start to cry. She had one day off each month; she refused to spend part of it like this. And then an idea occurred to her. Nikita! He would be her unwitting savior! She turned, backtracking toward the station.

From loudspeakers, a voice announced, "We have been informed that the Premier is on his way, coming through the Tsar's Tower now."

There is still time, she thought.

A band near the tomb began playing something martial, something she'd never heard before. So much new music in the weeks since Cherganyev had come to power, all of it drums and brass . . .

No one was looking at her. All eyes were on the hipped roof and white adornments of the ancient tower, a pinnacle from which Ivan the Terrible had witnessed the executions in Red Square.

"Yes, we can see him now—Sergei Ilyich, coming toward the granite steps of the Mausoleum."

Nona shouldered her way past a crowd of clerks. No one looked at her. She approached the entrance to the Metro, her heart galloping.

"Going somewhere, Comrade Inspector?"

The tap on her shoulder was hard, insistent. Nona turned and stared into the ascetic face of a man several inches taller than she.

She pointed down the steps. "I forgot my papers."

"Oh? Did someone ask to see them?"

"No," she said quickly. "I mean inspection forms."

"Why do you need them now?"

"I—I was in such a hurry to see the Premier that I forgot to sign them."

The *L* on the man's forehead seemed to burn. The slit eyes studied her. In the background, the loudspeakers announced Cherganyev's ascent up the short flight of stairs, his disappearance into the Mausoleum.

"A person in a uniform must not be seen leaving. You should be at the front ranks."

"If you will tell that to my supervisor, I will be only too happy to stay. Otherwise, he will be furious."

Where Nona found the courage, the voice just to address this man, she had no idea. She knew that she *sounded* sincere, at least; that part was easy, considering how demeaning Nikita could be on those rare occasions wl she slipped up on little things. She watched the man's eyes closely. They were thin, dark lines, like slivers of night. If he didn't believe her, she would be taken in for further questioning. If she was, she would certainly lose her job. Nikita would never back her up, say that he signed the form because she forgot. She quietly prayed the man did not decide to visit Nikita.

"What is your name?"

She heard the revolving door begin to move behind her. Oh God! What if it was Nikita?

"Nemelov. Nona Nemelov."

A man brushed past her—a well-dressed man she didn't know. There were no further sounds on the steps, and the knot in her throat went away.

The operative cocked his brow toward the stairs. "You may go, Comrade Nemelov. Only next time don't be so forgetful. I will be looking for you on Friday, at the front of the crowd."

"I'll be there," she said with relief and conviction. She *would* be there, too. Nikita would have to give her an hour off—orders of the KGB, she would tell him. Nona turned and rushed down the steps.

There was another way from the building, a service elevator that would bypass the lower lobby from which she'd just emerged. She went back to the lower lobby and headed directly for it.

The lift deposited Nona on Manege Street. This was actually better, closer to her apartment. She could change, take her time going to meet Georgi. She felt foolish for not having come this way before—punishment for her vanity. Georgi would just have to accept her in her old clothes.

Strangely uplifted for having *won* her first run-in with Lenin Utra, Nona walked toward the Sverdlov Square Metro. While standing in line at the escalator, she noticed a special edition of *Pravda* at a kiosk. Ambassador Anatoly Fedorsenko was being held prisoner in Washington, and United States Ambassador Isabel Kaplan had defected in shame.

Madness! she thought. Why arrest Fedorsenko, a diplomat who had served with such distinction—a lifelong friend of Cherganyev's? What was wrong with Alexander?

It was beyond her understanding, just as Stalin had been—arresting and murdering people when he could have talked to them. Reasoned with them.

Nona stepped onto the escalator and descended into the soft light of the Metro. There was nothing she could do about the government, so she refused to worry about it. She thought instead about her Georgi, wondered what she'd do if Georgi wasn't there. Go shopping *then,* she decided. But that wouldn't be nearly as satisfying. She needed to talk and be held.

She prayed that he would be at their spot. That he was in a good mood.

That his wife had not given him too much trouble about going out.

16

In photographs of the Oval Office, light was always lancing through the blinds. The air was always clear, the carpet vivid. The Presidents were pensive or smiling. Joseph remembered shots of JFK bouncing a young Caroline on his knee.

The room he entered was smoke-filled and gray. He'd once been on a sailboat in a fog at dusk; the room had that same eerie stillness, a sense of something ominous just out of sight.

President Alexander looked up. His expression was grave, the worse for not having slept. The other men in the room were almost as sober, slumped in chairs or standing and burning off nervous energy. Standing were National Security Adviser Romek Perkiel, a wiry, aquiline man with a frosty pad of hair on either side of his head; the very Ivy League Chief of Staff, Tim Moriarty; and the short, intense-looking Secretary of Defense, Vin Papa. The Vice-President shut the door and flopped on a sofa beside Secretary Lawrence; Press Secretary Joe Orlando sat in a wing chair across the room. Behind him, the volume turned low, a TV set was tuned to Russian television.

Clark nodded to Perkiel and stood beside him. Joseph went with him. He felt the way he did at cocktail parties—uneasy, an outsider trying to catch the drift of things. The President folded his hands on the desk.

"I've had Tim cancel all my appointments today. No sense trying to pretend it's business as usual." His eyes came up. "Jim, how the hell did you miss this? Why'd we have to hear it on Soviet radio?"

"Excuse me, sir—hear what?"

"The Russians occupied the embassy compound and took Ambassador Kaplan away," Lawrence said.

"Occupied? Not just sealed?"

"They took the damn thing over!" the President barked. "Just like Teheran in '79. And my intelligence experts didn't see it coming!"

Clark's normally impassive face looked pained. "Damage?"

"We don't know," Lawrence answered calmly. "I'm sure Kaplan's people started pushing paper into the shredder, but who knows how far they got."

"Anything come in over the private frequency?"

"Nothing. We assume that everyone there is being watched *very* closely."

The President folded his hands and stared at them. "Obviously, they want to limit our access to information on every possible front. Jim, how many people did we have airborne?"

Joseph knew he was referring to Americans who were

away from their home bases, floating through the city in restaurants, stores, museums.

"Fewer than usual, no more than fifteen or twenty at any given time. The same with natives."

"Natives" meant Russians or Eastern Europeans who were on the CIA payroll, as opposed to embassy personnel or journalists who did double duty. The United States wasn't as flagrant about spying as the Soviets, but did it just as diligently.

"I'm not making excuses," Clark said, "but that's one reason we've been so hamstrung. Not only has Cherganyev been playing things close to the vest, but even before the military moved in, the KGB and the Sredá-Grom had things sewn up pretty tight. Intelligence has been tough to come by."

Alexander shook his head. "So we acted as though nothing was happening, took no precautions?"

"What *could* we have done? Destroyed files 'just in case'?"

"You can bet your ass the Russians did, just as soon as Fedorsenko defected. Those sons of bitches have been a step ahead of us up and down the line!" The President looked at Lawrence. "Sam, I'd like you to respond to this. When's that AFL-CIO dinner?"

"Six-thirty."

"Call Lenny and have him give something short to the press. I want all military leave canceled—he can announce that. Maybe we can shake the Russians up a little. Use your speech tonight to tear into Cherganyev."

Lawrence reached for a phone on a small antique end table. "What can we say about Kaplan? Do we know if she was taken out at gunpoint?"

Alexander looked at Clark; the CIA Director went briskly to another phone and called his office. "We've got a woman at Tass. She might know which way the guns were pointing."

90

The President looked at Perkiel. "What'll the reaction be in Europe?"

"More sympathetic, I think, than if they'd done this before sending troops to the Finnish border." Perkiel spoke slowly and with a thick Hungarian accent, each word underscored with a roll of his hand, as though he were brushing water onto his chest. "But no one's going to protest *too* loudly. They have their own embassies to think about."

"Sam?"

Lawrence covered the mouthpiece.

"Make sure you get in a line about how Cherganyev has already shown his disdain for national sovereignty—that we're behind Finland and that our allies had better stick together on this."

Lawrence signaled okay with his fingers. The President looked at Joseph. "Dr. Rosenstock, give me the bottom line on this Leninism of his. Is Cherganyev really going to go as far as Fedorsenko says?"

Joseph was caught off guard. He'd been listening, beginning to think he was invisible. He coughed into the back of his hand.

"Well, Mr. President—I've been considering that myself, and I think he will. It's analogous to what Lincoln did during the Civil War. He shared the vision of the Founding Fathers, and when the Union was threatened he was willing to shed as much blood as it took to preserve it. He didn't want to have the legacy of Washington and Jefferson end with him."

"Even though it wasn't his fault."

"Precisely."

"But Lenin's legacy isn't threatened."

"Ah," Joseph said, "but as much as Lincoln loved the Founding Fathers, he was also in competition with them. In allowing the Union to fall and then be rebuilt, in his image—slave-free, industrialized, a world power—

he accomplished singlehandedly what Washington, Adams, Franklin, and a whole team of people hadn't been able to do. As much as Cherganyev loves Lenin, what we're seeing is common throughout history.''

''Who else?''

''Jesus and David, Nero and Julius Caesar, the need to do better than the father figure. Assuming that's what's happening here, it won't be enough simply to return the Soviet Union to Leninism. As Fedorsenko said, Cherganyev will risk all to spread Leninism throughout the world.''

Clark had hung up the phone. The President looked at him.

''Well?''

''Kaplan left with four men, each carrying a rifle. None was pointed at her, though.''

''So the Soviets will say the guns were just for her protection.''

''Of course.''

Except for the muted sound of the television, the room was silent.

Alexander sat back, hands folded on his stomach. ''All right, we've got two problems: regaining some initiative and damage control. We'll convene the Cabinet at two. Cabinet Room. Tim, ask Ruff and Erickson to join us.''

Ruff was Speaker of the House ''Ruff'' Dremlie, named for a cartoon bulldog whose manner he had; Erickson was Roy Erickson, majority whip.

''Is there anything we can tell them now? They'll be pretty pissed at having to wait.''

''Tell them we're still analyzing data and don't want to say anything until we're sure of our facts. Vin''—he faced the Secretary of Defense—''I'll want some options by then. See if the Finns will let us in. Let me know what we've got in the North Sea, the Baltic, and how fast we can be in the Gulf of Finland. Also, the Middle East.

Isn't the *Eisenhower* going to take part in that fiftieth anniversary thing at El Alamein?"

"She's already in Alexandria. I can have her moving within hours."

"Fine. Contrive something with the Egyptians and do it."

Perkiel seemed anxious. "Sir, you realize that you may be giving the Soviets a *reason* to go into the Middle East."

"If Fedorsenko's telling the truth and Dr. Rosenstock is correct, they're going anyway. I'd rather be en route than dead in the water."

The Secretary of Defense left, and the President eyed Clark severely.

"Jim, I don't care about the dangers. Get your people out of hiding. I want to know what's going on!"

"They'll do it, but there may be casualties. If they've been found out, the KGB will be watching them. As soon as they make a move they'll be arrested, given sodium amytal, questioned, then shot."

"I'm sorry, but I can live with that easier than I can having them alive and in hiding. Move them out."

Joseph could see that Clark was struggling to remain calm. He was being made the scapegoat, and his people were going to suffer because of it.

The President turned to his Press Secretary. "Joe, you're holding another press briefing when?"

"Two-thirty."

"Good. Lenny will give the press the basics, Sam will use the speech tonight to express our indignation. What do you think about playing up the Lenin angle, the compulsiveness?"

"To what end?" Joseph interceded.

"To embarrass him. Maybe branding him as a nut will make him retreat just a bit."

"Or it may end up pushing him in the other direction."

"Fine. If we're lucky, he'll rave a bit and show the world he isn't rational. Romek?"

The National Security Adviser winced. "I don't think it will make him behave any differently, but I'm not sure that name-calling is going to enhance *our* image."

"That's why God invented press secretaries." The President winked at Orlando. "Get someone to ask about it, Joe, maybe Dan Schwartz at AP. And make sure the Chinese press is there. It'll help, I think, if they see just what kind of a madman they've got on their border. Thank you, gentlemen. Romek, Dr. Rosenstock, I'd like you at the Cabinet meeting. Jim, I want to know the instant a Russian soldier budges toward another border."

The three men nodded and the President dismissed the group. As soon as the door opened, aides rushed in waving papers and files. Clark shouldered around them and headed silently toward his office, obviously annoyed; Joseph accepted Perkiel's invitation to lunch, and the two men made their way to the elevators that would carry them downstairs to the cafeteria.

But Joseph knew he wouldn't be eating much. He never did when he was in Washington. It never ceased to amaze him how much of government was reflex and instinct rather than carefully thought-out response. Alexander was a leader, no one could dispute that. But watching him at work, scattershooting and relying heavily on yes-men like Lawrence and Orlando, was not conducive to good digestion.

However, something the President had said triggered something. *He'll rave a bit and show the world he isn't rational.*

What would Cherganyev do, he wondered, if they took it one step further? What would he do if instead of taking on Cherganyev or his soldiers, they made Lenin himself their target?

17

The ship moved like a titan, the sea bending to its will.

Moments before, it had been rolling easily, ninety-five thousand tons at rest. Then, in a moment, the sea inhaled at the nuclear carrier's stern, leaving an eddy deep enough to suck down a yacht; before the whirlpool subsided, the thousand-foot-long vessel was six hundred feet from its berth and churning seaward. Behind it, the fifteen-story-high shipyard crane stood over the waters like an arm cocked in salute.

The ship dwarfed the crew that manned it: sixty-five hundred crewmen and two additional companies of marines. Those who were not engaged in taking the vessel to sea were busy working on the one hundred planes it carried in the 0-3 hangar deck; sweeping, mopping, and polishing floors; and operating roomfuls of communications equipment.

Overall, in the "island"—the command structure that towered ten stories over the deck—officers and noncoms studied radarscopes, reviewed charts and theoretical battle plans for the Mediterranean, and monitored the activities of the crew. Intercoms bleeped constantly, the officers answering in curt, low voices. Anything louder tended to blend with the ever-present roar of the sea.

Below them, on the stadium-sized deck, crewmen attended to the rows of fighters and search craft, readying them for flight. The men went about their work with careful steps; the nonskid surface of the carrier deck was extremely abrasive, and a fall meant a painful trip to sick bay.

Particular attention was paid to a sleek S-3 Viking that sat in a catapult, ready for launching. Crammed inside were radar gear, magnetic detectors, and infrared scanners. Tubes running through the fuselage held clusters of sound-sensitive buoys that it would drop in the sea to be monitored from the carrier. In the weapons bay sat four stubby bombs—each over a quarter-ton—and four torpedoes were pinioned beneath the wings. Once in the water, the torpedoes would use internal guidance systems to hunt like sharks for the enemy.

After the *Eisenhower* was fifteen minutes at sea, the S-3 sprang aloft over the bow, dipping once before heading into the darkening skies of early evening. The plane and its four crew members would be aloft for eight hours, searching for Soviet submarines. Upon finding one, they would mark the location with a buoy that would send back information that immediately became part of every computer in the Atlantic Command and in the mainframe computers of the Naval Operations Center just outside of Washington.

Immediately after the S-3 was airborne, a launch team guided a slender-winged E-2C Hawkeye to the next catapult. Fragile-looking, like a child's toy glider, the sixty-foot-long craft was topped with a flat, revolving radar disc some fifteen feet across. Flying a course four hundred miles in diameter, the Hawkeye would spend five hours scouting out all ships and planes.

Three decks below, in a gymnasium-sized chamber whose entrance was a lead-lined vault, brown canisters lay securely in steel cradles. All the men who worked down here held the conical shells in awe. Some measured their importance by reviewing what they'd rehearsed so often: the quick, careful loading onto planes in the event of a red alert. Others thought about their power, the ability to atomize enemy fleets or cities. Still others refused to think about them at all.

Two hours at sea, the escort ships churned toward them, spread across fifty nautical miles like a table setting, with the *Eisenhower* as the centerpiece. There were two missile cruisers, four missile frigates, two refueling tankers (some crew members were surprised; usually there was only one), two repair tenders (also instead of one, which not only surprised but alarmed some sailors), and submarines whose number and armaments were known only to a selected few fleet officers.

Three hours at sea, a slow-moving blip that had been on the Hawkeye's radar for two hours turned out to be—as expected—a Russian fishing trawler. Perched on the roof of the small cabin was a black radar scanner wide enough to bounce signals off the moon. The *Eisenhower* immediately sent four F-14 Tomcats screaming into the night skies.

The courtship between Tomcats and the many trawlers they encountered was ritualized. One of the thirty-five-ton supersonic attack jets would make a low, earsplitting pass over the topmast of the Soviet ship; more often than not, one of the Russian "fishermen" would jam a wrist into the crook of his elbow and thrust a fist skyward. Sometimes the obscene gesture would earn the ship a second, lower pass.

Today, however, there were no upraised fists. The fishermen looked up and returned to mending their nets beneath the ship's swaying lanterns. Or appeared to. They were busy looking out across the waters, studying activity on the carrier and its complement. This time it was serious, they'd been told. This time, any information they gathered was vital.

Inside the cabin, two seamen in rough clothing sat before sophisticated consoles feeding information into a computer: the time, their exact location, the ship's bearing (the Middle East, for certain). Men came and went from deck, relaying word about the number of frigates, tankers, cruisers. All of it was quickly encoded and sent rebounding from a satellite to a Russian receiver.

Unlike most encounters, the ritual was different in another way as well. The receiver was not on board a submarine or at a base along the coast. The information was going directly to the Kremlin, where decisions were quickly made on how to respond to the looming American presence in the Mediterranean.

The order came directly from Cherganyev to his Minister of Defense and Chief of Main Political Directorate, and it consisted of one word: *Iti*.

Go.

PART
TWO

1

"You are cleared for takeoff on Nine."

On the outermost runway at Sheremetyevo-2, the four whining turbofans of the light gray Condor suddenly changed pitch. They screamed, their noise causing the ground crews and TV camera operators to wince despite their padded earphones.

"We are with you in our hearts," the chief traffic controller added. "In our hearts and in the true spirit of Lenin!"

"Thank you," said the pilot as he edged the Condor forward. It rocked gently from side to side as it moved, as though testing its footing. Then, at his command, the aircraft kicked into motion, dragging behind it a V-shaped shadow of wings as wide as a soccer field.

The pilot gazed down three stories at the pale concrete unrolling beneath him. He grinned at his copilot. Civilian runways! Nine hundred meters. What kind of an amateur needed so much room? He throttled the turbofans to full thrust at the three-hundred-meter mark. The Condor nosed skyward.

Seated behind the copilot, the navigator glanced down at the cameras that were following their ascent. He sighed. "Very pretty. That will make a suitably impressive picture." He glanced over the copilot's shoulder, at the instrument panel. "But why only eight hundred meters a minute? I've seen pilots take the Condor up four times as fast."

"We are at maximum weight, Comrade, one hundred sixty thousand kilos. Fifteen thousand of that is the two hundred and twelve passengers we carry. The rest is explosive. I chose our rate of climb with extreme care."

The pilot kept his tone light, friendly. But inside he was more anxious than he'd ever been flying raids over rebel bases in Afghanistan. There was the mission, but there was also the navigator. The pilot and copilot, as well as the flight engineer at the rear of the cockpit, all knew each other. The beefy navigator was new to them. KGB, they presumed. Lenin Utra, most likely. *Stukach,* almost certainly. An informer.

Yet, what did it matter? they'd asked themselves before coming aboard. If any of them came back it would be a miracle.

The navigator turned back to the three radar screens set in the fuselage wall. "I understand your caution, of course. But I was thinking about the importance of the image we've left behind. This is a glorious mission; the picture the nation sees on television must be equally spectacular."

Looking up from his computer console, the flight engineer waited until the copilot glanced out the side window. He caught his friend's eye, pretended to spit at the back of the navigator's neck. The copilot winked.

"I believe we did quite well," the flight engineer concluded. "Too fast would have been showy."

The men fell silent then, busying themselves with instrument readings as the pilot climbed. The engineer had the most to do, just as he had been the busiest for the past twenty-four hours. His long day had begun when he supervised the loading of the armaments: six armorplated personnel carriers, a trio of self-propelled howitzers (none of them nuclear-capable, lest the Palestinians get their hands on them), two staff cars, and—stored in steel mesh hammocks suspended from overhead girders—crates of howitzer shells and Kalashnikov rifle rounds.

Now he was busy checking the weight distribution as they rose. He punched keys, the computer reading the signals from hundreds of pressure sensors and translating them into green dots on a picture of the aircraft. All secure. He repeated the check once every minute: the plane was indeed packed to capacity, and any change, any cargo that worked loose or shifted position, could jeopardize their stability.

Even the soldiers sat still, squeezed shoulder-to-shoulder on plastic benches that folded from the corrugated aluminum walls of the fuselage. Technically, the men—like the cockpit crew—were all ex-soldiers, having been mustered out of the military the day before. Technically, they were just two hundred volunteer riflemen. The green sweatshirts and camouflage-dyed jeans and combat boots they wore would not be found in any manual of Soviet military uniforms.

There was only one bathroom for the men, an open toilet in the rear of the plane; their rifles had more privacy, standing in a curtained-off section at the rear of the aircraft. The dozen officers also had more privacy and comfort, sitting in contoured plastic chairs that had been bolted in the night before. They also had a bathroom to themselves. One with a door.

At twelve thousand meters, the pilot leveled off in bright sunshine and headed southwest. He noticed, far below, a pair of blue specks bursting through the cloud cover.

"Visual on the escort."

"I've had them on my screen since takeoff," the navigator answered. "They're coming up like rockets, roughly eight thousand meters a minute. Foxbats."

"It must have been a wonderful shot for the television," the flight engineer pointed out.

The navigator ignored him.

Ninety minutes later, over Volsk, the cloud cover began to shred. Black fingers of smoke rose from cement factories on the shores of the Volga. The river itself snaked south beneath them, spinning off a network of brown ravines and tributaries.

The Foxbats peeled off, having nearly expended their fuel; two new jets from the Gurjev base immediately took their place. The pilot and planes repeated their welcoming ritual.

The copilot checked his clock. "Right on schedule."

"The spirit of Lenin is with us," the navigator said.

The Caspian Sea glistened to the east as they passed over the forested ridges of the Elburz Mountains into the lime-green foothills that marked the western border of Iran. The Foxbats waggled their wings, climbed, and banked north, their afterburners streaking the skies. The Kremlin had quietly obtained permission for just this one flight to pass over Iran and, briefly, through Turkey, then south through Iraq and west into Syria.

As for the passengers, once the plane landed in Damascus they were on their own. Overland to the West Bank. A patrol of peacekeepers.

Sacrificial lambs.

When the navigator left to go to the bathroom, the pilot leaned into the cabin.

"Does anyone want to wager how fast the spirit of Lenin abandons those poor bastards in the back?"

The other two shook their heads.

"These are all dead men we're carrying. Except for the ex-colonel. He's probably figured out some way to hide in one of our consulates until it's over. The others?" He leaned back into the controls. "They'll either be slaughtered from the front by the Jews or shot in the back by the moron Palestinians."

The Condor soared over the golden deserts east of Teheran. The navigator returned. No sooner had he sat down than his eyes went wide.

104

"Captain!" The navigator's voice was clipped, tense. "Two blips coming down from twenty thousand meters."

"Probably replacements based at Krasnovodsk. These grubby countries wouldn't say no to the Foreign Ministry."

"But wouldn't we have been told?"

"Not necessarily." The pilot saw the familiar shapes of jets approaching fast to the left and right. "A last-minute addition, perhaps. What with radio silence—"

He reached for the cockpit lights to signal. His copilot rested a hand on his.

"No, Comrade."

The pilot looked back out.

They were not swept-back, light blue, Soviet-made Foxbats. These were crouching, yellow-and-tan, American-made Eagles. But not American. Beneath the pilot's windshield on each jet was a Star of David.

"Shit."

In the cockpit of the Israeli plane, the pilot clapped his hands to his ears, hesitated, then spun a radio dial.

The Russian pilot understood and reached for his own dial.

The navigator's jaw dropped. "What are you doing? Don't answer! He has no right to—"

"Shut up!"

The pilot stopped turning the dial when the Israeli's voice, speaking excellent Russian, crackled through the cabin.

". . . if you read me. Come in, Condor, if you read me."

The pilot fine-tuned the receiver, then pressed his transmit button. "Condor here."

"*Shalom.* My name is Shmuel. My companion on your other wing is Moshe. Follow us, please. We have a runway waiting for you outside of Ashqelon."

"This is outrageous!" the navigator blustered. "Tell him we have mutual-defense agreements with the countries below. They will intercept and protect us."

"At fourteen thousand meters? Don't be ridiculous. Only the Israelis have planes that can fly at this altitude."

"Then call their bluff! They wouldn't dare shoot down a Soviet plane."

Though he didn't enjoy the prospect of being taken prisoner, the pilot took a perverse joy in his navigator's discomfort.

"Who'd know? Have you ever examined wreckage of a plane that fell from this height? There could have been mechanical failure, too much weight, a storm—any number of things."

"I won't allow this embarrassment to the Soviet people! If you refuse, I'll radio headquarters. Do you understand what I'm saying?"

"I understand. But what can even Lenin Utra do to dead men?"

Beside him, the copilot fingered his tie, a gift from his bride of less than a month. "Not much," he admitted, "but some of us have families—"

The pilot squeezed the wheel. "Damn." He shut off the radio and went on the intercom. "Strap in securely. We'll be climbing fast to avoid turbulent weather."

"A wise decision," said the navigator.

"A dangerous one, you mean," the pilot answered as he banked the Condor forty-five degrees and climbed.

Already near maximum thrust in the thin air, the straining turbofans growled like big cats. Despite the suddenness of the maneuver, Shmuel stayed wingtip-to-wingtip with the huge plane. Moshe disappeared.

"He's good."

"He's a Jew," the navigator said. "You are Russian. Beat him."

"Even if he were half-blind, they can climb twelve thousand meters a minute and fly at Mach two-five. We can't outrun them."

"Then get on the radio, call for help from Krasnovodsk!"

"And do you think they'll just let us wait here until—"

Something thumped on the starboard wing. The Condor shivered and dipped in that direction. The altimeter began to flutter. The pilot quickly throttled back and leveled off the big plane. The needle steadied.

His stomach crawling with apprehension, the pilot punched on the radio.

". . . holes in the starboard wing. I repeat, four twenty-millimeter holes in the starboard wing. Moshe avoided the fuel tanks—this time."

The pilot turned to the chalk-white face of his navigator and repeated the warning.

The navigator flushed. "Jew bastards!"

"That isn't in dispute. The question is—do we go down in one piece or in one thousand pieces?"

Behind him, the flight engineer jabbed downward with his thumb. The copilot nodded. The pilot looked back at the navigator. "Well?"

The navigator punched at the air. "Yes, dammit, do as they say. But when we're over the Mediterranean, veer away and—"

"You're not thinking of standard evasive tactic number three-oh-two, are you? Signaling for ships and ditching? Comrade, with what we're carrying, we could give a stone lessons on how to sink. There wouldn't be time to break out a single lifeboat."

Shmuel's voice intruded. "Fifteen seconds, no more."

The engineer licked his lips. The copilot mouthed a prayer. The navigator slumped in his swivel seat.

"Very well," he said quietly. "Do as they say."

The pilot switched the dial to transmit, politely accepting the Israeli invitation. Turning the big craft around, he headed northeast, and an hour later they touched down on a windswept airstrip nestled between orange groves.

Searchlights had been turned on to illuminate the Condor in the deepening dusk. Soviet vehicles rolled down the ramp into the hands of Israeli troops. A two-star general left the group by the jeeps and approached the pilot, who stood with his crew in a pool of light. The Israeli had a rugged face and a wry smile. He seemed pleased with his booty.

"Tell me, according to Soviet protocol, which of us has a higher rank? Do I salute you first, or do you salute me?"

"I am a civilian."

"*Sha, sha,* it's over now. Why keep up the façade?"

"I have no rank and no command. I am simply the spokesman for a group of Soviet citizens that you have unlawfully intercepted and detained."

The swarthy man pointed behind him. "Civilians don't travel with howitzers. Are you certain you don't want to declare military status?"

"We are civilians."

The general shrugged. "As you wish. You have no claim, then, to military rights or courtesies. You are, plainly and simply, international terrorists, dangerously armed, and will be tried as such."

The crew was somber, save for the navigator, who grinned. When the general walked away, he leaned toward his countrymen.

"Not exactly what we planned, but to die for Lenin will be an honor."

The other three men didn't share his enthusiasm. But as they stood shaking, their perspiration chilled by the brisk Mediterranean breeze, the pilot took solace in one thought. There were countless reasons the Israelis could put forth for having forced them down. They could claim invasion of airspace (the Israelis would tamper with the onboard computer program). They could say they'd been called in at the request of Iraq to prevent arms shipments to their foes in Iran (the Condor's destination could have been Teheran), or even—the truth—that they'd intercepted the Russians to avert trouble on the West Bank. After all, even Soviet television would reveal that the volunteers had been invited by Palestinian freedom fighters.

But regardless of what the Israelis claimed, this much was certain: the mission was still a success. Though they wouldn't be engaging them on the West Bank, the Israelis had still walked into one hell of an ambush.

2

They'd met because of a small patch of smeared white paint.

Nona had reflected many times in the past nine months that it was an odd way to meet a lover. But it had its own kind of romance, its own individuality. Leave it to her and Georgi to do things *differently*.

She'd been walking by the Kremlin wall on her way home from work. Sneezing because of the sudden smell of fresh paint, she'd dropped her clipboard and bent to retrieve it. As she rose, she noticed, to the side, a man with a blackened briar pipe. He had Asian almond eyes, a hooked nose, and a goatee. He was watching her harshly through light puffs of smoke.

Usually, Nona scurried away without talking to people. But something about his look bothered her. She retrieved the clipboard, hugged it to her.

"Is there anything wrong?"

The thin man started. "Pardon me?"

"I asked if there was anything wrong. You're looking at me very rudely."

The pellets of smoke rose more quickly. "My dear, I'm not looking at you at all. I was looking at the line."

Nona flushed. She felt foolish. Why would anyone look at her? But, curious, she followed his gaze.

"I didn't do that."

She pointed to the smeared paint of a traffic line just behind her. The man smiled paternally.

"I know you didn't. Soviet citizens don't. Neither do British, Vietnamese, Chinese, or Koreans." His words ascended like the pipe puffs—precise, holding their shape after they were uttered. "But Americans, Germans, French, Poles, Romanians—their minds are not on their surroundings. On the sights, yes. On their environment, no." He removed his pipe, pointed with the stem. "A Frenchman did that while he was talking to his wife. *'C'est très singulier! Starik,'* " the man said around his pipe, making as though he were flipping through a guidebook. " *'Son nom . . . est Starik.'* "

Nona smiled reflexively. The man's impression of a Frenchman's grand style was perfect.

Smiling back, the man settled down. He resumed puffing on his pipe. "They were so impressed with Lenin's nickname that they did this . . . without even looking back."

Nona regarded the man more closely now. He wore loose-fitting gray corduroy trousers, a white sweater, a black beret—and that smile.

He reached for his pipe. She noticed now that he also wore a wedding band. Her spirits sagged.

"I am Georgi Mikhailovich Tsigorin," he bowed slightly. "And you are Nona Pietrovna Nemelov."

Her mouth fell open. He smiled again.

"Don't look so surprised. It's stenciled on the back of your clipboard."

She looked dumbly at the bold black writing, then half-turned, embarrassed. He approached her, stepping high over the white line.

"Don't be ashamed."

She wasn't just ashamed, she wanted to cry. Not only was he married but she felt foolish, two swift stabs in the heart.

"Frenchman or Russian, Nona, we all become pre-occupied with what's right before us and not what's right around the corner or"—he tapped the back of the clipboard—"just out of sight."

She mumbled, "You don't, it seems."

"Oh, but I have a different kind of problem!" He swept his pipe in a wide radius. "I look around me, and do you know what I see? Not the world of today, but history. Brooding there by the Redeemer's Gate. Nestled here by the wall. Look at the corner, tell me what you see."

She looked to her right. "A kiosk," she answered carefully, though she knew she had probably given the wrong answer.

"There *is* a kiosk, but what I see are soldiers huddled over a fire, waiting to march against Napoleon. The cobbles beneath their feet are cold. The men are sad . . . clothes in tatters . . . one even has a bad cold."

Nona looked back at him. "Are you a writer?"

"No." He smiled. "A painter."

Her eyes sparkled with self-satisfaction. "I'm not surprised. You talk like an artist. What do you paint, portraits? Magazine illustrations?"

He shook his head. "White lines."

The satisfaction left her face. Nona's eyes fell to the traffic line, then returned to the man. "These?"

"Every one you see in the square, repainted once a month. Sometimes I stand here after work and look at the police pointing them out to motorists, automobiles obeying them, television crews taping them. It gives me a feeling of satisfaction."

Nona snickered. Georgi seemed wounded.

"You find me silly?"

"Not you," she insisted. "Me . . . if I tried to do that." She could just imagine going to Nikita's office and borrowing a chair, sitting out by the tracks as though she were vacationing on the Black Sea. He would have her institutionalized.

"Join me for dinner," Georgi said.

Nona declined. She said she had to buy food before heading home; the lines were longer here, but the vegetables were fresher.

"Then I'll wait with you."

She wanted to tell him he shouldn't, that he had a wife at home. But who was she to tell him his responsibilities? Besides, she found his friendliness and honesty appealing.

During the hour they spent in line, they talked about everything from history to science. Georgi was extremely well read. No one had ever talked to her like this before, explained things and asked her opinion. When she had made her purchases, he asked her to dinner again. This time she accepted.

They ate sandwiches on black bread at a small bakery. The caraway seeds got stuck in Nona's teeth, but she didn't dare pick them out. She suffered willingly, staring at her companion and listening intently. Then he asked about her, and the mood changed.

"What's the matter? Don't you like talking about yourself?"

She moved her shoulders indecisively.

"Is that a no?"

"What I do is not interesting."

He thumped his chest. "It is to me! Now I want to hear what you have to say—but first you have to do me a favor."

"What?"

"Look at me."

Nona realized that she was staring at her empty plate. She turned her eyes up. "I'm sorry, I'm being very rude."

"Not rude, unfair. I want to see your eyes."

She blushed; he smiled and she returned it. She didn't look back down.

"Much better. So—how long have you been an inspector?"

"Seven years."

"Do you enjoy it?"

"The discipline is severe. . . ."

Her voice trailed off. He smiled, and prompted her. "Severe, yes—and do you mind that?"

"No."

"You enjoy working."

"Very much."

"And the results are quite tangible. The trains run on time and the stations are spotless. You must take pride in that."

"I do, but I must admit I've never taken time to study my work the way you do yours."

Nona was surprised, though. What had struck her as absurd before no longer seemed quite so silly. She was willing to bet that this man could show her things in the Metro that she'd never noticed. Things she took for granted. The past. Stalin inspecting his tunnel. The future.

"It's a remarkable indulgence," he acknowledged, "especially if you let your mind go . . ."

He did something with his hands, opening them like flowers blooming, that reminded her of her father. Her throat grew tight.

". . . you can imagine people from other generations, horsecarts instead of trucks . . ."

His imagination, that was a large part of why she felt so comfortable with him. He was uninhibited, willing to dream and unafraid to share it.

". . . plains where princes once battled Teutonic invaders or Mongols . . ."

Alexander Nevsky! Just like her father's stories.

"And if you let your thoughts run wild, Nona, you can vaguely see the behemoths that roamed the earth before the coming of man. All from contemplating a smeared line in the Square. From realizing how fleeting it is, how fleeting *everything* is in the fullness of history."

The night ended with a peck on the cheek outside the Ploshchad Sverdlova Metro. His goatee had brushed her chin, tickling her. But she cherished the sensation, the closeness of a man.

As it happened, their lunch hours were nearly the same. They began meeting every day, and sometimes after work. On their third date—for she thought of them as such, even though he was married—he told her about his wife.

"Zoya married me because her father was injured in a fall and lost his job. She would have taken anyone, then, who had a roof over his head. Her neighbor, my cousin, introduced us and we were married after a b..ef courtship. For six years her interest in me has always been a distant second to her concern about her father."

"You have no children?" Nona asked.

"I would love children, but where would we put them?"

"Then why don't you leave her?"

Divorce was frowned upon, she knew, but to be unhappy like this . . .

"No," he sighed. "If I left Zoya, she would get the apartment. And besides," he said mysteriously, "there are other considerations."

"What?"

He didn't answer, not until their sixth date. And when he finally told her, she felt as if an awful new world had opened up, one of excitement and fear.

3

Their sixth date marked the first time they went out at night. Nona had been looking forward to it with excitement bordering on giddiness. Even Nikita was amazed by her changed mood.

First, it had to be canceled once. She stood in the Khudozhestvenny Cinema off Arbat Square for three hours, finally taking the Metro home. The next day, at lunch, Georgi apologized repeatedly. Zoya had been taken ill and he'd had to stay home with her. There had been no way he could get out and meet her, as much as he'd ached to.

They agreed to meet the following night, and this time he made it. His face glowed when he saw her. They went to the movie and, after a brief walk down tree-lined Suvorov Boulevard, he suggested (she quickly forgot under what pretense) that they go to her apartment. She readily agreed.

They made love.

Afterwards, while Nona lay cuddled against his chest,

Georgi did something that surprised her: he sat up, switched on a light, and said it was time he told her about his political views.

"What?" she rubbed her eyes. "Politics—now?"

"When else? I must leave soon, and it's a part of my life you must know about."

Sitting cross-legged on the bed, naked except for his pipe, he held her hands while he spoke—quietly, owing to the thinness of the walls.

"Cherganyev will soon come to power, Nona, and I fear for what will happen then."

The bluntness of the statement, as much as its content, caught her off guard.

"How do you know this?"

"There are signs—in the newspapers, on television."

Nona nodded; she was nervous and didn't know why.

"We watch these things closely," he explained. "I . . . and others. Zoya is not one of us, but she knows about the group. That is one reason I cannot leave her."

"The group?" Nona repeated. "You are all students of some kind?"

"In a way. We are students of history, but interested as well in certain freedoms we have lost. In literature. Speech. The exchange of ideas in and out of our nation. Freedoms that will be even more dangerously constricted once Lenin Utra officially comes to power."

Nona's stomach buckled. She felt a chill brush across her bare belly.

Georgi was a dissident.

During the next hour when they spoke—and in the hours she lay awake after he left—Nona had to radically change her thinking about what that word meant.

Georgi was not a shadowy figure plotting to bring down the government. He was the son of a soldier, a youth who had always wanted to be a teacher and poet. But after his father's death during Stalin's purges, the ten-year-old was given a choice: go to work in the Square or on a farm. A lover of architecture and museums, he had opted to work in the Square. He had been working there ever since.

And, while there, he listened to everyone who passed. Mostly what he overheard were tourists chattering, co-workers quietly complaining, officials blustering.

But sometimes he heard wisdom. Fresh ideas, always in hushed tones, like something precious. Some came from foreign journalists (who showed a courageous disregard for the KGB men who hovered nearby). Some came from people who taught in schools, worked in laboratories, wrote books. A few were priests. He got to know some of them, in much the same way he had gotten to know Nona, and soon he began going to their meetings.

"I hope, one day, that you will come," he said to her.

She never would, she knew that at once. Her spine grew cold at the thought.

"In any case, I hope you will keep my secret. You feel things very deeply, Nona, and I know this will trouble you more than a little. But I wanted you to know."

She said she was glad he'd told her. She lied. She couldn't stop thinking about her father, what it had meant to lose him because of his conflict with the authorities.

Why is every bright man in trouble, while every idiot like Nikita or Panas Pavadze has it good?

Georgi took her hands in his, and rubbed her fingers. She shut her eyes, savoring his touch.

"I think I knew I could love you the first time I saw you. I wasn't truthful, you know."

Her eyes snapped open. "When?"

"When I told you I was looking at the line and not at you. I watched you walk over. You looked so utterly full

117

of thought, as if you were in another world. A better world."

She thought back; her recollection of the moment was vivid. The smell of the paint had made her think of the tar her father had used to patch their roof.

"It was a perfect world," she admitted.

"And the sneeze." He smiled. "Like a witch's curse, drawing you back here. But I'm grateful, for it helped me to meet you. Our relationship means so much that if anything ever happened to me, I would miss you more than I'd miss anything else. Especially after tonight."

Nona opened her eyes. *If you feel the same as I do, then why not give up the other? It will leave more time for us.*

Though she thought it, she couldn't ask, which struck her as odd. She'd just made love to the man, yet she didn't think she knew him well enough to ask him to give up his political activities. Or was she afraid he'd reject her?

In one way, though, the revelation was an important one. Nona looked at each rendezvous as their last, and she treasured every moment. It made the relationship unusually alive and vivid, though it also left her severely depressed when they were apart. Life in the real world simply wasn't as interesting as life in the just, caring world they created.

End? Nona thought each time they parted. If anything ever happened to the relationship or to Georgi, she had no idea how she would face each day.

4

After fleeing Red Square and Cherganyev's rally, Nona went home to get dressed. They were going to the Bolshoi Theater. One of Georgi's "friends"—that's what he called the others in his group—had gotten him tickets.

"Good ones," he'd said with delight two nights before, "in the orchestra."

Nona laid her clothing out on the bed. The floral pattern dress. Black high-heeled shoes. A simple white hat with a veil. She napped, then dressed, snacking on a hard-boiled egg before putting on makeup. They would be eating afterwards, but she knew she wouldn't last until then.

Eating at the Azov, she thought. *Panas must see me on the arm of my gentleman!*

She listened to music as she prepared, humming along with "The Dance of the Tumblers."

Georgi was supposed to arrive at seven, and by six-forty-five Nona was staring out the window at the street. Any moment he'd come around the corner with his long-legged strides. She laughed. She, of course, would have forgotten the tickets at home. But not Georgi. He was brilliant, organized.

And usually prompt.

Seven o'clock came and went, and by seven-fifteen Nona was growing anxious. By seven-thirty she had forced herself to face the inevitable: he wasn't coming.

Nona continued to sit by the window until well after nine. Sweat stained her dress around the tight black belt, and her feet stung where the shoes compressed her little toe. Her makeup was still fresh and intact. She was too numb to cry; her face felt lifeless, like clay.

At ten, Nona pulled off the shoes. She did so with effort, fighting her shoulders; they wanted to pull her to the floor. But she knew that if she succumbed, she'd stay there all night.

So what?

No, that wasn't the way she should be thinking. She'd had a life before Georgi, she'd have one again.

And why was she thinking as if it were over? Something had come up, probably something with his wife. She couldn't begrudge him that, not after all the time he'd given her.

Shortly after eleven, Nona rose. The ballet would be out by now, people would be going to dinner. She wondered if Georgi ached the same as she did. Probably worse. He would have felt guilt on top of everything else.

She took off her dress slowly, painfully, and slipped on her housedress. Nona had come up in such a hurry she hadn't bothered to get the mail; she did so now. She lumbered into the hall to the steps, not caring what she did, but wanting to stay busy.

Busy at midnight!

It was a good thing she didn't have to go to work the next day. She didn't want to sleep, lie down, dwell on Georgi. She felt the way she had when her mother had died. She just wanted to coast through the hours until it didn't hurt so much to think. Then she could try to live with what had happened.

She walked slowly down the narrow corridor lit by a single hanging bulb. The mail bin contained three items. One was the Metro newsletter. One was a bill from the cemetery where her mother was buried.

One was a note from Georgi.

There was no postmark on Georgi's letter; he had obviously slipped it in sometime during the day. She slit

120

the envelope with care. The letter inside was folded once, crisply. There was a wrinkle in the back. A dried tear? She opened it slowly, scanned its single handwritten line:

It is best for you that we meet no longer. G.

Nona reread the note. She wasn't surprised. She was curious—what had happened?—but in a way she was also relieved. The romance was over. She could focus her sorrow, overcome it. She would never hurt like this again.

She slumped back against the wall. Pain cramped her stomach, grief pushed at her eyes. She raised her hand to her face.

"Georgi . . . I need you."

The words snagged in her throat. She loved him and hated him at the same time. Then all she did was miss him. And at last, she cried.

5

For Panas, the hours following the rally were a blur, stretches of goodwill peppered with bursts of sheer elation.

The rally had lasted a half hour, after which he had walked back to the Azov. Nothing bothered him. Not the crowds, not the soldiers who were massing in the streets— for what he presumed were other celebrations—not loud customers, not even the Supervising Director, who phoned twice that night to cancel visits, claiming to be busy with other matters.

Too busy!

But Panas knew the truth. The big man was afraid to come, afraid to confront a confident new Panas Pavadze.

His blustering would no longer frighten the manager, his threats would ring hollow.

And Alexei! The usually reserved headwaiter was disgustingly deferential. Not only had Panas become a friend of the Chairman but—a double miracle—he'd started the evening as a captive of the SG!

The next day Panas was even good to his wife. For sixteen years he'd treated Caterina the way the rest of the world treated him—with discourtesy, snapping at her and criticizing everything that displeased him. But not today. She always did everything she could to make her husband comfortable, but after seeing the rally when it was rerun on the morning news, she doted on him as never before. In return, Panas was complimentary to her. Only when Caterina was downstairs, using the washing machine, did she indulge *herself*. Then, in very explicit detail, she told her neighbors all about her husband's friend Cherganyev.

It was all quite a change, Panas thought, from the way things had been when he'd arrived in Moscow twenty years before. And when he went back to work the next night, the swaying of the Metro reminded him of something he hadn't thought about for years, a ride he'd hated, the rocking of another train. . . .

6

He thought back to the meadows that stretched endlessly from the boxcar. The fields spiky with harvested barley. The goats that looked up as the train rumbled past. The pungent smell of manure as they passed the cows in the field. The ramshackle barns.

But it was an improvement over what he'd been smelling just a few days before, his own excrement and that of others, a stench compounded by the closeness of a hot, windowless cell.

Panas had been mustered out of the navy with no more specific goal than to get as far from commanding officers as possible. Returning to Tara, he was cockier than when he'd left three years before; he'd seen the world, while all these people had seen was the inside of their homes and shops. He found them simple and simple-minded; as a joke, he stole from them. Wallets, food, watches, belts, even a Bible, once. Anything that struck his fancy.

The joke ended when the village innkeeper caught Panas in the shed with his daughter. To save her skin, the young girl told everyone that Panas had forced her to make love to him. Who would doubt her after considering his other misdeeds—which he'd confided to her and which she now rattled off without prompting.

Panas was sentenced to a year in jail and was sent to a prison in Omsk. There were four other men in his cell, and just two beds; the toilet didn't work. The warden was a former major who was especially hard on ex-soldiers who brought dishonor to their training; he whipped Panas with a bamboo switch once each week. His back still bore the scars.

When his father, a minor Party official, was finally able to obtain his release after two months, Panas was a frail, repentant young man. But the elder Pavadze had a surprise in store.

"You have shamed me in my home," he said, pressing a train ticket into his son's hand. "Do not return." That was all his father said before leaving him at the railroad depot.

The ticket was for Moscow. Panas spent the night alone at the station, waiting for the morning train. Thinking back, he didn't know which had been more sobering: the brutality of the warden or his father turning his back on him. They had not been in touch since.

Panas had reached Moscow penniless. He had used his military record to get work washing dishes at a small café on Gogol Boulevard, not far from the Central Chess Club of the USSR. Because he could play, he was able to establish a friendship with Boris Gurevich, a chess buff who was also an executive with the Young Communist League. It was he who got Panas a higher-paying job, washing dishes at the Azov—and who convinced him that to get ahead in any career it would be advisable for him to join a group of which he was a member. Thankful for the work, Panas had signed up without even knowing the group's name.

Lenin Utra.

The Metro train came to a stop. Panas stepped out, pushing against the tide of people heading into the car.

It had always pleased him that he'd been farsighted enough to join the group before it became so powerful. Well, if not farsighted, at least bold. He had attended secret meetings in people's homes (never more than ten people gathered, lest the KGB become suspicious); he had helped write pamphlets about Lenin (it was easy; he copied directly from textbooks); and, though he had no idea who the group's leaders were, Gurevich told him they appreciated his dedication.

That was fine, but his promotion to waiter at the Azov after just two years was even better. And the events that followed—Panas was extremely pleased with himself. He'd made the correct decisions right down the line, even to whom he'd chosen for his wife. Caterina was not particularly attractive, and she was not a passionate lover. But she had an uncle who was a clerk at the Housing Council of North Zmailovo, and that was not only rarer than a good behind, but more important. They'd gotten their apartment after waiting just eighteen months.

The only luck he'd had involved Yevgeny, the former manager. What had befallen him could not have been planned. Yet, if there was a God, and if Lenin was indeed looking down from Heaven, then perhaps even Yevgeny's misfortune had been brought about because of Panas's good work.

There were still soldiers outside the Metro station, in doorways and walking the streets, but only in groups of three or four. Most of the military vehicles were gone, leaving the air cool and sweet, the way Panas liked it. He exhaled loudly as he crossed the street and made for the Azov.

Behind him, in a shadowy corner of the tiered station, a man in a black trench coat noted the time.

7

"The point is," growled the German, "capitalism means more than just good plumbing!" Wine spilled from the side of his mouth, dribbled down his strong jaw. He poked at it with his napkin. "Sorry. One should never drink and pontificate."

His companion, a Russian with a woolly mustache and sad eyes, shook his head. "It's just you. Your mouth says one thing, but your actions say another."

"Oh?" The German's blue eyes sparkled at the prospect of a debate. "Explain yourself, Yuri."

"It's simple, really. If capitalism were all you say it is, your company wouldn't need to print its books here."

"Nonsense! Your *government* makes it worthwhile! They give me good prices just to get West German currency back into the country."

"Now who's talking nonsense? I think your brain has been affected by that *zmeyá* you've been dating."

"Virna? She's no snake, Yuri, she's a hardworking journalist."

"She's a snake who hides in the grass to ambush people. Reporters in Russia aren't like that. They're like our waiters and our bus drivers and our printers, civil and well-trained."

"Afraid and unambitious, you mean."

"I mean *professional!* The truth is, you come here because our work is better. And it's better because the inefficiency of printers in Western Europe is guaranteed by their unions. If they do poor separations, if the colors aren't saturated or are off-register, you have no choice but to accept the work."

"Or go to another printer—"

"Who is coddled by the same union." Yuri jabbed his fork at the German. "Admit it, Erwin. Capitalism invites mediocrity in every field. When was the last time a German or an American or even a Japanese train ran like the Metro?"

The German waved this off disgustedly. "You've never even been on one, Yuri. How would you know?"

"I read!"

The German snickered and cut off a piece of his salmon steak. "The truth, my friend, is that capitalism enables people to own automobiles so they don't *need* to ride the crowded Metro!"

"Automobiles that just sit on crowded highways."

"You're just jealous. Here, I'll prove it! Panas, come here!"

The manager looked over. He was chatting with two regulars, a deputy minister and his wife. The minister seemed distressed by the interruption. Panas held a finger toward his guest.

"A moment, Herr Reiner."

The German washed down the salmon with the Crimean wine. "You see, my friend, the difference. In West Germany, the attention of the manager goes to the patron who tips most lavishly, not to some government stuffed-shirt. One must *earn* someone's attention, not simply command it."

Yuri looked cautiously at the other table. "You'll earn a prison sentence if you're not quiet. And though I'm pleased to handle your printing business, I won't become involved in your legal affairs."

Reiner drained his glass. "You're an old woman, Yuri."

The Russian sat back, scowling. He didn't say what was on his mind, that if Reiner hadn't inherited the largest publishing house in Europe, he never would have amounted to anything on his own.

The men were silent until Panas approached. He stopped a discreet meter from the table.

"Is everything all right, Herr Reiner?"

The German pushed strands of black hair from his forehead. "Yes, the food is delicious as usual. What I have, my friend, is a simple question."

"A simple one? In that case, I should have no trouble answering."

"You're too modest," the German said. "But first, let me ask you—is your mind clear?"

"Clear?"

"Are your children well, is your wife passionate, is the Metro inspector you dislike keeping a discreet distance from you?"

Panas stole a look at Yuri, smiled benignly. "I'm very well, thank you."

"Excellent. It's important that your answer not be colored by anything. Now, Panas, my friend, think hard. The fate of two cultures rests upon your reply. If you had a choice, would you rather ride the Metro to work or own a car?''

"It's funny that you should ask, Herr Reiner, for just last week I was thinking of buying a Volga to take my family on trips through the beautiful Russian countryside.''

"A used Volga, and for three years' salary, right?''

Panas stiffened. "Not quite three—''

"Forgive me. For *Alexei* it would be three. For the manager of the Azov only two years, ten months. The point is, you would rather drive to work.''

Panas's mouth twisted. "I don't know. I enjoy the Metro. It gives me time to think.''

"About what? How you'd rather have a car?''

"No, Herr Reiner, about my work. My customers.''

"Thank you,'' the German said. Surprised, Panas bowed slightly and left; the German leaned toward Yuri. "You see?''

"See what? Panas disagreed. How does that prove your point?''

Reiner pulled his sharply defined chin into his neck. "Panas is an idiot. Ipso facto, my point is valid.''

The Russian threw up his hands in resignation as the German smiled to himself. After four years of diligent work, he'd worried that the new government would change things. They were arresting all Americans and many other foreigners; there was still a chance that he might be next. But even Lenin Utra needed foreign currency, and he felt that he'd be safe as long as he printed books here and brought in a great deal of that currency.

If only they knew what he took out in exchange.

8

The idea had come to Joseph like a bomb, whistling from far off before exploding full-grown.

While at the White House, every official tells the President's executive secretary where he is in case he's needed. Romek Perkiel had done that when they went to lunch, and, halfway through his salad, he'd been pulled from the cafeteria by a woman in a hurry. Joseph had started to follow, only to be told that his presence was not required. He'd sat back down and, to keep from being annoyed, began thinking about Lenin as a target, about how an anti-Lenin campaign could possibly be made to work in Cherganyev's Russia.

Then the bomb fell, the idea mushroomed. He'd rushed back upstairs, all afire, aching to share his idea.

That was nearly an hour ago.

Joseph was not an impatient man, but it was frustrating to know that right now the President was with his advisers and members of the Joint Chiefs of Staff, no doubt discussing military options prior to the meeting in the Cabinet Room. And for what? If the President would just hear him out, everything else might be academic. And they might even keep the world from going to war.

Joseph paced anxiously around the antechamber, rattling change in his pocket and muttering to himself. Almost as annoying as being shut out was the fact that the President had viewed the request for a meeting, shuttled in via Clark, with condescension. Alexander had agreed to try to make time when he could, but that wasn't good enough.

Joseph worried, too, that something new had developed, something that would push the President too far in one direction before he got his innings. The signs were everywhere. Rapid comings and goings of key people. The Cabinet meeting pushed back an hour. Clark rushing out several times to consult with personnel downstairs in the Sitting Room. The interrupting of his lunch with Perkiel.

Joseph paused to study the books lining the shelves of the antechamber. Plato. Caesar. Franklin, Churchill. Old, rare volumes, from the looks of the spines. His expression pained, Joseph looked away. He hated seeing them here, unread, while there were libraries around the country that could make good use of them. Worse, he felt like one of the books—full of knowledge, yet kept out here, unused.

The door opened. He looked over expectantly. It was Clark. He shut the door behind him, came over.

"No go, Joseph."

"What's no go?"

"A meeting. The President's got his hands full. The Russians sent up that planeload of volunteers Fedorsenko was talking about. The Israelis snatched them over Iran and forced them to land in Israel."

"How did they know about it?"

"There was a live broadcast of the plane's departure on Russian TV."

"Naturally. Lenin went heavy on the chest-thumping, too. But don't the Israelis realize—"

"That they were set up? Of course they do, but they're Israelis. They don't play footsie when it comes to national security." Clark cocked his head toward the door. "That's why you can't see the President. We've got the whole crew in there trying to persuade the Israeli ambassador to release the Russians."

"And?"

"So far, zilch. Ambassador Chazak didn't even want to take the President's call! *We* talk restraint, and he says there've been enough pogroms. You can't argue with that kind of mindset."

Joseph grabbed Clark by the arms, surprising him. "That's why I have to talk to the President. We don't have to argue with *anyone*, this is something we can do ourselves. Three, maybe four people."

Clark wrenched away. "What are you planning to do, go in and rattle the President too?"

"In a manner of speaking."

"You've been hanging around too many students, Professor. You're getting stupid—"

"And *you're* getting soft! A few hours ago you were ready to play 'Mission: Impossible'—"

"A few hours ago we weren't on the brink of war."

"All the more reason to get me in there!" Joseph backed away, held up his hands. "Look, I got carried away. I'm sorry. But you've got to believe me, Jim, I can *end* this thing. And I can do it without a single casualty!"

Clark's eyes narrowed suspiciously. "You've thought of something the rest of us have missed?"

"Don't act so surprised! How many of your people have spent time drinking with old-timers and talking to them in dialect? I know the Russians and I know how to *beat* them. Please—you said yourself you'd rather try something covert than bomb the Kremlin. Here's your chance. Just get me two minutes with the President. *One* minute. Christ, I'll even tell you, and *you* can brief Alexander."

Clark looked from Joseph to his watch. "All right, Professor. You've got one minute: talk."

"Thank you. Joseph dragged his hand across his mouth. "In a nutshell, I want to kidnap someone."

"Cherganyev?"

131

"No, someone bigger."

"Really. Who?"

Joseph told him. Clark's jaw fell.

"They're right about you, Professor. You're out of your friggin' mind!"

"I'm not. It can *work.*"

Clark shook his head. "I don't see how."

"As I said, you don't know Moscow. You don't know Moscow's *underbelly*. There's a way to pull this off."

Clark's features softened. He stepped back and sat on the edge of the table.

"All right, Joseph, I'll bite. Start at the top, I want to hear everything."

9

Nona sniffed back tears as she walked from the apartment building out into the cold.

Where to go? What to do?

It didn't matter. Wherever she went, Georgi would not be there. After nine months there was no longer anything to hold on to, no one to hold her, no one to talk to. Before, if she'd had a problem, she'd discussed it with Georgi. Now . . .

Now she wished she didn't have the day off. The last thing she wanted to do was *think*. The words—the handwriting itself—were burned into her brain.

It is best for you that we meet no longer.

After reading the note, she'd calmly torn it into a pile of small pieces, then swept them aside in a fit of anger. Like snow, the pieces fluttered about before settling on the floor.

She tried to tell herself that something must have happened, that maybe a member of the group had been arrested, or maybe Georgi felt he was being watched.

If only she could believe that. If only she could shake the suspicion that he had been using her. Comrade Elephant, the trusting soul the others always played for a fool.

She'd started to write back her words slanted with anger.

What do you mean by this? Did you lie about what you felt, about what you said you felt? How can you do this to me?

Then she'd stopped, thought again about what he'd written. *It is best for you . . .*

Something had happened to put Georgi in jeopardy, something that would also endanger her. He rarely spoke about his political group—her fears for him must have been apparent—but she suspected that was the cause. Were they under suspicion? Planning to become more militant now that Cherganyev was in power?

It is best for you . . .

If he really wanted to do what was best for her, he'd have given up politics and spent his free time at her side. Loving someone else made her as free as she needed to be. Why couldn't that be enough for him?

Feeling numb and rootless, Nona stood outside her apartment. Despite the bright sun it was chilly, and she buttoned the collar of her green winter coat. Tears formed. She wanted her lover, her father, someone strong. Why were all the men she knew so weak? Panas, a posturing fool. Nikita, a stooped fool. So many fools! No one to talk to, no one to admire.

She began to walk, making her way to the Metro. She knew she shouldn't go to the Square, that even if he was there he probably wouldn't talk to her. But at least she would see him, and that made her smile. Some of the weight rose from her shoulders.

133

She used her pass to get on. Her heart thumped against her breastbone. She sat impatiently drumming on her knees while the train made seven stops before reaching Sverdlov Square. She hurried off, picking her way through the sparse late-morning crowd. The escalator seemed slow. Old men and fat women stood in front of her. She couldn't run ahead.

She did anyway. There were scowls and mild oaths, but she had to see Georgi. She reached the landing walked past the GUM department store into the Square. She made her way through the thick crowds to the Kremlin Wall.

No one was working on the lines today, and she looked around for the distinctive red-and-yellow uniforms of maintenance personnel. She spotted someone by the Alexander Gardens along the Kremlin's north wall, a big man busy polishing the brass fixtures on the Gardens' iron fence. She hurried over.

"Pardon me, but do you know where Georgi Tsigorin is working today?"

"I have no idea."

"Have you seen him at all today?"

He shook his head, turned around.

"I see." Nona felt a chill unrelated to the wind drifting through the Square. "Will you give him a message if you do see him?"

He looked around again, his eyes severe.

"Would you tell him that Nona was asking for him?"

The man grunted and resumed his polishing. Nona thanked him and backed away.

Something was wrong. Georgi never missed work. He enjoyed being here too much, loved the sights and history, the escape. She felt sick.

She wandered listlessly through the Square, fighting the urge to go to his apartment. What would she do? Wait outside, hoping for a glimpse of him? And if he

134

came out with his wife, what would she say? It would only make Georgi uneasy. Then she'd feel even worse.

The sun was warm outside the shadow of the wall, and she walked slowly toward Lenin's tomb. Though it was smaller than the Kremlin Wall and the huge Senate Tower that rose behind it, the Mausoleum was the more massive and imposing edifice. Consisting of six flat, incrementally smaller levels stacked one atop another, it was capped by a pillared structure resembling a Greek temple; the whole thing had always reminded Nona of a squat, brown wedding cake topped with candles.

Though there was no ceremony today, a long line of people waited to get into the tomb. There was always a long queue, though it had grown noticeably since Cherganyev came to power. Nona stopped and looked. There were classes of schoolchildren, office staffs, workers, officials, soldiers, and tourists—mostly Asian, it seemed, and not as many as usual—all of them patient and organized. The line moved slowly but steadily, everyone having fifteen seconds—no more—to gaze upon the body.

Nona's shoulders heaved tremulously. Now that she thought about it, Georgi looked quite a bit like Lenin who was lean, older-looking than his years; prematurely aged from carrying the weight of the world on his shoulders; suffering three increasingly debilitating strokes before the age of fifty-two as he struggled to overthrow a government that had endured for centuries.

Maybe Georgi *was* a lot like Lenin. Confident, a dreamer, willing to take chances. Where had he gone wrong, then? Was it the times? Was Cherganyev so much more powerful than the Czar had been? Did Nicholas II have fewer spies than the KGB?

Nona started forward, toward the end of the line. She hadn't been inside the tomb for years, and now she wanted to lose herself for an hour, be with a strong man. She grinned. She'd have to imagine more than she did with Georgi, but that was all right. It was strength she needed, not fellowship or conversation.

10

The people waiting in line were orderly. If they spoke at all, they did so in hushed voices, instinctively, as they shuffled toward the red granite tomb. And no one spoke at all when the honor guard was changed every hour. As a child, Nona had noticed that even in winter, visitors hugged themselves to stay warm but didn't slap themselves or dance from foot to foot as they did while waiting for GUM or one of the museums to open their doors. The presence of Lenin commanded reverence.

Even here, it was difficult not to think of Georgi. They'd often met by the wall, frequently strolled through the Square holding hands. And when she didn't think of him, she thought of all the history he'd told her about the Square. It was first mentioned in chronicles written in the fifteenth century. All roads from all of Russia had converged here. A moat had once separated the Kremlin from the Square—a moat where Stalin's tunnel now ran.

She had first come here as a child in 1945, to the Victory Parade commemorating the defeat of Nazi Germany. With drums rolling, Russian soldiers tossed two hundred captured enemy flags at the foot of the Mausoleum. Everyone had seemed so tall, the press of people suffocating. But the cheers! They gave her chills. Raise to her father's shoulders, she could still hear his voice honoring his comrades.

In 1961, already enrolled at the Railroad Institute, she came for the celebration honoring Yuri Gagarin, the first man in space. And in 1963 for Valentina Tereshkova, the first woman in space. It had seemed that there was nothing she herself wouldn't be able to achieve!

But Nikita and others kept her down, and her mother required so much attention, and men just weren't that bright or understanding, weren't like her father.

Or Georgi.

The tomb loomed nearer, large and imposing. She saw the guards, stiff and fresh like toy soldiers. If she fell to the ground, would one of them help her, hold her? Did anyone really care about her except Georgi?

Tears pressed against her eyes. This couldn't be happening. How would she live without Georgi? More important, why should she live without him? Whatever had frightened him away, it couldn't be as bad as being apart. She could live with anything except *this*.

Nona walked through the bronze doors, her eyes slowly adjusting to the recessed lights in the low ceiling. She followed the slow-moving line down the black labradorite staircase. There were soldiers inside, sixteen of them, lining the steps.

The line she was in wormed downward into the darkness. At the foot of the stairs, it entered a large room. There were more soldiers here, each standing at a corner of the chamber. As Nona entered, the outside world and its problems suddenly ceased to exist. There was only Lenin.

The body lay inside a glass-covered bronze coffin. which lay tilted on a crimson catafalque. It was surrounded by decorative spears and somber red draperies that underscored the radiance of the face that literally glowed beneath a single spotlight. As she filed slowly past, Nona was mesmerized.

Though Lenin had died in 1924, the figure before her, lying peacefully on a white bed, covered to the chest by a silken coverlet, did not seem dead. Rather, he seemed to be . . . thinking. The face, as pearly as a mimosa leaf, was radiant; the light appeared to come *through* it. And there was intensity in the lines of the face, which had certainly commanded attention in life: the sharp nose and intelligent brow; the square lips whose words had shaken the world; the mustache and pointed goatee whose texture looked very much alive; the slightly arched brows that framed what must have been luminous eyes.

As a child, she'd wondered—actually, her father had wondered, so she had, too—if it was really Lenin in the tomb, or a wax dummy. According to what every schoolchild was taught, six days after Lenin's death, his organs and bodily fluids were removed by a doctor brought in from Germany. Then—over the vehement protests of Lenin's wife, Krupskaya—the body was mummified, injected with preservative fluids whose composition has never been disclosed.

She remembered things she'd heard, from her father and others. About how, in the 1930s, foreigners were invited to enter the tomb. An embalming chemist, Professor Boris Zbarsky, was permitted to open the hermetically sealed case and touch the body. He turned the head from right to left. Everyone there seemed satisfied that it was not wax, but the preserved flesh of Lenin.

Still, people had their doubts. The Egyptians had preserved bodies, yet those had been wrapped in fabric; shrunken heads could last for centuries, but in no way did they look lifelike. Not like Lenin. Flesh, even treated with some kind of preservative, wouldn't *shine* the way this did.

She moved past the body, then craned her neck to look back as she headed for the exit. Nona refused to believe that what she had seen was a mannequin. These were the actual remains of Lenin. She had touched the past, his power, the way Cherganyev did.

Her eyes hurt as she filed back into the sunlight. But

138.

she felt better inside, surer. She could muster as much courage as a man. As a cosmonaut. As Lenin. She would go to Georgi's apartment and ask for him, for what was the worst that could happen? She would tell his wife she'd come about official business, that Georgi had painted a line near a Metro entrance and it had gotten smudged. It needed to be retouched at once. All she needed was to be alone with Georgi for a few minutes, to tell him she would stick by him, no matter what. Just as long as he was hers.

Nona hurried toward the Metro, filled with new courage and a sense of worth she'd never felt before. She barely noticed the newspapers whose headlines screamed in red about "an unprecedented act of war committed by the piratic Israelis. . . ."

11

Vin Papa walked to a map of Asia. Beside it, on an easel, stood a map of the Middle East. The short, erudite Secretary of Defense seemed at ease, but the thirteen other men in the Oval Office looked on with expressions ranging from anger to dismay. The Secretary opened a telescoping metal pointer and glanced at a paper that Jim Clark had handed him before leaving.

"Here's the current situation as best Jim's people and mine can piece it together. As soon as the Soviet plane was forced down, Russian bases in An Najaf were put on alert." He touched the pointer to a spot in central Iraq. "A force was immediately mobilized, consisting of two batteries of seventy-three tanks and 365 men. The T-54s and T-62s are now moving through Iraq and, we suspect, will press on through Syria toward the West Bank. Here"—he pointed to the map of Asia, to the Black Sea—"the aircraft carrier *Minsk*— their latest and their most sophisticated—has left Odessa and is moving at thirty knots, flank speed, toward the Bosphorus and the Mediterranean. They should reach the straits by late evening. The helicopter carried *Moskva* and the cruisers *Kerch* and *Nikolaiev*—accompanied by one destroyer, three missile corvettes, and two attack landing ships—have weighed anchor off Crete and are also heading toward Israel. The landing ships are carrying a complement of six hundred men."

"And in the air?" The President's neutral tone belied the tension evident in his rigid posture.

"Several squadrons of MiG 21s and MiG 25 Foxbats are being readied in Iraq, at Jabal. At Mach two-point-eight, flying time to Israel is about twenty minutes. They can get more from the nearest base in Russia in about an hour. We've also seen a Tu-95 Bear bomber, which could do a hell of a lot of damage." The Secretary nervously fondled his pointer. "Frankly, Mr. President, if the Foxbats attack, the Israeli Kfirs, Mirage IIs, or even our own F-15s will be in no position to go one-on-one with them. The sons of bitches are too quick."

"How do the numbers stack up?"

"Right now the Israelis have a two-to-one edge. We've got a B-52G over there, which can do as much damage as the Bear, and there are one hundred Kfirs and about two hundred fifty H/N Skyhawks and F-15s."

"Which is fine for one hour. After that, the Soviets can bring in enough planes to flatten them."

"Correct. And though we haven't heard anything, I'm sure they'll do just that."

The President nodded. "What's the latest on the other Israeli forces?"

Papa read from the paper. "Their 138,000 regular

army troops are on alert, and they've called up the 375,000 men and women in the reserves. At sea . . ." He scanned the paper. "They've sent a pair of patrol subs from Haifa to intercept the *Kerch* and the *Nikolaiev* off Cyprus. Also, for what it's worth, the MIR space station crew has been told to skip their next rest period. We don't believe they'll go to the nukes, but they may be getting ready to take out some of our communications satellites."

The President reached for his Washington Redskins coffee cup. "Sam, what about Jordan and Egypt?"

Lawrence held up a telegram. "We have a cable from Hussein declaring Jordan's neutrality. I don't believe it, but we'll see. As for Egypt, they'll stay out of whatever happens, God bless Jimmy Carter."

A chuckle rose from the group. Only the President didn't smile.

The door opened. Jim Clark came back in and perched quietly on the arm of a sofa.

"Anything?" the President asked.

"Nothing vital. When you have a moment."

The President sipped coffee. His eyes stung and he clearly would have loved to shut them. He faced Papa again.

"How many of the Project 17 silos are operational?"

"Three. And we've learned they just put crews on around the clock to try to finish the entire network in a week."

"A month's worth of work in seven days. They'll probably do it, too."

"They'll come close. Just the three already on alert can cause ten to fifteen million fatalities right away, and God knows how many more from the ecological damage."

"What's the status of the Mobile Strike Force?"

"All 16,600 men will be leaving Fort Bragg for Germany within the hour, and we're still awaiting permission from Egypt and Kuwait to land if necessary.''

"Let me know what the Soviets have to say when they pick up on it. How are we in Germany?''

"The TOW and Dragon antitank missiles are primed, and we can airlift the Vulcan antiaircraft missile tanks. We've also readied the Pershings, Lances, and Honest Johns with nuclear warheads.''

"Double-key?''

"Absolutely. Two men to trigger them, only on direct order from you or the Vice-President. To wrap this up— ACE-NATO has been placed on alert, and we not only have the *Eisenhower* in the Middle East but also the *Nimitz* and the *Indianapolis* are en route.''

"What have we got in the Middle East to support the *Eisenhower now* if we need it?''

Papa consulted the paper again. "Three amphibious assault ships. The *Saipan* at Cyprus, the *Belleau Wood* in the Gulf of Aden, and the *Tarawa* in Oman. Each is supported by Belknap, Coontz, and Leahy-class destroyer leaders. Officially, all of that has been done at the request of the Israeli government. Finally, at your order, Mr. President, Stealth is being readied to fly from Edwards to Frankfurt. It will be there in five hours.''

"Dave,'' Alexander faced his Secretary of Transportation, "where do we stand on oil if the Arabs cut us off?''

The barrel-chested Dave Carlin cleared his throat and consulted a notepad. "We have 378.9 million barrels of crude, 265.9 million of gasoline, and 189.6 million of distillates. Enough to get us through the fall and start rationing, if we have to.''

"Who talked to Treasury?''

The Vice-President raised his hand. "Mike Schneider will brief you at the three P.M. meeting. He said he'll close the trading markets before we make any announcements about what the military is up to. He's going to try to get London, Bonn, and Tokyo to do the same."

"The gold markets too?"

"Here, yes. There, who knows?"

"Tell him to twist some arms. Or I will." He made a note. "What about Paris?"

"A definite no. They don't want to anger Moscow."

Stocky Secretary of the Army John Maher wriggled in his seat. "Now there's an approach we didn't think of. Cowardice."

The President nodded glumly. "It bothers me too. Almost more than Cherganyev does."

"At least you've got to admire that man's nerve," the Secretary noted, "which brings up the matter of our own response. Cherganyev has murdered people left and right, and while I think it's fair to say that he's out of his goddamned mind, he obviously understands power. We've got the navy, the marines, and the air force on alert. Why bother going tit-for-tat? Why not give him a conventional war *now,* and if he tries anything funny, *then* we hit him with Stealth."

"I considered it," the President said, "but even if we could sell the public, which I'm sure we could, we'd still have a problem convincing NATO. If they decide Israel isn't worth the bother, as France certainly will, or that the Israelis won't destroy the world, then we're in it alone."

"For a change," Maher complained.

"That isn't the point," the President went on. "Even if NATO *were* to stand by us militarily, we're still not equipped to sustain a war at the same level as the Soviets."

"I beg to differ—"

The President held up his hand. "The operative word is 'sustain.' You know we'd only have three, maybe four strong weeks, a little longer if the Israelis were with us."

"Exactly! And that's more than enough time to bang some sense into Cherganyev."

"John, even if we *could* match the Soviets," the President went on, "we're still faced with the old Truman question: Would I rather see a half-million American soldiers die, or a few million Russians? Hiroshima was the right decision then, and Stealth is the right decision now. Anyone disagree?"

Clark raised his hand; the President's brow rose with it.

"Jim, *you?*"

"Mr. President, you know how I feel about that bird, and ordinarily I'd be out there fueling it myself. But I've just had an option presented to me that—well, I feel merits consideration."

"Whose idea?" Lawrence asked.

Clark swallowed. "It was Rosenstock's."

Several men groaned. The President was one of them. "Are you serious?"

"I am, Mr. President. Very."

The Secretary of State sniggered. "What kind of idea? Unilateral surrender? Or maybe he thinks we should drop this in the lap of the United Nations Security Council for a fucking *debate.*"

Clark said without turning, "Don't do this, Sam. I'll go punch-for-punch with the Russians, and you know what I think about the UN. But we should be ready with an end-around, and Rosenstock has a good one." He regarded Alexander. "A *damn* good one. Mr. President, I'd be glad to brief you, but Rosenstock is right outside. I think he could answer any questions better than I could."

The President surveyed the room. "Anyone object to hearing a word from the other side?" No one did, and he pressed the heels of his hands to his eyes. "This had *better* be good. And Joe," he looked to the back of the

144

room at his Press Secretary, "make sure Flora Lewis at the *Times* hears about this. When we go head-to-head with Russia, I don't want to read about how I only listen to 'voices of fire from the right.' "

The men laughed again—Clark felt they would have laughed at anything to break the tension—and the CIA Director showed Joseph in.

12

The laughter died quickly, but Joseph felt it in the air. He watched the men as they settled back, arms folded beneath smug expressions, like cats who'd surrounded a mouse.

Never mind, he told himself. *You've had students who were this carnivorous.*

Joseph stopped in the semicircle of chairs and sofas. He faced the President, who sat forward.

"First, Dr. Rosenstock, forgive us if events have outpaced courtesy. I appreciate your having come for this morning's meeting, and I know the ambassador is grateful as well."

Joseph nodded. The President was playing the part of the Great Appeaser. Joseph was unimpressed.

"Dr. Rosenstock, Jim tells me you have an idea. If you wouldn't mind being brief, the floor is yours."

Joseph cleared his throat. "Mr. President, Jim told me that you've reviewed the psychological profile of Cherganyev that was prepared by the CIA and the State Department Division of Soviet Affairs when he came to power. I've read it too. In it, a battery of psychologists agreed that the Soviet leader is not a stable personality.

We touched on this before; there's a morbid, malignant relationship between Sergei Ilyich and Vladimir Ilyich. I mention this for the benefit of the gentlemen who weren't present earlier, and also to point out that your own people are very much aware of Cherganyev's sickness.''

"I think we're all aware of that by now. Your point, Dr. Rosenstock?''

"Just this. As Fedorsenko said, Cherganyev is feared by his own people: Aksakov, Kupala, Getman, Volin, others. Unfortunately, they can't do much—not unless they get a little push.''

"Are you saying there's a way we can help them?''

"Indirectly.'' Joseph clasped his hands behind his back, and as though addressing his students, he said with a certain buoyancy, "What we must do is push Cherganyev into instability by going to the source of his obsession. To stop Cherganyev, we must stop Lenin.''

"Meaning?''

"We must steal Lenin's body from its tomb.''

13

There was subdued laughter amid the general murmur of disbelief. Joseph and Clark watched Alexander closely; his expression didn't change, which was all that mattered.

The President rubbed his chin. "Go on.''

Two men, Secretary Lawrence and Chief of Naval Operations Burton Price, looked at the President oddly. The rest regarded Joseph with expressions ranging from impatience to amusement.

"Well sir, I haven't worked out all the details. But

basically, there's an abandoned Metro tunnel—a subway—that runs directly beneath the tomb. With the proper tools, I see no reason why we can't get inside the Mausoleum and take the body."

There was a moment of thick silence. It was broken when Lawrence smirked. "You can't be serious."

"Why not?"

"Christ, take your pick of reasons! Assuming you can get into this tunnel—let alone into Russia *itself*, which I doubt—what about the guards? If they didn't see you coming, they'd hear you. That tomb has to be wired nine different ways from Sunday. And even if it isn't, you'd be making enough of a racket to wake Lenin himself."

"Not necessarily," Joseph said, "especially if we use hand tools once we've cut away the roof of the tunnel. In any case, the walls are like sponges, designed to soak up sound and keep the mood reverent. It's unlikely anyone would hear us. As for alarms, the place is a fort, constantly under armed guard. I'd be surprised if there were any alarms at all."

"But you can't be sure."

Joseph frowned. "No, Sam, I can't. But even if there *are* alarms, there's no reason they should go off if we're careful."

"How can you be careful if there are sensors to detect body heat or motion—"

"They wouldn't *have* those in the tomb. It's a *shrine*, dammit, not a bank—"

The President waved his hand. "Forget about the alarms for now. Jim, what about the rest of the plan? Is it feasible?"

"I'll have to look more closely at blueprints of the tomb," Clark said, "but it has a shot. The manpower's there. Assuming they haven't been compromised, we have reliable contacts who are deeply entrenched in the black market. They'll do anything for a buck. Smuggle goods and people into and out of the country. Hide a body, if necessary.''

"Without the KGB finding out?''

Joseph said, "The KGB tends to leave the black marketeers alone. The whole society is geared to acquiring things under the table, from better apartments to theater tickets. Without the black market, the economy would collapse.''

The room was quiet; no one moved.

"Assuming for the moment that this is even doable,'' the President said at last, "how can we be sure that stealing the body will make Cherganyev anything but mad?''

"He'll be too confused to be angry,'' Joseph said. "During this Middle East crisis he'll be especially dependent upon Lenin. He'll visit the tomb for guidance, commune with the body, draw strength from it. But the body is not a possession, and losing it won't make him angry. The body is his god, and losing it will cost him far more dearly.''

"Specifically?'' the President asked.

"He'll suffer enormous grief and disorientation,'' Joseph said. "Enough, I think, to trigger a complete mental breakdown.''

"You think—''

"I earnestly *believe*, Mr. President. He already goes there twice a week, officially—''

"For the publicity value,'' Lawrence scoffed. "He just started visiting the tomb on Wednesdays at two because that's the day and time his party came to power.''

"That's only a small part of it,'' Joseph insisted. "Ever since 1945, when he first moved to Moscow, Cherganyev has gone to the tomb every Friday at noon. That's when he first saw Lenin as a child, and that time is sacred to him. Unofficially, he also goes there another two or three times a week. Believe me, Mr. President, the symbiosis between the Chairman and the body is absolute: If we violate Lenin's sleep, it's Cherganyev who'll have the nightmares. What's more, his trips to the tomb are televised. If we time the theft to occur right before Cherganyev visits the Mausoleum, he'll have those nightmares right there in Red Square, before the eyes of the nation.''

"And if he doesn't, there'll be hell to pay," the President said. "If there's one thing Cherganyev has shown us over the past few weeks, it's that he's not to be underestimated.''

"That's true," Clark agreed, "but then we don't go in without options. There's still Stealth.''

"The thing is," Joseph said, "Cherganyev won't be unfazed. He *can't* be.''

The President seemed unconvinced. "Even if he does break, what makes you think someone else from his organization won't just step into power?''

"None of his aides is that powerful," Joseph said, "and no one outside Lenin Utra wants it in control. So far, the purges have been limited to the military. But as Fedorsenko's defection suggests, Cherganyev will be starting on political rivals very soon. If we can get an overreaction from him in public, show Russia that their leader's confidence comes entirely from a dead man, it may be the impetus Aksakov and the others need to replace him—if not to save Russia, then at least to save themselves.''

"Another 'maybe.' " The President thought for a moment, then touched the intercom on his desk. "Sally?''

"Yes, Mr. President.''

"Get me Dr. Ogan at NIMH.''

Joseph's heart soared. He looked at Clark, who winked.

"Gentlemen, I'm not sold on the idea, not by a long shot. If nothing else, it's as ghoulish as sin. But before I make any decisions, I want to hear what Mental Health thinks of your scheme. Dr. Rosenstock, I assume you'd have to go over there to work on this."

Joseph nodded. His palms grew sweaty.

"Openly or covertly?"

"I haven't thought much about it, but I'm a little too well known there to just slip in."

The President smiled. "Editorials coming back to haunt you?" The phone beeped and the President picked up the receiver. After quickly reviewing what Joseph had proposed, he sat stiffly and listened. Joseph and Clark tried to read his expression, but it didn't change; after nearly a minute, the President thanked the psychiatrist and hung up.

"Ogan isn't buying."

Joseph slumped. "Why?"

"In his opinion, the worst Cherganyev would suffer is replacement. He says that strong personalities who lose someone close tend to channel their energies into something else—a cause, for instance. In this case, we have to assume it would be Cherganyev's holy war."

"Bull."

The President stiffened. "Excuse me, doctor?"

"Ogan doesn't understand the significance of Lenin. He's not a Kremlinologist."

"And when, Dr. Rosenstock, did you become a psychiatrist?"

The room seemed to tilt for Joseph. The President had him, and he shrank slightly.

The President tapped a pencil on the desk. "Sam, what do you think?"

"I think the idea's an abortion. If we fail, it'll be a hell of a mess to disentangle. Not just diplomatically, but ethically. This is a *corpse* we're talking about, a burial site. The Pope alone would murder us."

"True. Romek?"

The National Security Adviser stepped forward, his

hand churning before him. "I'm not sure I agree with Dr. Ogan, but—forgive me, Joseph—the logistics seem incredible. What Dr. Rosenstock proposes is comparable, I would say, to trying to steal Lincoln's body from a Washington under martial law. In my judgment, it can't be done."

The President nodded. "I think we've spent enough—"

"No!" Joseph interrupted. "Don't do this, not yet. Let's ask Fedorsenko what he thinks. No one we can talk to knows Cherganyev better, and he'd also have ideas on how we can go about this."

The faces of the President's advisers reflected their displeasure. The President himself was unhappy.

"Dr. Rosenstock, I'm not sure I trust him or the people *he* trusts. If Fedorsenko were to tell someone and word got back—"

"Then it would be *my* neck!"

"No. Sam hit it on the head, it would be a public relations holocaust. And if Ogan's right, Cherganyev might very well turn up the heat on his holy war."

"Which is when we use Stealth," Clark said. "And until we have a plan, it seems premature to anticipate failure."

The President considered this, checked his watch. "My gut still tells me no, but okay—put something together and we'll talk again at four-thirty in the Situation Room. Sam, Romek, I'd like you both to be there. In the meantime," he looked at the Secretary of Defense, "I want updates on the quarter hour as to what troops are where." He looked over at Joseph. "One question. I've heard that the body in the tomb isn't really Lenin but a dummy. What if that's true?"

"I believe it's real, Mr. President. Every year, usually late in November, the tomb is closed for several weeks. Ostensibly they do this to repair the stone, which is worn and cracked from the tread of so many million feet. But I also know that they check the body for signs of disintegration. Where the skin has worn thin or hair has fallen out, it is replaced with wax or implanted hair. Most of the body, I believe, is Lenin.''

''That's two 'I believes.' I'm still not convinced, but I'll reserve final judgment until later. Gentlemen, thank you.''

As the President rose to go to the Cabinet Room, Joseph felt as though he were being swept along without much chance to get his bearings. He suddenly understood what the commentators meant when they spoke of ''the tide of history.'' Joseph only hoped that he didn't drown in the tide, for he realized that if the President did approve their plan, it could well be *his* failure that sent an atom bomb whistling toward Red Square.

With him just a few meters underground.

14

Though Georgi's apartment was not far from her own, Nona had never gone to it. She hadn't wanted to see where he lived, to see his other life.

Now she had no choice.

The building was located on Ogaryov Street. A small brown structure with a dirty white stone canopy—a failed attempt to make the ordinary building seem ornate—it had a neat fenced-in garden out front, and she was not surprised to note that the paint was fresh on the fence and in the corridor.

Her heart slamming, she looked for the name Tsigorin

on the mailboxes. Apartment 3A. She hurried to the old wooden steps and ran up.

She had wondered all along what she'd say if Georgi's wife greeted her at the door.

Hello, I work with your husband. . . .

But what if Zoya knew Georgi's co-workers? Nona wasn't even sure there *were* women in that department. Should she pretend to be just a friend or a member of his political group?

Panting, she reached the third floor. Apartment 3A was at the end of the corridor, a corner room. She took a deep breath and walked toward it.

A friend, she decided. *I'm just a friend. We eat lunch together, that's all.*

She reached the door, took another breath. She knocked. There were footsteps on the other side.

Georgi's? No, they were too frail. The door creaked open, and a man's face appeared in the crack. It was a wizened face with thick white eyebrows. The body beneath it was cruelly bent.

"Yes?"

The voice was soft, barely above a whisper. Nona's wasn't much louder as it emerged from her clogged throat.

"My name is Nona Nemelov. I'm . . . I'm looking for Georgi."

The old man studied her up and down. "He's not here."

"I see. Are you . . . Zoya's father?"

The body straightened slightly. "Yes . . ."

"He's told me about you. You see, we have lunch together in the Square, and when he didn't show up—"

"I'm afraid I can't help you. You see, they took him with them."

"They? You mean his friends?"

153

The old man seemed not to have heard. "They took Zoya too. Why they left me, I have no idea."

Nona felt sick. "*Took* him? Who did?"

"Men. I don't know who they were, but they came early this morning and asked Zoya and Georgi to go."

"Go where?" Her voice was rough, urgent.

"I don't know that either. But they didn't look like police officers."

The KGB? The Sredá-Grom? Lord, no!

Nona was about to ask if Georgi had said anything, when she heard footsteps on the stairway. She turned and saw a shadow creep along the well-worn wood. It was a man's shadow.

A tenant?

"Excuse me," she said to the old man, "but may I come in and get a drink of water? I feel sick."

"Of course," he answered, shuffling backwards. "I'm not used to being alone, and it will be good to have the company."

Nona stepped in, pushing the door shut as the footsteps reached the landing; the door bounced back in as a toe was shoved between it and the jamb. Nona looked behind her, saw a hard young face glaring down from a black leather jacket.

A KGB jacket.

The man's cheeks were red, and Nona realized he must have been standing outside, watching the building.

"Good afternoon, Miss."

His voice had the same dark cast as his dress. Nona's body rebelled, her stomach falling faster, knees weakening. She had to urinate.

"Good afternoon," she said, her voice soft.

"You are a friend of Zoya Tsigorin?"

"No sir."

He seemed surprised by her candor. "Then why are you here?"

154

"I'm a friend of Georgi Tsigorin." She wouldn't deny him; she couldn't.

"You admit this?"

"Yes. Why shouldn't I?"

"What is your name?"

"Nona. Nona Nemelov."

The name didn't seem familiar, and he motioned her out with two fingers. "Come with me, Nemelov."

"I'm sorry?"

"I said come."

"Where, may I ask?"

It wasn't courage that made her stand her ground, it was sheer, paralyzing terror. Frowning, the man stepped to her side and gripped her arm tightly.

"We're going to see Georgi Tsigorin."

He tugged at her. Her loins trembling, Nona managed to remain upright as he walked her down the stairs. Only when she was seated in the waiting Moskvich, behind the partition of soundproofed glass and wire mesh, did she let go, weeping into the sleeve of her coat.

15

Panas awoke in a vile mood. He knew it at once from the tightness of his cheeks, the roiling in his belly. Where the contentment had gone, he had no idea. *Why* it had gone was also a mystery. All he knew was that the afternoon already seemed foul, and it was just a few minutes old.

It had started the night before. Reiner, with his humiliating questions. Panas had wanted desperately to tell him that he could well afford a car with the money he earned from selling food on the black market. It had hurt to hold his tongue. Then the Supervising Director had finally rescheduled his visit for the next night, for tonight. That meant two things. Not only hadn't there been any changes in the restaurant division—Panas ached just thinking of the money he'd have made at that job *plus* taking the Supervising Director's share of the ''spoiled'' food—but tonight would be filled with aggravation.

Then there had been little things, a succession of them. A steak cooked too rare for this one's taste. Wine that was a little too warm. A table too near the front door, another too near the lavatories. The worst were the four Vietnamese patrons, school officials from Haiphong, who argued about the bill. Not about the sum, but about the fact that their host from the Ministry of Education was supposed to have prepaid it. Panas gave them a bottle of wine, 1981 Madrese, to assuage them; for his efforts, neither he nor Alexei received a gratuity.

Even Alexei had been in a bad mood. Maybe he was as sad to see Panas still around as Panas was to see the Supervising Director.

Then there was the letter from his mother. She'd written to the Azov, fearing that Caterina—whom she'd never met—might not show it to him.

Your father is ill, she'd written. *Come and see him.*

''Come and see your grandchildren!'' Panas had snarled, crumpling the letter and throwing it away.

Finally, to top the night off, he'd encountered the bitch Nona on her way from the mailbox. Not only did her homely, sour face offend his sense of aesthetics, but last night she had fangs.

''Your children were playing outside my door—''

''It was raining.''

''Caterina took her bath on my floor, I had to wait—''

156

"Someone was using ours, and she prefers not to smell."

"And I don't hand out passes to the Metro, even to neighbors—"

"She was taking the children to the Mausoleum, and that can get expensive. Besides, I give out wine to many whom *I* meet."

Being civil was easy, he did it for hours every night. However, not hating people was impossible. He walked upstairs filled with rage against the misanthropic woman. Where was that scrawny boyfriend of hers? He wanted to punch him hard for allowing her to be such a miserable creature.

Now it was a new day, but the frustration remained. Panas pulled the blankets to his chin. At least Caterina was at work, the children at school. There was no one to set him off. He tried to buoy himself by thinking of the *good* things in his life. And as he did so, it occurred to him just what was wrong.

The glow of Cherganyev was fading.

He thought about it. In the leader's presence, everything had had an aura of importance, he'd been touched by the sun. And the warmth had lingered—until today, when it was finally obliterated by the small goals and niggling words of minor officials, by having to answer to mere patrons and neighbors after having answered the questions of Sergei Ilyich himself.

Had he been spoiled?

Oh God, no. Please let it be just a phase, the inevitable disappointment after such extraordinary elation. Things would balance out.

Yes, that was it. The pendulum going the other way.

A cosmonaut had once dined at the Azov. She'd said that as beautiful as the earth was, it was always difficult to return after having touched the heavens.

Panas's brow furrowed. The cosmonaut, at least, knew

157

she'd be going back to the stars. He was forever earth-bound, and the prospect was suddenly unthinkable.

Panas cried himself back to sleep, and when he woke his eyes stung and his chest felt empty. The mood hadn't passed, he was still steeped in depression.

It was early in the afternoon, just three, but there was no sense staying in bed. His movements numb and lack-adaisical, he went down the hall to shave and shower, then returned to the apartment to dress.

His thoughts ranged from desperation to anger.

Show the Supervising Director you have courage. Make changes without consulting him! He can't fire you, you know too much. . . .

Damn the foreign customers to hell! If they don't like the way I run my establishment, let them eat elsewhere. . . .

Don't be so accommodating! The first person who scuffs your shoes in the Metro, give him a piece of your mind!

Panas left an hour early, intending to walk to work, to think. He realized, however, that his prospects were poor. He could work as hard as he wanted for a promotion, but someone would have to die before he could move up; even if he took on more responsibilities in Lenin Utra, it would be years before he was *truly* important. He wanted—no, he *needed* to get back in Cherganyev's shadow *now.*

After a few minutes, Panas suddenly stopped walking.

All right, he told himself, *you can't stand with Cherganyev, be his friend.* But there was one thing he *could* do. Something simple but glorious. Something Cherganyev him-self did over and over.

Feeling a rush of excitement, the well-dressed young man surprised the other pedestrians by breaking into a trot and heading for the Metro.

Joseph and Clark entered the Situation Room, where Romek was sipping coffee and reviewing the President's schedule with an aide. The young woman left when the men arrived.

"I hate to say it," Romek said, "but before anything else happens we're going to be briefed—and a bit behind schedule, I might add. The President's still in with the Joint Chiefs of Staff and the Cabinet."

"New developments?" Clark asked.

"When I left twenty minutes ago, they were watching the Warsaw Pact forces. It wasn't clear whether they were just going on alert or being mobilized."

The National Security Adviser seemed to Joseph more subdued than before; it was ironic, he thought, that what tended to wear down men like Romek or Lawrence fired him up.

Clark sat, threw down his notepad. "I just hope they haven't already written us off."

"Is that possible?" Joseph asked.

"With Alexander? It's tough enough to change his mind when you have his complete attention, but if he's worried about another front opening up in Europe—"

Clark's voice trailed off and Joseph sat down. He checked his watch, reviewed his notes, and tried not to think of the project being shot down. If anything, he was even more enthusiastic than before. For three hours he and the CIA Director had sat upstairs in Clark's White House office with Deputy Director Paul Davids, reviewing maps and photographs and tossing around ideas out of sequence. Though the meeting was chaotic, what they came up with was not only workable it was inspired. Joseph couldn't recall ever having been so keyed up about anything. It was a chance to use everything he knew, to push himself mentally and emotionally.

A chance to make history.

He tried to stay calm by looking around.

The Situation Room was spartan and white, with a long conference table in the center and a half-dozen telephones and pull-down maps along one wall, five computer terminals along the opposite wall. Clark had told him that a code word opened each machine and was changed daily; each terminal accessed either a military, geographic, meteorological, personnel, or satellite database in a White House subbasement. The room was bombproof, and it was from here, in the early stages of a conflict, that the President would conduct the business of government in the event of a war.

Lawrence arrived at 4:50, his demeanor considerably different from before. His round face was drawn, the suit slightly rumpled. He greeted Perkiel, who was seated at one end of the table, then Joseph and Clark, who were sitting at the other end. He was followed in by a pair of youthful aides. One carried a cardboard carton, the other a large fruit salad. The aides set both on the table.

"Grass has not been growing under anyone's feet," Lawrence said. "I hope you'll excuse the President, he's been delayed; I hope you'll excuse *me* while I have my first meal of the day."

One aide left while the other opened the carton and passed around a seven-page document marked EYES ONLY in red across the cover and on every page. Each copy was numbered.

"Thanks, Terry," the Secretary said as he took a mouthful of cottage cheese.

Clark shifted in his seat. "Sam, what's the story? Is or isn't the President taking our proposal seriously?"

"I'll get to that in a moment," Lawrence said. "The first thing, he wants me to bring you and Romek up to date." He thumped the report with his index finger. "Your input on *this* is top priority."

Clark tensed his jaw and turned to the report. His heart sinking, Joseph did likewise.

"The printout will tell you where Soviet troop movements stood a half hour ago," Lawrence said. "The significant change from before is that Warsaw Pact troops have been mobilized in Poland, Hungary, Romania, Czechoslovakia, and East Germany. They're moving west, obviously to keep the pressure on NATO to break with us. The last page of the report is requests for materiel from Lieutenant General Ben-Avar, head of the Israeli Defense Force."

Despite his preoccupation, Joseph turned to the last sheet. The shopping list was streamlined but powerful: five F-115s, ten CH-53 choppers with night vision, six CH-47c Chinooks, ten Skyhawks, ammunition for M-16 rifles, M-72 antitank rockets, eighty-five TOW tube-launched missiles and nearly half as many Hellfires, and the Stinger handheld infrared homing device. The Israelis were obviously going for surgical strikes against the Soviets rather than an all-out offensive.

There was also, Joseph noted, a request for plasma and whole blood.

Lawrence touched a napkin to his lips. "The only immediate confrontation in the offing is in the Mediterranean, where the President has ordered the *Eisenhower* to set up a blockade to stop the Black Sea Fleet. That should happen around ten, our time, before any of the Russian tanks reach the West Bank. If the Russians shoot to kill, we're in it. If not, then we'll have to see what they do with the Israelis."

Joseph said, "They'll probably play chicken."

"If they do that, then everyone goes to the bottom. Our forces have been instructed not to let them through. We've got air time at eight tonight. The President is going to explain our position, then invite the leaders of the Soviet Union and Israel to an immediate summit in Stockholm. The Swedes are amenable, and so are the Israelis."

"Fat chance," Romek said.

"I agree, but the President wants NATO to see that no one but Cherganyev is being obstinate. As for our embassy," Lawrence went on, "someone finally managed to slip away from a guard and broadcast on our private frequency. Everyone's all right, but they weren't able to get much paper into the shredder before the KGB marched in."

Clark swore. "That'll cost us a lot of good people."

"All of them," Lawrence said as he chewed a slice of peach. "Since we have no way of knowing who's been found out, the President feels we should scrap the entire network and start from scratch. Is that possible?"

"I don't see that there's an alternative."

"What kind of downtime are we talking about?"

Clark thought. "We can have a skeleton crew working in a few days. All very good people, scientists and students we contacted when they were here."

"Their names aren't on file at the embassy?"

Clark shook his head. "Moles never are. How else can you spy on your own people if you have to?"

Lawrence made notes, then folded his hands. He took a deep breath. "That brings us to the next order of business, Dr. Rosenstock's plan. Jim—I'm sorry. The President feels it's just too risky."

Joseph's chest tightened. The CIA Director pushed his chair back in disgust.

"Give me a break! At least he's got to listen to what we have to say!"

"It doesn't matter. He's thought about it, and he's still worried for all the reasons he gave back in the Oval Office."

"What, that the Russians have our files? The time element? Cherganyev's reaction? Sam, the way we've figured things out, none of that works against us."

"Jim, please. I can't change things, and it's been a long day."

"Screw the long day! I'm in the doghouse because a new leader came in and beat the hell out of my people. Okay, *mea culpa!* But now it's our turn to catch *him* off guard. Look, we use agents who've worked exclusively for other NATO governments. One of my aides has already been in touch with an operative who's paving the way for us."

"How?"

"There's a woman we may want to work with over there, someone who can really make this project *work* for us. I don't have all the details yet, but the operative we contacted is already moving pieces around to make certain that we *get* this person. As for the time element, all we need is thirty-six hours from start to finish. Joseph was right. Cherganyev will practically be living at the tomb. Soviet TV says he's going back Saturday to honor the civilians captured by the Israelis—that's only a day and a half from now! We can be in and out while the military is still playing footsie in the Middle East."

"You hope."

"If not, it's all academic, isn't it? He bombs the Kremlin and that's that. But in the meantime, *what if we succeed?*"

Lawrence looked down, idly scanned the report. "I'm afraid we'll never know. What it really comes down to is the President doesn't think it *will* succeed. He gave it a shot—"

"You call one meeting a *shot?*"

"Not *just* the meeting. After you left, he had Ogan and two independent doctors work on this. Even if you can get the body—which the President doubts, by the way— the doctors agree that Cherganyev isn't going to fall apart. They feel that all you'll succeed in doing is waving a red flag."

"They're idiots!" Joseph snapped.

Lawrence froze. "They've got *reputations* in this town."

"They're still idiots."

Lawrence sat still for a long moment, then gathered up his papers. "Jim, again, I'm sorry. What the President *would* like is to get a makeshift intelligence network in place over there at once—anyone who can get us information on how Americans are being treated over there. The President is addressing the nation tonight and wants as much detail as possible. Dr. Rosenstock"— Lawrence rose and looked down at Joseph—"the President wanted me to extend his thanks for your having come down and to assure you that he'll be in touch if there's anything else."

"You mean the show's over," Joseph said bitterly. "He's gone through the motions of being openminded."

"Take it however you like. I think he's been more than fair with you."

Joseph wanted to say, "You would!" Instead, he sat in silence.

Lawrence thanked Romek and left; the National Security Adviser rose slowly. "I'd better get going. The Chief of Staff wants me there when the foreign ambassadors are briefed. From the sound of things, we'll be calling in a few favors." He paused beside Joseph. "I'm sorry this didn't work out for you."

"Are you? You didn't exactly help, Romek."

"I didn't exactly agree, Joseph, which isn't the same thing. I'm concerned about what's best for the country—and what's best for you. I'd hate to see you end up in a labor camp because your scheme backfired. If it's any help, do you know what I tell myself whenever the military wins over diplomacy or covert activities? That if Eisenhower had had Alexander's courage in 1956, and helped my people when they tried to throw the Russians out, a lot of suffering would have been averted. Hungary, Czechoslovakia . . . all of Eastern Europe might be free today. It's like Maher said before. All a tyrant understands is force."

Joseph looked up. "Dammit, why is it that no one seems to grasp that Cherganyev isn't a tyrant? He's an apostle. You can scourge him, you can starve him, you can crucify him—he's not going to stop."

Romek touched Joseph's shoulder. "He'll stop when he's dead, Joseph. And while I will grieve for many people, I won't grieve for him . . . or for the Russians who die with him. Forgive me for how that sounds, but it's the way I feel."

When Romek was gone, Joseph turned to Clark.

"It's a sick little group Alexander's put together. So much for all other options being considered."

"Fuck 'em." The CIA Director gathered up his papers and rose. "I worked on Stealth and I'm as proud of her as anyone, but these guys are trigger-happy. The only time they ever use my people is to drive in a wedge for the military—and I'm fucking *sick* of it."

"Join the club."

"To hell with the club. Come on, Professor."

"Where? If I'm not mistaken, I was just invited to leave."

"You *are* leaving, but you're not going home. You're coming to my office and then you're taking a trip."

Joseph shot him a glance. "Which trip is that?"

Clark looked over, his expression grave. "The one we planned, Professor. You're going to Moscow."

17

While they rode to CIA headquarters, Clark was on the phone with his Deputy Director, telling him to speed up the process of putting together a new spy network in the major Russian cities, even if it meant buying time from operatives employed by India, Saudi Arabia, and China, nations that had been unaffected by the arrests. Though Clark's uncharacteristic show of temper subsided quickly, Joseph could still see anger in his eyes, hear the tension in his voice. Clark was a diligent, hardworking ally; the President would find him a formidable foe.

Joseph, too, fully intended to rise to the task. With Clark's help, he would not only write history and answer a question that had puzzled Lenin scholars for decades—was the body real?—but he'd take Alexander, Lawrence, and their know-it-all psychiatrists down a few pegs.

Now the adrenaline was really beginning to surge.

Though Deputy Director Davids had the files of moles and espionage candidates at his fingertips, names of potential operatives were not discussed over the phone, nor, when Clark hung up, did he and Joseph talk about the mission to Moscow. Cars, Clark explained, were too easy to bug.

"The vibration of windows can't be read the way they can in office buildings," he explained, "because the engine causes them to rattle. But any of the cars on the road can be an enemy: a good agent with binoculars can read lips.''

He said that transmitters could also be concealed with no difficulty: pin-sized microphones fired by air rifles into a seat cushion when the door was opened; capsules dropped into fuel tanks. ''The best,'' Clark said with a trace of admiration, ''was when the Russians replaced a screw in an audio cassette with a microphone. The agent thought he was safe, turning up the music and talking. But the Russians had recorded the tape before replacing it and were able to filter it out of the guy's conversations. Neil Diamond cost us a top guy in Baghdad.''

When they reached the CIA's sprawling facility, the car went through three checkpoints, each attended by two armed guards. A photo ID was inspected at the first. Password at the second. Voiceprint at the third. If a guest was being brought in, he or she had to sign in at the last checkpoint.

''Sign in using my name,'' Clark said.

''Why?''

''Because if you'd coerced me into bringing you in, I wouldn't have told you that. When the guard saw an unfamiliar name, he'd call ahead and you'd be arrested the instant we got inside.''

Joseph was impressed. Between the codes and pin-sized microphones used by intelligence operatives, he wondered for the first time if his knowledge and bravura stood a chance against the KGB and Sredá-Grom.

What's the option? he reminded himself.

As they approached, Joseph could see five annexes behind the two-story main building. Trees were everywhere, along with picnic tables, a track, and a tennis court; it looked like the campus of a community college.

At the main building, Joseph was shown to a small cubicle where he was photographed, fingerprinted, and voiceprinted.

"Just in case you call from abroad," Clark said of the voiceprint, "we want to know for certain it's you."

Next he passed through a free-standing archway lined with sensors that looked like miniature radar dishes. Clark followed him through.

"It finds bugs," Clark said. "With the pin-mikes and fiber transmitters that look like loose thread, we can't just do a body search anymore."

After walking down a nondescript corridor, they reached Clark's office. Large and windowless, it was decorated with photographs of the planes he flew in Korea, as well as shots of Clark with every President since Kennedy. His medals were draped over a bronze bust of Aaron Burr, a distant relative.

Leaning over his desk, Clark pressed a button on the speakerphone.

"Eddie," he said, "ask Craig, Loree, and Erik to come in. Have them clear the decks."

"Will do."

"Also, have D.J. pack a suitcase." He looked over at Joseph. "Typical Ivy League professor, sixty, five-foot-seven, waist thirty-eight, neck seventeen, bow ties, not smooth." He spelled Joseph's name, then hung up.

Joseph scowled. "Typical, am I?"

"Don't take it personally, Professor. D.J. has to make it so that when the Russians go through your stuff, they'll think you brought the clothes from home. It cools the trail just a bit."

"Clever. And what, might I ask, is 'not smooth'?"

Clark smiled. "It means you've got zero color sense, Professor. D.J.'ll make sure that very little matches."

Clark's team arrived within minutes, all of them young and alert. Joseph had been impressed with Deputy Director Davids at the earlier meeting. He hoped these kids were as sharp.

After introductions were made, the lanky Craig sat

down at a computer terminal that was hooked to a fifty-inch monitor set in the wall. Through it, Joseph learned, Clark could access the entire CIA library: maps, histories, and even telephone directories of every city in the world, biographies of nearly a billion people from all walks of life, scientific and mathematical data, and such diverse facts as the schedules of trains, planes, and buses everywhere on earth, and the names and times of movies playing anywhere an agent might need to hide for an hour or two.

"The Central Omniscience Agency," a poli-sci professor had once called it. She hadn't been kidding.

After briefing the others on what had happened at the White House, Clark introduced Joseph.

"We'll go over the plan in general, to get a feel for it, and then we'll work out the specifics. Keep in mind, though, that not only do we have to move fast, but no one outside the team is to know about this." He said gravely, "We're going ahead without presidential approval."

The aides seemed unconcerned, and their think-tank calm impressed Joseph until Craig said, "At best, then, we save a few million lives and the President takes the credit. At worst, a few million lives are lost and *we* have to answer to a special prosecutor."

Erik and Craig laughed. Joseph was suddenly uneasy.

18

Clark was scowling. "All right, Craig, cut the crap. We've only got a few hours." Noticing Joseph's discomfort, he added, "Don't worry, Professor. These kids aren't quite as bad as your students. They're cynical but they really *do* know it all."

The room fell silent and Craig punched up a map of Moscow. He highlighted the Metros in red. Forcing a smile, Joseph stepped over to the monitor and pointed to an unlighted area of the map.

"Here is where the so-called Stalin Express starts and ends. Actually, they never did finish it; the tunnel just stops. It runs directly beneath Lenin's tomb, which is this rectangle over here, and it ends under the Moscow River. They never bothered filling it in, and I've been told that today it's used mostly for storage."

As Joseph pointed, Craig programmed in the Stalin Express. A small red line appeared on the screen.

Joseph moved his finger to a building a block from the tomb. "What we have to do is get over to the Council of Ministers Building here. There are a service elevator and a stairway, both of which access the Stalin Express."

"Can anyone just walk in?" Loree asked.

"No. There's no real security, but there are sure to be Metro employees on duty."

Clark said, "Erik, where do we stand on that? Did your contact work out?"

"Perfectly. His name is Reiner, a West German operative, and he stopped by the embassy there a half hour ago to bring me up to date. He's already moved to get us the person we want. Her name is Nona Nemelov, she's a Metro inspector, and she did indeed lose her father in the Stalin purges."

"Reiner did a rerun?"

The term, in this context, was new to Joseph. But he didn't like the sound of it.

Erik nodded. "Thanks to his tip, Nemelov's lover, a dissident, was picked up by the KGB. We'll tell her we can save him, which should push her into our arms . . . and get Dr. Rosenstock into the tunnel."

170

"Excellent," Clark said.

Joseph tasted bile. Some blameless woman was being hurt to serve their needs. Clark's words came back to haunt him: *That's why the Good Lord invented places like Cambridge.*

"Craig," Clark went on, "what did you get on the Mausoleum itself?"

A magazine page filled the screen. "This is an article from the Soviet magazine *Aftsa*. The walls are made of granite a meter thick, but the floor is less than three inches thick and covered with black and grey labradorite—easily penetrated. As for the coffin itself, the glass is bulletproof, over a half-inch thick, and the rest is solid brass. The way Engineering figures it, it'll take a high-speed diamond drill to get through the glass quickly and quietly."

"What about guards—number, locations?"

Loree said, "The guard is changed at exactly two minutes before the hour, each hour, every day of the year. What's important, however, is that the tomb is closed until noon on Friday, so that Cherganyev can officially welcome the public. At that time, there are only the two guards outside."

"So it has to be this Friday morning, then," Clark said. "Joseph, what do you think?"

Joseph was staring at his hands. It was difficult to concentrate. *What do I think?* he asked himself. *I think it's bad enough the Russians are suffocated by their leaders without Americans hurting them too. I think that what we're doing to this Nona Nemelov is criminal.*

He looked up, knowing that there was no choice but to press on. "I think we'll be fine," he said evenly. "Since work is done in the tunnel all the time, the noise shouldn't attract attention. Also, a band plays at the tomb for an hour before Cherganyev visits, which should help to cover any sounds we make once we're inside."

Clark seemed satisfied. "Erik, did you check our tool man in Moscow?"

"Yes, and there's bad news on that front. His name's on file at the embassy. But the *good* news is that our new friend knows someone named Lubchenko, a black marketeer who can provide the heavy drills and possibly electric stun guns. Also, when he makes contact with Nemelov he'll find out where tools are kept in the tunnel—just in case we need backups."

"I'm comfortable with that. How about you, Professor?"

Joseph nodded.

"Loree, get together the equipment we're likely to be using. Have Engineering put it through the rounds and clock it."

The woman left quickly.

"They'll duplicate the conditions you'll encounter at the tomb," Clark explained. "We'll know to within a minute how long this should take."

"The only thing we'll have to send over with Dr. Rosenstock is the diamond-tip drill," Erik said. "Reiner can't guarantee one to our specifications."

"No problem. We'll just have to think of a way to get it through customs. As for the body—Erik, you'll have to arrange for a car. Putting Lenin in a trunk may be disrespectful, but Joseph and I agree it's the most expedient way to go. Where they head after that is entirely up to Reiner." Clark paused. "That leaves just two problems, the first of which is how to get Dr. Rosenstock into Russia. Any ideas?"

"I've been thinking about that," Erik said. "Do you want to try something with balls?"

"Such as?"

"Parachuting him in."

Clark shook his head. "He'd be spotted."

"Not necessarily. Remember that German kid who managed to fly a Cessna into Red Square?"

"That's why he'd be spotted. Heads rolled at Air Defense."

"How about the press?" Craig asked. "Dr. Rosenstock's done a lot of writing. Can we arrange for the *Times* or the *Post* to send him over?"

"With all foreign reporters under house arrest? I don't think any newspaper will agree to send him over while their people are being held. What about a book?" Clark suggested. "Have you ever written one about Lenin?"

"I've considered it, of course—"

"Won't the timing seem a little suspicious?" Craig asked. "The United States and Russia are at each other's throats, and he decides that this would be a good time for a field trip."

"What *better* time?" Rosenstock countered. "I want to witness the rebirth of Lenin firsthand. I like that. I can make it work."

"You'll need a visa," Erik said. "Can you sell the Soviet embassy on that?"

"I think so."

"The thing is," Clark said, "I want you out of Washington with as little noise as possible. Have you ever gotten a Russian visa anywhere else?"

"In Helsinki, last year."

"They approved you with no problem?"

Joseph seemed slightly embarrassed. "None. Foreign Minister Aksakov is a fan."

Clark phoned his secretary and told her to book Joseph on a direct flight to Finland leaving New York around ten that night. He also asked her to have his helicopter on standby for the trip and to have five commissary sandwiches delivered to his office.

"You said there was a second problem," Joseph remarked.

"There is." Clark folded his hands on his desk. "Stealth. We've got to make sure that if we succeed, it'll be recalled."

"It'd be hell if we pulled this off and they dropped the bomb anyway," Erik noted.

Once again the humor eluded Joseph. "There must be some way I can signal the plane."

"Plenty of ways," Clark said, "but the pilot won't listen without a code, and only the President and the base commander have it. No, it'll have to go through me and I'll have to tell the President. Erik, get Dr. Rosenstock a transmitter, simple yes-or-no signal, hundred forty megaherz. We'll relay it right to my office at the White House."

The sandwiches arrived. Joseph wasn't hungry but he ate anyway. He was worried about Alexander.

"You're sure he'll listen?" Joseph asked. "You're sure that with Moscow in Stealth's sites, Alexander will really back down on your say-so?"

Clark nodded. "Even if he didn't give a damn about the Russians, there are eleven thousand Americans over there. One more thing," he went on, "but it's an easy one, Professor, and this one's all up to you. We need a name for the operation."

"A code name?"

Clark nodded.

Joseph thought for a moment. "If you don't mind, it would be fitting to use Lenin's nickname. It means 'the Old One.' Even when he was very young, Lenin looked like an old man."

"Fine with me," Clark said.

Craig cleared the screen and opened a new file. "Code?"

"Starik," Joseph said. "Operation Starik."

PART THREE

For once, Panas's heart didn't sink when Erwin Reiner walked into the Azov. This time the German didn't come with Yuri; he was accompanied by a woman, a statuesque creature who took Panas's breath away.

Her name was Virna, and she was about forty-five— a good age, as far as Panas was concerned, wise and not prudish. And she was very attractive, slender, with blond hair, high cheekbones, and hazel eyes; the crow's feet made her look sophisticated. Gazing at her cheered Panas—cheered him far more than what he'd done that afternoon.

He'd gone to the *Pravda* office three blocks from the restaurant and, introduced to an assistant editor, generously offered to write an article about the rally. Panas felt that if he could relive it, he could rekindle the glory of it.

"I'm sorry," the editor told Panas. "All assignments by non-staff writers must be approved by Lenin Utra."

"But that could take weeks!" he'd wailed.

"I sympathize," the young woman had replied, "but if you put in an application now, you may be able to cover another rally."

Panas left in a huff. He didn't *want* to cover a rally in five or six weeks. He needed to write *now*.

By the time the restaurant opened, Panas was not only depressed, he was angry. The Supervising Director was coming, normalcy was returning, routine was oppressive, and glory—sweet glory was slipping fast.

Except in Virna's smile. What excited him was that

she actually kept *looking* at him, and *in that way*—half-listening to Reiner while she studied Panas.

It couldn't be *him,* he knew. Reiner was more important, a VIP, and quite handsome with his strong jaw and blond hair. Maybe it was his suit? It *was* fine, having cost Panas two months' salary, was much finer than the drab jacket and trousers Reiner wore. Or perhaps she found out that he'd been on television with Cherganyev. That had impressed many women.

What did it matter, as long as she was attracted to him—as long as his spirits were lifted? Panas stopped at their table regularly, ignoring other patrons, to see how they were enjoying their meal.

"Just fine," she'd say each time, her Russian thick with a German accent. Seeing her big eyes this close, his heart would swell, his groin tighten.

The last time he'd gone over was after Reiner had had several glasses of wine too many.

"And what do you do, Virna, if I may be bold enough to enquire?" Panas asked.

Reiner answered. "She works for a newspaper bureau. God, how I wish Yuri were here. Do you know what I had to do to free Virna from house arrest? Hint—merely *hint*—that I'd take my business to the Chinese." He took a long swallow of the Crimean wine he favored. "Yet I wonder, friend Panas. Did I do the right thing?"

"I would say, sir, that if the authorities allowed it, then—"

"Wake up, Pavadze! I don't mean *legally!* Should I have had *myself* arrested *with* her? Can you imagine being locked up with nothing but a beautiful woman for entertainment?"

Whenever a customer said something off-color, Panas would look cautiously at the other tables to make sure no one had heard. Only then would he titter. Though he glanced around him now, he did not laugh.

178

"I'm sorry that I cannot answer, Herr Reiner, but there is a lady present." His voice was cold, critical.

Virna smiled and glanced stiffly at Reiner. "Thank you, Comrade Pavadze. It's refreshing to see that chivalry is not dead."

Panas bowed to Virna. "If you'll pardon me now, I have other guests to attend to."

Virna smiled sweetly as he left, a burst of nobility pulling his shoulders back. The fact that he had risked the handsome gratuity Reiner usually tucked into his pocket didn't bother him. He had earned this striking woman's approval, and right now that mattered more. For a moment his depression had been wholly and utterly forgotten.

Panas's sour humor returned with the arrival of the Supervising Director.

Pavel Lubchenko was a slender man of medium height and a round, red face. He was bald and had no facial hair, including eyebrows, having lost them to a childhood disease. His lips were thin and pale, his dark brown eyes perpetually bloodshot; he looked almost like a figure in negative. The impression was underscored by the fact that Lubchenko always wore black—trousers, shoes, jacket, overcoat, and gloves—which he wore late into the spring and early in the fall. It made him less visible in dark corners or behind shops when he made deals to sell the food they took from the Azov.

Lubchenko had a slow but imperative manner, and whenever he looked at Panas the manager felt the need to rush, although Lubchenko himself never did.

It was Alexei who came to the office to tell Panas of the Supervising Director's arrival.

"He may have been here for a while," Alexei said. "He was standing in the foyer, just watching."

Panas swore. All he needed was for Lubchenko to have heard the exchange with Reiner. It was more than a rule, it was a commandment that the manager was to withdraw rather than to criticize a customer. Panas had no idea how Reiner had reacted after he'd turned and left. If the German's face had seemed cross, or if he'd said something that Lubchenko might have heard . . .

Panas winced. The moment of pride he'd felt wasn't worth this rush of terror. Going to a safe and removing a private ledger, Panas straightened his jacket, paused by the sink to adjust his tie and comb his hair with his fingers, then strode into the smoke-filled room.

Panas peered into the foyer; Lubchenko wasn't there. He looked questioningly at Alexei.

"Out front," the headwaiter said behind his hand.

2

It was a shock, walking into the cold evening air, and goosebumps rose on Panas's chest, arms, and buttocks.

"Good evening, Comrade Director."

Lubchenko was facing the street. He did not turn when Panas came out.

"Pavadze, I have some unpleasant news. I'm afraid we must suspend our little deliveries for a while."

"Of course, Comrade. Whatever you wish."

Panas wasn't happy, but if that was all Lubchenko had to say, he'd be relieved.

"I don't wish it, but caution is necessary—at least for the next several weeks. After that, we shall see."

"I understand."

What Lubchenko probably meant was that although he'd survived the changes in his department, he was being watched. Perhaps not as closely as some, but watched just the same.

"I see that business is off."

"Yes. Without the Americans and other foreigners, we may even have to let some of the waiters go. It does not look to be a very comfortable time for us."

"No, it does not." The Supervising Director turned now. "In fact, Pavadze, you should know one thing more. The government needs money for its other projects. There may be a cut in salary."

"A cut?" Panas's voice broke. "But how will I survive? The children outgrow their clothes every month!"

Lubchenko shrugged, and Panas bristled inside. The paychecks came from the Supervising Director's office; there was no guarantee Lubchenko would not pocket the money himself.

"You won't be needing to see this, then," Panas said, tapping the ledger.

"Not for our private deliveries, no."

"If not that, then what?"

"More unpleasant news. You must begin to record the gratuities, I'm afraid. Henceforth, two-thirds must be turned over in taxes."

A trio of diners came out and Panas swallowed an oath. He smiled weakly at the customers, then glowered at the Supervising Director.

"This is ridiculous! We're already paid less in salary because of the gratuities!"

"I agree it isn't fair, but what can I do? You still have it better than many—it's just the way things are."

"To hell with the way things are! How will they—"

"Check up on you? People will come in now and then, posing as diners. They'll talk with Alexei, whose gratuities will also be taxed—and who, by the way, will have every reason to want to report you and move up to your higher salary. And they will look at the ledger at the end of the evening. If it doesn't balance with what is in your pocket, you will be dismissed and possibly arrested."

This was the last thing Panas needed to hear. Less money and more tension. It was all he could do to refrain from a second outburst.

Lubchenko stepped forward, put his hand on Panas's shoulder. "But don't worry, Pavadze. You know I would never let you be hurt."

"What can you do, Comrade Director? Is there another job?"

"Another job? No, and do you really want to leave the Azov? Few jobs are so clean, few restaurants so elegant. However"—he bent closer—"I'm working on something that will help you. Give me a day or two and I'll be able to tell you more."

"Can you tell me nothing now? I could certainly use a cheering word."

Lubchenko smiled. "A word, Pavadze? All right, I'll give you a word." He came closer still. "The word is money. A good deal of it. Does that cheer you?"

Panas's belly tingled with relief. "Very much, sir. Yes, it does."

"Excellent. Now go back inside and take care of your customers. I will tell you more tomorrow night. In the meantime, say nothing of the new project to Alexei or anyone else, including your wife. It is important that we keep this entirely to ourselves."

"I understand," Panas assured him.

"Oh, and Pavadze—"

"Yes, Comrade?"

"What you said tonight to Herr Reiner. That ill becomes the manager of the Azov."

Panas blushed. "I'm sorry. I know it was wrong, and it won't happen again."

"See that it doesn't. Reiner was drunk and may well

forget; next time you may not be as fortunate. Next time," he said, "*I* may not be so forbearing."

"Of course, sir. And thank you."

Lubchenko headed for his car, which was parked down the street, and as he watched the Supervising Director drive off, Panas thought, *This is a change! A beautiful woman's attention, and kindness from the Supervising Director.* Perhaps something *had* rubbed off from his brush with Cherganyev, after all.

Panas went inside, reluctant to give Alexei the bad news. As much as he didn't always trust the headwaiter, he was an excellent worker. If Alexei was unhappy, Panas would have to watch closely to see that he didn't slack off. Heading to his office, he placed the ledger on his desk.

"What's this?"

There was a note folded against the telephone. Snatching it up, he found an address inside, written in a florid script: 13 Vorovsky Street, apartment 10G.

He studied the writing, but couldn't tell if it belonged to a man or a woman. Then he grinned.

Vorovsky Street was near several of the foreign newspaper offices—including, he was willing to bet, those of West Germany.

The smile broadened. Virna. He *had* made an impression.

He tucked the note in his vest pocket, checked that the lavatories were clean, then made the rounds of the tables. When he was finished, he informed Alexei that there was something they had to discuss before he went home that night, and returned to his office.

Putting his feet on the desk, he had to admit that, all things considered, the day had turned out remarkably well.

And with any luck, the night would be even better.

3

The cell was small and windowless, the air stale; the only opening was the food-grate in the wooden door. She'd propped it open with her shoe. A bulb hung overhead, but it was operated from the outside and had been shut off; Nona had been informed that too many prisoners unscrewed them and tried to electrocute themselves. So she sat in the darkness.

Feeling her way around when she was brought here, Nona had found that the room's only furnishings were a toilet in one corner and a hard wooden chair in the other. Nona was sitting on the toilet because it was smoother and didn't rock on unsteady legs. She only hoped that the rats, which she heard in the walls, didn't get thirsty.

She had been taken to KGB headquarters in Dzerzhinski Square and, after being fingerprinted and photographed, brought directly to her cell. Nona had no idea how long ago that had been; they'd taken her watch, along with her earrings and the small amount of cash she carried. It may have been an hour or two, it may have been much more. In the dark, she had no idea.

She'd sat in silence, thinking about the good times she'd had with Georgi, wondering if he'd had a premonition that something was going to happen. She was content, at least, that he'd sent her the note because he was worried for her safety.

Then the taint of the prison set in, the distant slamming of doors and occasional shouts heightening her isolation. She thought of her father. Was this what had happened to him? Whisked from work and imprisoned, held for seven years until his death. He wouldn't have sat tamely as she was doing. Nona imagined his strong fists beating at the door, his deep voice bellowing. . . .

No. He would not have been there at all, but taken directly to some work camp. That was marginally better, working until he dropped instead of being left in a cell to *think*. To sour.

"Damn you all!"

Nona's own shout surprised her; her voice echoed briefly, then died. She lowered her fists, listened to her own uneven breath.

Stalin. Cherganyev. Two identical bastards.

To whom will they send the Certificate of Pardon when they realize that I am innocent? she wondered. To Nikita? To Panas, perhaps. She laughed at the idiocy of it all. They'd sent a pardon four years after her father had died. Her mother had torn it to pieces. A new regime may have wrought new values, but nothing could bring back her husband.

It was fitting, Nona thought. This kid of fate, his daughter following in his footsteps. They'd been close emotionally, intellectually, physically. In the dark she almost felt him touching her, reassuring her that being here was a mark of virtue, a sign that they feared you. . . .

Nona heard several sets of footsteps approaching, and rose. She turned to the door, listening carefully. She'd heard Georgi's footsteps frequently on the cobbles of Red Square; these were harder, faster. He was not with them. A key rattled in the door. The light blazed on.

Nona shielded her eyes and vaguely discerned two men. One wore a green uniform and police cap, the other civilian clothes. The man in the uniform shut the door behind him while the other pulled the chair to the center of the cell, beneath the light.

185

"Hand your clothes to Ivan," said the man by the chair. "Quickly."

Nona lowered her hand. "I'm sorry?"

"Strip!" he shouted. "I don't have all day!"

Once again, Nona was unable to move. The man jerked his head toward her, and Ivan came forward. Before she realized what was happening, he pushed her back against the wall. The impact knocked the wind from her.

"Take off your clothes," Ivan said, "or I will tear them off."

Nona slid to the floor. "Why?" she wept. But her fingers were already on her blouse, undoing the buttons. She squinted up at the other man's narrow face and dark, sunken eyes. She removed the garment, handed it to Ivan. *"Why?"*

Neither man answered. Still on the floor, Nona continued to undress. When she was naked, she huddled beside the toilet, her arms across her breasts.

"Get up."

She hesitated, then shook her head.

Ivan grabbed her arm, pulled her to her feet. She moaned from pain as, moving behind her and squeezing both arms, he walked her to the chair and forced her down.

His companion stood over her. Nona had crossed her arms again, and he looked down at them.

"On your head."

"What . . . ?"

He rapped her elbow. "Put your hands on your head."

Nona did so. The man made a point of looking at her breasts and she began crying openly; he walked away, began pacing. Ivan remained behind her, a gloved hand resting on the billy club slung from his belt.

"Are you comfortable, Nemelov?"

She shook her head. "Why are you doing this?"

The man stopped. He was outside the cone of the light

and she couldn't see his face, but she could hear the snicker in his voice.

"You're here because you're a friend of Georgi Tsigorin, and Georgi is a traitor, a criminal devoted to the overthrow of our government."

"No. Georgi is a gentle man who wouldn't hurt anyone."

"He's hurt many already by undermining the Lenin revolution, but that is not the issue. The question is, were you anything more than just his whore?"

Nona recoiled and spit, her actions reflexive; Ivan was nearly as quick. In an instant his arms were around her torso and she was pushed forward, kneeling. His boot on her neck pressed her cheek to the floor, and she gasped as something hard and wooden was shoved roughly between her buttocks. He pressed forcefully and pain shot up through her belly.

The other man squatted, his thin face close to Nona's.

"You haven't yet grasped the routine, have you, Nemelov? I'm surprised, since your employment record says that you are quite bright. Or at least you were, until you began associating with a dissident." He rose and glared down at her, lifted her chin with his toe. "The routine is this: I'll ask questions and you will answer them. Is that understood?"

Nona nodded briskly, the pain excruciating. Ivan withdrew the object and forced her back on the seat. Her vision was red and blurred for several seconds.

"Hands on your head," the man reminded her.

Panting from pain and fear, she obliged.

"Now then, how long have you been Georgi Tsigorin's whore?"

"Nine months . . . I think. Yes . . . nine."

"Did you know he was a dissident?"

"No . . . not at first."

"But later?"

187

"Yes."

"Yet you didn't report him?"

"No."

"Why?"

"I love him."

"More than you love your homeland?"

She hesitated. "Yes."

The man resumed his pacing. "How much do you know of his politics?"

"Nothing."

She flew forward, the wind pushed from her lungs. It took a moment for Nona to understand that she'd been hit from behind. Almost at once, Ivan was standing beside her, and she screamed as the object violated her again.

"How much do you know of his politics?" the man repeated calmly.

Nona's mind raced, but it was difficult to concentrate.

"He—he talked, but I—I never really *listened*. I didn't care!"

"Did he name any of his associates?"

Nona thought hard.

"Names!" he shouted.

Ivan withdrew the object. Nona relaxed until he drove it in harder. She collapsed forward, felt blood ooze from her anus. Ivan grabbed her hair and pulled her back to her hands and knees, the object still inside her.

"No names!" she cried. "Never! I d-didn't *care!*"

"Was his wife involved?"

"No! He said . . . she wasn't."

"Who were the others?"

Her back began to throb where she'd been struck. Her arms gave out, and Ivan had to yank her up again. She was vaguely aware of urinating.

"I . . . don't . . . know."

She was shifted back to the chair, and squirmed off

188

painfully. Ivan picked her up and held her on the seat. She wailed and pushed against his hands, the pressure on her buttocks unbearable.

"The others, Nemelov. Who are they?"

Her words were barely articulate.

"I don't know!"

The man stood back, tapping his toe. "Very well. Get him," he said to Ivan. "Bring Tsigorin here."

4

The man who was thrown at her feet looked nothing like the man who had made love to her just two nights before.

His naked back and buttocks were red with burns and welts. There were bruises on his face, his eyes and mouth badly swollen. When he dropped onto his side, she saw the burns and lacerations on his feet, genitals, and breasts. Caked blood was visible on his face and scalp.

Nona began to cry. "Oh my God—"

She forgot her own pain as she fell beside Georgi. She held him, but he didn't seem to be aware of it. He looked up through half-shut lids, his eyes staring vacantly. She clutched his head gently to her breast.

"Tell us about the others," the man said, "and we will see that he is cared for. Otherwise . . ."

Nona rocked as she held him. "You must believe me, I don't care about any others. Just about Georgi. I would tell you if I knew."

The man considered this, then nodded to Ivan. He pulled the dazed man from her arms and sat him in the chair. Nona stood.

"Please . . . don't hurt him—"

Ivan's arm came back like a piston and his fist landed flush in Georgi's face. Fresh blood coursed from his nostrils.

"*No!*"

Nona ran at Ivan and he pushed her into the other man's arms. Georgi's head fell forward, but there was no other movement. Ivan twisted Georgi's face around and punched him again. His nose shattered in a spray of blood.

"*NO!!*"

"Names," said the other man. "I want names."

"Take *my* name! I'm a traitor, I work for America— kill *me!*"

The fist jackhammered again. When it came back, Georgi's eyes were no longer open. Nona screamed. Her ears ringing, she felt as though her insides were going to explode; she was aware of vomiting, harshly, and then falling before her world went black. . . .

5

The apartment on Vorovsky Street was postwar and impressive. Panas took a moment to admire it. The streetlamps illuminated only the first story, but their light revealed the gleaming cleanliness of the white stone, the beauty of the golden terraces, the fine mosaic design— fishermen pulling nets—that framed the glass double doors.

"The press must pay well," he muttered as he walked past the concrete planters that lined a clean red carpet out front. He stepped into the foyer—and came to an abrupt stop.

There were three soldiers standing inside; all of them looked over at once, and Panas silently cursed himself.

How can I have been so stupid? This building is a nest of foreign journalists! I'll be arrested for sure.

Panas stood still, uncertain whether to stay or to try and leave; his mind was made up for him when one of the men came over.

"Can I help you?"

Panas's throat tightened. "I . . . I'm here to see someone."

"Who?"

"Just a woman," Panas croaked, "a customer at my restaurant. She, ah, left something there and I was simply returning—"

"What is her name?"

"I only know her first name, sir: Virna. Stupidly, I did not—"

"You may ring her."

"Excuse me?"

"Krauss. Apartment 10G."

The soldier turned and rejoined his comrades; Panas stared for several seconds.

That was a surprise! Virna must have bribed the soldier; she really *was* anxious to see him!

With a renewed sense of excitement, Panas went to a panel beside the door, lifted the receiver, and pushed the button beside Krauss.

"Yes?"

It was her voice. He melted inside.

"Virna? This is Panas. Panas Pavadze, from the Azov. I'm here about your note."

"Of course, Panas, it's good to hear from you. Come right up."

191

Giddy with excitement, Panas hurried through the lobby.

It occurred to him suddenly that he should have brought something from the restaurant, either champagne or wine. Where were his manners?

"No matter," he mused as he stepped into the elevator. "Virna will understand that I'm out of practice."

Or would she? It occurred to him that she might not know he was married. He didn't wear a wedding band when he worked, and Reiner may not have mentioned it. Panas quickly slipped off his ring and dropped it in his pocket. He'd tell her about Caterina, perhaps—afterwards. As for a gift, he'd bring something twice as fine next time.

Panas used the chrome railing inside the elevator as a mirror to brush his hair. He spit on his handkerchief and dragged it across his forehead and along the sides of his nose; he always got grimy walking the streets of Moscow. On the tenth floor, Panas made sure his bow tie was tightly knotted, checked his reflection once more, then turned right. He knocked once on 10G and waited. Footsteps caused the floor to creek. A bolt was thrown and the knob turned. The door opened.

And Panas looked into a face that was not Virna's, or that of anyone else he knew.

6

"Come in."

Panas looked past the man at Virna. She nodded and he entered, suddenly feeling unwell.

The man shut the door and stood spread-legged before

it while another man rose from a sofa and came over. This man didn't look even remotely friendly. He had a high forehead with an all-too-familiar Sredá-Grom scar in the center, and eyes that would look crossly at a baby. Panas could see several gold teeth through his slightly parted lips. The man wore a blue business suit and matching tie.

"Sit down."

The man gestured to a chair behind Panas, and he did as he was told. He stole a sidelong glance at Virna, who stood beside the man, her arms folded.

"When you and your Supervising Director stood outside tonight, what did he say to you?"

Panas couldn't have answered if he wanted to. His throat was frozen. He wished his bowels were.

The man lit a cigarette, then resumed. "I'll give you another opportunity to answer—just one. After that, you will be taken to SG headquarters for interrogation. Neither the room nor the company"—he bowed his scarred forehead toward Virna—"will be so pleasant."

Panas had no doubt about that. He swallowed hard.

"W-will I be punished, sir?"

It was Virna who answered. "No, you will not. It's the Supervising Director in whom case officer Glinka and I are interested. He and Herr Reiner. Reiner works for the German government, and we have reason to believe that both he and Lubchenko have agreed to work for the American CIA."

Panas momentarily forgot his discomfort. "Herr Reiner and *Lubchenko?* The CIA?" His eyes went wide.

"That's right. One of our people at the West German embassy reports that Reiner was there today, talking on the phone with the Americans. Then he and Lubchenko spoke together tonight, at the restaurant, after which you and the Supervising Director went outside. So you can see the importance of whatever details you can provide about their activities." She smiled warmly. "I assure you, Panas, our leaders will be most grateful for your help."

Panas breathed a little easier. Wonders, it seemed, would never cease. He wanted to get closer to Cherganyev, to his government, and now they had given him a chance. What's more, if he played his cards right, he could ingratiate himself with Sredá-Grom, perhaps even end up as Supervising Director himself.

But how to do it without incriminating himself? After all, under questioning, Lubchenko would tell about their black market activities. But then it would be the word of a traitor against the word of a patriot. Of course, if they checked his bank balance . . .

There was another way. He swelled with self-importance.

"Of course I will tell you all I can. I am, after all, a long-standing member of Lenin Utra. Sirs, Virna—Supervising Director Lubchenko has been forcing me to order more food than we need. When it comes in, we deliver the extra to—"

"We know about that," Glinka interrupted impatiently. "Tonight, Pavadeze. What did he say to you *tonight?*"

They know about the deliveries? Then they probably also knew that he made them willingly. Panas's chest deflated. He licked his dry lips.

"Tonight, s-sir, he said that we are to make . . . no more deliveries for a while."

"Was that all?"

"No. He said, sir, that he would have something else for me to do."

"What else?"

"He didn't say, sir."

The case officer approached and bent over Panas. He

held the cigarette between his thumb and forefinger. "Are you certain?"

Panas eyed the cigarette's red tip. "I *am*, sir."

Glinka blew smoke though his teeth. "I have been watching you, Pavadze—your comings, your goings. Your dealings with foreigners at the Azov. Did you ever suspect Reiner before tonight?"

"No sir. Never."

"Yet you knew his drunkenness was an act."

"Sir?" Panas was genuinely surprised.

"You've looked into his eyes, seen them watching . . . observing."

"No, never! I've heard him taunt our lifestyle, Comrade sir, but he always seemed to ramble. And I've never felt that the opinions of a German mattered."

"What of Lubchenko?" Glinka asked, the scar on his forehead becoming a deep blood red. "Do his words matter? What have you heard him say?"

"Nothing treasonous, sir. Never."

"Until tonight."

"Well, yes. If you say so. Please," Panas wheezed, "I will tell you *exactly* what he said. He told me that very soon he would have news about a new project, but he told me nothing about it—not a word. But of course," Panas laughed, "now that I know you're interested, as soon as *I* am told, *you* will be told. Every bit of it."

The man studied Panas a moment longer and then straightened. "Yes, Pavadze, I believe you. I believe you are too smart to risk imprisonment or death to protect traitors."

Virna moved between the men. "And Panas, you will say nothing to Herr Reiner about my activities?"

"Of course not."

"We date, you see. It would hurt Lenin Utra—he might even kill me."

Panas moved his thumb and index finger along his lips. "My mouth is zippered. It's our secret."

Virna smiled and kissed his cheek. "That's good. Come here again the next time he or Reiner says anything to you. Someone is here all the time."

Panas said he would.

As he rode the elevator, Panas had to admit it wasn't quite the night he'd had in mind. But at least the fire he'd felt at the rally had been rekindled. Nor had he been disloyal to Caterina. He quickly slipped his ring back on, telling himself he wouldn't really have made love to Virna.

And there was one thing more. Lubchenko and that bastard Reiner would soon be out of his life. That, more than anything, put a bounce in his step as he emerged into the cool, quiet night.

7

Another cell.

Longer than the other, this one had a barred window, and the heavy wooden door had bars across an opening near the top. Nona looked around. The cell had a toilet—it looked cleaner than the last one—a small writing table, and a cot, which she was on. There was no blanket or pillow, and she was naked.

It was still light outside, but Nona had no idea how much time had elapsed. Had it been a few minutes or was it another day? She wasn't hungry, but that told her nothing. What kind of appetite could anyone have, after what had happened?

Georgi!

Nona's own pain was quickly forgotten as she remembered what they'd done to Georgi. Marshaling her strength, she swung her feet to the concrete floor and stumbled toward the door. She squeezed the bars.

"Is anyone there?"

Nona's throat was raspy. She pressed her face to the bars and peered down the gray, dimly lit corridor.

"Can anyone hear me?"

No one answered, and returning to the cot, she lay on her side and examined herself as best she could. The bruises she could see were full and dark, the cuts scabbed. From the way her upper back and buttocks hurt, she didn't have to see those wounds to know how ugly they were. Then she thought again of Georgi's suffering and began to cry.

Keys rattled down the corridor, and a door squealed on stubborn hinges. Two pairs of footsteps echoed closer. She stifled her sobs and looked up. Two shadowy figures stopped in front of her door.

One of the figures walked in; it was the man who had supervised her torture. The door shut heavily behind him.

"You've been sleeping for several hours. How do you feel?"

Nona looked away, pulling in her legs and curling against the wall.

"No, I didn't expect you'd want to talk to me. But would you feel any different if I told you you're free to leave?"

Her expression changed. "With Georgi?"

"No. I'm afraid Georgi will remain with us for a while. He has broken the law, after all."

"How long is a while?" Nona's bluntness astonished her. Her jailer merely seemed amused.

"That's not your concern. If you wish to go, I'll bring your clothes."

Nona looked at him, then nodded once. He motioned to the man in the door, who walked in with a neatly folded bundle. She recognized him at once as Ivan, the brute who had violated her. She started to cry.

"I'm sorry we had to bring you into this," the other man said. "You're not, we're happy to say, one of the dissidents."

Her eyes blazed. "And will you give me a certificate that says so?"

The man motioned for his aide to leave. Ivan placed the clothing on the bed, then hurried away.

"Do not mistake our clemency with you for weakness. Tsigorin confessed to his crimes and named his accomplices. Though you're not one of them, I can, if I wish, see to it that you never leave here. Is that what you want?"

Nona said nothing. She pulled her dress toward her with a finger.

"You still have your job and your life, Nemelov. Enjoy them instead of mourning for a traitor."

Nona rose. *He's invisible,* she said to herself. *Have courage and ignore him. His words don't matter.* She stepped into her dress.

"Do you disagree?" he asked.

The blue flowers of the fabric seemed warm and friendly.

"Well?" he pressed.

She leaned against the wall for support. Each move she made exacerbated the pain in her thighs.

Tell him! Tell him to go to hell!

The words pushed at her lips. Nona looked up as she buttoned her blouse. She thought about Georgi, and almost spoke. Then she thought about where she was. About the man at the door. How would it serve anyone if she died like the rest of his friends? She remembered a fable her father once told her. A lamb was slaughtered in the fox's den. Instead of following it in, its mate waited until nightfall, then lured the foxes to their death by bleating beside a cliff.

You cannot win here. Look past this. . . .

Nona mustered all her will. "Yes, Comrade, I will forget him. He is dead . . . to me."

The man smiled. "Very good, Nemelov. We've made some progress here today." He called to his aide. "Open the door for the Metro inspector."

Nona draped her coat over her arm, and her captor stepped back, allowing her to pass. She refused to look at Ivan.

"Good day," Ivan said with a grin.

She wept openly and limped down the corridor of the holding area. Through her quiet tears she saw that the seven cells she passed were full, people lying on the cots and staring out the windows. She wondered how many were Georgi's friends, waiting their turn with the inquisitor.

A guard at another door let her out. He was an old man, his wrinkled face impassive. If he had ever been shocked by what went on here, that time was long past.

Nona made her way down a short flight of steps and through a narrow foyer to another door. The guard at the top of the stairs buzzed her out. She stepped into the twilight.

"Damn them," she muttered as she pulled on her coat and drew up the collar against the stiff wind.

Her tears turned cold; no one who passed seemed to notice them. Then again, had she ever noticed anyone else? How much suffering had gone on around her without her being aware of it? How many Georgis had there been in the last week, the last month . . . the last *day?*

Nona hurried away, wincing from pain. A man bumped into her without excusing himself. Everyone was mad . . . insensitive. She had to get away. She needed

199

to get home and sit in a bath, and hoped that no one was using it.

Hope? she thought bitterly. A waste of energy. She'd "hoped" often, that one day she might have a child with Georgi. What good had it done? Few fantasies ever truly die, but this one had—killed, today, by the KGB. Like life itself, hope seemed pointless now that Georgi was not there. So much hurt her, inside and out, it was all she could do to keep from shrieking.

But she knew she mustn't. As she'd done in the cell, she must be civil. She didn't want to end up like Georgi. Yet . . .

When her father had been taken away, Nona had been too young, too overwhelmed, too concerned for her mother's well-being to do anything. This time she had no reason to hide.

No reason except fear. For as much as she wanted those men to suffer, she could live with hatred; she had done it before. But to live in terror was more than she could bear.

She was tired, confused. She had to think. Or maybe she had to *stop* thinking. But she could never stop feeling, and right now her soul screamed out for vengeance. . . .

8

Clark tapped a button on his desk, muting the sound of the video monitor.

"Does anyone really care what Tom Brokaw and John Chancellor think the President will say?"

Eddie chuckled. He'd come in when Loree returned, helping with the team's last-minute needs. He was the only one who heard Clark. The others were huddled with Joseph, three chairs pulled in a semicircle before his sofa; they were like an ogre with a wide body and three heads, all of them battering each other with data and questions.

"And if there happens to be a citywide power failure?"

"That shouldn't affect you—"

"Right," Craig cut Erik off. "The electricity comes from the Kremlin itself, which has its own emergency system."

Joseph's pug nose was wrinkled, and deep trenches ran from his eyes nearly to his ears and across his brow. His mouth was more lopsided than usual, as though a hook were dragging it down. He had been listening hard since the computer spit out the last of the data about Moscow, trying to remember all the details and at the same time fit them into the broader picture. He was still worried about what the computer scan of textbook cases by CIA psychologists had shown, that mental damage in the destruction of a symbiotic relationship was significant in only thirty-four percent of the cases. There really *was* a chance that Cherganyev wouldn't fall apart at the tomb and emerge in a childlike state.

In which case, Joseph had reflected, *I won't be emerging at all.*

Fortunately, there hadn't been time to dwell on the odds.

"The floor is made of one-by-one-inch blocks held in place with cement and rubberized sealer," Loree said. "The best place for the drill bit is just to the right of here"—she pointed to a chart—"where the electric wires enter the tomb. . . ."

"According to blueprints obtained during the war," Craig showed him another diagram, "you'll need to go down a catwalk of the nearest Metro exactly 280 meters. There is a door there that leads to an electrical transit box shared by that Metro and the Stalin tunnel. Proceed 160 meters . . ."

Joseph nodded.

"If there's a repair crew there, evaluate," Erik cautioned. "Can you overcome them? Convince them there's a gas leak? Tell them they should be at the rally?"

The three aides spoke evenly, each filling in details the others had left out. As the night waned, their voices ran together.

". . . Drilling on a simulated wall with the kind of equipment you're likely to have, we were able to punch a one-foot, four-inch hole in a similar setup in just under fifty minutes. . . ."

". . . Reiner says Lubchenko has a Mercedes-Benz— a supercharged Model 75 engine if you need horsepower, and a trunk with a false bottom. . . ."

". . . They will be responsible for bringing the equipment to the site and then getting you away. . . ."

". . . Lubchenko told Reiner he can get everything we need. You'll have to take over the money to pay. . . ."

"The equipment will be in three cases. The first case will have four battery-powered stun guns, each with two insulated delivery wires and a range of one hundred meters. They shoot nets attached to the delivery wires, not barbs or burrs, and they leave no marks. . . ."

". . . . The second case will contain oxygen masks in case you need them in the tunnel. . . ."

". . . In the third case will be two miniaturized, high-speed, battery-operated drills."

"What about alarms?" Joseph asked. "Were you able to find anything out?"

"Yes." Craig riffled through the blueprints. "At the doors, but not downstairs, around the tomb, or—as far as I can tell—in the sarcophagus."

"If there *are* wires in the glass," Erik said, "you'll

202

have to make an arc. Strip the wire in two places and—"

"Strip it with what? Forget it, I'll just be ready to run like hell."

When the review of the Metro and the Mausoleum was over, Clark sat forward in his chair. He stood a piece of equipment on end.

"My turn," he said, pushing the object forward.

Joseph studied it, enjoying the respite. "It looks like a cassette recorder."

Clark smiled. "It is." He slipped off the back panel and removed the C batteries. "These are what I want you to see."

He set two of them aside and unscrewed the jackets of the other two. "This one"—he held up the first—"is your transmitter. You pull up the terminal, which releases the spring-mounted antenna. Then you press the base like so"—he pushed hard with his thumb—"and the transmission begins automatically. Bounces from you to a satellite to me. There's nothing else you have to do to signal success."

Joseph grinned. "Impressive. But how do you know I won't signal success even if I fail?"

Clark's expression didn't change. "Because you know that won't do a bit of good for anyone—especially you. Better to die with Lenin than with the Sredá-Grom."

Joseph hadn't considered that. He tried to shrug off his concerns. "And if I fail, at least I've got something there to record my last words."

"Don't laugh. The recorder works. We rearranged some things inside and put the real batteries there. As a reporter, you'll have every reason to carry it around."

Clark set the first battery aside and picked up the second. He pressed the base and the cylinder telescoped to nearly a foot in length; it ended in a cone with a fine point.

"As I said before, a diamond drill is the only thing we can't count on Lubchenko obtaining. Besides, I trust NASA's gadget guys more. They developed this compact unit for satellite repair. The beauty of the whole setup, obviously, is that if you're searched and they see it's only a tape recorder, they're sure to let it go. As I said, it works, so they shouldn't suspect anything."

"Real James Bond stuff."

Clark grinned. "Where do you think we get our ideas?"

Joseph couldn't tell if he was serious, and didn't want to know. He had heard that the CIA had consultants from every field working for them, with everyone from movie special-effects personnel to comicbook writers pitching ideas. He just didn't want to think that his life might depend on a piece of equipment that had only been tried in a "Dick Tracy" strip.

But he was impressed—at least with the details.

"I suppose you also have a contingency plan in case this Reiner doesn't show at all. Or Lubchenko."

Clark grinned. *"You* are the contingency, Joseph. That's why we're sending you instead of letting them handle it alone. It'll be what we in the trade call 'tea time.' "

Joseph frowned. "I'll bite. Tea?"

"Try everything, anything. It's like football. Sometimes the desperation pass works better than the diagramed play."

"That's *sometimes.* "

"Yeah, there's always a chance you'll fail. I'll tell you this, though. Attitude trips up more people than the enemy does. Some nervousness we expect, even from seasoned people. But if you doubt yourself, you *will* fail. Worse, if you *think* too much, you'll really screw up."

"Think? Are you telling an academic not to think?"

"What I'm saying is to *do*. If you think too much—mark me, Professor—you'll shit your pants."

Eddie received a call and left quickly; when he returned, he held a thick folder that he handed to Joseph.

"Bathroom tissue, just in case?" Joseph quipped.

"Close," Clark said. "Your manuscript. About Lenin."

Joseph flipped through it, openly amazed. "Christ, this is incredible! It looks like my own writing."

"We used the sample you gave at the front gate," Clark explained. "A writing machine interfacing with the Library of Congress did the rest."

Joseph read a few paragraphs. "I can even live with this. You stole from some good books, including a few of my own."

The President had begun his address; Clark asked for silence and punched up the sound on the TV.

". . . aim of our great nation is not to provoke the Soviet Union into a war that no one wants. However, the Soviets must understand that they cannot bully us or our allies into submission."

Alexander's face shrank suddenly, reduced to the lower right-hand quarter of the screen. The remaining portion of the screen was being used to give an accurate accounting of whose armies were where and what they were doing. Joseph looked up as animated red tanks rolled through the Middle East. Blue ships steamed toward red ships in the Mediterranean. Red and blue planes prowled the skies over Iran, Afghanistan, and Turkey. Everything was present and accounted for—except Stealth.

Alexander briefly explained the nature of the Soviet aggression, after which the map disappeared.

"We invite the Soviet Union to turn back from the course on which it has placed itself," he said with an edge of hope. "We invite the Soviet Union to pull back its armies from the borders of Israel. We insist that

Chairman Cherganyev release Americans and other foreigners from Moscow, where house arrest has kept families apart and deprived our citizens of their fundamental rights. We ask him to restore normal relations with nations that desire only peace and friendship. And finally, we *implore* him to begin his rule with the reputation for being a peacemaker, not a peacebreaker."

"Nice line," Erik noted.

"Tomorrow's 'Quotation of the Day' in the *Times*," Craig said.

"Our nation will not accept ultimatums, but it *will* accept mutually satisfactory agreements, settlements arrived at openly and without malice. God willing, the Soviets will respond to these overtures. God willing, both nations may soon turn their considerable resources from confrontation toward other, more productive areas of endeavor. God willing, we can do this before it is too late.

"Thank you," Alexander said, "and good night."

Clark hit a button and the monitor went black. He rose. "Okay, people, you've had your pep talk. Now let's show the bastard up. Any last comments or questions?"

"Just one," Joseph said, rising. "Is there a phone I can use?"

9

Even as the telephone rang, Joseph had no idea what he was going to say.

What do you tell a woman in whom you've always confided everything? *I'm sorry, darling, but I won't be home for a while and can't tell you why?*

What was the phrase he'd once heard in Walt Lee's sociology class? *Pitch a bitch?* That's what Lil would have every right to do. Hopefully, she'd pitch such a bitch that she might even forget to yell at him for not having called.

He consoled himself with the thought that as worried as she'd be, she'd worry even more if she knew what he was really doing. Each time he thought about it himself, he couldn't believe it. He was glad the last few hours had been so hectic. He'd been too busy to think.

The telephone rang once, twice. Joseph looked around the spartan office he'd been given, savoring the momentary respite, the quiet.

The tomblike solitude.

Joseph pressed the phone to his ear. Three rings, four. He checked his watch. Nearly nine P.M. Lil should be home. If she wasn't, there'd be no other chance to talk; the helicopter was waiting to ferry him to JFK.

His eyes stung. Too many printouts, too many maps, too many photographs: high-altitude shots of the area between the Rossiya Hotel and the Karl Marx Prospekt; Red Square; buildings where he might be asked to meet his contacts; even doorways and alleys off Red Square where he could hide, if necessary. Photographs taken that day, showing Moscow as it looked right now.

Then there were pictures of his contacts Erwin Reiner and Pavel Lubchenko, which had come from the Western German Embassy. As far as the embassy knew, the CIA was only looking to fill an intelligence gap while a new team was put together. Only the two men themselves were told about Operation Starik, lest some ambitious diplomat leak it to State or the White House. Reiner and Lubchenko cared about money above all; they could be trusted to keep a secret and do a thoroughly professional job.

If that were true, then only one thing could ruin them: timing. According to the latest information, Stealth would be arriving over the Kremlin when Cherganyev was at the tomb. It was the only time they could be certain he'd be in Moscow. If anything held them up, even for just a few minutes—

"Hello?"

Lil had picked up. Joseph cleared his mind, tried to sound cheerful.

"Hi, Lil. It's me."

There was a moment of silence that seemed much longer. When she spoke, Lillian's voice was brusque.

"Do you know how worried I've been?"

"I can guess. I'm sorry."

Another silence. It was a coin toss whether she'd yell or cry. Her next words took him by surprise.

"How bad is it, Joseph?"

Since he'd been closeted with Clark's people, Joseph had forgotten there was an outside world, one with its own sources of information. She was probably frightened as hell.

"What have you been hearing?"

"Mostly the things that the President said. That the Russians are converging on Israel and we're trying to intercept them. There's talk on TV of blockades, of limited nuclear strikes in the Middle East." She laughed uneasily. "People at the club are talking the way we did during the Cuban Missile Crisis, remember? Everybody hoping that we'd get hit first."

"Nobody's going to get hit," Joseph assured her. He shut his eyes. He wanted to hold her, reassure her; it wasn't fair that she had to go through this alone.

"Maybe not, but it's scary up here."

"Scary?"

"Like *On the Beach*. Quiet outside, no traffic, no joggers." She choked, hesitated. "Joe, would you mind if I came down there?"

"To Washington?"

"Even if I just stay in the hotel it will be better than this. I won't feel so lonely."

Joseph shut his eyes. "Honey, you can't. I won't be here."

Her voice seemed to shrivel. "No? Where will you be?"

"Russia, hopefully."

Silence again, even longer. She finally managed a weak "Why?"

Joseph swallowed. He hated to use her, but he had no choice. Clark had come close to calling off Operation Starik when he realized that the press had seen Joseph leave the White House. If the Russians had seen him too, he was vulnerable; certainly they'd have tapped his phone. Joseph had implored Clark to let him handle the Russians.

"Why? Because do you know what happened when I got to the White House? The President listened to what I had to say, he smiled, and then he threw me out. He doesn't want to hear anything from anyone who supports Cherganyev."

"Joseph, what are you saying? You don't support—"

"The President in anything, I know. So it occurred to me that the American public needs to be educated. I've got my notes on the Lenin book. I'll go over, do some firsthand research, maybe get a few interviews, and come home with enough material to finish the book and also write a series for one of the newspapers."

Joseph squeezed the receiver. *Don't ask any more questions!*

"You're just upset," Lil said. "Come home."

"I can't, Lil. I need to get this information firsthand."

"But it's dangerous over there for Americans."

"I was born there. They'll love to have me back."

"And then they won't let you go! What if they decide

to hold you like they're holding all those reporters and the ambassador?''

"They wouldn't dare. I've still got umpty-seven thousand distant relatives over there. One false move and we restage the October Revolution. Besides," his voice lowered, "they're not stupid. They want their story told. Who knows? If I'm lucky, I may even get to see Cherganyev, talk him out of this madness."

He could hear Lil's strained breathing. "Joe—"

"Trust me, Lil. I know what I'm doing."

"How—how long will you be gone?"

"A few days. I'll be back Sunday—Monday at the latest. In time for my evening class and then our stroll around the campus."

"Will you be able to call me from over there?"

"I don't see why not."

"Will you? No matter how busy you get?"

"As soon as I reach the hotel."

"Even if you have to wake me."

"I promise." He glanced at the wall clock. Forty-five minutes. For the first time he was beginning to get restless. "How are the boys?"

"Nervous, like everyone else. Jonathan says he's going to try to put together a "Movie of the Week" about this. Barry says he's just trying to get in as much skiing as he can before the bombs fall."

Joseph chuckled. "My sons the activists. Twenty-five years ago, kids would have been throwing rocks at the Soviet Embassy."

"Like Neanderthals. Like the Soviets. This is better."

Joseph didn't agree. He'd choose the playing field over the sidelines any day.

Responsible people should.

But this wasn't the time to argue.

"I've got to go, hon, but you take care. It'll all be history before you know it."

"And we'll all still be here? I can tell my friends that Dr. Rosenstock says so?"

Her voice was lighter now. Joseph smiled.

"Monday-morning aerobicize will be held as usual. I promise."

There was more silence, though the mood was different now. "I love you, Joseph, and . . . I'm proud of you. I married a very brave man."

He kissed the mouthpiece and Lillian did likewise.

If only you knew the half of it, he thought as, eagerness welling within him, he hung up and hurried back to Clark's office.

10

Clark met him at the door. He seemed relaxed, his expression composed.

"How did it go?"

"Fine. If the Russians were listening in, they'll roll out the red carpet for me."

"Excellent."

He handed Joseph a pouch containing his tickets. Joseph slipped his passport into the packet.

"Well, Professor, everything's ready out back, so unless you've got any second thoughts—"

"I've got plenty of those," he admitted, "but Stealth is a powerful incentive."

Clark extended his arm down the corridor and they walked toward the door that opened onto the helipad.

"I hear it's cold over there," Clark said. "I told them to splurge and get you a real nice winter coat."

"And a bearskin cap, I trust."

"But of course."

Their voices, like their footsteps, were muted owing to the sound-proofing in the walls. Above were banks of fluorescent lights with a slightly bluish cast. All the red light had been filtered out; the alarm system, when activated, was sensitive to anything at that end of the spectrum, flesh and lips included.

Reaching the end of a short hallway, they stopped at a guard post to exchange their Main Building badges for helipad badges. Clark used his to open the door, then followed Joseph out.

A two-seat F-28F helicopter sat on a brightly lighted pad, its rotors spinning. They walked toward it, heads bent. Clark yelled to be heard over the din.

"Just don't forget to be at the Azov for dinner tomorrow night, eight o'clock. If for any reason you can't make it, the fallback time is ten. Listen for someone yelling about whiskey; that will be Reiner. Use the code word and he'll take care of the rest."

Clark clapped his companion on the arm and opened the door.

"Good luck, Professor. Godspeed, and remember: Don't think. *Do.*"

Joseph gave him a thumbs-up and stepped in; the helicopter rose at once, angling swiftly as it climbed. Joseph yelped, having expected a smoother ascent than he got from the rattling two-seater. But his cry was swallowed by the thwacking drone of the rotors, and he settled down—*You're supposed to be brave!* he reminded himself—and managed to enjoy the view as they banked north and soared over the brilliant lights of Washington.

11

It was early morning when the *Eisenhower* and its escort fleet sailed by Jabal, well within sight of the shore. Palestinian patrol vessels rushed by, the sailors making obscene gestures at the Americans.

If the Americans noticed, they made no response. Several hours before, the *Minsk*, the *Ivan Rogov*, and their support ships had passed single-file through the Bosphorus. Now that they'd been sighted, everyone was at his battle station. In contrast to the swaggering and the harsh words of the Palestinian, the Americans were quiet and alert.

It was standard practice to establish sector screens of two hundred miles, which the ships defended territorially. Both fleets violated those sectors as they coursed toward one another. No one fired, but no one stopped.

On the bridge of the *Eisenhower*, Captain Hank Adams watched as the Russians launched a plane. He scratched at the leather armrest of his chair. "What is it?"

A picture was beamed from the Argos IV satellite 170 miles overhead, translated from laser beam readings into computer signals and hard copy. Lieutenant Commander Warren pulled the photo from the printer.

"A Foxbat, sir."

"No bombs, just air-to-air missiles," Adams muttered. "All right, let them have that. Concentrate on the blockade."

The vessels surged ahead, just over forty miles separating them. Then, when the U.S. convoy was just passing the boxy white houses of Netanya on the Israeli coast, visual contact was made. The frigate USS *Truxton* spotted the Soviet destroyer *Chiecherin* and radioed the sighting to Captain Adams.

"Understood," he replied evenly. "Proceed."

Neither convoy slowed. Soviet and American fleets always worked in close proximity and there were frequent collisions, not just between vessels but even between jets and helicopters. It was Superpower Tag.

But the situation was different today. Emotions usually didn't run as high as they did now, and contact of any kind might well trigger an exchange of gunfire. So why wasn't he slowing? Where was the sanity the pundits said would ultimately triumph in the nuclear age?

But this *was* sane, he told himself. The Russian ships would create a far more dangerous situation if they were allowed to pass.

The navigator kept him apprised of the bearings of the two lead vessels. Adams sat stiff and still, jaw set, gray eyes stern beneath his slicked-back silver hair. Warren stood to his right, hands clasped tightly behind his back. Both men stared at the straight line of the horizon, where faint gray dots had begun to rise and fall.

The Soviet fleet.

These were not fishing vessels or isolated convoys, but state-of-the-art craft with enough guided missiles among them to obliterate every building in a state the size—and distance—of New York. And below, just behind them, prowled an *Oscar*-class submarine carrying twenty-four nuclear antiship missiles. Even with the submarine, the fleets were evenly matched—depending, of course, on who struck first. Adams would deploy the blockade and, after so informing the enemy, fire only if the Russians came within thirty feet of any vessel. With fifty feet between each American ship, it would be impossible for the Soviets to pass. And if they tried to go around, the Americans would shadow them.

The gray dots took on faint shapes. They became one-third as large as the distant *Truxton,* then a half, then two-thirds. The two lead ships would pass in approximately fifteen minutes.

Adams picked up the telephone on his armrest. He ordered communications to raise the *Truxton.* Seconds later, Commander Abraham Burroughs was on the line.

"Yes sir."

"Commander, inform the Soviet captain of our intention to conduct maneuvers in this area and establish your perimeter. Inform the Soviets that unlike the two-hundred-mile limit, this one will be rigidly enforced. Follow SOP unless you hear directly from me."

Burroughs acknowledged and signed off.

Standard operating procedure. The Russians, eavesdropping, would know exactly what that meant. If they crossed the perimeter by thirty feet—an acceptable margin of error—they would be disabled by gunfire. Adams wasn't sure what the Soviets would do, but he knew what he'd do if it were necessary.

Suddenly the radar screen went wild with blips from the shore. When the nearly twenty newcomers had been identified, Adams realized with alarm that the rules had abruptly been changed.

12

The five Israeli corvettes sliced low through the water, foredecks boasting gray missile tubes twice as long as conventional launchers. Small and maneuverable, they had the ability to sting hard and hurry away. Adams had seen them earlier, close to shore, but had been assured they would stay well away from the action. Now that a squadron of Israeli F-15s had arrived, the equation wasn't so cut-and-dried.

The fourteen jets screamed low overhead, toward the Soviet fleet. Adams snapped up his receiver then set it down. Warren regarded him with concern.

"Sir, aren't you going to raise the Israeli leader?"

Adams shook his head. "He won't tell us anything with the Russians listening in. We'll just have to watch and see what they do. Have four of the boys from air cover peel off and follow them."

"Shall I scramble replacements?"

"Not yet. Just be ready to."

Within an instant, the Israeli jets were visible only by their contrails as they streaked toward the Soviet fleet. Four American Tomcats roared by in pursuit.

A communications officer looked from his console to the captain. "Sir, the Russians are scrambling four Foxbats."

"Just four," he muttered. "Daring the Israelis to shoot them down."

"The Israelis may take them up on it," Warren said.

Another officer—monitoring land communications only—turned to the captain. "Sir, there's a major confrontation under way ashore. The Israelis and a full Soviet tank regiment, just north, in Lebanon, at En Naqura."

Warren whistled. "That's eleven thousand Soviet troops. They mean business."

"Which means those F-15s do too," Adams said urgently. "They want to keep the fleet from getting involved."

The communications officer continued. "The Soviets just learned of the confrontation ashore. Sixteen more aircraft are being scrambled."

"Flight plan?"

"Eight here, eight to En Naqura."

"This whole area's going to blow," said Warren, "with us in the middle."

Adams snapped up the phone.

"Israeli squadron leader, open channel, on the double."

The call was put through. Adams prayed the Russians were listening.

"*Eisenhower* to Israeli leader, do you copy?"

The earpiece grumbled with static.

"We read you."

"Your presence here endangers American maneuvers. Request that you withdraw at once."

"Negative, *Eisenhower.*"

The communications officer said, "Four Foxbats launched, intercept course with the Israelis."

Adams placed his hand on the mouthpiece. "Get eight of our boys up." He spoke again to the Israeli leader. "I repeat, we are on sensitive maneuvers. Request that you leave immediately."

There was no response. Dark gray puffs exploded just above the horizon. The sound of antiaircraft fire from several of the Soviet ships reached them several seconds later. Radar showed the Russian aircraft approaching the Israelis.

To the left of the tower, the first of the Tomcats shrieked into the skies. Adams looked at the flight officer, who sat by his console awaiting instructions. The second Tomcat shot out over the water. Adams replaced the receiver, then sat back.

"Who knows, this could be a blessing in disguise. Use an open channel. Tell our boys to run interference, and that if they must fire to shoot only at the Israelis."

"At the Israelis," he repeated with a trace of disbelief.

"That's right."

"Yes sir."

The Pentagon had come up with this contingency during the war between Iran and Iraq. The idea was to fire on your friends in order to convince your enemies you wouldn't hesitate to shoot at them. Ironically, it was called the Messala Option, inspired by the Roman who betrayed his best friend, a Jew, in *Ben-Hur*.

Adams looked at Warren. "What do you think? Will the Russians get the message, or will they think we're weak for not backing the Israelis?"

"I think they'll realize that what we said to the Israelis holds true for them, that we intend to hold our ground."

"Let's *hope* they understand that. Wilson, patch us in to the Argos IV. I want to see what's happening in Lebanon."

The communications officer swung a keypad from beneath the console. He typed in several code words, and a map appeared on a console monitor. Adams walked over.

Behind him, the flight officer said, "There's gunfire. One Israeli plane, one Soviet plane hit, both returning to base. Thirty seconds until we make contact."

Adams studied the map. Read by satellite, the battle site was translated into computer images that resembled a child's videogame screen, the tanks and their movements represented by pinpoints on a map grid—red for the Soviets, green for the Israelis.

"Twenty seconds."

At this resolution the confrontation was a jumble, but data at the bottom indicated that hits were being scored regularly by each side. The casualties would be heavy, with one difference: the Russians had a lot more tanks and men where these had come from. And the chances were good that more jets from the fleet would join the battle if the F-15s retreated. He regretted having given the order to turn on a brave ally, but his course, he told himself, was the sane one.

"Ten seconds."

"Put it on visual," Adams said, and sat back down.

The flight officer punched keys. A grid appeared on the monitor: Argos's overhead view of the perimeter. The American ships were white, all others blue.

"Nine . . . eight . . . seven . . ."

Before them, the air was a web of fleecy contrails that stretched toward the horizon.

"Six . . . five . . . four . . ."

Adams stared ahead. *Artificial clouds ridden by guardian angels . . .*

"Three . . . two . . ."

. . . while the gods below make decisions about life and death.

"One."

Adams watched the monitor. The bridge was quiet, save for the whisper of the air conditioner—and the throbbing of blood behind his ears. He said a silent prayer for his fliers.

The flight plan was uncomplicated. The eight American jets entered the fight flying intrusive patterns: four in vertical figure-eights to divide the combatants, while two zig-zagged above and two below. The latter four began to come together slowly, creating a wall of hardware that effectively blocked the other planes from maneuvering. The only options for the Israelis were to retreat or to shoot the planes down.

The Israelis began talking to one another in Hebrew. Adams glanced toward Lieutenant Hadley, who was seated beside the communications officer. Every major vessel carried crew members fluent in most of the world's languages; Hadley spoke virtually every Middle Eastern tongue. Next to him, also on a headset, was Lieutenant Tracy, who was fluent in Russian.

"The Israelis are staying," Hadley said without emotion. "Their orders are not to let the Russian planes reach the shore."

Warren exhaled slowly. "The sons of bitches. They're outnumbered. What're they going to do, start scatter-shooting?"

"I wouldn't put it past them," Adams said.

The men watched the grid as the Israeli and Soviet squadrons flew tight patterns inside the Tomcat box, like bees in a hive.

"Sir," said the flight liaison, "the Israeli squadron leader wishes to speak with you."

Adams snapped up the receiver. "Yes?"

"Eisenhower, recall your aircraft."

"Negative."

"Then I cannot be responsible for any damage they incur."

"Squadron leader, listen to me. Pull back and we'll contain—"

The line went dead; Adams hung up.

"The damn fools!" Warren's neck was flushed, his nostrils wide. "What do they think they're doing?"

"Sacrificing themselves to keep their ground forces from becoming sitting ducks. I can't fault that."

"Then what are you going to do?"

"Just what I said I'd do, with one small loophole." Adams swiveled to the left. "Open channel. Tell the wing to hold their positions and get another two squadrons airborne. Send 'A' group to the Russian fleet, have 'B' group set up an aerial blockade along the shore. 'A' is to shoot any Israeli jet that hits one of our boys. 'B' is to let the Israeli jets retreat, but allow nothing else to cross the perimeter. That means the Russians. Also, tell 'B' that if the Israeli corvettes fire on any of our people, they're to blow them out of the water." He looked out toward the dim white lines marking the distant standoff. "I admire the hell out of the Israelis, but I'll be damned if anyone's going to threaten my pilots."

Warren seemed to approve, and both men watched the

digital clock on the captain's right armrest as its red numerals marked off the seconds.

Now that he'd made the decision, Adams thought it through. He was allowing the Israelis to return to the battle in Lebanon, and also to back off with their security uncompromised; *he'd* keep the Russians away from the fighting at En Naqura. At the same time, he wasn't doing anything to the Russians that he wouldn't have to do eventually. His orders had been to blockade them; the only difference now was that that included keeping their planes away from Israel.

Nearly a full minute passed before the Israelis, with half their planes shot down or having turned back, broke off the engagement. They doubled back toward the *Eisenhower* in a V formation.

"Think they're going to attack *us* now?" Warren asked.

"Not if he understands what I've done for him."

Adams watched, smiling when he saw what he'd been waiting for: the squadron leader dipped his wings slightly as he passed over, signaling his appreciation. To the Russians it would appear as though the low pass were the angry buzz of a bested foe.

As the Israelis headed for shore, Adams immediately turned his attention to the Russians. "Recall the first group and order 'A' to join 'B' along the shore." Adams watched the monitor. "Now it's all up to the Soviets."

The Foxbats were soon alone in the sky above the fleet. His own planes were in position along the Israeli shore; whatever happened now, he knew it was a prelude to what would happen when the fleets themselves drew near.

The Russian planes regrouped at ten thousand feet and then headed east, toward the shore.

"Get me Secretary Papa's office, on the double."

If it became necessary to shoot down a Russian plane, the Pentagon must know at once. Adams's heart began to race. His own planes were circling the shore four miles away; he watched as the Soviets approached.

"I have Deputy Secretary De Falco, sir."

Adams turned to Warren. "Brief him, then stay on the line."

Warren nodded and went to the headset. Adams resumed watching the monitor. The wedge-shaped objects were moving quickly, would meet in seconds. Superpower Tag. He faced the flight officer, who pressed the earphones to his head.

"Squadron leader has the Russians in sight. Descending to intercept the lead Foxbat."

"Order him not to fire unless fired upon."

The officer did so. Adams peered toward the distant coastline. He didn't think the Soviet planes would try to punch their way through. Giving the United States cause to become involved at En Naqura would far outweigh the advantages of having the Foxbats partake in the battle.

On the other hand, Israel had hijacked a Russian plane. Did the Soviets *want* the United States inextricably tied to pirates for the public-relations value? If so, this was the way to do it.

The monitor was a blob of mixed shapes. They had to have closed by now. Adams grew impatient.

"Well?"

The flight officer sat half-turned, staring into space and listening intently. "Nothing yet, sir."

"Gunfire?"

"Not that I can tell."

Adams looked ahead. The *Chicherin* and the *Truxton* were nearly the same size. The Russian destroyer would be able to pass the American vessel at a safe distance before running smack into the four ships behind it. The captain ordered the fleet to slow from twenty-five knots

222

to five. He folded a stick of gum into his mouth, wished he had never given up smoking.

"Captain! The Russian planes are turning back!"

"All of them?"

Silence. "Yes sir. Squadron leader reports all Foxbats returning to the carrier."

"Helmsman, what about the fleet?"

"Down from twenty knots to near zero, sir. They're stopping."

Adams sighed through his nose, his only outward sign of relief. Warren was more demonstrative. He shook a clenched fist in the air.

The room suddenly seemed cold as the sweat cooled on Adams's body. He sat back and listened to the distant, muted sounds of artillery fire, knowing that the respite here was only temporary. If the Israelis managed to get the upper hand ashore, the Soviet fleet would have no choice but to act. And if the Israelis were in danger of losing, they might well call for help under the terms of the 1983 Mutual Assistance Pact. Either way, a confrontation in which the Soviets would *not* back down still seemed inevitable.

Adams shut his eyes and savored the sultry breeze. Folding his hands before him, he also took a moment to pray.

13

Joseph learned of the battle after landing at Helsinki Airport. The London papers were full of it: IT'S WAR! screamed one headline. USSR STRIKES BACK! announced another. Joseph bought a copy of each paper and read them as he took a cab for the twelve-mile ride from the airport to the Russian consulate. The half-hour trip seemed longer as he worried whether anyone would be allowed in or out of the Soviet Union while a state of emergency existed.

His mouth went dry as he read the newspaper accounts. A small Russian patrol had crossed from Lebanon into Israel, by mistake it was said; instead of capturing them, as they'd done with the civilians on the plane, the Israelis had wiped them out. The Russians had responded by moving a tank division south in support, the Israelis had countered with a division of their own and three fighter squadrons, and all hell had broken loose when they converged at En Naqura. The Israelis had had the upper hand until another Soviet tank division was moved in. Casualties were very heavy on both sides, but Joseph was relieved to see that at least there had been no formal declaration of war.

It was just after 1:00 P.M. when Joseph reached the pastel-yellow Soviet Embassy. Ordinarily, it opened at 10:00; however, a press conference had been scheduled an hour hence, and only invited reporters were being admitted.

His heart racing, Joseph got past a guard by pretending to be Russian, then approached a young man seated behind a desk in a sumptuous foyer. He had a trump card to play, and he prayed that it worked.

"Excuse me," Joseph said, "but I'd like to see someone on the ambassador's staff."

"What is your business?" The youth's voice was flat, unwelcoming.

"I need a visa," Joseph said. "It's rather important."

"No visas. Come back in a week."

"I don't *have* a week. Please, let me see one of your superiors."

The Russian didn't look up from his paperwork. "I'm sorry, but they're not seeing anyone."

"They'll see me," Joseph said.

"Yes?" The young man finally glanced up. "And what makes you think so?"

"Because I've just been with Anatoly Fedorsenko."

Five minutes later, Joseph was seated in the office of Deputy Ambassador Kuldonov. A phone call to Foreign Minister Aksakov himself cut through what Joseph had once called "Red-squared tape"—the delays one encountered when dealing with the Russians. A visa was granted in what Joseph believed was record time, and two hours after reaching the embassy he was on an Aeroflot jet to Moscow, reading *Pravda*'s account of how the Soviet navy had blockaded the Mediterranean so that U.S. forces couldn't interfere in the fighting at En Naqura.

Now only two things troubled him. Kuldonov had informed him that the Foreign Minister himself would meet Joseph at the airport "to greet a respected authority on Soviet-American relations." An official welcome meant that he would probably be assigned a full-time chaperon. He'd known that the KGB would be watching from afar in any case, but having someone at his elbow would make things that much more difficult.

Then there were the larger problems an official welcome created. He suspected his arrival would be played up in the Russian media as an example of an American scholar's disenchantment with administration policy. Joseph had a wide readership in West Germany and France, and this would drive another small wedge between the United States and its NATO allies.

Worse, however, was the fact that press coverage meant Alexander would learn he was there. If Clark disavowed any knowledge of what Joseph was up to, the President might well assume he'd gone to warn the Russians about Stealth. That would leave the President with two options. One was to call off the attack. The other was to order the plane to take off at once.

Joseph knew which option the Chief Executive would pick. He hoped that Clark would have the good sense to tell the President everything—and that Alexander would have the good sense to wait until Friday afternoon before deploying the bomber.

Glancing down at the front-page photograph of Russian soldiers gathered around a blown-out Israeli tank, Joseph hoped one thing more: that the beleaguered Israelis would wait that long before resorting to their *own* doomsday weapons.

14

Nona lay in the white porcelain tub, the pink curtain drawn entirely around her. She leaned against the rim, her head on a neatly folded bath towel; the edge of the cloth hung in the water, which reached nearly to her chin. An old, wet washcloth was lumped on her left breast, over a bruise. Another was folded beneath her, cushioning her. Perspiration rolled from her shoulders to her chest, from her forehead down her temples and cheeks. It felt good, oddly purifying.

She ignored the people who came and went outside her little shell: the noisy Pavadze children, whom she had beaten to the tub; the tenants who came and went to wash or use the toilet or see if the shower was free. She didn't care who had to bathe, she needed the warm water and intended to keep it as long as it eased the outward manifestations of pain and anger: the tightness in her chest, the knot in the back of her neck, the bruises and welts that throbbed every time she moved.

But nothing could relieve the pain she felt inside. Nona was at once empty and filled with rage. Fury enveloped her whenever she thought of the faces of the KGB men, of her interrogators, of Cherganyev. She relived, over and over, the moment she had spat at her captor. For a moment, she had been a hero.

Yet the hate wasn't as devastating as the emptiness, for the void was beyond her means to fill. She had not only lost a lover but a guide, a light. And there was so much, still, she'd wanted to give him. She'd given him love and maybe, in that way, she'd also given him courage. But she'd wanted, just once, to make him proud—to outguess him, to catch him off guard, to say something he hadn't thought of. To fly, the way he did, through history and through thought.

She wept, bending her face to her hand. God, how she would miss him.

In the distance, a clock tower chimed. Ten o'clock. She'd been in here nearly two hours. She hadn't washed or moved, but merely confronted her agony—as if she could have avoided it. She also thought about the future.

They would be watching her, she was certain of that. And they would not hesitate to arrest her again, to abuse her more harshly than they had today. Even the thought of what had happened caused her breath to come in small, frightened gasps. She couldn't endure torture again, and didn't think she had the courage to take her life to preclude it. So her thoughts were all she had—her fantasies about what she would do *if* she could.

Nona stirred. The rippling of the water was gentle, delicate. She looked down, turned quickly from the tenuous laces of blood between her legs.

What they did *to me* . . .

She sat up slowly and washed herself carefully. She

remained sitting instead of standing when she rinsed her hair, it being easier to move her head than to twist her body.

Than at last she returned to her room, and lay on her bed clutching Georgi's last note to her breast. She was not a terrorist looking to die, or a martyr able to suffer. But for what Georgi had given her, how he'd made her feel, she could manage to be both.

She would go to work for a while, be a model citizen once again. And then, somehow, she would—

Do what? Become a terrorist? A murderer? Go down to the Metro storehouse and take dynamite, blow up a government building, or—

Dear God!

Fear shot through her as she remembered something her interrogator had said. He'd mentioned her employment record. *They'd been to see Nikita!* Would she even *have* her job in the morning?

To most employers, investigation by the KGB was equivalent to a guilty verdict. To a man as spineless as Nikita, having her around might be perceived as unpatriotic, rebellious.

Nona couldn't wait. She had to see Nikita now.

She ignored the pain brought on by each movement. Hair wet, clothes damp, she folded herself into her coat and hurried into the night.

15

With consummate authority, Alexei supervised the staff of five in their nightly cleanup. He checked the storing of leftover meat and cheese, the scrubbing of dishes and kitchen utensils, the mopping of the floors and polishing of the tables.

He also watched his superiors.

Panas and Lubchenko were seated at a table near the front door, far from the kitchen and well out of earshot. Though the head waiter couldn't hear what they were saying, Panas knew the looks were his way of letting them know that he realized *something* was up. They were his way of saying that since their black market activities had been suspended, he'd say nothing to the authorities of this new intrigue—as long as he got a fair share of the profits.

"A simple pickup," Lubchenko said over a dim candle. "Tomorrow you will take my car out to Klin, to an electronics shop named Klyazma. There you will pick up several cartons."

"What is in these cartons, Comrade Director?" Panas tried hard not to appear as smug as he felt. He was working for the KGB, a confidant of the people in power. With a word, he could crush the man sitting across from him, the official who had caused his own throat to tighten so often.

"The cartons contain electronics," Lubchenko said with a shrug. "Digital goods. That isn't important. What *is* important is that we keep to a very strict schedule. My client is eager to have the goods tomorrow night, and I intend that he should have them."

"I understand," Panas said solemnly, though he was grinning inside. *He is eager to commit treason. Will he be so eager to face a firing squad, I wonder?*

Lubchenko sat back and lit a cigarette. "I would go myself, Panas, but I must be here to arrange the transfer. The client will not be free until then." He leaned forward again, jabbing with his cigarette. "I cannot stress enough, my friend, how important it is that everything go as planned. Any delay will cost us our entire fee."

"Which is?"

Lubchenko allowed himself a rare smile. "Your cut, friend Panas, will be one thousand rubles."

It took several seconds for the figure to sink in.

"That's right," Lubchenko smiled. "A year's salary for one night's work."

Panas shut his eyes. The self-importance had fled, replaced by the desire to run screaming into the street. He doubted the KGB would pay him anything, let alone that kind of money. Why did this have to happen to him?

"You don't seem pleased," Lubchenko prodded. "Is something the matter?"

"No, Comrade Director, nothing. I—I'm just a little stunned, that's all."

Lubchenko flicked ashes into a crystal ashtray. "But, Panas, I repeat—if anything goes wrong there will be no payment, no recompense whatsoever. You'll be ready tomorrow night when we close?"

"Tomorrow night. Yes."

"Excellent. And eat a hearty dinner. You'll need your strength."

"I will."

"Panas—you *are* pleased, aren't you?"

"Yes, extremely. Thank you, Comrade."

Lubchenko ground out the cigarette. He stood, stretched, and pulled his greatcoat from the back of an adjoining chair. It had a fur collar, which he fastened close to his neck.

"I needn't remind you that you aren't to breathe a word of this job or your destination to anyone. If your wife asks, tell her we will be working late at my office, going over the books."

"She won't ask," Panas assured him, his expression still dazed, his mind reeling. *One thousand rubles!* He could easily afford a car with that much money. Was there some way, he wondered, that he could take the money and still not cross the KGB? *Better not even try,* he cautioned himself, and his heart ached anew.

Making a perfunctory check of the restaurant, Panas left to report to Virna and her people. He took the long way to her apartment, not minding the frigid winds that knifed up from the Moscow River.

Why me?

A new client, the U.S. government, a bottomless pit of capitalistic money—gone. Plucked from his pocket by the KGB because he happened to be the kind of man they could trust. There was the punishment, the sacrifice he had to make for the privilege of belonging to Lenin Utra.

The visit was brief. It felt good to tell Virna and Glinka what he knew, to have the undivided attention of people so important—though he had to admit to himself that it did not feel as good as one thousand rubles folded into his hand.

"Tomorrow night," the KGB officer said thoughtfully when Panas had finished. Pacing the room, he pulled on his cigarette, firing smoke from his nostrils. "Did Lubchenko give any clue as to *why* the schedule was so important? Is someone leaving Moscow with the goods? Is something going to happen in the city itself?"

"I don't know, sir. All he said was that I would not be paid if I was late. That's all."

The Sredá-Grom official looked at Virna. She cocked her head to the adjoining bedroom and, smiling at Panas, retired with Glinka. She shut the door behind them.

"So, Comrade Glinka—do we tell him to get a flat tire, or do we allow him to make the delivery?"

"We don't really have a choice. A flat tire will net us whatever he's carrying and whoever he got it from, but that's all. It won't tell us anything about the plot in which Reiner and Lubchenko are involved."

Virna chewed her cheek; her companion seemed annoyed.

"You don't agree?"

"It isn't that. I'm just concerned that we may be giving them too much leeway. I don't understand why we can't simply take the cargo and arrest Reiner and Lubchenko."

"Because it won't enable us to apprehend anyone else who may be involved. What's more, if we catch them in the midst of espionage, it will do enormous damage to the CIA—publicly and in the eyes of the intelligence community."

Virna rubbed her bare arms and, nodding reluctantly, returned to the living room. There she told Panas to proceed with the operation—and slipped him ten rubles for his trouble.

Panas forced a smile, which faded the instant he was back in the corridor.

16

Nikita's house was in the Reutov suburb, a white cottage that his father, a war hero, had purchased when the postwar community was first built.

It took Nona nearly two hours to get there. She took the Arbatsko-Pokrovskaya line out to Shchelkovskaya, the last stop, then walked the rest of the distance. The three-mile trek was a nightmare. The bruises had become extremely sensitive and her legs ached terribly; just the pressure of her stockings caused pain, and she removed them halfway to her destination, preferring the cold. She had to stop repeatedly during the last mile, huddling against the odd statue or automobile to get out of the wind. She stumbled several times, weakness and exhaustion taking their toll.

When she finally reached Nikita's home, it was after midnight. There were no lights on—the entire block was dark, save for a few streetlights—and now that she was here she wondered what she was doing. If she had lost her job, this wouldn't get it back; if she still had it, her standing with Nikita certainly would not improve by waking him.

She began to shiver. Her hair, damp when she left, was now stiff from the cold. Tears flowed as she tried to understand how she'd come to this—confused, freezing, in constant pain. She looked back down the long, dark road. It would hurt to go back, but at least the pain in her body kept her from dwelling on Georgi.

No!

She would not leave. She had to know now. Pushing through the gate, Nona crossed the straight concrete walk to the front door. She wrapped a gloved hand around the knocker, and rapped it twice. A light went on inside, and behind her, a lamppost in the center of the walk flashed on. A woman drew back the curtain. Her gray hair was tucked in a sleeping cap. Beneath the frill, her eyes were half-shut.

"Who is it?"

"It's Nona Nemelov. I must speak to Nikita."

The woman shielded her eyes from the glare of the lamppost. "What do you want with my husband?"

"I work with him. Please, it's urgent!"

"Just a moment."

The woman left. Nona hugged herself against the cold. Now that she had stopped moving, the temperature seemed to plummet.

The woman returned quickly. "I'm sorry," she said, her stern expression belying her apology, "but my husband says you are to leave. He says that you do *not* work for him.''

The words took a long moment to register. By the time Nona understood what she'd been told, the woman was gone, the lights had been shut off, and she was once again in darkness. She remained there, staring at the curtain, numb and unable to move.

He's done it, she told herself. *Nikita has abandoned me.* She felt ill and saw a hail of white streaks; her knees gave way and she was only vaguely aware of a man in a black coat standing behind her, arms catching her as she fell. . . .

17

Her cheek stung.

"Miss Nemelov. Nona! Can you hear me?"

It was more than the bite of the wind. Someone was tapping her fragile, frostbitten cheek. She could hear it but not feel it. The air around her was warm, comforting. In the distance were other voices, someone talking about war in the Middle East. She opened her eyes.

The man standing over her had a kindly face. Sad blue eyes, a square jaw with red cheeks, soft blond hair, cut short. His lips were thin and pulled into a gentle smile. He was holding one of her hands in his.

The smile broadened. "Welcome back, Nona. How do you feel?"

Feel? Not as bad as she should have, she had to admit. Her legs and thighs were numb from the cold, and it felt so good to be lying down.

But—lying where? She looked around and saw that she

was in the front seat of a car. The heater was on and so was the radio; hence, the other voices. It was still dark, and a light snow fell beyond the open door. The man's back was flecked with white, but he didn't seem to mind. He continued to look at her.

"Poor woman," he said. "Are you sure you can make it?"

Nona bit her lip and rested her weight on her hands, lowering herself slowly to the seat. The softness of the cushion failed to ease the pain.

"I'll be fine," she said.

With a reassuring wink, the young man shut the door and hurried to the driver's side. He put the car into gear and turned up the radio.

"Sorry about the din, but it's necessary. It'll confuse them if they're listening in."

"Who?"

"The KGB. I didn't see anyone, but that doesn't mean they aren't here. They may have seen where you went and parked a few blocks away to listen. With a directional antenna, eavesdropping wouldn't have been a problem."

The man's kindness and fearlessness caused Nona's heart to swell. She felt safe; someone strong had been watching her, had lifted her, as her father would have done.

But why?

She regarded her companion. "Are you a friend of Georgi's? Is that why you were following me?"

The man drove down the broad but deserted avenue. "Who I am isn't important. Let it suffice to say I have no greater desire than to see Cherganyev and his hooligans overthrown."

He stole a glance at Nona. She looked down at her hands, fidgeting with the belt of her jacket.

"Does that alarm you?"

It did, and she hated herself for it. The anger was still there, gnawing at her—but so was the memory of her punishment.

"A little," she admitted.

"Would it make you feel better if I told you that Georgi was still alive?"

She looked over sharply. "How do you know that?"

"From my sources. Early this evening he was moved to a mental hospital in Shcherbinka. It won't exactly be a holiday for him there, but at least he's alive."

A lump formed in Nona's throat. "The interrogation—it will continue?"

"It will, but with somewhat more restraint. What they do is try to force out information at first, before trails can grow cold. When they have all they feel they can get, they fall back on chemicals and psychological means. To clean up any residue their torture failed to dislodge."

Nona tasted vomit; she cracked the window and sucked down the cold air.

"I know this isn't easy for you," the man said, "but you must bear with me. You see, I'm working on a project that, if successful, will very likely mean freedom for Georgi—and before the week is out."

"How?" There was uncharacteristic defiance in her voice. She was surprised to hear it, just as she was surprised by the paranoia that suddenly overwhelmed her. "And how do I know *you're* not with the KGB yourself, trying some other way to get information from me?"

"You don't. It's just something you'll have to believe."

"Believe?" she rasped. "Why should I believe you when you won't even tell me your name?"

"A name can be made up. Is that what you want? I haven't given my name because, should you be questioned again, it would put me and my associates in danger."

236

"Your voice," she said, "I can tell them you have an accent."

He smiled with amusement. "By the time they checked every foreigner visiting Moscow, I'd be long gone."

"But if they're watching me they'll have seen you, seen your car."

"It's stolen," he said. "As for seeing me, from so many blocks away they'll see nothing distinguishing."

Nona shut the window. "Why did you follow me, then? Obviously not just to help me."

The man recoiled. "You do me an injustice! I may not be a saint, but don't take me for a devil, either. I'm not as bad as the people who hurt you—or the bastard we just left. One thing you'll learn about me is that I don't abandon my friends."

Nona looked away. She felt an increasingly familiar welling of hatred in her stomach. After all those years she and Nikita had shared—the happy experiences, the birth of his children, his promotions—he wouldn't even come to the door, wouldn't even see her, ask how she was after her ordeal.

"I'm sorry," she said. "So much has happened, so much hurt. You've helped me already, and I *am* grateful for that."

"And I'll help you again, but we have to act quickly. For the sake of my comrades—and for Georgi."

"But I thought you said—"

"That he's in no immediate danger, which is true. But he won't receive medical treatment or anything except rice and water to eat. The longer we wait, the worse are his chances of recovering. You hold a key to overthrowing Cherganyev," the man said. "You are someone whom the KGB and your frightened little employer have severely underestimated."

They turned and headed along the Yauza River, a twining body of water that ran southwest into Moscow.

237

There it met the wide Moscow River and took on a new importance.

Like me, Nona thought as she stole a glance at her companion. If he was telling the truth, he could be her salvation. And if she helped him and they failed, the KGB would have her again.

But as frightened as she was, she knew that there was no more hiding, no more shutting herself up in her own world. Without work—and, worse, without references—she would lose her home and be sent to a labor camp.

"What exactly do you need from me?" she asked.

The man used his gloved hand to rub condensation from the window. He switched the car's heater to defrost. "I need someone to take me and my associates through the Stalin Metro."

"Through the Metro to where? It ends under the river."

"We won't be going that far. We only need to penetrate a few hundred meters."

"Why?"

"I'd rather not tell you yet. However, I promise that absolutely no one will be hurt. In fact, we'll be trading death for life."

Death for life. It was a poetic phrase, like something Georgi would say. Nona looked over at the man. Of course it reminded her of Georgi. All men who yearned for freedom, who were willing to fight for it, had spirit and sensitivity far greater than that of other people.

"I *could* help you, yes. But—"

"What's wrong?"

"Please, I need to know more."

"I've already told you, it would be better for all concerned if details of the undertaking were to remain a secret until—"

"Not about the job. I need to know more about *you.*"

"Such as?"

Nona wasn't used to haggling, nor had she any idea what would reassure her.

"Show me something with your name on it. The KGB won't hear . . . and if I'm questioned I'll do my best to say nothing."

The man laughed. Nona's eyes shrank to slits.

"Why is that funny?"

"You don't understand. What you're asking could compromise more than just this project. All of my contacts would be in jeopardy."

"Not if *you* don't talk."

The man regarded her with surprise. "Touché. That was *very* good. Are you saying, then, that if I do as you ask, you'll help me?"

She lowered her chin, then raised her eyes.

"Is that a yes?"

She nodded with greater conviction.

The man thought for a moment. "I can't," he said, but his eyes told her differently. "It's just too dangerous." While he spoke, he stuck one hand into his coat pocket and flipped her his passport.

Nona stared at the cover for a long moment, then opened it, glanced at the photograph, read the name Erwin Reiner, and pushed it back toward him.

"Does this mean you won't help?" he asked.

"I just want to be left alone," she said weakly, then looked up. She nodded once, then took a deep, calming breath.

The German smiled as they rolled down Komsomolsky Prospekt and over the bridge into Moscow.

18

The men in the KGB vehicle followed well behind Reiner until he dropped Nona at her apartment. One of the men got out and stood in the shadow of a building across the way while his companion returned to KGB headquarters.

Imagine, he thought excitedly, *we follow Reiner and catch a second spy!* He could already hear the accolades, taste the caviar.

He parked by the curb and hurried toward the Vorovsky Street apartment building, racing not from fear but from excitement. He hated the way the SG had muscled in on this case, but now that he had news it didn't seem to matter.

Reiner and Nemelov had met. The radio had garbled reception, but obviously whatever Reiner was planning involved the Metro. That was big news, and it was *his* news. There might well be a commendation and a bonus for it.

Just before he reached the front door of the building, the agent ran into a wall. At least that was what it felt like: his face stopped and he flew backward, stumbling away from the door. He was vaguely aware of being grabbed from behind and pulled into an alley; the last thing he knew was a hot, stabbing pain at the base of his skull and bright red lights flashing all around him. . . .

19

Reiner removed the tapered, four-inch shaft from the back of the agent's neck. He wiped the blade on his own shirt and then touched the top of the instrument; the blade snapped back and Reiner slipped it into his pocket. He'd need it again for the man who'd been left to watch Nona's apartment. Reiner had expected to be followed as a matter of course; he was, after all, a foreigner. However, when he doubled back to see where the car had gone, he saw them set up a watch at Nona's apartment and knew they suspected something was afoot.

Reiner was careful to hug the man's head to him and take all of the blood on the front of his coat. Killing was an accepted part of the espionage business; leaving a mess was not.

Checking first to see that there was no one coming, Reiner scooped up the agent and threw him back into his car, blood seeping along the backseat onto the floor. In the dark, no one would see it. On the front seat was a remote-ear listening device attached to a microcassette recorder; after removing the tape, Reiner searched the man for any notes he may have taken. Then, laying his victim out beneath his coat as though he were asleep, the German drove off.

Reiner had deposited his own car around the corner. Using this one, he'd lure the other man over, then dispose of it and the KGB men together in the junkyard just northeast of Odintsovo, where Lubchenko had said he'd meet him to bring him back to the city.

All in all, Reiner reflected, it had been a profitable

day. If the arms and equipment pickup went as planned, and Nona didn't change her mind, they might actually pull this off. The man coming from America was an amateur, he'd been told, so this would be his show entirely—his chance to get out of the nickel-and-dime information peddling he did for his own government and become a truly global figure.

A Swiss chalet. A week alone with a woman like Virna. He enjoyed the hunt, the chance to use the skills he'd acquired during his years with the UN armed forces. But the rewards would be truly breathtaking.

Tomorrow, at the Azov, he would meet his CIA contact. The next day, the mission. In forty-eight hours he would be on top of the world.

Or else, he thought pragmatically, there would be no world.

PART
FOUR

1

The jet eased onto the runway just after 6:00 P.M. Thursday, Moscow time.

Joseph slept for most of the flight and awoke rested— but concerned. Years ago, when he was a student, Joseph had learned never to cram for a test. Masses of information always took at least a day to sink in; better to cram two days before. Now he found that he couldn't remember many of the details that had been worked out for Operation Starik.

He assumed it would all come back to him before he had to use any of it. But what if it didn't? What if the incalculables—pressure, fear—kept it from bubbling forth?

No, that won't happen. Not unless you talk yourself into it . . .

"Dr. Rosenstock?"

Joseph looked up into the smiling face of a pretty young stewardess.

"Yes, I'm Dr. Rosenstock."

"Sir, our pilot has just been informed that when we reach the gate you're to go directly to position number five in the passport area. Your party will meet you there."

Joseph thanked her, though it was an effort to smile. That wasn't what he'd wanted to hear.

Whenever he had met officials in the past, they were always waiting outside the terminal. If Aksakov was coming inside to greet him, they intended to make an even bigger fuss than he'd imagined.

Which means there's no way the White House won't find out I'm here.

Joseph fretted about the problem as the plane taxied to a stop; his only hope was that the lateness of the hour would work in his favor.

Crossing the tarmac into the terminal, Joseph went straight to passport control, five green metal cubicles set side by side, a small path separating each from the next. Inside, young men in poorly fitting uniforms stood on foot-high platforms behind a high pane of glass. More authority. It didn't matter who had it, as long as authority was in evidence. Passengers waited silently in long, orderly queues while the officials examined their passports and visas and asked with disinterest if they had any currency to declare. A few of the new arrivals stared vacantly past the iron gate that separated them from the vast customs area; long lines awaited them there, where every piece of luggage was examined at the dozen stalls.

Glancing toward position five, Joseph saw that his "party" was not one person but seven. The moment they saw him, a man stepped from the group and stopped the line. He motioned Joseph over; presenting his passport to the agent, Joseph was ushered right through. None of those who had been held up complained; several, however, followed him with their eyes, obviously wondering who this person was, that he'd been allowed to bypass the bottleneck. Joseph looked at them as well, envying their anonymity.

The members of the welcoming party were all dressed alike, in black coats and matching sheepskin hats; the grimly set faces were also identical and resembled other long, official faces typical of the Soviet Union. The only one Joseph recognized was Foreign Minister Fyodor Aksakov. Like the people Joseph had left behind in Washington, Aksakov looked tired.

Like Fedorsenko, Aksakov had been with Cherganyev

for most of his political career. Also like Fedorsenko, he was one of the few members of Lenin Utra who did not fawn on Cherganyev in public. He had many friends in the Politburo, people whose support had been critical in the last few steps of Cherganyev's rise to power. In the late 1980s, Gorbachev's swing toward capitalism had allied the traditional Marxists and the more radical Lenin Utra forces; the alliance had been uneasy, and only Aksakov and Fedorsenko had kept it from coming apart. Fedorsenko's recall had obviously been Cherganyev's way of seeing just how far the Politburo would go in backing the ambassador and the foreign Minister. Fedorsenko's defection was his way of signaling the Politburo to resist. The purges were Cherganyev's way of reminding them who was in charge.

Small and bull-like, with an aura of volatility, Aksakov was far from anyone's notion of a diplomat. That was where Deputy Foreign Minister Valentin Zhukov came in. Tall and physically refined, the deputy was Aksakov's public arm.

Joseph extended his hand as he approached. Aksakov did likewise.

"Comrade Minister," the American said in Russian, "it's a great, great pleasure finally to meet you."

"I share your delight," Aksakov said without smiling. "The enlightened views of Dr. Rosenstock are held in very high regard in the Soviet Union."

"I'm honored."

"Be more than that," Aksakov didn't so much say as order. "It is unlikely that anyone but you would have been allowed to come here."

Joseph bowed slightly. He yearned to tell him that no one else would have been as reckless. As had been the case at the CIA, it took all of Joseph's effort to concentrate; now that he was here, now that the countdown had begun, he felt as though he were electrified.

Aksakov released Joseph's hand and stood before him, his arms rigid at his sides. Joseph thought there was something *stiffer* in his manner—was it wariness or simply a more obvious show of dignity?—than he could remember ever having seen on newscasts.

Aksakov introduced Joseph to only one of his aides, a young woman named Serafina Nazvanov. Pretty and tall, with raven-black hair and angular cheekbones, she was the Kremlin's equivalent of Julie Roberts, overseeing matters of protocol.

With the woman to his right, Aksakov on the left, and the others behind, Joseph walked through the glass-walled terminal. Smiling warmly, Serafina professed to have read two of Joseph's books—then surprised him by summarizing the thesis of his first, *The Ideological Foundations of the USSR*. Whether she'd actually read the book or had been briefed solely to impress him—something his students often tried to do—he was still enchanted. He suspected that he was supposed to be.

Near the front of the terminal, the group was approached by a pair of reporters. This was what Joseph had been waiting for. He studied the badges clipped to their shirts.

One was from *Pravda* and the other, with a microphone, was from the TV program "Rasti." Joseph did some quick calculations. *Pravda* was published in the morning, and "Rasti" didn't air until 7:00 A.M. That would make it around midnight in Washington before anyone learned that he was here. If the President was told at once and immediately dispatched Stealth, it would reach the Soviet Union sometime between eleven and twelve.

It would be close, but there was a chance. He breathed a little more easily.

Aksakov raised his hand and the reporters stopped. He turned to Joseph.

"Would you mind answering their questions, Comrade Rosenstock? It would help both our countries, I think, if the Russian people saw that all Americans are not warmongers."

"I'd be delighted," Joseph said. Aksakov lowered his hand.

The two reporters took turns asking Joseph questions, primarily about his meeting with the President and the reasons the United States was supporting the piratical Israelis. Joseph's answers were vague and peppered with praise for Lenin and descriptions of the articles he intended to write. Neither journalist inquired about Fedorsenko, but that didn't surprise Joseph. Cherganyev had almost certainly decreed that, officially, the ambassador no longer existed; for all practical purposes, the purge had been successful.

The interview lasted less than five minutes, after which Aksakov walked him toward a waiting limousine. The car was a Chaika, a considerable step below the ZIL that a visiting head of state would have been given. However, when the driver came around and opened the door, Joseph noted that the car had electric windows; at least they considered him an *important* low-ranking figure.

Aksakov faced Joseph stiffly. "I'm sure you would like to rest and perhaps get something to eat. We have a suite of rooms for you at the Rossiya Hotel. Your luggage will be sent separately. There is no need for you to wait here while it goes through customs."

"I understand."

He did, completely; each of his bags would be examined and possibly bugged. His only concern was that no one had left a receipt in his new clothing. Tracing it to the store, a KGB plant in Washington might be able to find out who had purchased it and nail down the CIA connection with a MasterCard slip signed by someone in Clark's office.

He was being paranoid, he knew. But the Russia to which he was accustomed had at least put a pleasant face on Big Brother. Cherganyev's Russia was different. It wanted you to *know* just how implacable it was.

Except for Serafina, whose pleasant manner snapped him from his musings.

"Dr. Rosenstock, if you don't mind I'd like to go with you, to make sure that everything is in order at the hotel."

"Thank you, but that isn't necessary. I've been there before."

"But never as our guest. Please, I'd be unhappy if everything weren't right."

He couldn't refuse again. "Of course," Joseph said with a smile.

Aksakov made a sound that signified his approval. "Comrade Nazvanov will also be happy to assist your research in any way she can. However, there is one favor I must ask."

"By all means."

"You've been invited to attend a meeting tonight."

"Tonight? Actually, I was rather hoping to be out then, reacquainting myself with one of Moscow's finer restaurants."

"I'm afraid that will have to wait," Aksakov said. "Your meeting must begin precisely at eight. You see, Dr. Rosenstock, Chairman Cherganyev does not like to be kept waiting."

2

Joseph's jaw clamped shut.

Aksakov allowed himself a small smile. "You're surprised. I don't blame you; the Chairman grants very few audiences. Yet, when he was informed that you were coming, he insisted on seeing you."

"I never expected such an honor," Joseph muttered.

"Then you understand that I had to fit you in when there was time in his extremely crowded schedule. I hope it won't prove inconvenient."

"Not at all."

"Excellent."

Aksakov's expression was suddenly—*jolly* was the word that came to Joseph's mind. Whether the Russian saw in him an ally or prey, Joseph couldn't be sure. Nor did Joseph dwell on it. His stomach was in knots.

Aksakov bowed slightly, then left with his entourage. Joseph remained rooted to the ground. He didn't know what concerned him more, the fact that he would miss the early meeting with Reiner or that he would be visiting the man he had come to stop. The last thing he wanted to do was expose himself to Cherganyev's charisma, fall under his spell. He was afraid he'd lose his nerve and tell him about Stealth.

Serafina held a hand toward the open car door, but Joseph insisted she enter first. He slid in after her, still stunned.

Why does Cherganyev want to see me? There's no propaganda value in that. Yet he's making the time for a reason. . . .

"I understand your reaction," Serafina said as the

limousine pulled from the curb and headed for the two-lane Yaroslav Highway. "I would consider it the crowning achievement of my life to be granted a private audience with the Chairman."

Her selfless devotion only troubled him more. Joseph looked out the window, trying hard to fight down his fears and doubts. He reminded himself that as difficult or distasteful as it was, and regardless of all distractions, the crowning achievement of *his* life must be to *destroy* the Chairman.

3

When Clancy Jones was growing up in New York's Hell's Kitchen, he'd carried an Urban Pal in his pocket. The grip held inside the fist, the razor blade poking between the index and middle finger, the Urban Pal was a compact but deadly weapon. He'd throw an uppercut, letting the knife just graze an adversary's cheek or ride up under his ribs, depending on the situation. No one ever saw it coming; sleek, thin, cloaked by his palm, it was more effective than the switchblades the other kids carried.

The plane inside the nondescript hangar was like his old blade in every way. He'd felt that the instant he was transferred to it from the F-16s he'd been testing. No one could see the F-19 coming. The strike could be surgical or deadly. It even had the same shape: like a teardrop, the nose sharp but tapering into a broad, flat fuselage. From any side, the sixty-foot-long fuselage was just under six feet high, save for the twelve-foot horizontal stabilizers that sloped inward, nearly touching at the top.

Clancy approached the door of the hangar. Two airmen stood stiffly on either side of the entrance, while seven others with dogs patrolled the perimeter. Above, a pair of choppers sent out microwaves to scramble satellite photos of the facility.

Of the F-19.

Of Stealth.

Though the guards had seen Clancy leave when he flew the plane into Frankfurt from Edwards Air Force Base, they checked his credentials again. That meant one of them putting aside his Uzi while the others held his at the ready. The weaponless man then put Clancy's palm and fingers on a white screen beside the door; it changed to blue and he was admitted. Or rather, the plane had admitted him. The palm and fingerprints of Clancy and four other men were recorded on Stealth's onboard computers; only they could activate the four computers and one backup. Without those units, the aircraft could not be flown. Mechanical linkages from the controls had been abandoned for electrical ties to reduce weight; the computers funneled everything from the stick and rudder pedals to the plane. Moreover, the F-19 was simply too unstable for a human to fly. Balance and aerodynamics had been sacrificed for speed and invisibility; constant adjustments had to be made to keep it aloft, since its seamless, multilayered skin of bubbles and intricately woven fibers not only absorbed radar beams, but sucked up air; as one engineer had put it, flying Stealth was "like flying a sliver of pumice."

But Clancy didn't mind the computers. A child of the sixties, he had rarely driven a manual-shift car and had no aversion to being helped along by machines. The Air Force had made sure of that; half the month of psychological tests he'd undergone were designed to root out any deep-seated distrust he might have of high technology, a cockeyed notion that human reflexes were somehow better. The other half of the testing was devoted to his competitiveness. And he'd had exactly what they were looking for, apart from the basic piloting skills. He wasn't afraid to put his life on the line on a mission or in keeping the plane aloft.

Which was fine with Clancy, a fair price to pay for the satisfaction of having whipped the other Top Gun champs to land this assignment, beaten them just as he used to beat the kids in Hell's Kitchen only five years before.

Clancy approached the plane to run the daily battery of computer checks and weapons tests. Three technicians were already overseeing maintenance on the ground and would be using a battery of computers sitting beside the craft to troubleshoot if need be.

Clancy greeted them, then mounted the crane that would lower him into his seat. It would be devastating to the plane's effectiveness if a dirty footprint were to be left on the fuselage.

Clancy rubbed his sweaty palms on the legs of his speed jeans, the tight pants that would keep the body from dumping blood into his legs due to the G-forces and the legs' adrenaline-dilated blood vessels. He liked to wear them to stay in the mood, in character.

Soon, he told himself. A quick trip just under the speed of sound so that no one would hear him coming, and then a return home to a hero's welcome.

As he climbed from the bucket into his seat, Clancy Jones found himself hoping once again that this was all for real, that he'd get to go through with the mission. Not only had he trained for it, but it appealed to him enormously that, of everyone in the military, he had been selected to fly this super-tech Urban Pal east. To take the controls in his palms and, in a swift, catlike move, punch a big hole under some Soviet ribs.

4

During the forty-minute ride through heavy late-afternoon traffic, Joseph alternately stared out the window or made polite conversation with Serafina.

Small talk was an effort, though not as difficult as he'd imagined; without realizing it, Serafina managed to rekindle a small part of Joseph's resolve.

The woman was somewhere in her midforties, having been born after the Second World War, yet she had a clear recollection of once meeting Stalin when her father, a military officer, had been decorated by the Premier during a May Day celebration. She had joined Lenin Utra with her father's encouragement, and had worked as a secretary at the Mosfilm movie studio until Cherganyev came to power. Her experience in communications and in dealing with actors had made her ideally suited to the job, and she had taken to it with no difficulty.

No college, as in America; no summer internships. Just hard work and singlemindedness.

Perfect fodder for Lenin Utra.

Cherganyev *had* to be stopped. Otherwise, the growing network of acolytes like Serafina could never be.

5

The Rossiya was typical of the newer hotels in Moscow, pale and monolithic on the outside, stately on the inside. There was an intricate mosaic of life in the fields behind the reception counter; the subdued lighting made the yellow floor tiles seem golden, the marble of the columns and lobby walls liquid.

Serafina walked to a grumpy-looking woman and, signing a registration form, cheerfully accepted the key.

"Number 2101," she said approvingly as they walked toward the elevator. "Top floor, sitting room, southern exposure. You've an excellent view of the Square."

And they of me, he reflected.

After making sure the room was clean. Serafina left promptly, promising to return in a half-hour.

Sitting on the edge of the double bed, Joseph still felt lost. Meeting Reiner later would help, he suspected, but he still had the hurdle of Cherganyev to get over.

He needed to get back into the mission, to recapture the enthusiasm he had felt in Washington.

Reaching into his jacket pocket, Joseph withdrew the tiny cassette recorder. Clark had told him that the room would be "dirty," the KGB listening in. As he would have done on a research trip, Joseph began reciting details of his arrival.

"I came here to study Lenin more closely," he began, "and I've no doubt that the astonishing good luck of meeting with Cherganyev will permit me to do that. . . ."

While he spoke, Joseph drew the blinds to make certain he wasn't being watched, checked behind a large mirror for "peeps"—cameras—then shut off the lights. Only then did he open the back of the recorder and remove two C batteries.

He needed hands-on reassurance, a sense of the mission.

Still dictating notes, Joseph unscrewed the jacket-tops of both. He examined the drill. Facts about it began to return. It's powered by a millimeter-wide cadmium cell; one hour of drilling time. . . .

He reassembled it, picked up the transmitter. Positive terminal extends into the antenna; base activates. Press two times, pause, then two more times, to signal Clark of success.

Joseph stopped talking and held the device, admiring it. The CIA's long-range radio expert, an old OSS pro named Hal Turner, had told him that as soon as he activated the signal, everyone from the KGB to the local radio station would pick it up.

"But don't worry," he'd said. "A one-time broadcast won't give them enough information to triangulate your position."

"I hope not," Joseph had replied. "By then it won't matter."

Joseph smiled.

Hope.

All his life he'd put more credence in knowledge than in anything else. The appropriate fact, the learned quote, the clever riposte. Now, away from the ivory tower, he began to see how important the intangibles could be.

Joseph folded the antenna away and returned the batteries to the machine, then tried to relax by strolling around the room. The decor was tacky rather than elegant. Tan wallpaper. Two standing lamps of highly polished brass. Inexpensive carpet with a pair of low, brown velvet armchairs. Brown drapes, a desk chair, and a bedspread all made of the same fabric as the armchairs. It looked very much like the room he and Lil had had when they honeymooned at Niagara Falls.

Lil . . .

No, he wouldn't call her now. There were too many things on his mind and she'd sense it, start asking questions. Listening in, the KGB might get suspicious.

He sat on the bed.

Still feeling tense, Joseph turned on the Russian-made TV. It received two channels badly, and Joseph shut it off. As soon as he did so, however, other facts he'd studied started to return.

Clark had warned him about this. . . .

The Azov. Reiner. Nemelov. The equipment. He began to worry about timing, teamwork.

And luck. They'd need it.

Joseph tried to stop, but his mind wandered.

He thought about more than just the scope of the job. There was also *what* he was doing, desecrating the Soviet holy-of-holies. It had made so much sense at the White House cafeteria, but it seemed crazy now. How would he feel when he actually put his arms around Lenin, a man who had died decades ago?

No!

Clark had told him not to think, just to *do*. Otherwise he would be overwhelmed, paralyzed.

Joseph felt himself slipping into a state of anxiety worse than before, and squeezing his eyes shut, he curled up on his side. The coarse bedspread scratched his neck and he pulled over a pillow; within minutes he was asleep.

There was a knock on the door. Joseph started, looked at his watch.

Seven-ten. Too early for Serafina. Who, then?

He slid from the bed and pulled open the door.

A young bellhop in a gray uniform stood in the hallway beside Joseph's two suitcases.

"Your luggage, Dr. Rosenstock."

His mind swimming, Joseph stepped back and admitted him. What he saw snapped him back to reality.

The youth walked with a pronounced limp, and there were long, deep scars on one cheek and just above his tight collar; judging from his age, Joseph guessed that the boy had been wounded in Afghanistan. He went over and tried to help the boy with the heavier case.

"Please, sir!" the youth exclaimed. "It's my job to do this, and yours to be our guest. Let us each do those jobs the best we can!"

Although tipping was frowned upon officially, Joseph rewarded the bellhop generously.

While Joseph unpacked, he distracted himself from *thinking* by admiring the CIA's handiwork. Not only were there no sales tags, but everything there had been "aged." The fabric of his shirt collars was slightly worn inside, as though it had been rubbed repeatedly against his neck. They'd popped a belt loop of his pants and sewn it back with thread of a slightly different color. Even the bristles of his new toothbrush had been pressed down, used. When he went to brush, he couldn't help but wonder what they'd rubbed it against to wear it down. Even the roll of dental floss they'd packed had had several yards removed.

They'd also given him a fresh tube of Crest, though from the looseness of the cap Joseph surmised that the KGB had looked inside—probably to make sure the tube wasn't filled with plastic explosives. He couldn't decide who was madder, the Russians for checking toothpaste tubes for tools and weapons, or the Americans for hiding them, instead, inside batteries.

The surrealism of it all made him laugh, and, thankfully, he was able to hold on to the mood as he showered and shaved.

7

Serafina came at precisely the appointed time.

The ride to the Kremlin took just over ten minutes. Unlike the bellhop, the driver was a middle-aged man, poised and silent—KGB, undoubtedly. Stopping by a small white guardhouse, the driver presented his papers and they were admitted, not through the main gates, but through a small wrought-iron gate between the guardhouse and the larger gate.

As they crossed a quiet courtyard, Joseph admired the massive complex to which they were headed, the boxlike Grand Kremlin Palace with its sloping, green copper roof attached to a series of stately, gold-domed cathedrals. Before this, he'd only observed the structures from the other side of the high Kremlin Wall; now he was about to enter them, walk into history. Like a paleontologist who'd just discovered a living dinosaur, Joseph didn't even try to fight the tears that formed in the corners of his eyes.

He turned to Serafina, who had been strangely quiet for most of the ride.

"This is magnificent," he said. "Working here must be quite exciting."

She shook her head. "Sadly, my office is near Gorky Park. I've only been here once, and Cherganyev wasn't here then." Her voice grew reverent. "It *is* magnificent, but it's different now, knowing that he's inside."

That explained her silence. Again he felt the awe. She was beginning to scare him, and he looked away.

The sense of history was even greater inside the Grand Palace. The dry taste of antiquity hung much heavier than it did at even the oldest buildings in Cambridge. It was not as if the young had chased out the old, as at the school, but as though the ghosts were all still here and running things. And the smells—there were no air fresheners, perfume, or cologne, just the dust of the ages. Joseph grasped, with frightening swiftness, why Lenin still lived for Cherganyev.

Not that there weren't concessions to the modern era. No sooner did they start down the corridor, with its finely worked parquet flooring, than they had to pass through a metal detector. Joseph's heart jumped; he had the tape recorder in the vest pocket of his jacket, and it was sure to sound the alarm. He didn't intend to use it, but hadn't wanted to leave it at the hotel. If he showed it to them now, he was afraid they might confiscate it.

Damn it! Why wasn't I thinking?

At Serafina's invitation, Joseph was the first one through the metal detector. He sneaked a look at the guards standing on either side. Each man carried a bayoneted carbine slung over his shoulder; there were no nervous hand movements as there were with the Secret Service agents at the White House. These men made no secret about their weapons or what they would do with them if necessary. A tight band seemed to encircle his chest; Joseph swallowed hard and walked through, braced for a buzz or beep.

Nothing happened. Fighting down a smile of relief, he turned and waited for Serafina.

It occurred to him, then, that the drill was plastic and that Clark's people would have removed any significant pieces of metal from the recorder. Their attention to detail no longer seemed mad. Not at all.

The hallway led to a pine-paneled elevator with a large, framed photograph of Lenin on the rear wall. As they stepped in, Joseph noticed the cyclopean eye of a security camera glaring down from the ceiling. He realized from its position that the portrait of Lenin would also appear in the TV picture; even the security guards must never forget who they served.

On the second floor, Joseph and Serafina stepped into a wide corridor with more superb parquet underfoot. As they walked in silence, Joseph couldn't help thinking that if the Czar had spent less on the floor and more on his people, the Romanovs might still be in power.

The corridor was lined by a squad of soldiers pressed from the same rough clay as those below. Ahead, a tall, granite-faced major stood with his legs apart, his Makarov pistol unholstered and poked into his belt.

Serafina stopped. "Go with the major. I will be waiting for you here when you are finished."

There was sadness in her voice, and her eyes were distant; Joseph was glad. Distracted, Serafina wouldn't see the disgust in *his* expression, the anger that what should have been a high point of his career was something base, something carnivorous. The hunter meeting his quarry.

The click of the major's boots echoed sharply as he stepped forward and ordered Joseph to follow him down the windowless corridor. Now and then he caught the glint of lenses amid the flowers of the floral-design molding that framed the ceiling.

More cameras.

Joseph nearly stopped then, as a numbing thought occurred to him. What if there were cameras in the tomb? Why hadn't Clark or his damn computers thought of *that?*

He pictured the Mausoleum, couldn't imagine where they would be concealed. What's more, snapshots were forbidden within the tomb, and Joseph told himself that the Soviets would never permit an electronic image to be sent from the inside. The signal could be taped, recorded, and broadcast. That would be a sacrilege.

Still, as he thought of the picture in the elevator, of the TV camera, he realized what it would mean to Cherganyev if a monitor constantly showed the preserved body of Lenin. It was ghoulish, it was possible—and it was one more thing that could trip them up.

But there was nothing he could do about it now; deciding to leave the problem in Reiner's hands, Joseph forced it from his mind as the major pushed open a door at the end of the corridor. They entered a small, dark room. There was a second door in the wall across from them; music filtered through it, Ukrainian folk melodies. Joseph recognized them at once; they were from the soundtrack of Kasparov's famous 1933 documentary film about Lenin.

"Sit there," the major said gruffly, indicating a wooden chair beside a plain oak table. Joseph sat, perspiration fogging his vision. Everywhere in Russia it was too cold; this room was warm, almost stifling. He sat down carefully on the fragile-looking chair, looked around.

And drew breath sharply. *Christ.*

Four unlit candles stood watch over a pair of inkwells at one end of the table. There was a potted palm tucked in a corner. Old books and magazines were piled on shelves. Joseph recognized them, knew where he was.

Lenin's private study.

The candles, inkwells, table, and brass lamp had once been on exhibit in the one public room of the palace. Now, with modern pens, paperweights, and other stationery items scattered among the artifacts, this served as Cherganyev's office. The Chairman was playing at nothing, the mania was *that* complete. Cherganyev not only revered the past, he was living in it.

To the left, behind the desk, Joseph noticed a shadowy photograph of Lenin. Ornately framed, it had been retouched in the manner of a dime-store painting of Jesus, a faint halo shining from behind his head.

Joseph leaned forward, scowling at the hardwood floor. The high walls, the security, the soldiers, he was used to that. Even Cherganyev's adoration of Lenin he could understand. But he wasn't prepared for this kind of shrine—

"Are you ill?"

Joseph looked back to where the guard had positioned himself, several paces beside the closed door.

"No. Just a little warm."

Joseph removed his coat, folded it in his lap. He felt in the pocket, to make certain the recorder wouldn't slip out; the major stirred, his medals clinking faintly. Looking back, Joseph saw that the officer's hand was resting on the butt of his pistol.

"Just looking for my handkerchief," Joseph said.

The guard continued to stare as Joseph reached into his trousers pocket, withdrew a handkerchief, and mopped his forehead.

Joseph looked at his watch. He grew anxious again as he realized that, had things gone as planned, he would have been at the Azov waiting for Reiner. The mission would be under way instead of being stalled.

Had things gone as planned.

Already, the first task he'd had to accomplish had been bungled. It was no one's fault, but he began to wonder if *anything* would go right for them. Sweat stung his eyes and he dried his brow again.

What if the West German wasn't there at ten? Could he find this Nemelov on his own? What would he do with the body, even if he *could* get inside?

It was a nightmare, with monstrous impasses everywhere he turned. There *had* to be another way. Maybe he *would* say something about Stealth to Cherganyev. Talk to him, try to reason with him—

The music halted suddenly. Behind Joseph, the major snapped to attention. A lock clicked.

The door to the other room opened slowly.

8

For a moment, Cherganyev was framed in the bright lights of the room behind him. Then he came forward, pausing to shut the door. In the brief glimpse he'd had of the other room, Joseph had seen a spacious chamber with a massive teak armoire, velvet couches, and a jewel-encrusted samovar resting on a scrolled sideboard. Relics of the Romanovs that even the strict Leninist had not discarded.

Broad, tall, his round face at once serene and intelligent, Cherganyev approached behind an outstretched hand.

"Dr. Rosenstock. I am delighted."

Joseph rose. Their hands locked tightly. Cherganyev had a grip like a workingman.

"The pleasure is mine, Comrade Chairman."

Joseph bowed slightly to the larger man. His spine tingled, more than it had when he met the President; a presence had come into the room. The mission suddenly seemed remote, almost unthinkable.

Cherganyev's bushy brows sought the major. "Leave us, Kozlov. Dr. Rosenstock is *ta'varish.*"

A comrade, a trusted friend. Cherganyev might be mad, Joseph thought, but he was no fool.

The Chairman released Joseph's hand and invited him to sit back down. Cherganyev himself took a seat in the wooden chair behind the table. He gestured disdainfully behind him.

"The other room is more comfortable. Like the White House, we have historic rooms here, functional rooms, rooms with electronics. But as you can well understand, I prefer this room." He laid his palms on the desk, as though he were at a séance, and looked around. "Tell me. How does it affect a scholar such as yourself to be in the very surroundings where Lenin worked?"

"Intimidating," Joseph answered truthfully.

Cherganyev smiled, and when he did so his lower lip hung down almost comically. Joseph understood now why Cherganyev was never smiling in photographs.

"It is that, Dr. Rosenstock. Sometimes I feel at home here, sometimes I feel like an intruder with no right whatsoever to be among these things."

He rubbed his hands slowly from side to side, as though savoring the touch of the table. Joseph guessed that he was completely unaware of doing it.

"Sometimes," Cherganyev went on, "I sense that Lenin is here. I can feel his eyes. His left eye squinting, right eye transfixing. Head held close. I'm told he made you feel as if you were the only person that mattered to him."

Cherganyev seemed, at the moment, sane and rational; yet Joseph knew that Hitler could also kiss a child or lead a sparkling dinner conversation, and a minute later order a foe garroted, the death filmed so that he could watch it later.

Cherganyev moved back, using both hands to lift the chair and shift it away from the desk. Reaching into the drawer, he withdrew a thick envelope and handed it to Joseph.

"Sadly, we have business other than Lenin. I am told that you have access to Comrade Fedorsenko. Please deliver these to the traitor." Cherganyev used the words as casually as he would any adjective. No malice, no disappointment, just a fact. "You may look them over, if you wish. They are letters from schoolchildren."

Joseph turned the envelope over in his hand. Before revealing anything important, he decided to see just how rational this man was. "I'm not sure, Comrade Chairman, that that would be appropriate."

"And why not?"

"If I'm not mistaken, such a request should ordinarily be made through our ambassador."

Cherganyev spread his hands before him. "But your ambassador has defected. I am asking *you.*"

"With all due respect, sir—under the circumstances, then, the task would fall to the deputy ambassador."

Cherganyev's brow darkened. Sweat trickled down the small of Joseph's back.

Cherganyev pulled in his chair. "Take the envelope," he said severely. "Take it and deliver it. Men like you and I do not follow protocol. Men like you and I make our own rules."

Cherganyev's cheeks were flushed, his neck ruddy where the tight collar of his shirt rubbed against it. He looked like a man who could turn entirely red and make others feel it.

With a sigh, Joseph slipped the envelope into his

pocket. He had no choice; in a fit of fury, it was conceivable that Cherganyev might expel him from the Soviet Union.

Joseph looked up. In the yellow light of the desk lamp he saw the red drain from Cherganyev's face. Khrushchev had been ousted after failing to stand up to Kennedy. That was not a weakness Cherganyev would ever show. Joseph's spirits sank even deeper.

"Thank you," the Russian said warmly. "You are a more reasonable man than those in your homeland. But then, you were born in the Soviet Union. And now—you've come back. A Jew who has returned to the Motherland."

Joseph felt queasy. Something was up.

Cherganyev studied Joseph with interest. "You are a scholar, Dr. Rosenstock, one who is respected here. Yet you are scorned in the United States. Why is that?"

Joseph wiped his moist palms on his trouser legs. "Americans have no sense of history. Their perspective is solely on the present."

"And you urge them to look back in order to see ahead." He smiled. "In a way, our messages are the same. As you drove through the gate this afternoon, did you not *feel* the history?" He made a fist, shook it before him. "Did it not reach out to you and *hold* you tightly?"

"Very much so," Joseph answered truthfully.

Cherganyev eased back and laid his hands on the desk. He seemed to be drawing strength from it.

"Of course it did. Unlike Alexander or Fedorsenko, you are a man of depth and vision. Tell me, Dr. Rosenstock, do they understand, in Washington, that the fighting is the result of Israeli aggression?"

Joseph weighed his words with care. "The President knows the Israelis are stubborn, but the consensus is that in this case they were baited."

"Baited? By whom?"

"By your volunteers."

The red returned to Cherganyev's cheeks. "Do *you* believe that?"

"Is there another interpretation?"

"There are the facts! Our people were *requested* by the Lebanese to help liberate them from Israeli terrorism."

Cherganyev's bullying was beginning to annoy him. "That's precisely the point, Mr. Chairman. Your people were en route to fight the Israelis, so how can they be faulted for—"

"Forcing down one of our planes? No!" he sliced the air with his hand. "The Israeli barbarians will release our crew and our aircraft, or they will cease to exist. And if your fleet tries to stop us from rescuing our people, they *too* will be destroyed. Can a man of your background, of your scholarship, fail to see the czars that lie in wait beyond our borders? The tyrants who would prevent us from bringing the truth of Lenin to the savages in Lebanon, in Israel, in India, must be *stopped!*"

Cherganyev didn't thump the desk—he wouldn't dare!—but he did drive a fist into his open palm. Joseph looked down at his lap.

Non sequiturs. Flashes or rage. Joseph had heard and read speeches like this before. The man had substituted Leninism for Aryanism, but he was still every bit as mad as Hitler. And Caligula. And Nimrod. If Joseph were to tell him about Project 17 or Stealth, Cherganyev would move against his enemies and the results would be the same: worldwide destruction. There was nothing to do for now but to placate him.

"I see your point," Joseph said weakly, "but what I can't agree with are your methods."

"Death?" Cherganyev dismissed the subject as though it were yesterday's weather. "Great men and women die for what they believe in. The heroes of the Revolution demonstrated the nobility of that, and we can—we *will*—do no less."

"Even so, Mr. Chairman, others *will* resist you. And if you move to stop them, the result could well be the end of civilization."

"Only if *we* let that happen. Will your President launch a nuclear war? No. Certainly not without NATO accord, and they will not agree. The Western Europeans are cowards. At worst, there will be limited nuclear exchanges in the Middle East—but that is a small price to pay to bring Leninism to the backward peoples of the world."

"And eventually to other nations?"

Cherganyev hesitated, then thrust up a thick hand. "Yes, why deny it? You are a colleague. You understand. And you will find, I think, that most people will accept Lenin before death. What was the quaint expression your people once used? 'Better Red than dead'?"

It didn't quite translate into Russian; it came across as a favorable option rather than the lesser of two evils. In any case, Joseph knew that what was true in the early 1960s wasn't true in the late 1980s. The maxim now would be "Better them dead than us Red."

But there was no point in explaining that, or anything else.

Dear God, Joseph thought, *Stealth is starting to make sense!* He hoped he didn't look as sick as he felt.

Cherganyev was sitting back, once again rubbing his hands on the desk. If he noticed anything unusual in Joseph's manner, he gave no sign of it. His expression was peaceful, satisfied, like a great dog by the fire.

"So now you understand, Dr. Rosenstock. But I asked you here not just to say these things—not just to allow you to enjoy Lenin's study with me." He looked around, savored it himself. His eyes returned dreamily to his guest. "No. I invited you here because I want you to

270

have a chance to make history instead of simply recording it.''

Someone had done his homework. Joseph felt naked, vulnerable.

''I want you to join us, Dr. Rosenstock, to become a member of Lenin Utra. I want you to return to the United States when you have completed your research and help to establish our party *there.*''

The suggestion was so brazen that Joseph literally recoiled. He struggled to collect his wits.

''Comrade Chairman, forgive me, but what you're asking isn't possible.''

Cherganyev's expression didn't change. ''Anything is possible if you revere Lenin.''

''I do revere him, greatly. But I could never serve him as you do.''

''*Shum!* You've served mediocre Presidents.''

This line of debate was a dead end, Joseph knew. He was talking politics and Cherganyev was talking religion.

''The problem isn't with Lenin, Comrade Chairman, it's with me. I can't be a rabble-rouser. As much as I want to make history, I'm more interested in making peace.''

''And you can do both,'' Cherganyev insisted. ''You see that our course is set, that we cannot be stopped. Your goal, now, should be to see that losses are minimized. You can do that by establishing our party in America. You are an articulate man with access to the press, to young minds at your university. Talk to them. Persuade them. Write your articles. Tell the American public that Alexander's policies will plunge the world into war.''

''Even if I were to do so, my voice is only one of many.''

''But it will be the loudest,'' Cherganyev promised, ''after tomorrow.''

"Tomorrow?"

"In the morning. You will breakfast with the American ambassador. You will speak to her, and Comrade Kaplan will tell you why she decided to defect. Then you will join me at the Mausoleum."

Joseph smiled crookedly. "Excuse me?" It was all he could say before he felt his world collapse, all purpose and thought sucked out of him.

"I want you to be at my side when I honor Lenin. A large crowd will be mustered, and television coverage will be sent throughout the world. You will grant interviews and pose for photographs before I arrive. Afterwards, I will release all of the journalists whom we have detained. They will be free to return to America, in your company—your trophies. Your voice will no longer be one of many," Cherganyev said confidently. "Yours, Comrade, will be the *only* voice."

Joseph was numb, save for a very real sickness in the pit of his stomach. Cherganyev's plan was brilliant. He got what he wanted—the reporters out of the country—while his rivals at home and abroad would laud his compassion.

It was a devious joke on the world, and Joseph was horrified at the mere thought of being a part of it.

"Your silence—I take it, Comrade Rosenstock, that you're pleased?"

Joseph tried to speak, but his voice was a cracked whisper. He nodded.

"You above all men can appreciate what I'm doing," Cherganyev said, rising. His voice was loud, arms held aloft as though he were addressing a crowd in Red Square. "I'm seizing the moment as Lenin did, writing history with lightning."

Joseph tried to collect his wits.

"And you'll be part of it—" Cherganyev bellowed.

No, Joseph admonished himself. *Don't think. Do!*

But how? Alexander would bomb the city. Clark might pull a gun. What was Joseph's weapon, except for his mind?

"—part of our history—"

Then *use* that weapon. There must be a way. He was not the only member of the Operation Starik team. The plan couldn't be done according to their timetable without four people, but maybe Reiner could find someone else.

"—a part of the land that gave you life—"

A professional would have reserves, *must* have them.

"—a part of Lenin!"

Cherganyev looked down at him, and Joseph took a strained breath.

"You cannot be unmoved," Cherganyev said. "You cannot be blind."

"You're right, of course, Comrade Chairman. We must end the hostilities."

"Then you will become one with us?"

Joseph rose unsteadily. "I will come to the ceremony tomorrow. I will see the people . . . go inside the tomb. Then I will decide."

Joseph hadn't wanted to capitulate too easily, and Cherganyev seemed to accept the compromise. The Chairman's face became tranquil then, and his hands began moving in a sweeping motion up and down the sides of the chair. It struck Joseph as a masturbatory act, and as he looked at the strong worker's hands he thought about Vera.

There had always been questions about the death of Cherganyev's mistress. She had been murdered, strangled, but the killer was never found. It was presumed to have been the act of one of Cherganyev's rivals, but now Joseph wondered—

Cherganyev could only have one lover, and his fidelity must be absolute. Had he killed her himself? Had she been the first one purged, his companion of over twenty years?

Joseph didn't want to believe it, but as he watched Cherganyev there was no escaping the obvious. The undreamed of. Even Fedorsenko hadn't entirely understood.

Lenin was dead, so Cherganyev revered death. To kill others was not a sin, it was to make them more like Lenin. And if he couldn't convert the world, he *would* destroy it. Think like Lenin or die like Lenin, it didn't matter to Cherganyev.

Joseph felt ill.

With a smile, Cherganyev came around and suddenly embraced his companion. Joseph was caught off guard, both by the hug and by his initial reaction: he knew, without any doubt, that if he had a knife he could easily twist it into the monster's back.

Calling to the major, Cherganyev neither spoke again nor looked at Joseph as he returned to the back room—in which, Joseph now noticed, several heavily decorated Soviet officers were milling about. No doubt they were monitoring events in the Middle East, preparing military responses to Israeli and American actions.

Doing without thinking, he though bitterly.

"Come," the major said sharply. Snapping around, Joseph picked up his jacket and followed the officer into the corridor.

Rejoining Serafina, Joseph asked if they could take a short drive through the city. "I need to be reminded of its beauty," he said truthfully.

The woman readily agreed and he suggested offhandedly that they visit the north side of the city. There he would "happen" to spot the Azov and tell her he'd heard of it and would like to dine there.

Alone.

"After all," he would say to her, "if I'm to appear

274

with Cherganyev tomorrow, there's a lot I have to think about.''

As he stared out the window of the automobile, Joseph realized, suddenly, what Clark had really been trying to tell him. Thinking too much wasn't the problem; thinking about *failing*, about dying, was the problem. Cherganyev was strong because even his own life didn't matter. That gave him a powerful advantage over those who wanted to live.

Like Aksakov. Like the leaders of NATO.

Like Joseph.

But what Joseph had witnessed in that room was also a powerful motivation. Cherganyev was a living obscenity, insane and inhuman. Joseph had always wondered what he would have done, given the chance to go back in time and kill Hitler or Amin—even if his own life were forfeit. Now he knew.

Cherganyev must be stopped.

Away from the closeness of the room, Joseph's mind began to clear. Seeing pockets of soldiers outside foreign news bureaus and apartments angered him. Fire and indignation joined the fear in his belly, and that pleased him. History had repeatedly borne out Coleridge's observation that what begins in fear usually ends in folly. Operation Starik would not end in folly. One way or another, he and Reiner would find a way.

They *must* find a way.

9

The Azov was still crowded when Joseph arrived just before ten.

Though Serafina had understood when he said he needed to be by himself, Joseph knew he'd be watched or at least listened to, in some way, by his driver. Reiner would know that too, and Joseph hoped he would take precautions.

Serafina came in to make certain that Joseph was treated well, and he was shown to his table by a small, prim man with darting eyes. The man introduced himself as Panas, the manager, and he was refreshingly eager to please. Joseph ordered a beer, which he nursed with disinterest. He wasn't sure he could keep anything down.

At precisely ten o'clock, the door opened and a tall blond man strode in. He didn't wait for Panas to greet him but walked briskly toward the dining area; he had an aristocratic bearing, and even before he pulled off his gloves and revealed the inkstains on his hands, Joseph knew this had to be Reiner.

"Pavadze, I'm back and I'm cold! I need a whiskey!"

"You also need a washcloth," Joseph commented as the man passed. He segued into the code word: "Filthy. Your fingers, my friend, are filthy."

"It's a filthy business I'm in," the man responded as he was supposed to. "Pavadze!"

The manager came scurrying from the back, followed by Alexei, who headed straight to the bar.

" 'Dobrij 'vechir!' " Panas declared.

"A good evening it is *not*," Reiner replied, removing

276

his overcoat and handing it to the manager. "That's why I'm back, Pavadze. To *forget* what a bad evening it's been. Yet, not only is it cold outside, not only did that idiot Yuri misplace the boards for a chapter of a book, but the moment I walk in your doors *this* man insults me!"

Panas shot a concerned glance at Joseph. "There must be some mistake. Dr. Rosenstock is a great man and an honored guest of the Chairman. I'm sure he would not have been so unkind."

"He *was* unkind, *most* unkind. But if he will consent to buy me my drink, I might—just *might*—forgive him."

Panas wrung his hands. "Comrade Reiner, if you would come with me, *I* will buy you your—"

"Nonsense," Joseph said, rising. "I'm alone and fellowship would be welcome. Even the company of one with dirty hands and a sour disposition. Comrade Panas, would you do the honors?"

"Eh?"

"*Introduce us,*" Reiner said.

"Ah, but of course. Immediately. Comrade Dr. Rosenstock—"

"Joseph, please."

"Uh . . . Joseph, yes. Comrade Dr. Joseph Rosenstock, may I present Comrade Erwin Reiner."

Reiner shook Joseph's hand. "A doctor, are you? What kind of doctor? Medical? Psychiatric?"

"Neither. I'm a professor of Kremlinology."

"But an American," Reiner said as Panas slid away.

"That's right."

The men sat. Reiner undid his red scarf, but left it draped around his neck. "And you are a guest of Cherganyev?"

"I am. Would you believe, in fact, that I've been invited to stand with him tomorrow at his visit to Lenin's tomb?"

"Oh?" Reiner's pale brow arched.

"And before that, have breakfast with United States Ambassador Kaplan."

"Have you?" Alexei brought Reiner his regular drink, but the German ignored it. "That's quite an honor."

Joseph studied Reiner's expression. The newcomer didn't seem pleased. His own weakened spirits plunged.

Reiner looked down at his drink and swirled the contents of the glass. "The limousine outside, is it yours?"

"It is."

Reiner pointed to the door, then to his ear; the driver would be listening, probably with electronics. Joseph had expected as much and nodded with understanding.

"The car is very handsome," Reiner went on as he removed a felt-tipped pen from the pocket of his double-breasted black sports jacket. He began writing on the paper napkin beneath his drink. "In fact, if the car is at your disposal, here are a few places you absolutely *must* visit if you have the time."

Reiner began writing in English. Joseph turned his head slightly, reading as he wrote.

We can't do it with just three people.

Reiner rotated his hand in front of his mouth, meaning that his companion should talk. Joseph nodded again.

"I've heard of that," he pointed to the note. "Quite a lovely museum."

Reiner wrote again. *Can you get out of* A.M. *meeting? Sickness? Other business?*

"No, that one's out of the question. No time."

Must we proceed?

"Oh, without a doubt. Top of the list."

Reiner sat back, tapped the pen to his chin. After a moment's reflection he wrote, *Need you inside tomb with other man. Woman meeting us in tunnel to look out but not to stop intruders. I must be out there to keep watch.*

"Isn't there someone else who can—"

278

Reiner held a finger to his lips: Joseph shrank back, having forgotten himself.

Reiner wrote, *No. Free-lancers scared. KGB and SG are everywhere.*

Joseph leaned forward, resting his forehead in the crook of his hand. After a few seconds he snatched away the pen, turned the napkin over.

If I go back to Rossiya after breakfast, can I get out unseen?

Reiner thought for a moment, then nodded. *Express Bar, ground level. Storeroom behind bar leads alley. We meet there 9:30?*

Their eyes locked. What would Cherganyev do if Joseph disappeared two hours before the ceremony? Would he call it off? It was doubtful, Joseph decided. There had been too much publicity. After a moment, he nodded.

"A unique restaurant, you say? I'll try it. I'll definitely try it."

Reiner sat back and swiped at his drink with his arm. The contents spilled over the napkin, causing the ink to run; Joseph hopped back with his chair.

"Damn!" Reiner shouted, grabbing the cloth napkin and blotting up the mess. *"Damn!* Panas, Alexei! Bring napkins—and a refill!"

The paper napkin stuck to the tumbler and Reiner pulled it off in clingy, ink-discolored pieces.

"I'm sorry," Reiner said. "This just hasn't been a good night."

Joseph sat back. He didn't agree: for the first time since he'd left the airport, he didn't feel as if things were totally beyond his control. For the first time since he'd left Cambridge, he didn't feel quite so alone.

"Don't worry," Joseph said as Alexei came over. The waiter began to blot up the spill. "I'm sure that things will be better tomorrow."

"Let's hope so," Reiner said solemnly, and when the head waiter scurried to get more napkins, he wadded up the napkin with the writing and slipped it into his coat pocket. He raised his empty glass to his companion. "In the meantime—to you, Dr. Rosenstock. To your health . . . and to the success of your visit."

Joseph drank to the toast with all his heart.

10

After Reiner left, Joseph sat and picked at his meal.

The men had chatted about their lives and work, with only a few notes passed about the mission. It was their conversation that reassured Joseph more than anything. He had a knack for judging people correctly on first impressions, and Reiner impressed him as a meticulous, ambitious man.

Reiner could pull off the scheme if anyone could. And if Lubchenko held up his end of the bargain, acquired the tools and weapons they would need, the operation might actually succeed!

Only now, on his way back to the hotel, did Joseph *really* consider what they were about to do. His stomach was seething again, and he realized that it wasn't just the pressure making him anxious. It was also the fact that he would soon have the answer to a question that had haunted Lenin scholars for decades: Was it, in fact, Lenin's body that rested in the vault, or was it a fantastic fake? And if it were a fake, did Cherganyev know the truth: If he did, would the theft of a mannequin matter to him? Would violating the memorial be enough to bring him down?

He didn't want to consider that now. He was too tired. *What you need to do now isn't to think or do but sleep.*

Unfortunately even there he faced obstacles. Returning to his room, Joseph found that he had company—Serafina.

"I hope you don't mind," she said quickly, "but I asked the manager to let me in. With people milling about downstairs, I was afraid I'd miss you."

The young woman rose slowly from the edge of the bed, where she'd been perched with her legs crossed below the knees; she was still dressed in her smart Western-style outfit, her portfolio tucked under her arm.

Joseph closed the door. "No, I don't mind. Why did you want to see me?"

Serafina slipped her hand inside the portfolio. "To give you this agenda. I was told to make certain there was no confusion about the times."

She handed Joseph a typed schedule and stood watching him while he read it; she hadn't been wearing perfume before, but Joseph could tell that she was wearing it now.

" 'Breakfast with Ambassador Kaplan at eight-thirty,' " he read aloud, " 'the ceremony at noon.' Was Aksakov afraid I'd forget?"

"He wasn't sure what the Chairman told you," she said. "He wanted me to check."

Joseph laid the paper aside and walked to the closet, wondering if she was here to pump him for information, make sure he'd be in a good mood come morning, or enable compromising tapes to be made should he prove uncooperative.

Probably all three, he concluded. And knowing that, he was able to fight down the temptation to let her stay, to let her help him shake the tension he felt.

"How was your dinner?" she asked.

"Delightful. It's been years since I've had a lamb kebab that good." He hung up his coat then went toward hers, which was lying on the bed. "In fact, I'm embarrassed to say that I ate so much all I want to do is crawl into bed.''

Serafina smiled. "I understand."

Much to Joseph's surprise, she really seemed to.

"I'll call for you at seven," she said formally, putting on her coat and turning to face him. She held out her hand and he shook it. "Until then, sleep well and—thank you."

"For what?"

"For giving me faith in the future of our two great nations. It takes more courage to make peace than to make war: both you and the Chairman are courageous men."

As Joseph undressed, he began sorting through the conflicting signals the woman had given—and realized that confusion had been the whole point of her visit. It was the same tactic used in the first stage of brainwashing: disorient the victim. If he'd come on to her, she certainly would have spurned him—and indignantly. The following day, under her icy stare, he would have said things he didn't quite believe just to redeem himself.

It wasn't a terribly sophisticated tactic, but it worked. He was glad he'd been too paranoid to bite. As he buttoned the shirt of his pajamas—amazed that the CIA had gone so far as to put a memo about a lecture in the pocket to show that he'd worn them before—he was glad of one thing more: that he was too tired to be bothered by the sexual itch Serafina had left behind.

Panas locked up the restaurant and bid Alexei good night. Bundling his coat against the stiff wind, he walked toward the Metro; when Alexei had disappeared around the corner, going in the opposite direction, Panas doubled back and headed toward a side street not far from the restaurant. That was what Lubchenko had told him to do earlier, when he'd phoned; Panas, in turn, had immediately telephoned Virna. She thanked him for the information and told him to come by the apartment when he was finished to make his report; her voice was so sweet, so appreciative, that he momentarily forgot how much money he'd lose without Lubchenko around.

Panas yawned. It had been a long day, a nearly sleepless night followed by a typically large Friday-night crowd at the restaurant. He wished he didn't have to go through with whatever Lubchenko had in mind, but that he could just turn the information over to Virna and be done with it. But that was not the way the KGB wanted things done. Thinking of the KGB, Panas quickened his pace.

Lubchenko was where he said he'd be, sitting in his car at the far end of the street. Behind him was another car, a compact white one.

"How was your evening?" Lubchenko asked when Panas hurried over.

"Fine," Panas shivered, swatting his gloved hands together. "Very fine."

"That's good."

Lubchenko handed Panas a folded slip of paper and a key ring with two keys.

"You're going to take a little drive, Panas. Here's the address. When you get there, you are to pick up four suitcases, which you must then bring back here."

"Just four, eh?"

Panas was relieved. Sometimes, when they shuttled foodstuffs around, there was crate after crate to load and unload. It could take hours. He might yet be home before dawn. He opened the paper Lubchenko had given him; his mouth sagged when he saw his destination.

Lubchenko scowled. "What's the matter?"

Panas read the address again. Noginsk. "It's nothing, Comrade Director. Nothing."

Noginsk. Two hours north of the city, at the end of a long, straight, boring, two-lane road. He looked back. The car was Czech, probably didn't even have a radio.

"I—I just hadn't expected to be making such a long trip at two in the morning."

"So? You have urgent appointments?"

"No sir," he said, averting his eyes.

"Besides, Panas, you will be well paid for your troubles—assuming, that is, you get the suitcases here intact. If the electronics inside are damaged, our client will not pay us. You must be very, very careful."

"I understand completely," Panas said. Then, thinking to get as much for Virna's people as he could, he asked. "If I may inquire, Comrade Director, just who *is* the client?"

"That's not your concern," Lubchenko said. "But I'll tell you this much. If we succeed in this, there's a great deal of work that we'll get in the future. Money the likes of which you've never imagined."

Panas felt a welling of regret. The job sounded easy, the future would have been bright. He folded the address into his pocket; Lubchenko snapped his fingers once and held out his hand.

"Memorize it, Panas. You can't keep the paper."

284

"Why not?"

"Because if you have an accident or heart failure on the way back, and the cases are inspected, the man at this address will be in jeopardy."

Panas nodded and handed over the slip. Lubchenko folded it in quarters and tore it into small pieces. He stuffed some in the ashtray, threw the rest out the window.

"Drive slowly, Panas. Carefully. We don't want you being stopped by the police."

Panas snickered to himself. *If you only knew, you fool, that Panas Pavadze is immune to all danger. . . .*

"Above all, be *careful* with the merchandise!"

"And where do I take these suitcases after I have them?"

"Back here," Lubchenko said. "Just leave the car with the keys in the ignition. Someone will come for it."

The inside of Panas's mouth felt stringy. He wished he knew when Glinka's people would strike. They wouldn't take Lubchenko here, since the Supervising Director probably had to inform the electronics dealer that the car was on the way. But when? After he got back from Noginsk? When Lubchenko came to pay him? Panas hoped not. It was no triumph to betray him, and he didn't want to see that kind of condemnation in Lubchenko's eyes.

Lubchenko took out his handkerchief, poked it up a nostril. "You look uneasy, Panas. Is anything wrong?"

"No, Comrade. Nothing."

"You understand that I am not going myself so that *you* can be a part of this. You do understand, Panas, that I'm doing this for you?"

"Of course. You're very kind."

"I want you to be happy, to be able to give your family special things. I'm a generous man, but also a demanding man." Lubchenko examined the contents of the handkerchief, then folded it away. "Do the job, Panas, and do it *well*."

"I will. But I've been meaning to ask," Panas said thoughtfully. "I wonder, Comrade—is there any chance that I could get part of that money . . . tonight? A few hundred rubles, perhaps, something modest?"

Lubchenko scowled. "What's the matter, you think I'm not good for the money?"

"It isn't that, Comrade, and you insult me for suggesting that! No, I just thought—well, that it would bring a whistle to my lips as I drive."

"Come now, Panas, I *know* you. Just *thinking* about it will make you happy enough." Lubchenko turned on the car's headlights. "Job first, money second. But nothing at all if you fail, understood?"

"Perfectly."

When the Supervising Director saw that Panas's car had started, he drove away. Too miserable to enjoy the thrill of being behind the wheel of a private car, Panas followed Lubchenko into the street; half a block back, Panas noticed a pair of headlights flick on. Though he'd been half-expecting them, Panas's spirits sank as the car began following at a discreet distance. He felt as if he were on a leash.

Why can't things be the way they were a few days ago? Panas wondered. Who'd decided that he had it too good and should be a patriot instead of comfortable? *Damn Lubchenko, but damn them more.*

To distract himself, Panas switched on the radio; it didn't work. Squeezing the wheel hard, Panas damned everyone he could think of as he drove through the night.

12

Nona lay awake, staring at the ceiling. The pain from her bruises was constant, and the chemist had been out of aspirin. Not that her mind would have allowed her to rest.

The note tucked into her mailbox had been typed and obscure: *At the entrance. Nine.* But she'd known what it meant. She was to wait for Reiner just inside the Stalin Metro. The note was on top of the rest of her mail; whoever had delivered it had come after the postal carrier. It was ironic, she thought, that the authorities had probably read the rest of her mail and found nothing but news of a friend in Leningrad and a card from a former co-worker who was on vacation and obviously hadn't heard that she'd been fired. The real conspiratorial message had been missed entirely.

She wished Georgi were here to see this. She wouldn' have had the courage if it weren't for him; ironically, she wouldn't have had a reason, either. Now she wanted to hurt them for what they'd done to him, regardless of the consequences.

Hurt them, but how? What was Reiner going to do?

There was only one thing she could think of: nine o'clock was not long before Cherganyev would be coming to the tomb. Whatever they were planning probably involved him. Even if it were his death, she told herself, she would not care. Better that than a future filled with victims like her father and Georgi.

Besides, Reiner had said that Georgi might not be dead. If they succeeded, he could be found; there was no question in her mind about trading Georgi's life for Cherganyev's.

Nona could not sleep, but not because she was anxious.

For the first time in years, she was hopeful.

13

Captain Hank Adams was awakened with the shocking news: the Syrian and Libyans had joined the battle in En Naqura, and, vastly outnumbered, the Israelis had called for American military assistance.

The President had agreed to provide it.

Adams read the decoded message. They were being upgraded from a Code Yellow hold to a Code Green: they were being ordered to scramble as many squadrons as Adams thought necessary and strafe—not bomb— enemy positions. If the enemy refused to retreat, or if resistance was offered, Adams was to use "any and all means to hold the Israeli line."

Adams hadn't bothered to undress before retiring. Reaching for the phone above his bed, he raised Warren on the bridge.

"Yes sir?"

"I'm coming up. We've got a Code Green. Destination . . ." Adams leaned toward his desk and checked the computer terminal. "Destination is seven-niner."

Warren confirmed the target, and Adams signed off. He pulled on his cap and headed down the brightly lighted corridor toward the elevator.

Ten minutes from now, twenty-four Tomcats would race into the skies. When the Soviets saw where they were headed, the Foxbats would follow. No doubt they'd intercepted the message from Washington and put their pilots on alert.

Ten minutes later, the Tomcats would attack. The Foxbats would in all probability defend. And for the first and perhaps the last time in history, the United States and the Soviet Union would be at war.

As he rode to the bridge he didn't pray, now, for sanity. It was too late for that. What he prayed was that after all the talk and training and years of remilitarization, his pilots were sharp enough to take the Russians out of the skies. Because if they didn't, he knew that one way or another the Israelis would.

14

The reports that reached the President were not what he'd hoped. Instead of backing down, the Russians had engaged the U.S. forces in the skies over En Naqura. Losses on both sides were heavy, though at the moment the fleets had not engaged, nor was there any shelling.

"The important thing," the weary President said to Lawrence in the Oval Office, "is that we keep the Israelis from going crazy until tomorrow morning."

The phone rang. Lawrence answered.

"Yes?"

"Mr. Secretary, Mr. Clark is here."

Lawrence looked at the President. "It's Jim."

A few moments later the door opened. The President touched a button on his desk.

"We just taped this down in Communications. Want to explain it, Jim?"

Clark looked across the room where a television had winked on. Beside it, a videocassette machine was playing. The tape showed Joseph Rosenstock being interviewed at the Moscow airport.

"Well?"

Clark looked back. His gaze was steady. "I'm sorry, sir. I had to try it."

The President angrily punched the TV off. "Then you *did* send him over. The damn fool didn't go on his own initiative."

"Everything was in place. It made sense—"

"To *you!*" the President slammed his hand on the desk. "Dammit, Jim, we've engaged Russian planes in the Middle East, and you've got one of my leading critics standing there with Aksakov *praising* the bastards!"

"We hadn't planned on that, sir. But that doesn't invalidate his mission."

"His *mission?* We don't have time to play games with Lenin's body! We've got an undeclared war on our hands!"

"Please, Mr. President, we only need a few more hours—"

The President shook his head, reached for the phone.

"What about the Americans in Moscow? The reporters, the Embassy staff, the tourists, for God's sake—"

"I've got a fleet in the Middle East, and protecting *that* is my primary concern. If we lose military access there, every shithead terrorist in the Middle East will start killing Americans—not to mention Israelis. And you know where that will lead."

The President's executive secretary came on the line. Alexander put his hand over the mouthpiece.

"We go back a long way, Jim, and that's the only reason I'm asking for your resignation. Otherwise, I'd throw you the hell out of here."

Clark struggled to stay calm. "I don't care about the

290

job, Mr. President. *You're making a mistake here.* We've *got* a shot!''

"What you've got," the President snapped, "are your orders. Now get out."

When Clark was gone, the President took his hand from the mouthpiece.

"Sally, get me General Tunick at Alpha Base in Frankfurt."

15

It was early morning when Clancy Jones hurried out to his plane. He'd left his breakfast the instant the orders came; his hunger was forgotten in the rush of adrenaline that followed.

The strike was in four hours. Air Command feared the Russians might have been told he was coming, so he had to take a longer flight path, one that would bring him in from the east. An hour of prep, three hours in the air. Then *bango*.

This was it. Unlike last year's run, when Al Milgrom had buzzed the Russians, this was for real. They'd eat shit back home over this, it was something they'd be talking about on the street for as long as there *was* a street. The hometown boy, Clancy Jones, was about to take out the Soviet Union all by himself.

And the Russian fucks deserved it. Twelve pilots dead, eighteen planes downed before the last six Tomcats finally made it to their target. Twelve dead for *what?* The fucking Arabs scattered when they saw the Tomcats coming. The Israelis were able to hold. What the hell was wrong with the Russians, siding with losers?

Some of the dead guys he'd known and trained with. He only wished there was time to scratch their names on the bomb. They'd have appreciated it.

The Russians deserved it, all right. And if he didn't get the recall smack on the money, he was going to give it to them.

PART
FIVE

1

Joseph's watch beeped moments before Serafina called.

"Good morning, Dr. Rosenstock. I wanted to make certain you were up."

He was. All the facts and figures about Operation Starik had started coming back to him when he lay down, and for most of the night he had lain on his back, running them over in his mind.

Strangely, though, he wasn't exhausted. Not physically, at least.

After informing Serafina that he'd be down in twenty minutes, Joseph sat on the edge of the bed and began to cry. It was nerves, he knew, and he didn't fight it. He didn't even care what his hosts would think, listening in. He just put his face in his hands and, his shoulders heaving, allowed himself this release.

It was today. A miracle wouldn't intercede. He and Reiner would have to make their own miracle. And even though everyone knew what they had to do, even though everything was in place, so very much could go wrong.

"No." He sucked in a breath. "No, you mustn't think like that. You can't afford to."

He shut the larger picture from his mind. One step at a time. After breakfast he'd return to the hotel, ostensibly to freshen up. Instead, he'd change clothes and, rather than take the elevator back down, use the stairwell. Then over to the kitchen and out the door. If anyone stopped him, he would claim to be a delivery man. "Come and see my truck," he would tell any inquisitor—at which point Reiner would have to intercede.

There's no reason it shouldn't work, he assured himself as he pulled his rubbery legs beneath him. He rose. *No reason at all.*

Running into the bathroom, Joseph threw up his kebab. Then he stepped into a hot shower.

2

Shortly after six o'clock, Nona gave up trying to sleep. She dressed, made herself tea, took a tin of sardines, pulled on her coat and kerchief, and went downstairs.

For years, the cats that frequented the alley outside her room had annoyed her. Today, though, she decided to make peace. She needed to know that someone, at least, would want her to come through this day alive.

3

Panas climbed from the Metro station, his feet literally dragging and his eyes half-shut.

It had been an awful night.

The broken radio had been just the beginning. The heater hadn't worked either, and he'd gotten a flat tire on the way up; on the way back, he was pulled over by the KGB. They inspected the suitcases, noted the contents. They didn't disarm the weapons because, he assumed, Lubchenko would check them before setting off. The KGB obviously wanted to catch them in the act.

After making him stand a half hour in the freezing cold while they sat inside the car—"security," they said, but he knew it was spite—the three men let him go. By the time he reached the outskirts of the city, early morning traffic was beginning to build, which made the trip even longer. All he wanted to do now was sleep. Sleep and forget he'd ever heard of Virna, Lubchenko, and even Cherganyev.

And then he saw Nona.

She was seated on an old milk crate, feeding sardines to the cats that gathered around her. He didn't recognize her at first, her features seemed so dark and puffy. When he came near, he saw that the darkness was bruises and the puffiness was swelling. He couldn't imagine what had happened, and tried not to stare.

"Comrade Nemelov, good morning. No, ah—no work today?"

She was silent for a moment, her eyes on the cats. "Not today, Panas. Not any day."

"No?"

"I've been dismissed."

He was startled. "You? After so many years? For what cause?"

She looked up now, and he winced when he saw the even darker discoloration under her eyes and along her left cheek. "For loving a man who the state did not love. Prison was not hell enough. They sodomized me, beat me, then fired me."

"God, I'm so sorry!" The sentiment was heartfelt, the horror in Panas's eyes real.

Nona resumed feeding the cats. "Forgive me for being blunt. I shouldn't have troubled you."

"No, it's quite all right—I listen to problems all the time. But—my God, what are you going to do?"

"I have no idea." She glanced up again. "Would you hire me?"

Panas started to nod, but then his eyes dropped.

"Of course you wouldn't. No one would—except the hotels. I can work as a whore or I can go to a labor camp."

Panas looked around, then said quietly, "There are ways of getting new identity papers."

"And then what? Live in fear, waiting for the day I'm discovered? I'll go to prison then, Panas. I've been there once, and it was enough."

"But . . . did you even share this man's beliefs?"

"I shared his bed and his heart, nothing more."

"Yet you knew . . . you *had* to know what he was. Why did you bring this on yourself?"

She put the tin on the walk and stood, favoring her left leg; the right leg smarted where it had been smacked behind the knee. "I stayed with the man I loved. If that is now a sin in the Soviet Union, perhaps it's time to do something about it."

"Do something?" His gaze pinned her. "Comrade, what are you talking about?"

Realizing she'd said more than she should have, Nona excused herself and began walking away. Panas grabbed her by the sleeve.

"Comrade Nemelov, wait. Please explain yourself."

"Why? So you can run and tell your friend Cherganyev, appear with him on television while someone beats me with a broom handle?"

Wrenching her arm free, Nona limped toward the doorway. Panas watched as she disappeared into the building, then stood in the street for a long moment, bewildered.

Was she planning something? What could Nona Nemelov possibly do to hurt Russia? And yet . . .

He was a group leader with Lenin Utra. If she did something crazy, and they found out he'd been talking to her just before, they'd want to know why he hadn't

noticed anything odd about her. Perhaps they'd inter-
rogate him as they'd questioned her. Maybe he'd lose his
job as well.

But if he reported her, what would he say? That she
was acting strange? Who could blame her, under the circumstances? The KGB did not appreciate frivolous com-
plaints.

Deciding that it was best to ignore what he'd heard,
he headed inside for some much-needed rest.

4

Down the street from Nona's building, the KGB agent
who'd been assigned to follow Panas had been listening
with interest. Having heard enough of the conversation,
she turned and headed into the Metro at the corner,
making quickly for the nearest telephone.

5

Clancy Jones waited patiently for final clearance. Cool
in his stiff black pressure suit, the big mask feather-light
around his nose and mouth, he had cleared his mind of
everything but flying. There was a technique to that,
which he'd been taught when he'd joined the exclusive
club that had graduated from F-16s to F-19s three years
before: the eject button doesn't exist.

It did, of course, and he was free to use it; but he

wouldn't. Once the multifaceted mission canopy was shut, its flat faces protecting him from radar like a dozen shields, he was in for the ride.

There was no voice communication, not this close to Eastern Europe. Instead, the instructions came to Clancy Jones over his computer terminals. The three screens formed the vertices of a right triangle, with the darker green situation-display indicator between them; all now went from light green to black to amber at the same time.

He moved the control stick ahead and the plane rolled forward, accompanied by the utter silence of the engines. With deft movements he brought the plane into position on the runway. The twin tailfins were in an upright position; once he reached Mach-2 they'd fold in, forming a squat pyramid.

The amber went briefly to black and then to red. He was cleared for takeoff. The next time the screen changed, at 1100 hours, it would be to blue—the signal to proceed as planned. To drop a nuclear bomb on Moscow exactly one hour later, with Red Square as ground zero. He'd been told that the chances of receiving a recall were low.

Jones touched a flat white button on the fuel-management panel to the left of the stick. The panel went red. The engines were being fed. He guided the bomber swiftly and silently into the black skies.

6

The limousine pulled up to the Kremlin's main gate, the Borovitskaya Square entrance built into the Borovitskaya Tower. Serafina and Joseph stepped out, the

American trying his best to smile for the Russian TV crew and press photographers.

They were met at the iron gate by a pair of fair young men wearing the drab green uniforms of the ceremonial palace guard. With a youth on either side, they were ushered along the cobble walk to the Grand Palace. There, after Joseph was searched—a process none of the cameras recorded—he was allowed to keep his tape recorder and enter.

Breakfast was being held in the main dining hall, a room where the Czars had entertained visiting heads of state. It was filled with rich tapestries and finely wrought mosaics, the colors reflected in the highly polished flatware. Joseph wasn't touched by history as he'd been the day before. As the cameras moved in and were positioned for the arrival of the American ambassador, he could think of nothing but getting out of there.

7

Nona changed into baggy gray pants and a full white blouse she'd once bought for a play the railway workers had put on two years before at the Arbatskaya Metro, a skit about the railroad's role in the Revolution. She'd played a peasant whose one line had been, "My husband has left our fishing village to fight with Lenin. Now I gladly pull the nets in his place."

She'd felt so brave in that short role. So noble.

As she laced the boots she wore whenever there was a leak in one of the tunnels, Nona heard a series of car doors slam outside her window. Taxis were rare, and no one she knew owned a car; with a strange tingling at the base of her neck, Nona went over to look.

Two identical black cars had pulled up outside. She drew breath sharply. They were KGB vehicles.

The occupants had all left, but the motors were still running; they didn't expect to be there long.

Had they come for her? Had Reiner been captured? Or—

Panas, she concluded. The little viper Panas must have done this.

Nona ran for the door. She pulled it open just as four men stepped onto the staircase.

She froze as they came toward her.

8

"Panas, what do you think?"

Panas had been in the bedroom undressing when the cars arrived. He'd seen at once what the men were and watched more intently as they hurried out. Caterina had walked in then, having put out the children's breakfast, and followed his gaze.

"Panas, I asked what you think! They're from the KGB, aren't they?"

He nodded.

"Is there someone here important enough to be purged?"

"Not purged, no."

"Then what?"

"Tikhi!" he said, silencing her and padding into the small living room. There was concern in his face, wari-

ness in his manner; bending by the door, he listened as the footsteps grew louder on the stairs.

Caterina stalked over. "Don't hush me! You're *frightening* me. What's the matter?"

"I think they've come for Nona Nemelov."

"Nemelov? Whatever would they want with her?"

Panas explained about Georgi. When he finished, Caterina nodded self-righteously.

"So *that's* the man I saw her with. A dissident! I suppose that was the best she could do. She *is* a very plain woman."

Panas ignored her. He listened as the footsteps approached the landing, waiting to hear which way they went down the corridor. Their arrival suggested that someone had been watching Nona. Or perhaps the tail hadn't left him after his job was finished.

What if someone saw me talking to her!

The footsteps went in *both* directions. There was a knock at his door. Panas straightened, stared at it.

Caterina knit her fingers. "Why do they want us?"

Panas said nothing. The knock came again.

"Open the door, Pavadze. We wish to speak with you."

The children sat still over their toast. Caterina laughed nervously.

"Perhaps they want a witness to Nemelov's crimes. Could that be it?"

"I—I don't know."

The knock became a pounding. Caterina started forward. Panas started back.

"Yes, I'm coming!" the woman said. "There's no need to break the door down!"

Panas licked his lips while Caterina undid the chain. Though the room was cool, sweat began to spot his T-shirt.

She opened the door.

Two young men in black trench coats stood outside. Beyond them, Panas could see two other men approaching Nona, who stood stone-still in the doorway of her own apartment.

"Panas Pavadze, you are to dress and come with us."

He looked up at the man who had spoken, a tall man with humorless eyes. "Come where?"

"With *us*. Immediately."

There was a scuffle down the hallway. Caterina and Panas watched as the men took Nona by both arms and forced her from the room.

"No, I won't go back there!" she screamed. "I *won't!* Let me *go!*"

The other rooms were unnaturally quiet; people were listening, holding their breath.

Panas began buttoning his shirt. "This is pointless, Comrade. I haven't done anything wrong."

The man instructed Caterina to get her husband his coat.

"I'm just her neighbor," Panas went on. "In fact, this is worse than pointless, it's mad! Crazy!" Caterina handed him his coat and stepped away. "Don't you two realize that I have been on *television* with the Chairman? What will happen if you embarrass—"

Nona screamed as she fought to keep from being taken to the stairs. But her captors wrestled her forward, one of them grabbing her by the hair and pulling her around.

"Is that really necessary?" Panas asked, pulling on his coat. "She's hurt—"

In response, one of the men grabbed Panas's arm and led him into the corridor. The other man stood behind him.

"That *certainly* isn't necessary," Panas pointed to his arm and tugged lightly against his captor. "I'm not a crim—"

The man behind Panas drove a fist into his back. The wind rushed from him and he fell to his knees.

"You are being arrested for conspiring with a dissident," the tall man said. "Any further protests will be dealt with accordingly."

Somewhere in the distance, Panas heard Caterina gasp.

"Conspiring?" he said, still on his knees and unaware that he'd spoken aloud. "I was simply—"

The man's heel smashed hard into the back of his head; Panas sprawled forward. The other man still held on and yanked him up. Behind him, on the steps, Nona was screaming for someone to help her.

"Up!" the other man said, tugging on Panas's arm again.

Caterina called his name softly and started toward him; Panas turned and saw the man behind him look menacingly in her direction. She stopped. The other agent pulled roughly at his arm.

"Up, or you'll get more."

He rose. He didn't understand. He'd helped the KGB last night, and now they were beating him. Worse, he was letting them take him to another beating. How had things changed so suddenly?

Everyone was watching him. His employees would find out, and so would his regular patrons; even if he still had his job, how would he be able to do it effectively?

As they ushered Panas down the stairs, he frantically considered his options. And he decided, at last, that there was only one.

He had to escape. If he could get to Virna, she would help him. After all, he had impressed her, led her to Reiner's supplier, and she *did* seem to have influence.

If he had any chance of fleeing his captors, the time was now. Panas stopped suddenly at the top of the stairs.

"I—I don't feel well. I may get sick."

"I don't care. Let's go!"

305

The man gave him a tug and Panas seized the moment to throw his weight against his captor; the two of them went tumbling down the short flight. Behind them, the other man came running.

The agent took the worst of the fall, Panas having tucked his shoulder into a crude roll; the thick jacket helped to pad his fall. Upon hitting the landing, he scrambled to his feet, spun around the corner, and ran down the second half of the flight. The other man leapt over his moaning comrade and bolted after him.

"Stop! I'll shoot!"

Panas wasn't going to stop, not for him—he had nearly a full flight lead—or for the men holding Nona just below, one of whom had heard the commotion and looked back just as Panas spun around the second floor landing. The agent released Nona and braced himself for Panas. But Panas had the momentum and, flinging himself down the last three steps, he pushed the man face-first into the corner.

Turning on the man holding Nona's hair, Panas locked his fists and swung at him; the man jerked back and Panas missed.

Nona, however, did not.

With her free arm she hammered his face as it cocked away from Panas. She threw a second punch; the snap of bone announced that she had shattered his nose. Easily wrenching free, she hurried down the steps, followed by Panas. A bullet pinged off the metal banister just behind him as the man from upstairs came swinging around.

On the first floor, Nona continued running while Panas ducked under the steps. He realized they'd be dead if their pursuer followed them into the street and got a clear shot; he remembered most of the combat techniques he'd learned in the navy, and hoped to God that surprise would make up for his staleness.

The agent saw the glass outer door shut and ran toward it; as he did so, Panas rushed out, driving the side of his fist into the man's spine and sending him sprawling. With a cry, Panas kicked the side of the man's head. It was a crude but effective maneuver; the agent didn't move.

Panas heard footsteps on the stairs, the other agents coming after him. He dashed into the street.

9

Nona ran toward the Metro station. Her eyes stung from tears. She was frightened, the last few minutes a blur, but she was free.

And Panas had helped! That seemed ridiculous, since he was the one who had certainly called the KGB. Had he suddenly found his conscience?

"Nona!"

She looked back without stopping. Panas was hurrying after her. When she saw that no one was behind him, she slowed, walking backwards, seemingly propelled by her quick, small puffs of white breath.

"Nona, where are you going?"

She waited until he was near. "I have an appointment."

"Forget it. Come with me. I have friends who might be able to help us."

Panas was breathless, his face flushed and his hair mussed; for the first time Nona could remember, he didn't seem like a foolish little fop.

"I can't," she said, "I have an appoint—"

Nona bit off the rest of her sentence. Her eyes had been on the apartment building three blocks back, and she saw men burst from the foyer. Nona resumed running and, throwing a quick glance over his shoulder, Panas continued after her.

The Metro crowds were light, but so was the train schedule. Racing down the marble steps, they just missed the 8:07—why, she wondered, *this once,* did the Metro have to run on time?—and Nona knew the men would arrive before the next train. Grabbing Panas by the hand, she pulled him toward an unmarked gray door beside a bronze statue of a soldier of the Revolution. The door, as always, was unlocked; anyone who wanted to haul the mop bucket or spare trashcans through the turnstile and up the escalator was more than welcome to them.

Slowing, walking over as if they belonged, Nona opened the door, looked back toward the stairs, and waved Panas into the small chamber. She turned on the light and locked the door.

"We should be safe here. The janitor doesn't come to work until nine, and we'll be gone by then." Her eyes narrowed. "Why did you call them, Panas?"

"What?"

"Did your night with Cherganyev go to your head? Did you have to send the KGB after me?"

Panas seemed mystified. "What are you talking about? I didn't call anyone."

"It had to be you! I heard some of the things you were saying to them—"

"What things?"

"About working for them. And I talked to no one else, told no one how I was really feeling."

Panas's eyes fell beneath her gaze. "It's true, I . . . *have* helped them. I led them to a smuggler last night, but that's *all* I've ever done for them."

"I don't believe you. You and Caterina have always had such nice things, more than you could afford on your salary."

"I—I have done *other* things," he admitted, "illegal things—which is how I *got* into the fix last night. But I didn't send them to get you! If I had, why would they have taken me too? Why would I have *helped* you?"

"I've been thinking about that—"

A train came rumbling into the station, but Nona waited. As much as she wanted to get away, to be with Reiner, the KGB agents would have arrived and would be watching for them.

When the train pulled out and the platform was silent, Nona's gaze returned to Panas. "Georgi told me about the psychological tricks the KGB plays. They want me to trust you, lead you to my confederates. Then you'll call and have them arrest me and my partners."

"That's idiotic! Can't you tell how scared *I* am?"

"You always look scared, Panas. Even when you strut like a lion, you have the eyes of a rabbit." She looked at her watch. "I'm leaving. Stay here if you like. Just keep away from me."

She turned off the light and went to open the door; Panas grasped her shoulder and pressed something into her hand. She shuddered.

"I picked it up back there. Do you know how to use it?"

Nona turned the light back on, stared down at the nine-millimeter semiautomatic.

"No," she said.

Panas took a step closer. "It's simple. All you do is release this catch"—he pointed to the safety—"then aim and squeeze. I don't think this weapon will kick much, so you shouldn't have any trouble hitting anyone at close range."

She studied the six-inch gun, then slipped it into a pocket. She looked up. "If you're telling the truth, why did they come for you?"

Panas shook his head. "I've been trying to figure that

out. I was followed last night, perhaps I was followed again today. Or maybe you were. Maybe they thought I was joining your group. That's funny, because what you say is true. I am not a brave man. I never have been." He grinned. "That's not true. A few nights ago I stood up for a woman, I told off the man she was with. The joke is that *she* was the one with the KGB, and Reiner was the victim."

Nona shot him a look. "Who was?"

"A German. Erwin Reiner."

Nona's face drained of color.

"Nona, what's wrong?"

"Erwin Reiner—he's one of the men I'm to meet."

Panas grabbed her. "Then you mustn't go. They're going to arrest him and his partner, Supervising Director Lubchenko."

Nona spun toward the door. "No, that can't be. Without them, everything is lost."

"*What* is lost? What are you talking about?"

Instead of answering, Nona shut off the light and opened the door. Panas followed her into the station.

"Nona, where are you going?"

"To my meeting place."

She shouldered her way to the front of the platform and looked impatiently down the tracks. Panas stepped up and leaned toward her; the commuters stood in silence, reading their morning newspapers.

"Please," he urged, "let's go see my friends."

"Get away from me."

"You're being foolish! They can *help!*"

"Then *you* go. And while you're there, sell them someone else for your own benefit. Turn in your head waiter or our landlord, I'm sure you can come up with a reason." She glowered at him. "Lubchenko was good to you, Panas. Whatever trouble he was in, he deserved your loyalty."

310

"I've got a family, Nona. I had no choice!"

"And were you thinking about your family when you fled just now—"

"Who else?" Panas looked around to make sure that no one was listening. "What will happen to them if I'm taken away?"

"What will happen to them *now?* Don't you realize they'll question Caterina the way they questioned me?"

"That's *why* I need to get to my friends!"

"Your friends!" Nona sneered. "They won't get involved. Georgi was right, no one has friends in Russia. The generals had friends. Gorbachev had friends. Where are those men now?"

A rumble echoed along the tunnel. Moments later the tracks turned light gold around the distant bend and then the train's headlight was visible.

Panas shifted uneasily. "God, why did this have to happen? Everything was going so well!" He looked from the train to Nona. "Please let me go with you. If you have a plan that can change things, I want to help!"

Nona stared at Panas as the train rolled into the Turgenevskaya Station. They were one stop from Red Square; there wasn't much time to think. He *had* given her the gun, but what did that prove? Maybe he wanted them to shoot at her instead of him—

She shook her head. "They have your family. You'll betray us."

"No! What I did to Lubchenko was wrong, I see that now. Let me do something to make up for it!"

"You've done enough, Panas. Just stay *away* from me!"

"Nona, wait!"

The doors opened and he impulsively grabbed her arm; Nona shoved him back a stepped onto the train. At the last moment, Panas jumped in beside her.

311

10

Reiner stepped from his apartment holding two suitcases; the doorman carried the other two, helping him to the idling Mercedes.

The German was dressed smartly, no overcoat, just a gray business suit; there were airplane tickets tucked into his lapel pocket. The clothing wasn't especially stylish, but it said what he wanted it to say: that he was a businessman about to return home. And if for any reason—a spot check by police while he was sitting at a light, a curious security guard spotting him as he took the cases from his car in the alley outside the hotel—there was always the P7 automatic tucked in the pocket of his jacket.

Loading the trunk, Reiner thanked the doorman, told him he'd see him in a month, and headed down rustic Frunze Street to pick up Lubchenko.

Three hours, he thought as he glanced at the digital clock in the dashboard. Lubchenko was only in it for the pay, and for fifteen years, money had been Reiner's prime motive as well. But that was secondary this time. As the moment grew near he could *taste* the glory. He would be liberating one nation and celebrated in countless others—even in Israel, the irony of which was not lost on the German.

Just three hours.

He only hoped that Nona and the American didn't botch their end of it. Without their help, he couldn't be famous in two hours. Without them, he could very well be dead.

11

The phone beeped and the driver snapped it up.

"*Da?*"

"A-two; M-twelve."

Every case had a supervisor at KGB headquarters; each day the supervisor's code designation changed, along with that of every operative. Only those working for the supervisor knew his designation, and only the supervisor knew the code for each agent.

The code was correct. The driver waited.

"Quarry is apparently not headed for Red Square. He has turned into an alley off Stoleshinkov."

The driver frowned at the man sitting beside him. They'd been hoping to capture the men while the TV cameras were watching. The publicity would have been good for the KGB at a time when the SG was getting all the praise. On Stoleshinkov, only the rats would see them.

"It's presumed he'll go to the hotel," the supervisor continued, "and that a sniping or bomb attempt will be made on the Chairman's life. You are to join Rukhlyadev at the school bus and apprehend him before he enters the building. We can't take a chance on losing him inside."

"Understood."

The driver signed off. At least they'd be getting credit for the job—though he wouldn't put it past some arrogant SG swine to try to find a way to steal it from them.

Refusing to think about that, and concentrating on the prospect of seeing action and perhaps even saving the

Chairman's life—good for a commendation and extra food privileges if nothing else—the driver shifted the car into gear and picked his way through the mounting traffic on Gorky Street.

12

Joseph sat at one of the eight settings clustered in the center of the large table. As he sat there with Serafina and two of Aksakov's deputies, Ambassador Kaplan and her Russian hosts entered. The ambassador was seated directly across from Joseph.

After introductions were made and photographs taken, waiters came around to serve the meal. All the while, Joseph studied the ambassador carefully.

"So, Dr. Rosenstock, you've come to research Lenin?"

"Yes, Madam Ambassador."

"I understand even the Chairman shared his thoughts with you. That's quite an honor."

"I'll never forget it," Joseph replied.

Ambassador Kaplan seemed cheerful and alert. There was nothing distant or distracted in her manner, nothing to suggest brainwashing or drugs. Still, he couldn't believe she'd defected willingly.

"He has remarkable presence," the ambassador said. "More, even, than Alexander." She smiled. "How is our lunatic President?"

Joseph couldn't believe what he was hearing. "Preoccupied," he said, "and, to tell you the truth, a trifle confused by what you've done."

"Is he?" she laughed. "Well, tell him not to mourn for me."

"It isn't a question of mourning—"

"I think it is."

The laughter was gone from her eyes. The change of mood caught Joseph totally off guard.

"In any case, I hope you'll do me a favor, Dr. Rosenstock. The embassy staff will be released today, but they don't understand. When you go home, explain to the President and to the public why I decided to remain here."

"And exactly what *is* that?"

"As I said, the President of the United States is a madman. I simply can't be a party to anything he might do."

Her gaze was still hard, her tone was grave.

And suddenly Joseph understood.

The ambassador knew about the Stealth option, and knew that the President wouldn't hesitate to use it. She wanted her people out of Moscow, and their release was obviously contingent upon her defection.

"Of course, Madam Ambassador," Joseph said. "I'll make certain they know what you've done . . . and why."

She thanked him with her eyes, and Joseph had to look away. She didn't know about Operation Starik, about why he was really here. All she knew was that in a few hours she would probably die with her captors. Yet she hadn't told the Soviets about Stealth, not even to save her own life. For several minutes, Joseph was too moved to speak.

Talk over the meal was of the new ballet season and of the huge fair that would be built outside the city to mark the seventy-fifth anniversary celebration of the Revolution. A week before, Joseph would have been excited by the prospect of such a fair.

But not now.

All he could think about was Isabel Kaplan's courage. And how he must find it in himself to be just as brave over the next few hours.

13

Captain Adams was in sick bay, visiting with three pilots who had been fished from the ocean after bailing out of their stricken fighter.

Adams was proud of his ship, his men, and his country. But nothing would make him prouder that day than to withdraw. There was only one way any further escalation could end, and it had very little to do with fighting men or conventional weapons.

At least it was calm now. He'd been ordered to wait, told that further instructions would issue directly from the White House, which was engaged in a critical operation of its own; he'd also been told that the Russians seemed to have something of their own brewing: broadcasts intercepted from Soviet TV indicated that the American diplomats and journalists being held captive in Moscow would be freed within two hours "as a show of trust." Coincidentally, that was when the White House action was due to occur.

Someone was in for a big surprise.

He hoped, for once—just this *once*—that it wasn't Washington.

14

A half hour out of Frankfurt, Clancy Jones activated the communications computer.

ACTIVATED appeared on the monitor.

He pressed in a code.

INPUTTING now appeared.

To prevent any information leaks on the ground, the aircraft's exact flight path was not known to the pilot or the aircraft until it was well aloft. Then, bypassing Frankfurt, the coordinates were fed directly from the White House into the plane's computer.

Jones stared at the screen. As the figures came in, he checked them on his map terminal. He was to head due north at latitude twenty-five degrees, longitude sixty, which would carry him over Helsinki, then fly east to latitude forty. Precisely over Sokol he was to spear southward, circle four hundred kilometers wide around Moscow, and approach heading due west.

Analyzing the latest data, the computer projected his ETA.

By noon, Moscow time, he'd be directly over the target.

Two minutes later, the target would no longer exist.

15

Reiner nosed the car up to a large brown dumpster and left it. He looked back down the alley to see if anyone looked at him as they drove past. Cars, delivery trucks, a school bus—all went about their business. He and Lubchenko hadn't been followed.

Stepping from the car, Lubchenko rapped on the kitchen door. With his identity papers, the Supervising Director was permitted to enter any restaurant in Moscow. He would go inside this one and, while pretending to be checking cleanliness, wait for Rosenstock. He looked at his watch. It was 9:20. With any luck, they would have just a few minutes to wait.

16

The group moved down the Palace corridor with painful slowness. Serafina stood to Joseph's left, Ambassador Kaplan to his right. The rest of the Soviet party followed behind.

At least the pace seemed slow to Joseph. He was so full of energy now that he felt certain he could run the half-mile to his hotel.

As they neared the door, he tapped Serafina on the elbow: "Do you think there's time for me to go back to the hotel?"

Her penciled-on brows dropped unpleasantly. "What's the matter?"

The side of his hand hovered just above his belt. His cheeks filled and slowly deflated. "My stomach. I think it was the sour cream."

Serafina looked at her watch. "It's getting late."

"I know, but . . . I'd hate to embarrass myself while the Chairman honors Lenin."

The woman stopped and half-turned toward a winding staircase behind them. Joseph and Ambassador Kaplan stopped several steps ahead.

"Come with me, please."

She intended for him to use the lavatory at the Palace. His mind worked fast. The discomfort in Joseph's own face became very real.

"It isn't just . . . that." He gestured ahead of her. "I need my stomach medication."

"Medication?"

Serafina's expression was difficult to interpret. Was it displeasure at the schedule's being jeopardized, or suspicion? She might well have gotten a complete accounting of what had been in his luggage, and if so, she might well remember that there weren't any pills.

The seconds moved like a winter storm; he was relieved when she strode forward. "I'll come with you. Can you at least put on a pleasant face for the cameras outside?"

Joseph said that he would try.

17

Agent Rukhlyadev threw aside his driver's cap when the teacher had left with her students, and pulled a satchel from under his seat. In his ear was a small device that looked like a hearing aid; it was, in fact, a radio receiver. The night before, he'd placed a bug behind the steering wheel of Reiner's car; while Rukhlyadev drove, he'd listened to everything the German and his companion had said.

Followed by a driver whom he was allegedly training, the KGB operative walked briskly down the block, heading for the alley into which Reiner had pulled.

"Lubchenko has already gone inside."

"What about the cases?"

"Still in the trunk." He'd placed a small transmitter on the inside; if the trunk had been opened, a light in his wristwatch would have gone on. "My guess is Lubchenko's clearing the way or else meeting an accomplice before Reiner joins him."

They reached a doorway beside the alley, and Rukhlyadev bent and opened the case. While the other man hovered behind him, facing the street, the agent withdrew a pair of holster-sized submachine guns. Rukhlyadev rose, using his body to shield the weapon from passersby; his companion turned and accepted one of the guns, which he held close to his waist.

"Mikhail—go around front and move toward the kitchen, see what Lubchenko is up to. If you don't see him, go back and cover the front. If you do see him, follow him. When backup arrives, I'm going to move in on this side.''

Mikhail rose and walked back in the direction of the bus. Rukhlyadev waited until a car pulled up across the street, out of view of the alley. Two of his colleagues emerged and walked briskly toward him. His palms grew sweaty. They would follow his lead, go in and shoot at Reiner's legs to bring him down. Then they would question him. He had every confidence that the days of surveillance would finally pay off with a very important catch.

18

Nona squeezed from the Metro before the door was completely open. Panas scurried after her.

"Not the steps!" he said in a loud whisper as she headed for the staircase. "You'll attract attention!"

Nona slowed. He was right. Only lunatics ran up the four hundred steep steps. Time was important, but if she was caught, nothing mattered.

She turned toward the adjoining escalator and stepped on, Panas standing next to her. She could stop him if need be, she had the gun.

Assuming, of course, that she could bring herself to use it. On Panas, perhaps not, but if someone was interfering with Reiner . . .

She repeated to herself that this chance, however slim, was *all* she had left in life. Nothing would stop her, not even if she had to kill someone.

When she reached the top of the escalator, Nona slipped her hand into her pocket. Holding the gun, she walked briskly toward the front of the government building where she was to meet her accomplices.

19

The limousine pulled up before Joseph's hotel and, much to his alarm, Serafina got out with him.

"No need for you to come up, Comrade Nazvanov. I'll be right back."

"It's my job to see that you have everything you need. There's a chemist in the hotel, and if you can't find your medication—"

"I'm sure my wife packed them. They may be buried inside socks or a handkerchief, but I'm sure they're there."

He smiled reassuringly, then headed for the door. Serafina started after him and he stopped again, stepping back as a bus driver plowed through the revolving door.

Joseph scowled at the woman. "Comrade, you're making my stomach worse. I will take my pill, use the lavatory, and come right back."

"Forgive me, Dr. Rosenstock, but it seems as if you're trying to get rid of me."

"Precisely! When you get to be my age, you'll find you're very private about what you must do to maintain your body."

She regarded him coldly.

"Three minutes," he said, smiling. "I'll be back in three minutes. Please, we're wasting time."

Joseph started in; Serafina followed him.

"I'll wait outside your door," she said. "That way, if

you're detained, I'll be able to inform the Foreign Minister."

Sighing in resignation, Joseph entered the lobby, the pain in his stomach now very real.

20

There was no longer any need for caution. The two backup men took up positions on either side of the alley, their automatics drawn. Nodding to them, Rukhlyadev went in.

Reiner saw the motion in his rearview mirror. Spotting the men, he immediately threw himself flat on the seat and pulled out his own pistol.

"We have you closed in," yelled the man who was approaching. "Don't attempt to resist."

Reiner swore. *How the hell did they know?*

It didn't matter now. At least they hadn't fired; they obviously wanted him alive, and that meant he had a chance.

If I can just make it to the street—

Reiner had left the car running. Shifting into reverse, he reached down and pressed his left palm to the pedal; the Mercedes shot backwards.

He clipped the nearest agent, who flew to one side, and the other two jumped onto the sidewalk. They fired at the car. Reiner heard the tires pop, but kept going. Careening off the wall of the hotel, he twisted the wheel and spun into the street.

And crashed into a delivery truck.

Uninjured, Reiner bolted upright. Tires screeched and another car slammed into the truck. The impact tossed

Reiner against the steering wheel. Though the wind was knocked out of him, he threw open the door and jumped out.

The two backup agents were running toward him. Reiner ducked behind the door, fired, and missed. Their return fire rattled the car door.

Reiner looked behind him. Pedestrians had scattered and there was a clear path to St. Basil's Cathedral. Behind it was crowded Red Square. They wouldn't dare fire there. If he could just make it to the corner . . .

Clutching his chest, Reiner rose. He sprayed gunfire toward the alley and the two agents ducked behind cars. Turning, Reiner ran.

Limping, Rukhlyadev emerged from the alley.

"Stop!"

Reiner reached the opposite sidewalk, his legs churning madly. Rukhlyadev fired a burst from his submachine gun.

Reiner's shins and feet exploded. The impact spun him around and he landed on his back; the pain was intense, but it was secondary to the helplessness he felt. Groaning, he tried to wriggle ahead.

Rukhlyadev hobbled over and straddled him. He disarmed the German, then shoved the submachine gun under Reiner's belt.

"Don't move, Comrade. I will not shoot to kill, just to maim."

Across the street, the other two agents ducked back into the alley to cover the kitchen door.

"Tell me what you were up to, *svinya!* Where are your accomplices?"

Grimacing in pain, Reiner felt the hot muzzle of the gun pressed to his testicles. He knew that, one way or another, he was a dead man. Better to die here, he decided, than after a few days of Soviet hospitality.

At least he could still be a hero.

Reaching down, Reiner grabbed the muzzle of the gun with one hand and pointed it toward his face. With the thumb of the other hand, he pressed on the trigger.

Rukhlyadev's scream of rage was lost in the stream of bullets that drilled through Reiner's chin and up into his brain.

21

Joseph heard the short staccato drone from behind the hotel and looked with alarm toward the ground floor restaurant. He saw the bus driver break into a run and pull out a pistol. A moment later a man in a gray sweater came running from the restaurant; the bus driver halted and called out his name. Joseph's heart stopped when he heard it:

Lubchenko.

A panicked look on his face, Lubchenko stopped and whirled with a pistol in his hand. Without hesitation, the bus driver fired. Lubchenko spun and fell just as two other men ran in from the restaurant.

Joseph's stomach gurgled. *God . . . they were waiting for them out back.* Somehow the KGB had found out.

Joseph noticed Serafina standing with her mouth open, and realized they probably didn't know about him. If they had, Serafina would have been informed. She would have expected something.

Joseph's mind reeled. *Without Lubchenko and Reiner, what chance do we have?*

A better one, he told himself, than if he did nothing. Reiner had said there were others who would meet them at the tunnel. Maybe they hadn't been arrested. Maybe they had the tools and were waiting for him.

Maybe.

Don't think!

Around the lobby, everyone was frozen. Joseph looked back. If he could make it to the street—

Muttering a quick prayer, he sprinted toward the door.

"Dr. Rosenstock!"

Joseph broke into a run. He hit the revolving door and rushed outside, holding his breath to keep from hyperventilating. Turning east, he made for the nearest cross street. He had a good head start. If he could just get around the hotel to the Square he might elude them.

Again, just a chance. Another *maybe*.

His chest stung with every cold breath. But he didn't dare slow—not yet. The clock in the Czar's Tower chimed. Nine-thirty. Cherganyev would be arriving in two and a half hours, and Stealth—he didn't know when. A few minutes before? A few minutes later? He refused to worry about it. That, at least, was out of his hands.

He reached Manege Street, spun around the corner, and was in the clear. He slowed now, wheezing.

Muscovites regarded him curiously, some with amusement. His hair was wet with perspiration. His mouth hung open as he gulped down air. He stopped and suddenly threw up. The few pedestrians who still watched him quickened their pace or sneered; but Joseph felt much better, and wiping his mouth with his handkerchief, he patted his vest pocket to make sure the recorder was still there, and continued toward the Square.

22

Nona tarried by the Rossiya Cinema, nearly a block from the Council of Ministers Building. She pretended to study a billboard, but was watching the front of the Council building from the corner of her eye. The street was unusually deserted.

Panas was looking at the building more overtly, rubbing his hands to keep them warm. He seemed to read her mind. "Do you know what I think? It's quiet because people have already gone to the Square, to be as close as possible to the Mausoleum. I don't think the KGB came by and told everyone to stay away, they have a spy to catch."

Nona looked at him, reluctantly acknowledging his presence. Perhaps she wasn't as courageous as she'd thought.

"But why would they leave so early?"

Panas seemed pleased to have her attention. "I read yesterday in the newspaper that today's ceremony is a special one, that they want as many people as possible to attend. People would rather stand in the cold and wave little banners for two hours than work. Believe me, most of my waiters would."

If that was true, Nona was glad. Her former colleagues at the Metro would be the first to take advantage of such an option, which would leave a clearer path to the Stalin Express.

Assuming, of course, Reiner even came.

"The men coming for Reiner—will they be in cars or on foot?"

Panas blew on his hands and rocked from foot to foot. "Cars, I think. The plan was to follow them until they reached their final destination."

"But did they know the Council of Ministers Building was his destination?"

"I didn't tell them. I didn't even know."

Nona started toward the Council building.

"Wait! What are you doing?"

"Maybe he's watching the building like we are. I've got to go over there and wait for him."

"But if the KGB comes for him, they'll take you too—"

Nona continued walking. Panas ran after her.

"Don't come with me," she said, "they may recognize you."

"I'll stand behind those trees," he indicated a row of oaks by the corner. "I'll keep looking at my watch, as though I'm waiting for someone. Believe me, I don't want to be recognized."

She wanted to say that she still didn't trust him, but what was the point? If he was still in league with the KGB, her protests wouldn't send him away. And if not, conceivably he could help.

As they crossed the broad street, Nona noticed a man hurrying toward the building from the opposite direction; he was the only person moving away from the Square.

Panas followed her gaze. "Is something wrong?"

"That man seems to be in a hurry. Could he be one of Reiner's people?"

"That's strange," Panas said.

"What is?"

"I know him. He's a distinguished American scholar. He was—Oh God."

"What?"

"Last night. He dined at the Azov. With Reiner."

328

Nona ran the rest of the way across the street. She reached the curb and continued jogging ahead, breathing heavily. Panas didn't even caution her to slow down; if anyone from the KGB was watching them, yelling would have drawn as much attention as her pace. Instead, he just shook his head and laughed.

"Can't wait to get a good spot to see our beloved Chairman, can you? Well go ahead, I'll catch up."

Nona hurried toward Joseph, who stopped and watched her warily.

"Excuse me," Nona blurted, "I must talk to you. You are an American, yes?"

"Yes . . ." There was no reason for caution.

"This man saw you at the Azov restaurant last night, dining with a friend of mine."

She pointed behind her; Joseph regarded Panas and his eyes wrinkled as though he'd heard a wrong note on the piano.

"Are you by any chance here to meet my friend?"

"You are . . . ?"

"Nemelov. Nona Nemelov."

Joseph exhaled loudly. "Comrade Nemelov, I'm *so* glad to see you." He frowned. "I'm sorry to say that I *was* to meet Reiner, but he will not be here. There was shooting. His partner is dead, and I believe Reiner is too."

Panas jumped onto the curb. "His partner? You mean Lubchenko is dead?"

"I saw him shot, Comrade Pavadze, with a machine gun." Joseph looked behind him again, then gently took the woman's hand and began walking with her. "Comrade Nemelov, do you still wish to help?"

"Anything," she said. "I'll do *anything!*"

He regarded Panas. "And you?"

"Yes."

In response, Panas stepped to Joseph's side. He ig-

329

nored Nona's critical stare; his frown told her that he didn't need to be reminded of the role he'd played in their deaths.

"We don't have much time," Joseph said, oblivious of the tension between his companions. He pulled them closer to the doorway, away from the few pedestrians. "Comrade Nemelov, Reiner had the tools we were to use. He said that you work for the Metro, and you know where we can get more—picks, shovels, a drill."

"We can get them in the tunnel. There's a supply car where tools for all the Metros and trains are kept. I'm sure they're older than the ones Reiner was bringing—"

"No matter. They'll have to do."

"What are you planning to do?" Panas asked.

As casually as possible, Joseph said. "We're going inside the Lenin Mausoleum to remove the body."

Panas gasped. "Remove Lenin's *body?* Good God, what for?"

"If we can get inside before Cherganyev does, imagine what it would *do* to him."

There was understanding and then triumph in Nona's expression as she realized what Reiner had meant the other night. *Death for life.* Dead, Lenin would actually cause Russia to be reborn. "If anything were to happen to the body, Cherganyev would be overcome! It would *cripple* him, and in front of tens of millions of eyes!"

"You're crazy!" Panas declared. "How will you even get *near* the tomb?"

Nona said, "The Metro tunnel runs right beneath it. The rock is soft." She thought for a moment. "But—I was just at the Mausoleum. How will you get into the coffin itself?"

"I can take care of that," Joseph said, clearly not wanting to reveal too much in front of Panas.

The young man was still shaking his head. "Why not

just *shoot* Cherganyev? You'd have a greater chance of succeeding."

"That wouldn't do the job," Joseph said. He moved closer. "Even if we had the weapons, death would make Cherganyev a martyr. Lenin Utra would continue."

"But stealing the body—it's mad!"

Nona said to Joseph, "We're wasting time. We'll find a way to do this alone."

"I'm not so sure," Joseph said. "Panas, don't let the job frighten you. We worked it out in Washington, and it can be done."

"Did you work it out with the KGB looking for you?"

"That isn't a factor. The only other people who knew about the plan are dead. Once we're inside, no one will find us." Joseph glanced at his watch. "Make up your mind. Are you coming?"

Panas stood stock-still for a long moment, avoiding Nona's damning eyes. "Yes," he said at last, "I'm coming."

Without another word, the three hurried toward the building's revolving door.

23

The escalator led to the chrome-and-tile lower lobby, which, like the lobby above, was not as crowded as usual. Windowless and serviced only by a pair of elevators—the only access to the offices above—the cavernous room seemed to close in on Joseph. He felt like Dante descending into the heart of hell, but welcomed the distraction; it took his mind off Reiner and Lubchenko.

The Metro platform was also deserted, though Nona slowed as they approached the turnstile.

"What's wrong?"

Joseph followed her gaze toward a booth several meters down the platform.

"My former supervisor works here. I don't want him to see me."

"Do we have to go that way?"

Nona nodded. "The tunnel that leads to the Stalin Express is there." She pointed toward a latticed metal walkway that paralleled the tracks roughly a meter above the railbed. To get to it, it was necessary to step off the platform and climb a short flight of stairs.

"I see." Joseph looked ahead. "Is your supervisor there?"

"I can't tell. The lights are reflecting off the glass. It's best to wait for the Metro. He usually comes out to chat with the engineer."

The wait was not a long one. The train rattled in and deposited a mass of riders bound for the Square. Joseph and Nona peered through the crowd while Panas stood in the shadows beside a life-size bronze statue of a factory worker.

"Nothing," Joseph said as the few waiting passengers boarded. The train pulled out and the tunnel was silent.

Her chest tight, Nona led the way toward the end of the platform. The box-shaped booth seemed like a sleeping dragon to her, impersonal but dangerous. The reflected light began to recede as they approached, exposing more and more of the interior. Her breath came in low gasps. She saw the rack of keys, the filing cabinet, the clipboards hanging from the wall, the small desk—

"Empty!" she said. She picked up the pace. "Come on. He's probably inspecting one of the other lines. They'll expect him to do my job until they name a replacement."

"How do you know he won't be where we're going?" Panas asked.

"He only goes there once a month, for inspection, and we just did that."

"What about work crews?" Joseph asked.

"If anyone is there, they won't bother us."

"Why not? Reiner intended to shoot them with a stun gun."

"It would have been a waste. These men are half-dead when they work, drinking vodka between each swing of their picks. Even so, you're dressed like a supervisor," she said admiringly. "They probably haven't heard about my dismissal, and Panas looks as if he belongs down here. No one will give us a second glance."

They reached the end of the platform and hopped down. Then they were up the steps and around the bend on the catwalk before any other passengers had reached the platform.

Joseph decided this was not where he'd want to be when a train came by. The catwalk rattled, held up by thin struts along the outside, and the train's headlight had to be blinding in the close confines of the tunnel. He understood now how a deer could be paralyzed when it saw a car approach at night, and was relieved when Nona pointed to a black door set in the white tiles of the well-lit tunnel. When they reached it, she bent beside the combination lock and twisted the dial.

"Did Reiner plan to shoot this as well?"

"Lubchenko would have opened it," Panas said glumly. "He—he could do such things."

Joseph recalled Panas's surprise at the mention of his murder. "You knew him, I take it?"

"I worked for him."

"In the black market?"

Panas nodded. "That, and also at the Azov. He gave me my job there."

"I'm sorry."

Nona turned the latch. The door creaked open on rusty hinges and she stepped in, the others following. They were in utter blackness, the air stuffy and rank.

"The Metro is straight ahead," Nona advised them. "Just keep your head low and watch your footing. There's a lot of moss on the rocks."

Joseph didn't need to be told about the moss; it smelled like Coney Island under the boardwalk in the heat of summer. He used the walls to feel his way; they were clammy, like the air. His head began to pound, as it did whenever he came in from the cold Cambridge winters to the hot halls of the school.

"How long is this thing?" Panas asked. "My feet are already wet."

Panas was between them, assaulting Joseph with an unpleasant mix of fading cologne and body odor. Joseph slowed a few steps, preferring the smell of the tunnel.

"It's about thirty meters," Nona said.

"Why so many curves?"

"In case of pursuit, Stalin didn't want his enemies to have a clear shot at him. That's also why the ceilings are so low—so they couldn't straighten up and aim."

The passageway was remarkable to Joseph as a monument to Stalin's paranoia, which was greater, in its own way, than the tunnel itself. This would make for the most incredible Stalin paper in decades; he'd survive this and get back home if for no other reason than to publish it and leave his rivals in awe.

A faint yellow glow appeared on the rocks.

"This is the last curve," Nona said. "The tunnel is just ahead."

They rounded a sharp bend and squinted in the light of a bright bulb hanging a few meters ahead. It was high, and several meters beyond the mouth of the passageway;

334

below it, Joseph could make out a dirty metal cart and the smudged wooden slats of a platform.

"The wood creaks," Nona said as they neared the opening, "but it will hold the three of us. We put in new supports just last year."

"Why bother?" Panas asked. "This place is like a bad dream."

"For fifty years they haven't known what to do with the tunnel," Nona admitted—answering for the same reason that Panas had asked, to try to keep her mind occupied. "Too costly to fill, too costly to complete, too dangerous to leave unattended. So they use it mostly for storage and repairs."

The trio crossed the planks and climbed aboard the cart.

"The fact that this is here is a good sign," Nona said. "It means that if anyone's in there, they didn't go very deep."

"How deep are we going?" Panas asked.

"Deep," Nona said. "Nearly to the end."

Kneeling, she reached around the side and felt for the starter handle. She gave it a tug; the engine growled and stopped. She tugged again and it ground more vigorously, then stopped.

"Damn this!"

"It sounds wet," Joseph said.

"It is."

"Why don't we use the catwalk?" Panas asked.

"Because when we get to the tools, they'll be heavy enough without having to haul them an extra two hundred meters," Joseph explained.

"I'll carry them," Panas said bravely.

Nona snickered. She pulled again and the engine refused to turn over. Leaning over the side, she checked the fuel gauge. It was full.

"Come on, you cow!"

"Can I help?" Joseph asked.

Nona ignored him. She stood, bent, retrieved the handle, put her foot on the engine, and yanked hard. The engine spit a dark cloud toward the catwalk, fired another, and finally puttered to life. Allowing herself a smile of satisfaction, Nona jumped up, switched on the lantern, then handed it to Panas so they could see the walls instead of the tracks. She pushed a red button on the front handrail and started the cart down the tracks.

24

Lubchenko was propped on the floor in a corner of the hotel manager's office. Neckties had been knotted around his thighs to stop the bleeding from the bullet wounds in his legs; his shirt had been torn away from the gashes in his side. His wrists were handcuffed behind him, and the belt from his trousers had been looped around his throat like a noose.

Serafina and three KGB men stood around Lubchenko in a semi-circle. Rukhlyadev squatted beside him, next to a floor lamp. Across the room, Case Officer Glinka was on the telephone.

In the absence of truth drugs, it was common practice to cut off a suspect's air to make him talk. Garroting made the victim light-headed; that, plus the pain of torture, was usually sufficient to obtain whatever information was needed.

"You were here to meet someone," Rukhlyadev said calmly. "Who?"

Lubchenko was gasping for breath. "No . . . one. Just . . . drop off."

"You were to leave drills and stun guns here, but you don't know for whom. Or why."

Lubchenko nodded vigorously, his jowls and cheeks reddish purple.

Rukhlyadev studied him for a moment. "I'm sorry, but I find that difficult to believe."

The agent calmly reached out and tightened the belt a notch. Lubchenko gasped. Veins stood out on his forehead. His temples pulsed visibly.

"This was not one of your typical black-market operations, Comrade Director. Not with Reiner involved."

"P-Please . . ."

"Were you here to try to assassinate the Chairman? What were you going to do with the drills?"

"Break . . . safe . . ." he said.

Rukhlyadev rubbed his chin. "Here? Now, with security forces everywhere? I don't believe that. Why suffer like this, Lubchenko? Tell me what I wish to know and you'll be taken to a hospital, your wounds treated." He grabbed the end of the belt and pulled Lubchenko toward him. "Who else are you protecting? Was Rosenstock involved? Is that why he ran?"

"W-who . . . ?"

"Why are you stalling? *We have your equipment.* What can your accomplices do now?"

"No . . . accomplices. No . . ." Lubchenko's tongue fell from the side of his mouth. He wheezed horribly.

Rukhlyadev loosened the belt a notch, then rose. "You're lying. You had gas masks but no gas. Why would you have needed those to break into the hotel safe?"

Serafina looked at a desk clock. Her normally unflappable features were lined with concern. "Comrade Rukhlyadev, it's less than two hours until the ceremony. I suggest we use drugs."

"Drugs obtain answers, but only to questions that are

asked. Besides, in this man's weakened condition, drugs might kill him.''

''But what do I tell my superiors about the ceremony? Should it be postponed?''

Glinka hung up the phone. ''All the rooms facing the Square have been searched by my SG men, so there's no danger from snipers. The sewers have been checked by your people, Comrade Rukhlyadev, so I can only assume there are no explosives.''

Rukhlyadev bristled, but said nothing.

Serafina regarded Glinka. ''So—we can proceed?''

The SG officer looked at Lubchenko. ''Proceed, for now, but not because the rooms and sewers have been secured.'' He walked over to the lamp, removed the shade. ''You may proceed because long before the Chairman arrives, we will know exactly what Lubchenko and his confederates were planning.''

25

Concerns about the mission faded as Joseph looked down the dank, craggy tunnel and felt history touch him again. The rocks glistened with moisture, and the railbed—gravel and dark sand—was damp from the river. Overhead, bare bulbs were strung every twenty meters from a single wire. The light they provided was stark and unearthly.

''It's magnificent,'' he said.

Nona throttled the engine to throw off the remaining moisture. ''All Nikita talked about was how awful it was to dig it. They only used explosives for the first part, up to the bend, then they had to go by hand because of the river. Men died of pneumonia, and there was always flooding."

"I understand what he meant," Joseph said reverently. "It's sinfully magnificent. This is a monument to vanity as great as that of the Pharaohs who raised the pyramids."

Panas's nose wrinkled. "Why are we using petrol to run the cart? It stinks terribly. Don't the tracks have electricity?"

"They do, but it's only on when they're doing repairs on cars or on the tunnel. The controls are in Nikita's booth. Would you like to go back and turn them on?"

Joseph asked, "If there's no electricity, how are we going to work the hammers?"

Nona pointed to the ceiling. "These lights and the outlets are all run directly off the Kremlin's generators. That was how Stalin wanted it, and no one has bothered to change it."

"Amazing," said Joseph. "He was *that* afraid someone would try to stop him from getting away."

"If I had been older, and known what he'd done to my father, I might have tried to stop him myself. He was a monster, every inch as foul as Cherganyev."

Joseph saw Nona brighten when she said that, said something *openly* against the Chairman. Come what may, he reflected, at least that had made her feel *good*.

Joseph saw a Metro train car sitting on the sidetrack. It was at least a quarter-century old, and rust covered its iron flanks like scales. Most of the windows were broken, the rest mossy and streaked with dirt. Here, amid the stone, it looked like a dinosaur, somehow bigger than it would have seemed in its natural surroundings. Joseph wondered if Cherganyev had ever taken this ride. He'd have enjoyed it—more unreality for his imagination.

As they passed the car, Nona stopped the cart and hopped off. "Another good thing about not having electricity," she said, pointing toward a rail beside the other two. "The third rail. You don't have to be careful where you step."

Joseph followed, watching the change that had come over her. He'd imagined her a quiet woman, and he was rarely wrong about his impressions. Here, however, in her element, she seemed to be coming more and more alive. That was good, because with every passing moment Joseph's own strength was waning. Part of it was the physical stress, to which he was unaccustomed. But the mental strain was worse. The fresh doubts.

With all the shooting at the hotel, the KGB would certainly assume an assassination plot was afoot. They wouldn't cancel the ceremony, but they might decide that Cherganyev shouldn't go down to the Square. They might ask him to remain atop the Kremlin Wall, where he could be better protected. Or they might delay the ceremony until they could better secure the area. With Stealth on the way, even a fifteen-minute delay could be fatal.

Joseph was thinking again, but he couldn't help it. He wasn't used to so many variables, or being at the mercy of others. In the past, whenever something didn't suit him, he walked away from it.

But how do you walk away from apocalypse?

Nona stepped over the rail and headed toward the car. "They keep tools in here," she said.

She climbed onto the coupling and pulled herself up to the car. The back door had been removed, and Joseph could see the equipment stacked or leaning in the shadows.

He smiled. The equipment really was here. Though Nona had said it would be, the way things had been going, he simply hadn't believed it.

Panas looked displeased. "With all of this here, why did your people have to go and get fancy equipment?"

340

Joseph looked at him oddly. "How do you know about that?"

"Lubchenko had me drive hours out of Moscow just to pick up your gear. Why, when this was just lying around?"

Joseph hoisted himself up to the car. "The equipment he had you get would have been far easier to handle." Joseph took a jackhammer. He felt its weight in the small of his back and quickly passed the tool to Panas. "Hold this for a few minutes and I think you'll understand."

Joseph took the second jackhammer from Nona, and dragged it to the back of the car. He handed it down.

"I still think it was a big risk for nothing," Panas said. "This scheme was ridiculous enough without adding smuggling."

"I'm sorry," Joseph said. "I know how you must feel."

"I don't think so," Nona said, handing picks to Panas.

He shot her a look. "I suggest you shut up, Comrade Nemelov. You don't know anything."

"What?"

"You don't know me, and you're in no position to judge me. The mistakes *I* made were honest ones, but what about you? *You're* the one the KGB arrested for dating a traitor—"

The words were barely out of Panas's mouth when Nona threw herself at him. Panas stumbled back, dropping the picks; Joseph jumped between them, restraining Nona. She reached out to claw at Panas.

"You *pig!* Don't *ever* talk about my Georgi. *Don't you dare!*"

"Calm down," Joseph implored.

"Georgi was a saint! He wanted only *good* for people!"

Joseph impulsively pulled Nona to him. She struggled in his embrace.

"Let me go!"

"Nona, don't do this—"

"*Let me go!* He didn't know Georgi. No one did. They killed a blameless man."

Joseph felt ill, knowing the part Reiner and the CIA had played in her suffering. He held her tighter. She pushed away, facing the train.

Joseph took a few steps toward her. "Please, Nona, I know you're hurting, but the enemy isn't here. He's above us. And if we don't stop him, how many more will suffer the way Georgi did?"

Nona said nothing. But her shoulders relaxed, and after a long moment she returned to the cart. Joseph sighed with relief.

Behind her, Panas stared down at the tracks. "I'm sorry, Nona," he said quietly. "What I said—I didn't mean it."

Nona remained silent, but Joseph didn't care—as long as she did the work. "Come on." Giving Panas a reassuring pat on the back, he helped him recover the picks and finished loading the cart.

When the cart set out again, Joseph found that they were traveling at a slight incline, a precaution the builders had taken in the event of serious flooding. The deeper they went, the more girders Joseph noticed supporting sections of the tunnel. The river probably caused considerable erosion; proximity to the river would also account for the sudden drop in temperature, which left Joseph shivering.

Just now, Joseph could have lived without the chill. His own doubts and Panas brooding beside him were distracting enough. Now his head was chilly and his bare hands smarted from the cold metal rail. He began to flex his fingers in anticipation of having to hold a drill. He told himself what he always used to tell his children—not to complain, that things could be worse.

Not much, he admitted, but at least they were down here with tools to do the job.

He forced himself to think about the mission. "How far in would you say we are?"

"Nearly three hundred meters."

Joseph looked up, began watching for the spot the blueprint said would tell them they were near the tomb. He didn't think it would have changed, given the way things were patched rather than ever really improved down here—

A few meters ahead he saw it.

"Stop the cart!"

The wheels creaked to a halt. Joseph held up the lantern. Overhead, a thick knot of cables intersected the wire, each cable converging from a different direction.

"That hole for the wiring is supposed to lead to the tomb."

"It does," Nona said, cutting the engine. "Nikita was telling me about it just the other day."

From somewhere up ahead, they heard water dripping. It always amazed Joseph that a sound that was so soft up close could be so loud at a distance; growing lightheaded from the fumes, he took it as an omen, that a drop of water from the West would prove louder than all the noise Cherganyev intended to make.

Assuming, of course, they could get through the wall. Joseph had begun to feel confident as they neared their destination. Now, looking at a stone wall instead of at a blueprint, he was no longer so sure. The people who'd clocked the drilling at the CIA were strong young men. He was neither strong nor young, and he wasn't sure how his companions would bear up.

He stepped off to the left, bending under the rail that led to the catwalk.

"Be careful," Nona said, "it's slippery."

Joseph held the rail for support, and lifted the lantern

343

over his head. The thin film of slime that covered the walk had frozen into a gritty surface like frosted glass. It cracked under his tread, releasing in concentrated puffs its foul, mildewed scent.

Panas backed away. "It smells like the garbage we leave out during the summer."

"Breathe through your mouth," Joseph advised as he glanced at the ceiling. "I only wish the stench were our worst problem."

"Why?" Nona asked.

Joseph pointed with the lantern. "For one thing, we'll have to hold the hammers over our heads and at an angle. That won't be easy. For another, look at the hole. It's only five or six inches wide, but we have to have both jackhammers working at it, widening it."

"You also have to make sure you don't hit the wires," Panas said, stepping over. "If they were to snap—"

"I was just thinking that. Someone upstairs might notice."

"*Would* notice for sure," Nona said. "I'm certain one of those powers the alarm at the entrance to the tomb."

Joseph swore. He would have traded an arm for the light drills that Reiner was to have brought.

"Tell me," said Panas, "those jackhammers are probably a great deal stronger than the drills you were going to use. Do you think we can get away with using just one?"

Joseph brightened. "With two of us holding it?"

"In a way. What we did in the army when someone had to work at an angle or use heavy equipment was to have one man brace the other, back to back. We'd switch off every ten minutes or so."

Joseph looked back at the jackhammer. "Hook it up," he said. "At this point, I'll try anything."

26

Lubchenko had never thought of himself as brave. Even now, in his lucid moments during torture, when the belt was loosened to keep him from passing out, he didn't think of himself as a man of courage. He was simply a survivor.

He knew he had only one chance of living through this, and that was for the American's plan to succeed. Even without Reiner and him, Rosenstock might still find a way—and every moment Lubchenko stalled these people brought Rosenstock closer to success.

Rukhlyadev bent the lamp forward again. The bulb seared the flesh of Lubchenko's cheek.

"Your accomplices," the operative said. "And your mission."

Serafina had left to help arrange last-minute details of the rally, and the other agents had gone to help police the Square. Only Glinka remained. He was smoking a cigarette and watching the torture with disinterest.

"He's stronger than I thought. I'm calling for chemicals."

Rukhlyadev set the lamp aside. He yanked the belt tighter. Lubchenko gagged. His eyes bulged.

"You hear that, idiot? You'll be given sodium amytal. You'll talk anyway, or you'll die. Why do that to yourself?"

The flesh of Lubchenko's face burned. Through flashes of pain he saw Glinka pick up the phone. There was no sense delaying any longer. He couldn't speak, could barely breathe; he nodded limply.

Glinka set down the phone. "Yes, Comrade?"

Rukhlyadev loosened the belt.

"I'll . . . tell."

"Talk, then," Glinka ordered.

"M-my hands—"

"You don't need them to tell us what we want to know!" Rukhlyadev barked. He grabbed Lubchenko's hair. *"Talk!"*

Lubchenko drew air through his mouth. "We . . . were to meet others and drive . . . to the TV tower at Ostankino. Blow it up."

"The tower?" Glinka said. "Why?"

"So you couldn't broadcast. Show lies . . . to world."

Glinka withdrew a slip of paper from his coat pocket. He studied it.

"There were no explosives in the car. What were you planning to do, *shoot* it down?"

Lubchenko shut his eyes, breathed heavily. Every delay ate up seconds and gave him a chance to think, to embellish his story.

"The explosives were delivered earlier," Lubchenko said.

"By—?"

"A friend . . . of Reiner's. She didn't know what she was delivering."

"Name?"

He thought one up, a name certain to be plentiful in Moscow. "Mazurov. Tonia Mazurov."

"Where does she live?"

"I . . . I don't know. Reiner never told me."

Glinka weighed what Lubchenko had said.

Rukhlyadev stood. "I don't believe him."

"I don't either, but we can't afford not to check." Glinka looked at his watch. "If Rosenstock took the Metro to the tower, you can still get there ahead of him.

Take some men and go. Phone me when you've searched the tower.''

Rukhlyadev left, and Glinka phoned his office. He told his aides to find a Tonia Mazurov who knew Erwin Reiner, and asked for truth serum to be sent over. Then he regarded Lubchenko.

''If you're lying, Comrade Director, you'll find me a most unforgiving man.''

Lubchenko slumped to one side. The gunshot wounds and the burns on his chest and arms stung severely, but he was too weak from the loss of blood to cry out.

One eye was swollen shut, Rukhlyadev having pushed the bulb against the lid. But as he looked across the room, his good eye noticed the clock—

Just ten-thirty? They would get to the tower and report back long before noon. How could the time have passed so slowly?

Lubchenko knew there was no way he could endure any more suffering and, letting out a small moan, he fainted.

27

The day was overcast, which suited Foreign Minister Aksakov's mood.

So Rosenstock was gone. It didn't matter that much from a political standpoint. Even without Rosenstock at his side, Cherganyev would release the Americans. Show the world that he was a reasonable man, willing to make peace.

At least, with NATO and Japan.

Aksakov rose from behind his desk, wondering where

Rosenstock had gone, and why. Surely he wasn't going to defect. Remaining in the Soviet Union wouldn't accommodate the man's needs. Aksakov suspected that Joseph Rosenstock enjoyed being an underdog, an outcast. Here, he would simply be preaching to the converted.

Shaking his head, Aksakov slid into his greatcoat.

If he'd known what Rosenstock was going to do, he might have gone with him. Lose himself in the countryside, on a farm somewhere. Even in Siberia. Somewhere the madness wouldn't reach.

With Fedorsenko gone, he was alone among the Lenin Utra outsiders. Politburo members dined with him less frequently, even within the halls of the Kremlin; his own deputy, Zhukov, was more and more Cherganyev's puppet. He was watched constantly whenever he left his office, or at home in Moscow and abroad.

The Foreign Minister looked contemptuously at the large portrait of Cherganyev behind his desk. This was the first time he had been invited to join Cherganyev at the tomb. He alone among the ministers would stand beside him—but not for the sake of their long friendship, or because they shared a common love of Lenin. Aksakov was ordered to be there to show the world that Fedorsenko had had no reason to defect, that he obviously had been coerced by the Americans.

Aksakov took his fedora from the coat rack, pulled it down snugly. His soul as dark as the morning sky, the Foreign Minister left his office and headed for the limousine that would pick up Cherganyev for the short ride to the ceremony. He had the impression that this would be his own last ride with the Chairman, though he felt worse for the nation than he did for himself. His suffering was about to end. The carnage against the Russian people, and people everywhere, was just beginning.

28

The men carried the tools to the catwalk while Nona walked the electrical cords back nearly five meters, to an outlet that hung from one of the cables.

"Ready," she said.

"Damn!" Joseph put the tool aside and fumbled around in his pants pocket.

Nona hurried back. "What is it?"

Joseph pulled out a handkerchief. "Panas, do you have one?"

Panas drew one from his back pocket, dangled it like a white flag. Joseph tossed his own over.

"Tie them together."

"Why?"

"That's something else Reiner was bringing. Face masks. The dust will be suffocating."

Panas knotted the ends while Joseph yanked out his shirttails, tearing off the bottom of his undershirt. He extended it toward Nona, then withdrew it.

"What's wrong?"

"Reiner had planned to have somebody watch the tunnel. We should do the same."

"Why bother? Wouldn't we see or hear someone coming?"

"Not with the hammer going."

"Then *you* go back," Nona said, "or Panas. Let me stay."

Panas grabbed one of the jackhammers, leaned on it as if to say they were wasting time. Joseph began knotting the mask around his mouth.

"Nona, you know the tunnel. You'd see and hear things we wouldn't." He looked at his watch. "We've got an hour and twenty minutes, assuming we don't stop to argue. Please—"

"Please!" Nona sneered. *"Drugóy czar!"* Stalking back to the cart, she started it up and threw the gearshift into reverse. The cart crept back along the tracks.

"Another czar, eh?" Panas said. "She can be a difficult woman, but you have to admire her courage."

"I do," Joseph admitted, "and I'll appreciate it even more when we're safely out of here. Let's get going."

Panas hooked his fingers through the handgrips. "You support me first. I'll widen the hole so you'll have a ledge to rest the jackhammer on."

Joseph agreed. With one jackhammer as a crutch, wedged between his chest and the ground, Joseph bent so that Panas could lean on his back.

The puttering of the cart receded, but the dripping water was no longer the only sound. Joseph and Panas were loudly sucking air through their masks, and Joseph was amazed at how many images their gasps caused to flash through his mind. Divers, high altitude pilots, surgeons.

Men on their deathbeds, fighting to the last.

The pictures evaporated when Panas finally hoisted the jackhammer up and, grunting, switched it on.

As he stood there, shaking from the vibrations, Joseph kept himself busy by considering a problem he'd been avoiding: just what they'd do with the body once they got it.

29

A bomb squad from KGB headquarters met Rukh-lyadev at the TV tower. They didn't evacuate the 533-meter-tall structure, not even the sumptuous Seventh Heaven Restaurant on top. If tourists or government officials were alarmed by the arrival of the dogs or metal detectors, they said nothing, but sat quietly and continued eating their meals.

After three quarters of an hour, the ten-person squad declared the tower clean. Rukhlyadev ran to the telephone in his car; two agents waiting at the Metro reported that Rosenstock had never arrived. With an oath, the operative called Glinka.

30

The jackhammer was modern, with a plastic motor housing and guide cylinder to keep the weight down. But the meter-long tool still came to over twenty-five pounds, and when Panas hit the operating lever on the handgrip, the tool seemed to have a life of its own. The jackhammer rode down the wall in three great hops, and though Panas managed to hold on, he jumped back so the drumming point wouldn't strike his feet; Joseph fell to one knee, ripping his pants and skin.

Panas shut off the jackhammer. "Are you all right?"

Joseph hadn't scraped his knee since he was a boy, yet it was amazing how familiar the sensation felt. He rose. "I'll live. Let's go."

Panas spread his legs and leaned against Joseph's back. He started the jackhammer again, but this time he pushed hard; the unit stayed up against the wall. Joseph felt the motion from his feet to his head. His nausea returned. But he smiled. Chips were tumbling around him, and dust swirled toward the railbed in a thick cloud.

They were *doing* it.

Panas said something Joseph couldn't hear, but his tone was unmistakable. He was also excited.

Up and down the tunnel the stone walls shuttled the sound of the hammer until it was a roar. . . .

31

Nikita was late, but it made him feel powerful to know that he was *allowed* to be late. He looked around at the other passengers on the Metro, wondering how many of them had been with someone important today. He hoped that sometime during the day one of the engineers driving through would ask, "Where were you this morning, Nikita?"

It would be a privilege to tell them.

He would thump his chest and say, "Comrade, I was with the Director of Public Transportation. Yes, Krimsky himself. He wanted to tell me to make certain that whoever I hired to take Nemelov's place would be good enough to take *my* place one day." He would smile knowingly. "No, Comrade, not because I will be dismissed. Krimsky has confided in me that he has *plans*. Great plans, to move me into repair management of transcontinental express trains."

He still couldn't believe it. More prestige, more money, the right to have certain foods held for him at the stores so that they were never sold out after he had waited in line.

He shook his head. *Stupid Nemelov! What she would have had!*

The Metro arrived and people emerged. Nikita checked his watch. If he went directly to the Square, he would be assured a relatively good position for the ceremony today. But if he did his paperwork, he could have it on Krimsky's desk by the afternoon, assuring the director that he deserved the great man's trust.

Unlocking the door of his booth, Nikita pulled the gunmetal stool to his drawing table and reached for the folder containing the rundown of the morning's mechanical evaluations.

He began to read the inspectors' reports. All tracks clear. All engines running. No lightbulbs requisitioned. No injuries. Only Stokowski's report was missing, which was understandable since he was doing Nona's job as well as—

Nikita looked up. What the *hell* was that?

He stepped from his booth, listened. He couldn't hear anything out here. Just inside. He went back.

It was still there: a low humming. He looked around.

The sound was coming from behind the wall, the wall his booth shared with the tunnel itself. He looked at it, trying to decide what it could be.

He noticed, then, that the overhead lamp was shaking—the green metal hood, the bulb, the wire from which they hung. The electrical line came through the eighth tunnel. What could be going on in there?

Nikita ducked outside again, pulled a clipboard from its hook, and ran a rigid finger down the list of names.

Everyone had signed in and checked off the assignments he'd left for them. Adabashian had gone to check the fishplates that had rusted in tunnel five. Lyubshin and Gurchenko were replacing several crossties in tunnel three. The others, too, were where they should be. No one should be in tunnel eight.

Flashlight in hand, Nikita hurried down the platform and to the catwalk that led to tunnel eight.

32

Nona was still angry. The two men had looked like American bandits, almost comical; both were half a head shorter than she was, and Rosenstock was probably weaker. Who were *they* to send her away? She was sorry that there hadn't been time to show them—and herself— that she could do the job.

She pushed Panas and the American from her mind, concentrated on the job at hand.

Overhead, the swaying bulbs caused the tracks to appear to undulate.

Side to side and back—they reminded Nona of giant snakes. And all around her, the echo of the jackhammer was the snoring of the master they served, the dragon.

That's what her father would have said. She had the faintest recollection of him once taking her on a handcart down the above-ground tracks where he worked. She didn't recall much about the trip, but she remembered when they'd stopped near a station and he'd put his big arms around her and whispered in his deep voice, "See the trains over there? They're only dragons disguised as trains to try to fool the hero Mourometz—"

One of the snakes suddenly called to the dragon. Nona was instantly alert. She listened.

It had sounded like the door to the passageway slamming shut, but now there was no way to tell. If there were any footsteps, they were lost in the din of the jackhammer. And if someone *was* coming, he'd find the cart missing and report it.

Nona stared ahead, trying to imagine who might be making his way through the passage. It usually took her five minutes to walk this far with a light. She waited. She began to relax, to think she'd imagined the noise.

And then a light struck the track from the side, causing its shadow to rise against the far wall of the tunnel. A faint crescent of light rose above it, growing fatter.

The beam of a flashlight!

Nona ducked under the railing of the cart, sliding to the railbed and nestling in the shadows beneath the catwalk.

33

The drug was sodium amytal, and the KGB physician administered the injection while Glinka stood back.

"I'm giving him a small dosage," the doctor said. "In his condition, even a small overdose would kill him."

The case officer was frowning. He looked from the Supervising Director's battered face to his own knuckles, which were red with Lubchenko's blood. Glinka had been careful not to strike Lubchenko in the mouth; he wanted to be able to understand what the traitor said. But he had hit him hard about the eyes and nose. He didn't want him to die without pain.

The chemical took effect quickly. It both anesthetized and stimulated Lubchenko; he stirred groggily.

Glinka stepped forward.

"Where is Rosenstock?"

Lubchenko's lips moved. Glinka leaned forward. The Supervising Director fell still.

"*Rosenstock!*" Glinka screamed. "Where is he?"

"Tu . . . tun . . . nel."

"*Tunnel,*" Glinka snarled. "Which tunnel?"

"Stal . . ."

Glinka straightened, his face screwed in thought. "Stall? Or—Stalin? *Stalin?*"

Lubchenko nodded once.

"Stalin tunnel," Glinka said. "The abandoned Metro line?"

Lubchenko nodded again.

"But why would Rosenstock go there? To hide?"

"D-dig."

"Dig for what?"

"Bo . . . body."

"Is someone buried there?"

Lubchenko just lay there, too weak to nod.

"Who is buried there? *Who?*"

"He . . . is."

"Did you kill someone? Are you *going* to kill someone? The Chairman?"

"He is there."

"Who is—"

Glinka shot upright. He realized, suddenly, who was buried there. With an oath, he rushed to the phone and ordered all SG shock troops in the Kremlin sector meet him at the Council of Ministers Building.

34

Eyes slitted, Nikita stood at the mouth of the passageway, studying the circle of track beneath his light.

"So—someone is here," he said, turning both the beam and his weasel face into the tunnel. He snapped off his light, noticed the bulbs swaying overhead, and stepped onto the catwalk. *"Hello!"*

His voice echoed, was swallowed by the distant drone.

"Someone is either very industrious or very stupid."

The orders he'd written out the day before had been plain. No one was supposed to be here. Unless there had been an emergency while he was away . . .

"Shit. That's all I need."

He started down the catwalk. The thought that a subordinate might do something wrong made him shiver. It would reflect badly on him, and perhaps even change the director's mind about promoting him. He quickened his pace.

Reaching the bend, he saw the cart and stopped.

"Now *that* makes no sense."

His nose wrinkled. The tunnel smelled of petrol; someone had used the cart recently. That made even less sense. He flicked his flashlight on again, sent the beam poking around the cart.

"Is anyone there?"

What a fool! he told himself. No one would be here. The droning was much farther along. The cart must have broken down and been abandoned. He shut off the light again and continued down the catwalk.

35

Huddled against the stone wall, Nona listened to Nikita's approach. She had recognized the voice, and wondered how far in he intended to go. She got her answer when the sound of his footsteps changed.

He had left the catwalk and gone to inspect the cart. He would smell the fumes, feel the heat of the engine, and realize that it had been used recently. And he would certainly hear the rattling of the jackhammers.

She listened as he looked around, muttering to himself. *This seems okay, that seems okay.* She heard the starter handle thump against the side of the engine as he reached for it. He pulled and the motor took.

"There's nothing wrong with this!" he said over the roar. "Something's going on here—"

There was no choice now. Nona knew she had to stop him.

She slid from beneath the catwalk and approached the cart from the rear. She reached into her pocket and withdrew the gun. She waited until he turned, then scurried toward him. She was able to press it to Nikita's back before he knew she was there. He began to turn.

"Don't!" she warned. "I have a gun."

He was half-turned and rolled his eyes back.

"Nemelov?"

She slapped off the engine. "I'm glad to see you're feeling better than you did last night."

"What?"

"When I came to see you. Your wife said you were ill."

"Oh," he said anxiously, "I was. A virus, I think."

"I think it was cowardice. After all I've done for you, letting you take credit for things I did, for ideas I had, how could you refuse even to *see* me?"

He swallowed hard. "They . . . they may have been watching."

"Damn you, it was cold. I needed to sit, to *talk!*"

"Nona, please—I had my own position to consider."

"What about your position *now?*"

His shoulder twitched nervously. He started to look back, but checked himself. "I'll give you a job," he said, "I promise. It will be a good one."

"You're a liar."

"No, really. I'm to be promoted soon, to the express trains. I'll take you with me. Assign you to another city. No one will ever know."

"I don't believe you. And even if I did, I have *other* work to do."

Nikita grasped the flashlight tightly. "The noise down the tunnel—do you have something to do with that?"

"That's none of your business. Just start the engine again and take us back there."

"What are you going to do?"

"Put you in the equipment car until—"

The flashlight came around so quickly that Nona saw it and felt it at the same instant. There was no pain; her left ear went numb and she stumbled to the right.

Nikita pushed her back and she fell onto the tracks. He bounded onto the catwalk and began running. Nona heard him and struggled to her knees. She had managed to hold on to the gun. She raised it, threw the safety as Panas had told her. Part of her went quickly through the reasons for preventing Nikita from leaving. He'd bring others. They'd be arrested. Cherganyev would continue. But part of her was merely an observer, horrified when she pulled the trigger, then pulled it again.

The tart smell of the gunpowder startled her from her stupor. In front of her, the smoke dissipated. Beyond it, Nikita was still running. She had to chase him, to shoot again.

Nona tried to stand, but black circles swirled in front of her eyes. She dropped the gun, then fell back to the railbed, the left side of her head throbbing. Suddenly, quickly, she was swallowed up in darkness.

36

It was a small militia that surged into the Council of Ministers Building.

Five cars had screeched to a stop outside the door, where they waited for the case director. Glinka and Rukhlyadev arrived separately within moments of each other, as the strategic weapons crew was handing out gas masks. It was an eclectic group, most of them plainclothes but a few wearing uniforms; all, however, moved with the restrained economy of motion that typified their breed. Most had red *L*'s burned on their foreheads.

Several people stopped and stared as the operatives made their way down the escalator, through the lobby, and then to the Metro platform. The fourteen men and one woman didn't seem to notice; at least they didn't acknowledge the onlookers. Glinka had briefed them as the masks were being passed out, and they grasped at once the importance of why they were here.

Glinka was the first one down the steps leading to the catwalk. He reached the platform just as Nikita burst from the door leading to the passageway. The officer put his hand on his gun.

"No, no!" Nikita yelled, waving both hands frantically. "The people you want are down there."

"How many are there?"

"I only saw one—a former inspector, Nona Nemelov."

"Nemelov?" Glinka raged. They had had her in for interrogation on the Tsigorin matter. How had they missed this? "Is she armed?"

"She has a gun, she even *shot* at me. But I hit her with my flashlight. I think she's hurt."

Glinka grabbed Nikita's arm. "Lead the way. Show me."

"Back there?" Reluctantly, Nikita turned. "Yes . . . yes, of course. At least as far as the tunnel, eh?"

The men moved quietly, double-file behind Nikita.

"How far up was she?" Glinka asked as they neared the opening.

"About thirty meters."

When they reached the end of the passageway, Glinka pushed Nikita onto the catwalk. "Show me where."

Trembling, Nikita openly wondered if he might get a commendation for this. That was clearly the only thought that kept one foot moving in front of the other.

"Was she on the walk or on the tracks?"

"On the tracks. She was kneeling. I think she was bleeding. As I said, I hit her very hard."

Glinka asked for a flashlight, and one was passed up. He shone it on the railbed, and as they came around the bend, the hint of a smile touched his lips. He stopped, training the beam on the prone figure of the woman.

He turned to the man directly behind him. "Stay with her."

"I'll stay," Nikita offered. "There's no need to waste a man."

"You're leading us into the tunnel." Glinka listened. "That's a jackhammer, is it not?"

Nikita nodded.

"Is the power off on the track?"

He nodded again.

"Excellent." Glinka weighed having the overhead power switched off, but decided the sound of the jackhammer would cover their own approach. He addressed the rest of the agents. "We'll go on foot along the railbed, which will make less noise than the catwalk." He drew his pistol. "They're trying to steal Lenin's body. Shoot to kill."

Glinka vaulted the railing, and the others followed behind.

37

A rush of fresh air greeted Panas as he broke through the floor of the tomb.

He had wielded the tool almost until they penetrated the soft rock; then Joseph had taken over. Using the jackhammer, they had progressed more rapidly than they would have with Reiner's drills; however, it was so heavy that after just fifteen minutes Joseph's arms were screaming from pain. Having rested enough, Panas took the tool and pushed it through. Pieces of tile now joined the slabs of rock that fell around them, covering the catwalk with debris.

"Stop!" Joseph yelled over the din.

"Not yet, it isn't wide enough!"

"That's why I brought the picks. Someone up there may hear."

Panas set the jackhammer aside. Joseph straightened and looked up.

"Magnificent work," he said. "Just magnificent."

"Thanks." Panas handed Joseph a pick. "You start, my arms are numb."

Joseph began hacking at the mouth of the hole, careful to avoid the bundle of cables that ran through it. Gradually the foot of the hermetically sealed glass and bronze sarcophagus came into view.

"I can see it," he said in an excited whisper.

Panas bent under the hole. "Give me a hand, I think I can make it through. It will be easier and faster if I hack at it from the inside."

Joseph laid the pick aside and knitted his fingers into a stirrup-like cup. He hoisted Panas up, and the younger man grabbed either side of the hole. Wriggling through to his waist, he put his hands flat on the floor; the rest was easy.

Joseph passed the pick through. "Can you hear anything outside?"

"Barely."

"Good. Just keep it slow and easy."

"How much time do we have?"

Joseph looked at his watch. "It's eleven-fifteen. If the CIA engineers are right, it should take twenty minutes to cut through the glass."

"We're going to make it, then," Panas said.

The young Russian began chopping at the floor. He kept glancing toward the steps and the sarcophagus. He couldn't decide which made him more anxious: the thought of being alone with the body or of someone walking in.

Below him, Joseph stood aside as the pieces of black labradorite and decorative ceramic tile fell from the edges. He eyed the hole.

"I think I can make it through now! Help me."

Panas straddled the hole and reached down. When Joseph hopped up and grabbed the sides, Panas dragged

363

him in. Both men pulled off their masks and looked around. Still on his hands and knees and panting from the exertion, the American shone a flashlight about the room. When he saw no cameras, he rose. There was a dimmer switch beside the drapes. He punched it on and turned it up full.

The light in the tomb was dim, provided by two rows of recessed bulbs. The bulbs were frosted, their glow diffuse. Holy. Yet Joseph could see clearly, his eyes having become accustomed to the darkness of the tunnel.

There was nothing in the room but the ten-by-four foot case and, tucked in a corner, the brass poles and blue velvet ropes put out to control crowds. *Mute sentries for a dead ruler,* Joseph thought. He looked at the figure reposing in the sarcophagus.

Joseph had seen him before, many times. But he had only gotten a glimpse while passing through with the rest of the crowd. In this setting and at this angle, viewed against the darker walls, the body was eerily aglow. It had to be a trick of the glass, a filter, or else it was not Lenin but a replica made of some luminous yellowish polymer. Either way, Lenin was flawless, like an icon. Joseph understood how a fatherless boy could latch on to him, make him his personal god.

"You have a drill, you said?"

Though muffled by the mask, Panas's voice was clearly shaky. Even among the nominally converted, Lenin was a figure of inordinate power.

Joseph reached into his vest pocket and withdrew the tape recorder. Oddly, the danger of what they were doing was no longer foremost in his mind. Professional curiosity took over; he was about to find out whether the body was real or not.

And if not, he worried again, *how will Cherganyev react?*

Joseph paused at the foot of the monument. Loree had told him what kinds of sensors to look for to see if the

364

sarcophagus had an alarm. Hair-thin filaments in the corners. Small, round sound detectors in the heads of screws.

He shook his head. Outside, the band was playing. Even if there was an alarm, he didn't have time to deactivate it. Cherganyev would be arriving shortly.

Unless my escape made them change their plans.

That was ridiculous. A worldwide audience was tuned in, and Cherganyev would lose face if he called off the ceremony. Joseph chided himself for thinking too much, again.

Don't think. Do!

He removed the battery, extended the drill, and put the tip to the glass covering, a few inches from the top. He pressed the base and the bit began to spin.

He moved the drill counterclockwise, in a broad rectangle. The diamond bit sliced a groove in the half-inch casing. He didn't have to go back and deepen the cut; the drill penetrated on the first pass. He moved slowly, squinting through the cloud of dust. Perspiration made the mask stick to his face.

After nearly twenty minutes, a panel roughly the width of the body fell outward into Joseph's hand. He leaned it against the bronze base.

A sickly sweet smell drifted from the opening. Joseph suspected that it was a preservative of some sort, pumped into the case during periodic maintenance. It was colorless, but the glass was not: seen through the opening, the body wasn't quite so golden. The case polarized the light in some way.

Panas squatted beside Joseph. "Tell me, Comrade. Was stealing the body your idea?"

Joseph put the drill away. "Yes. Trust me, though, it was either robbing the dead or *being* dead. And we're not out of the woods yet." He pulled off the white sheet that covered Lenin's feet, and handed it to Panas. "Here. Spread it out, we'll need it."

Joseph looked at Lenin for a moment, then leaned against the glass. He put his arms around the legs.

"Christ. Jesus Christ."

"What—?"

"The legs are soft. It's him. It really is Lenin."

Joseph gulped back the sour taste in his throat. He was unable to look away. The veins on Lenin's temples were even more visible in natural light. Never mind necessity, he was about to become the most notorious ghoul in centuries.

Upstairs, Joseph heard a band begin to play. He glanced at his watch. Twenty minutes until Cherganyev arrived.

"What are you waiting for?" Panas asked.

"Waiting?"

"You're just standing there! It's disgusting, but let's *do* it and get out of here."

"Yes," Joseph said. "I'm sorry."

Joseph slid the body forward. The arms remained stiff at Lenin's side, the sleeves of the jacket having been sewn to the hem. The fingers dragged slightly, as though resisting.

"Take the legs," Joseph said to Panas.

The Russian hooked his arms around them and pulled. Joseph put his hands under Lenin's shoulders. He looked down into his face.

Lenin's eyes were shut, the lips pressed together, the beard neatly trimmed and still shot through with gray. Somehow the Russians had actually preserved the body. The sweet smell was stronger now, where the gas had clung to Lenin's clothing and flesh; but there was also a faint odor like that of formaldehyde rising from the body itself.

They lowered the body onto the cloth, and while Joseph took a step back Panas pulled the ends of the fabric around the body, knotting the sides in the center.

"I gutted beef when I first went to work at the Azov," Panas whispered, "and I once carved a boar for a Politburo member. Until now, there was no mistaking something dead for something living."

Joseph nodded in agreement. The red of Lenin's face. The smell like a garden where every flower was in bloom.

"Lenin Utra," Panas mumbled. "Lenin Awake. It wouldn't surprise me." He looked over at Joseph. "Are you all right?"

"Just weak."

"You're telling me? My arms are dead weights—"

"No, I mean I'm queasy. I didn't think he'd be so lifelike."

"What were you expecting, a dummy?"

"More or less," Joseph said. "Anyway, let's not worry about that now." He looked away as he stepped around the body. "You take the legs, I'll take the shoulders."

"What are we going to do with him?"

"We were *supposed* to have a car. Now I suppose we'll have to take him to the equipment car."

Panas dropped to one knee and put his arms under the knees. "Yes, we can prop him against the crates of dynamite. Comrade Lenin, be careful not to smoke. We don't want Cherganyev to have to put you back togeth—"

He fell silent.

"Panas, what's wrong?"

The Russian scurried toward the hole. "I thought I heard something."

"What?"

"Footsteps."

"Nona's?"

Panas shook his head. "It sounded like there were more than one."

367

Joseph listened. After a moment he heard the unmistakable crunch of shoes on the gravel of the railbed. The men exchanged worried glances.

"From the sound of it," Panas said, "there are a *lot* more."

Joseph looked around. A pick, a pane of bulletproof glass, and Lenin's body, those were all they had. Whoever was coming would make short work of them. He grabbed the pick and handed it to Panas.

"Take this. Maybe you can get out."

Panas clutched the pick tightly. "With any luck, they'll just be trainmen. We can hit them and run."

Joseph didn't believe that. If they were Metro employees, Nona would have warned them. More than likely, one of them had been followed.

Joseph pressed his hand to his forehead. The vaunted Dr. Rosenstock, a mind like a machine, a debater without peer. Cool when other heads were hot. Why weren't ideas flowing? He always did his best thinking, his best writing under pressure. He had all the answers when his reputation was at stake. Now that the fate of a city was in his hands, he was paralyzed.

No! There has to be something!

There must be something he could use. The transmitter! Could he tell them he had a radio-controlled bomb?

No—that would keep Cherganyev away. And eventually they would call his bluff. Or Stealth would arrive. They had to kill whoever was coming, and they had to do it quickly.

But how many are there? And was the pick enough? If only they had a gun.

Guns. Joseph brightened.

The newcomers would have them. The hole was only big enough for one. Whoever came in first would have one. If they could just get it . . .

Of course.

368

Motioning to Panas to get on the other side of the hole, away from the sarcophagus, Joseph hurried over to the body. Squatting, he reached into his pocket.

38

Nona twitched. Her cheek felt cold from the muddy soil, her temple hot from the blow. Her head throbbed.

Suddenly there was a sharp pain in her scalp, and her eyes snapped open. Someone was holding her by the hair, peering down at her with angry eyes.

"Get up."

It wasn't Nikita. She noticed the holstered gun, the gloves, the gas mask. The telltale *L*.

SG.

So they had failed. . . .

The man pulled again and she squealed.

"Get *up!* We'll be leaving when your friends arrive."

She pulled her knees in, rose on her forearms. He'd said *when* her friends arrived. She no longer heard the jackhammer, but that didn't mean they'd been taken. Perhaps they'd already gotten inside the tomb.

She knew she couldn't have been unconscious long; the smell of gasoline still hung in the air. Up ahead, she saw the cart. The KGB operatives had gone on foot. That meant they might still be on their way.

Nona had an idea. She looked along the tracks.

"Come on!" the agent yelled. "Move your fat ass!"

She saw what she'd hoped to see. What they *hadn't* seen.

"Yes, Comrade. I'm sorry. I—I'm coming."

She feigned dizziness and suddenly slumped back, falling on her elbow.

"Forgive me," she said quickly, holding up a hand so he wouldn't come over. "Give me just another moment."

Now she was on her hands and knees, facing the other way.

Facing the gun she'd dropped.

Scurrying forward, she grabbed it—

Nona turned, firing twice. The agent never knew what happened. One moment he was glowering at her, the next he was gone, propelled backward by two funnels of red. She'd struck him twice in the chest.

Nona climbed slowly to her feet, averting her eyes from the body.

I had no choice!

Her head was pounding as she half-walked, half-stumbled to the cart. She leaned on the railing to muster her strength. She told herself that the life she took was in exchange for Georgi. The SG made the rules, and she was simply playing by them.

She yanked the cord and started the engine. There was no time to think, to doubt. Her head throbbing worse than before, she sent the cart forward and slumped to the floor.

39

Glinka paused. Hearing the shot, he assumed Nona had tried to escape; hearing the cart, he assumed the agent was coming to join them.

He hoped that if Rosenstock heard the noise, he would assume it was Nemelov.

Not that it mattered. There was no way the intruders could escape now.

Glinka peered up into the pale yellow light of the tomb. A circle of men with submachine guns stood beneath the hole, just out of view from the inside. Other agents were behind them with canisters of tear gas and automatic weapons. Back several meters, Nikita stood watching, his arms folded tightly against his chest.

There was muted talk in a corner of the Mausoleum. Could it be that Rosenstock still hadn't heard them? Glinka squeezed the butt of his pistol.

If they'd caught Rosenstock in the tunnel, Glinka would have used the gas. But uncorking it up there would send acrid clouds rolling from under the doors. Cherganyev would have him shot.

He would have to go up there. He couldn't be sure whether Rosenstock had a weapon, but he could hear where he was up there. All he had to do was get up and draw a bead. . . .

Rukhlyadev came forward and indicated that he wanted to go up first. Glinka knew why: the KGB man wanted to show up the SG. But that was fine. He would also draw their fire and probably wouldn't survive to tell about it.

The case officer nodded and motioned for an agent to cup his hands and help Rukhlyadev in. Pointing to himself then, and to two other agents, the SG officer indicated that they would follow him in turn.

Putting his toe in the agent's hands, Rukhlyadev leaped up.

40

Rukhlyadev followed KGB procedure. He hit the floor of the Mausoleum, rolled on his shoulder, pulled his feet underneath him, aimed at the voice. And fired.

At a tape recorder.

Behind him, Panas swung the pick. The agent's head exploded in blood and bone and he fell back through the hole.

With the gun.

Joseph swore. Running from behind the coffin, he stopped as a second man came up through the hole. Still holding the pick, Panas swung at him; he was too late. Glinka ducked, then jumped up when the path was clear. Crouching behind his gun, he trained it on Panas. Panas dropped the pick, held up his hands. Joseph, too, froze as another man climbed in. Then another. Glinka yelled down for the rest of the team to remain in the tunnel.

"You are both *vile,*" Glinka sneered, circling Joseph and backing toward the door. He looked with open horror at the body, and ordered Panas and one of his men to replace it.

There was a moment when Joseph was convinced that the man was going to shoot him. Glinka's entire body grew taut; his eyes burned with anger. But just as quickly he eased, apparently realizing, as Joseph did, that if there was no one left to punish, he might well draw all of Cherganyev's wrath for having failed to prevent this.

"*Skawruh!*" the Russian barked, hurrying the men along. "I must inform headquarters what has happened."

41

Nona stopped the cart by the supply car and staggered off. Her vision was blurred, and she had to concentrate hard to find what she wanted.

A bucket. Matches.

Dynamite.

She used a crowbar to wrench open a wooden crate of the explosive, which had been used to excavate a new Metro trunk before the 1980 Olympics. The train crews didn't lock it up because the tunnel itself was locked. And so few people knew it was here that it would be simple to find the responsible party if any of it turned up missing.

Nona put five sticks in a metal pail, grabbed a box of wooden matches used for the older lanterns, and returned to the cart.

The cart clattered along, the cool breeze refreshing. She thought about what she had to do.

Even if Rosenstock and Panas had gotten inside, there was no way they'd get the body out now. And the body, as Rosenstock had said, was the key to destroying Cherganyev.

There was no choice but to blow up the Mausoleum.

Nona realized that she had to keep going at all costs, even if there were men in front of her. She thought back, counted how many bullets she'd fired. Four in all. That left two. Those should be enough, at least, to clear anyone off the tracks and get her under the tomb.

She came around a turn. Fifty meters ahead was another bend, and then the last stretch of track before the

373

Mausoleum. She laid the gun down, took out a match. She didn't think about dying, only about succeeding.

And she thought, too, that never before had she felt more worthy and more alive than she did now.

42

Joseph watched with awful sadness as they cradled the body in the sheet and carried it back to the sarcophagus. Cherganyev would be furious, of course, but he'd probably be able to control any public displays of emotion. They'd think up some excuse, and the ceremony would be delayed. But the mission had failed. Millions would die because a corpse had been apprehended.

Joseph turned to the hole in the floor. There was a commotion below, a clacking on the tracks, shouts from the men.

Glinka yelled down, "What's wrong?" The answer was a gunshot; he bolted toward the hole.

And stared in horror and confusion at one of his men holding his abdomen and writhing beside the track.

43

Nona hadn't known whether the young man intended to shoot her or whether he was aiming at the car's bright light. She couldn't take the chance. She'd fired, he'd fallen, and the others had scattered. As she closed in on the opening, she saw the job Rosenstock and Panas had done. It was too bad they'd been stopped. Kneeling, she struck a match and lowered it toward the pail.

Nona felt the punches in her side just as she heard the low roar of the submachine gun. Her lower back and midriff went numb, but her thigh was warm. Blood.

She'd been shot.

A burst from the other side hit her arm and stomach. She went down, slumping over the pail. She lost the match on the tracks.

The cart rolled on and she thought she heard men running after her. She wanted to stand but couldn't feel her legs. The lantern exploded in another burst of gunfire. Sparks flew from the metal of the cart where bullets hit.

Nona felt dizzy. She hadn't expected so many of them, and now she could barely breathe, let alone stand and throw dynamite back at the Mausoleum. Her throat was clogged with blood; she began to choke.

The cart jolted to a halt and she slid forward. The pail spilled onto the frozen railbed. There was nowhere to go, she'd reached the end of the track. She felt cold, more than the cold of the tunnel. Her right arm was covered with goosebumps.

The bucket.

The dynamite.

The end of the track.

The matches were still in her hand. Nona marshaled her strength, pulled another match from the box.

There were footsteps behind her, men were shouting that she was still alive. Was that a surprise?

She held the box on its side, and the matches spilled out. Her arm fell, her hand landing on the matches.

They'd shot her. She understood that, but it didn't hurt. Could she really be dying?

It didn't matter. Without Georgi, what did anything

matter? She pinched a match between her fingers, scraped it along the pitted metal of the cart. It flared. She extended her hand toward one of the sticks of dynamite lying on the tracks. The fuse sizzled.

Brightness.

Nona stared at the sparks, thinking back to when her father had once made fireworks for her, to celebrate her birthday. She'd been so impressed at the way he'd packed the gunpowder in a container, knotted the fuse, and left just enough to let them get away after lighting it.

She smiled. And the dynamite exploded.

The blast ignited the other sticks; the roar broke the eardrums of the men nearest the blast. But none of them knew it. A few fell as shards of cinder block were ripped from the end of the tunnel and peppered them with death; the rest were beaten down by the rush of water.

The Moscow River surged through the hole in the wall, smashing away the rest of the cinder blocks and sweeping through the tunnel. Caught in the torrent, the cart spun end over end, gouging huge pieces from the walls as it led the onslaught. Men struggled futilely to stay afloat, but they had nowhere to go as the water rose to the ceiling. Feet and arms flailed, surfacing occasionally as the water crested and troughed. Soon the only motion was that of the raging waters.

44

The telephone beeped as the limousine turned into Red Square. Aksakov picked up the receiver.

"Minister Aksakov?"

"Yes."

"Chief Basmanov, SG. One of the guards at the Mausoleum reports an explosion."

"Where?"

"Below the tomb—apparently in the Stalin tunnel."

Beside him, Cherganyev looked up from the speech he was studying. "What is it?"

Aksakov's voice was relaxed, almost casual. But his eyes watched Cherganyev intently. "There's been an explosion, it appears, in the Stalin tunnel."

Cherganyev started. *"Where* in the tunnel?"

"They believe it came from below the tomb."

The red of the Chairman's cheeks spread quickly to his neck and forehead.

Aksakov asked the caller, "How soon until you have a report?"

"Our men were at the site when it happened; they believed the American, Rosenstock, was down there. I'm trying to raise them now. In the meantime, the guards want to know if they should go in."

Aksakov hesitated. "No, not yet. Wait until you've heard from your men, then call me."

He hung up. Cherganyev's jaw was taut, his breathing more like a wheeze.

"What is it?"

"There were agents down there. Rosenstock may have been there as well."

"Rosenstock!" he erupted. If any American would have known about the tunnel and its route, it was Rosenstock. "No," he muttered, "it couldn't be. No one would *dare.*"

"Comrade Chairman, are you all right?"

"Rosenstock. He's down there. He was *sent* there."

"Sent?"

Cherganyev drove the side of his fist against the window. *"He was sent to hurt Starik!"* Half-standing, the Chairman yanked open the glass partition and grabbed the driver's shoulder. "Get me there, *quickly!"*

"Where, Comrade—"

"To the tomb!" he screamed, then fell back in the seat.

45

Joseph didn't know what caused the explosion, but he recognized a godsend when he saw one. The floor of the Mausoleum had heaved with the blast, tossing Glinka to one knee; the other two agents were staring aghast at the rushing water.

Joseph wasn't. He was looking at the pick.

With surprising agility, he scooped it up and swung at Glinka. The side of the metal head caught him from behind and the case officer sprawled sideways.

Panas dropped Lenin's body and threw himself at the man across from him. Raising the pick, Joseph ran at the third agent.

The agent aimed his gun.

Don't think! Joseph screamed inside.

With a snarl, Joseph threw the pick at the man. The handle struck the agent, who fell back, his gun discharging wildly; recovering the weapon, Joseph shot him in the chest. He looked across the Mausoleum and saw Panas flailing with both fists at his own adversary. The agent had pulled a knife; aiming the pistol, Joseph fired. The agent shuddered and collapsed as the bullet bored through his temple.

Panas pushed the dead man aside. He staggered to his feet.

"Thank you, Comrade."

Joseph dropped the gun, turned away.

"What the hell happened down there?" Panas walked

toward the hole, shaking his head as though he were in a daze.

Joseph didn't answer. The floor seemed to shift, the entire structure creaking. Though the rush of the water was loud, the floor kept most of the sound back; Joseph heard the girders below the building groan. Outside, he could hear the blare of a car horn getting louder each moment.

He returned to Lenin's body and tried to lift it onto his shoulders.

"Help me, Panas."

Panas looked back. "Help you do what?"

"Get him out of here."

"And go where?"

The body was too heavy and Joseph laid it down. He started pulling it toward the hole. "The catwalk. If it's still there, it's our only chance of getting out."

Panas came over and lifted the legs. Reaching the hole, Joseph looked down. He squinted through the spray of foul water.

Twisted metal supports poked from the stone wall. The catwalk was gone.

Joseph stood. Outside, the car horn fell silent. There were muffled shouts. Bolts were thrown and the great doors opened.

Panas knelt nervously beside the hole. "I say we swim. At least down there, we stand a chance."

Joseph looked at his watch. It was 11:55. So close. They hadn't gotten away with the body, but seeing the destruction, Cherganyev would still break.

He hoped.

"I have to do it."

"Do *what?*"

"Send the signal."

Joseph ran to the cassette recorder and retrieved it. And gasped.

379

The first agent had shot at it. Hit it. Destroyed the back. Pieces of the transmitter dangled from the casing.

"Oh God. God."

Light streamed down the stairs. A guard stood silhouetted against it, a carbine slung over his shoulder. Seeing that neither of the men in the tomb were armed, he stepped aside, saluting smartly.

Footsteps clattered on the stairs. Cherganyev rushed past, and three more guards came down behind him.

Joseph's mind raced frantically. There had to be a way he could get in touch with Clark. If he could get past Cherganyev, talk to Aksakov or someone—

His stomach burned. He moved forward. The guards all raised carbines and Joseph stopped.

"Please," he said to them, "I must get upstairs. There's something worse than this—"

"Worse?" Cherganyev said. His voice was high, broken.

The Chairman took several steps and seemed to waver. He stopped, staring at the body wrapped in the white cloth. Joseph couldn't see the Chairman's face, only his big frame. It was stiff and erect, almost bloated. The structure moaned again, but Cherganyev didn't seem to be aware of it. He began to come forward again in small, shuffling steps.

He passed under one of the lights, his face illuminated by the dull glow. His mouth hung loose and his eyes were wide; the color had seeped from his face.

He'd been right. Cherganyev was near collapse.

But what good will that do if I can't get to Clark?

Joseph studied the guards. "You've got to listen. There's a bomb. Upstairs. Only I can defuse it."

The men looked at him. Their faces were stony. None of them moved.

The Soviet leader reached the body, fell to both knees. He touched it through the cloth, his fingers brushing the

380

outline of the face, down the rigid nose and along the beard.

"Starik—"

Joseph licked his lips. He looked at his watch. The carbines were still raised. Even if they shot him, he'd have to try to get upstairs.

"I beg you," he said to the guards. "Please, one of you go up and get the Foreign Minister. Tell him Rosenstock must speak with him!"

The guards looked at one another, then at Cherganyev on the floor.

"What has been done?" the Chairman whimpered, both hands hovering over the cloth. He reached for the knot. The covering fell away and he looked into the face of his god.

Lenin's head was turned to the side, away from Cherganyev, the chin upturned. As though the dead Lenin were rejecting his spiritual heir.

"I'm sorry. I've failed you."

Cherganyev seemed to recoil slightly as he noticed a deep gash behind Lenin's head. It ran down his neck, revealing a rod that had been placed inside the body to keep the spine rigid. Cherganyev looked pitifully at it, pushed back the hair that had parted around it. Several strands came out in his fingers.

"They've hurt you. They must suffer. . . ."

One of the guards turned suddenly and started up the stairs.

Joseph regarded Cherganyev. He could see the boy in the Russian leader. The lonely child who had latched on to the sarcophagus and wouldn't let go. In spite of everything, Joseph's heart went out to him.

There were more footsteps. Aksakov appeared in the doorway, his face registering shock as he surveyed the carnage. He looked from Cherganyev to Joseph, not with hate but with questioning. Then he walked toward Cherganyev.

"Comrade Chairman, are you all right?"

The Russian leader ignored him. He brought his hand to his face, clutching the hairs as he rose. He pressed his cheek to them. His eyes suddenly grew wild. They found Joseph.

"You *dared* to touch him?! You dared to *profane* him?" Cherganyev strode toward the guards. Tears trickled down his cheeks. *"Shoot* him! Kill him *now!"*

"No!" Aksakov stepped between Joseph and the carbines. "No, Comrade Chairman, don't do this."

"What?" Cherganyev's face melted with anger. *"Are you mad?"*

The accusation brought Aksakov's shoulders back. "I'm thinking of you, Comrade Chairman. This is not dignified—"

Cherganyev wagged a thick finger accusingly. "You and Fedorsenko, you planned this. You planned this *sacrilege* together."

"We planned nothing."

"A *lie!*"

Cherganyev backed toward the stairs. "You never believed in Lenin, in his eternal life!" He stumbled over the bottom step, then rose. "Kill them!" he yelled to the guards. "Kill all of them!"

The guards raised their weapons.

"You don't deserve to share in his glory!" the Chairman raged. "The *world* doesn't deserve Lenin! My own brothers . . . look what they did to him! Metal and wax . . . they took away his dignity. *Look what has happened!"* He held out his fingers, and the strands of hair fell from them. "I'll kill them *all* for this! *Everyone will suffer!"*

Joseph's knees were shaking. The clock in the Spassky Tower signaled noon. Joseph looked from Cherganyev to the guards. The men seemed to waver.

Aksakov went to them. "Put down your weapons. Comrade Cherganyev is not well."

Cherganyev raised his fists. *"I said shoot them! Now!"*

"No! It's over, Comrade. Come upstairs with me. Use the ceremony to make a new beginning. Tell the world it's over, the insanity."

With a cry, Cherganyev turned and ran up the stairs. As he passed, the guards lowered their weapons.

Aksakov ignored him and turned urgently to Joseph. "What is it, Rosenstock? What is this about a bomb?"

His heart slamming in his throat, Joseph told him.

Together, the men rushed upstairs.

46

Clancy Jones's instruments indicated that he was twenty-four miles from Moscow. His fail-safe point.

Removing his glove, Jones put his thumb on a small white square. The sensor scanned his fingerprint. It turned green.

TWO-MINUTE CHECK appeared on the monitor.

The screen cleared and Clancy Jones waited for final instructions from the White House.

47

. At the entrance to the Mausoleum, Cherganyev was screaming at a line of guards.

"How did you let this happen? How did they get inside?"

Tears flowed freely, and Cherganyev grabbed the green tunic of the nearest guard. "Where were you? Does Lenin mean nothing to you? *Didn't you know? Or you?"* he screamed at a woman whose badge, hooked to her belt, identified her as a reporter for *Pravda.* "Did you see? They dared to touch him!"

Her notepad and pen hung limply at her sides. Cherganyev looked up at the platform behind her, into the black eye of the Vremya television cameras. The spotlight was blinding, and he held up his hands. A few strands of Lenin's hair still clung to his palms. Staring at them, he sank to his knees.

"My father . . . my loving father . . ."

Cherganyev folded toward the ground, his sobs echoing through the silent square. People watching television monitors that had been erected throughout the Square looked uneasily at neighbors and then away, anywhere there wasn't a face to share their discomfort.

For over a full minute no one moved or spoke as Cherganyev cried bitterly on the cobbles of the Square.

Except for Aksakov. Emerging into the sunlight, he saw Cherganyev and, forcing back his own tears, hurriedly led Joseph to the limousine.

48

It was nearly 4:00 A.M. in Washington. Jim Clark had gone to clean out his desk at the White House—and stayed. If Joseph's signal came at all, it would come over his private line.

For the last hour he'd paced the room. Waiting. Worrying. Second-guessing. Silently swearing. He dragged his hand through his hair, drummed on his desk.

And leaped from the seat when the phone rang.

He snapped up the receiver. Instead of the distinctive transmitter tone he was expecting, he heard a voice muffled by static.

"Professor?"

Joseph had to yell to be heard. "Jim, the transmitter was destroyed but—we did it."

"Cherganyev?"

"He's in the Square. Crying."

"Christ!" Clark looked at the clock on his desk. It was a minute before four. Sixty seconds until the President gave the final order . . .

Dropping the phone, Clark bolted from his desk and ran down the corridor.

49

The President was seated in the Oval Office with his advisers. The mood was somber. In the adjoining communications room, an aide was seated at a computer, giving Stealth the final go-ahead.

Clark burst in; Alexander rose indignantly.

"I'm sorry," Clark said peremptorily, "but Rosenstock's succeeded."

"What?"

"Cherganyev's finished." He glanced past the President toward the communications room. *"For God's sake, stop the bomber!"*

Lawrence jumped to his feet. "Bullshit. It couldn't possibly have worked."

Clark ignored him. "Mr. President, at least *postpone* the run until we can confirm. The ceremony is being broadcast—*put it on!*"

Alexander looked at his advisers. Lawrence sat heavily. No one else protested. The President turned to his aide.

"Put Stealth on hold," he said.

The young woman nodded and fed in the instructions. Clark fell into an empty seat.

"God help you if you're wrong," Alexander said as he asked Chief of Staff Moriarty to switch on the television.

50

Joseph climbed from the limousine and watched as Aksakov stepped to Cherganyev's side. The Foreign Minister motioned to several of the guards.

"Help him to the car," he said.

A pair of Sredá-Grom operatives pushed their way through the crowd. They told the other men to get back; Aksakov ordered them to stay.

"We'll handle this," the Foreign Minister said quietly.

The men glowered at him. "I think not. The security of the Chairman is our jurisdiction."

"Not anymore," Aksakov said.

One of the men looked down at Cherganyev. "No? Comrade Chairman—come with us."

Cherganyev didn't answer. He was sobbing piteously, his face in his hands.

"Comrade Chairman!"

Aksakov stepped between the operatives and Cherganyev. "I said *go.*"

"Go?" one of them said. "And if we don't?"

"I'll have you arrested."

The *L* on his forehead flushed. "You won't succeed with this, *Comrade* Foreign Minister. You'll die—"

"It's possible. But Lenin Utra will die as well. Henceforth, Lenin lives only in here." Aksakov touched his chest. "You won't corrupt him anymore with your purges and wars."

Joseph watched as the operatives' eyes searched the row of guards for support. Joseph knew that the operatives carried weapons; for a moment he thought they might use them.

But the men found no encouragement in the eyes of the Mausoleum guards, and without looking down at Cherganyev, they turned and strode away. The crowd parted to let them pass.

Joseph exhaled.

Aksakov faced the two guards who were standing by Cherganyev. "Do what I asked, please. Help him."

Shouldering their weapons, the guards raised Cherganyev to his feet, his cries echoing through the otherwise silent Square. As the men led him away, Cherganyev's driver came from the car to help.

The Foreign Minister turned to Joseph. The American held up two crossed fingers; Aksakov nodded grimly, then walked toward the microphone that had been prepared for the Chairman.

51

The men in the Oval Office watched as Aksakov addressed the crowd in Red Square.

"Comrades. Today our nation has suffered a great tragedy. Chairman Cherganyev has long borne the weight of Lenin Utra on his shoulders, carried the burden for us. Now it is our turn to repay our debt to him, but in a way that relies more on belief in the words of Lenin than in the force of arms. . . ."

Alexander shook his head. "Incredible. Simply incredible." Turning to the communications room, he ordered the bomber recalled. A small round of applause filled the Oval Office. Even Lawrence was clapping.

The President regarded Clark. "I've got to tell you, your methods leave a hell of a lot to be desired. But there's no arguing with what you accomplished. Congratulations—and welcome back to the team."

Clark smiled and thanked him.

PART
SIX

The wind rushing across the airfield was unseasonably warm, and the smell of diesel fuel made it seem even warmer.

It also, Joseph thought, made the air seem friendlier. The fuel told him he was going home.

"You look like a very contented man."

Joseph looked over at Panas.

"I am. And you?"

"I'm feeling . . . not bad," he replied, his lips puckering.

Panas looked across the field, frowning pensively as the big jet pivoted from the landing strip toward the terminal. He couldn't read what was written on the side, but he'd been told that this was Air Force One, the jet of the President of the United States.

"I'm glad that only Ambassador Fedorsenko and your Minister of State are on it," he told Joseph, "and not the President himself. Otherwise I'd have been forced to give the man a piece of my mind."

"You'd have had every right to," Joseph said.

"Drop an atomic bomb on Moscow. The man is madder than Cherganyev ever was."

Rosenstock didn't disagree. He regarded Panas warmly.

Joseph's admiration for the Russian had increased enormously when, after Aksakov had finished speaking, Joseph had gone back into the tomb.

He'd found Panas sitting on the floor, crying.

Joseph sat beside him, and without prompting, the

Russian proceeded to tell him everything that had happened with Virna; Joseph's own sons had never confessed so readily or completely to him.

"You were doing what you thought was right," Joseph had said when Panas was finished.

"No. I was afraid of them."

"There's no crime in that."

"No crime, just shame. Nona wasn't afraid. She was made of iron."

Joseph had smiled. "Nona wasn't made of iron. She was in pain. You could see it in her face."

Tears had formed in Joseph's eyes as well. Whatever the reason for what she'd done, and however she'd done it, Nona had saved them . . . and the mission. He smiled when he thought of how she and Panas had distinguished themselves when the professionals had failed.

Joseph watched as the door of the aircraft opened and a staircase was wheeled over.

Thanks to Aksakov's intervention, the government wouldn't take any action against Panas. Still, Joseph wondered what would happen to him. He was still a pivotal figure in the day's events, a simple man thrust into history. In America he would have written books, given lectures, become a millionaire. Here, Panas would find day-to-day survival a struggle. He would have to endure the questions and accusations of those who felt he had betrayed Russia.

But if Panas's smile wasn't as quick as it had been at the Azov, if his manner was less cocky, he was now a man who would notice what went on around him. With Lubchenko's death, he would probably be given the post of Supervising Director; that would change him too. And in the future he would dig in his heels a little harder, and not allow himself—or his nation—to be pushed toward Armageddon.

Like all of Russia, all of the world, his eyes had been opened by these past few days.

As the reality of what had transpired settled in, Joseph still couldn't believe how close the world had really come to disaster.

In a television speech the night before, Aksakov had announced that he was withdrawing his ships from the Mediterranean and recalling his troops from the Middle East. Having described Cherganyev's fall as "the final purge," he moved quickly to consolidate his power in the Politburo; with Fedorsenko's help as President, he would put the cult of Lenin behind them. Aksakov had even announced that the Mausoleum would be closed for several months. No mention was made of the body's having been disturbed, but only of the collapse of the tunnel. Joseph suspected, though, that when it reopened, the tomb would be more a monument than a shrine.

And maybe, he thought, some of those uppity dictators in the Middle East had been sobered by war and would show less appetite for it.

It was a long shot, but then Operation Starik also had been a long shot.

2

The American journalists who were to have been freed by Cherganyev had been released by Aksakov. They had been given the option of remaining in the Soviet Union, and had accepted; most of them had come to the airport. Joseph had given several interviews when he arrived, and now they were talking with Ambassador Kaplan, who had also come along. Her praise for Joseph and his team had been effusive, and he'd walked away, embarrassed.

Fedorsenko appeared in the doorway of Air Force One. He stood there for a moment, the hem of his greatcoat whipping in the wind; he breathed deeply before starting down the stairs, followed by Lawrence with a small army of aides. The ambassador did not carry his cane.

Joseph stepped onto the red carpet which had been unrolled on the tarmac, and the airport police officers quickly shut the door behind him to keep the reporters back. Only cameras from Vremya were on the field.

Fedorsenko's eyes never left Joseph as he approached; his smile never wavered. Their hands met in a warm clasp.

"I don't know how to thank you." Fedorsenko's eyes moistened. "I was *right* to ask for you."

Joseph grinned. "I'm not so sure I was right to accept. Making history isn't easy."

"Nothing of value ever is." Fedorsenko looked past Joseph. "You are Pavadze?"

"Yes, Comrade Ambassador."

Fedorsenko motioned him over, and shook his hand. "It's an honor to meet you. What you did was very courageous."

Panas seemed uncomfortable. He bowed silently.

Lawrence approached, a smile on his face, his hand extended. "You worked a miracle, Joseph. Just an incredible job."

"Thanks, Sam, but it wasn't only me. There were others—Russians. I hope the President realizes that."

"He does, though you'll forgive him if you're the only one to whom he gives a government post."

"Which post is that?"

"National Security Council. He thinks you'd be a valuable asset to the team."

Joseph couldn't suppress a smile. "You're kidding."

"The newspapers are calling you a hero," Fedorsenko said. "The President won't let you go."

"Unfortunately, my wife won't either." The smile refused to go away. Joseph stared along the red carpet. "I'll have to talk to her. Maybe after a dinner or two at the White House . . ." he said, his voice trailing off.

Accepting Fedorsenko's thanks once again, Joseph embraced Panas and then headed for the plane. At the top of the stairs he looked back. Beyond the airport loomed the Moscow skyline.

A hero? Joseph smiled as his eyes roamed the towers and churches . . . the history.

Panas was the only hero. The rest of us . . . we were all just desperate lovers of one kind or another.

Even Cherganyev.

3

He was wearing a bright blue robe, the belt of which was knotted loosely about his waist. His big hands, extending from the full sleeves, lay limply on his lap. He sat on the wooden bench staring at his hands—but seeing something else.

Some*one* else.

A pale face with an angular jaw, a neatly clipped beard, a look of complete repose.

He wished he could be like that. Just rest. Sleep.

Forget.

Yet, Lenin had done *his* work, earned his repose. He had not.

Not yet.

Cherganyev smiled.

The bench was bolted to the floor. He'd found that out earlier when he tried to use it to hit at the door of the hospital room. But it could still be used. In his own captivity, Lenin had written on walls, on the floor, anywhere he could write to help crystallize his thoughts.

Cherganyev pulled back his full sleeve, put the nail of an index finger to the bench. He scratched down hard, forming the words slowly. Splinters gashed his fingertip and drew blood, but Cherganyev didn't mind. His eyes reflected the contentedness he felt as he wrote:

Lenin Lived. Lenin Lives.

Lenin Will Live.

He sat still, admiring his handiwork. Back straight, head held high, he confidently added one more word.

Again.

ESPIONAGE FICTION BY WARREN MURPHY AND MOLLY COCHRAN

GRANDMASTER   (17-101, $4.50)

There are only two true powers in the world. One is goodness. One is evil. And one man knows them both. He knows the uses of pleasure, the secrets of pain. He understands the deadly forces that grip the world in treachery. He moves like a shadow, a promise of danger, from Moscow to Washington—from Havana to Tibet. In a game that may never be over, he is the grandmaster.

THE HAND OF LAZARUS   (17-100, $4.50)

A grim spectre of death looms over the tiny County Kerry village of Ardath. The savage plague of urban violence has begun to weave its insidious way into the peaceful fabric of Irish country life. The IRA's most mysterious, elusive, and bloodthirsty murderer has chosen Ardath as his hunting ground, the site that will rock the world and plunge the beleaguered island nation into irreversible chaos: the brutal assassination of the Pope.

Available wherever paperbacks are sold, or order direct from the Publisher. Send cover price plus 50¢ per copy for mailing and handling to Pinnacle Books, Dept.17-270, 475 Park Avenue South, New York, N.Y. 10016. Residents of New York, New Jersey and Pennsylvania must include sales tax. DO NOT SEND CASH.